25/3

Rupert Smith is the author of *I Must Confess* (Hamish Hamilton), a pastiche showbusiness autobiography. He writes regularly for the *Guardian* and *Radio Times*; contributed to *The Gay Times Book of Short Stories: New Century, New Writing* and wrote *On the Edge*, the book based on the BBC dot.com drama *Attachments*.

Fly on the Wall

RUPERT SMITH

for Marcus

First published 2002 by GMP (Gay Men's Press),
PO Box 3220, Brighton BN2 5AU

GMP is an imprint of Millivres Prowler Limited,
part of the Millivres Prowler Group,
Spectrum House, 32-34 Gordon House Road, London NW5 1LP

www.gaymenspress.co.uk

A CIP catalogue record for this book is available from the British Library

ISBN 1-902852-35-4

Cover image © Getty Images

Printed and bound in Finland by WS Bookwell

Distributed in the UK and Europe by Airlift Book Company,
8 The Arena, Mollison Avenue,
Enfield, Middlesex EN3 7NJ
Telephone: 020 8804 0400
Distributed in North America by Consortium,
1045 Westgate Drive, St Paul, MN 55114-1065
Telephone: 1 800 283 3572
Distributed in Australia by Bulldog Books,
PO Box 300, Beaconsfield, NSW 2014

Preview

Meet Serena Ward. In many respects, she's just like you: hard-working, fun-loving, still single at 35, constantly battling with her weight, fond of chocolate, shopping and the odd boozy night out with the girls. Unlike you, she has a pronounced taste for getting shagged roughly up the arse by men of the blue-collar type, a hang-over from the time when she was a teenager – more to the point, a teenage *boy* – plying her trade round the public toilets of suburban south-east London. But for the time being, this piece of information is strictly embargoed. You're the first to know. The public at large won't even begin to find out until week six of *Elephant and Castle*, the new fly-on-the-wall docusoap from Kandid Productions.

Yes, Kandid Productions – the people who brought you *Check-Out Girls*, *Waiting Room* and the Bafta-winning *Sprayers*, which, as you recall, followed an insecticide hit squad during a hectic summer and made a star of Dave 'Missed It!' Merryweather, who accidentally poisoned an entire family by spraying deadly chemicals through their kitchen window and went on to a successful career as a stand-up comedian.

Serena is just one of the larger-than-life characters who live in London's never-fashionable Elephant and Castle. Across the road there's Jamie Lord, the hunk of the show. Twenty-two years old, fresh out of the army, celebrating his new-found freedom with a cheap bleach-job to complement a growing collection of tattoos. Six foot tall with a simian cast of features, long of limb and narrow of hip, he dreams of a job at the local gym. There's 'Maureen' and 'Muriel', two elderly homosexuals whose overdecorated eyrie on the upper floors of Beckford House affords them a commanding overview of the comings and goings beneath them. And here's their neighbour Mrs Renders, who was once on the stage, who remembers the Elephant and Castle 'before all this'. And still to come: drug dealer Daryn and his tearaway six-year-old, Ben; sexy schoolgirl Debbie Wicks who lives with her publican parents above the Princess of Wales; Fat Alice, who'll do anything for attention…

Within a few weeks, they'll seem like family. The viewing millions will take them to the collective bosom, suffering as they suffer, gasping at each new twist in the 'real-life' drama. And you – because you have shown such excellent judgement in buying this exclusive tie-in publication – will nod in the certainty that they ain't seen nothing yet. That's the kind of special added value that we aim to give you in the following pages as we take you behind the scenes of Elephant and Castle – or, rather, *Elephant and Castle*, for the tv series and the place itself are two very different things, as you are about to find out.

Part One

Meet the Stars

One

The doorbell rang in Serena Ward's flat at 7.30am. Less organised neighbours might have emerged crumpled and blinking into the grey morning light; not Serena Ward, who had risen even earlier than usual to present an immaculate facade to her visitors. Her hair was washed, conditioned and brushed up into a neat little chignon. Her (minimal) make-up looked dewy-fresh. Her grey suit was innocent of crease or stain, her legs almost prosthetic in their sheer smoothness. For ten seconds she stood in the gloom of her hallway, eyes closed and arms extended above her head. She wanted her pupils to appear wide and inviting, her hands pale and veinless. When she opened the door to the camera crew, she was radioactive with good grooming.

Not so bearded, sensitive Steve Soave, freelance director, or burly, shaven-headed Nick 'Nicko' McVitie, jobbing cameraman, neither of whom had known at nine o'clock last night, when they sat down for the first of many beers, that they would be up and about, let alone working, so early the next morning. Both of them felt fuzzy; Serena, on the other hand, was in sharp focus.

'Good morning, gentlemen.' Her voice, something above a whisper, promised more than it said. She peered into Nicko's lens. 'Is that thing on?'

'Yes, I'm afraid so.'

Serena popped a finger in her mouth, moistened the tip and ran it across the eyebrows that marched in single file across her forehead. 'In that case,' she said, pouting a little, 'I must be sure to look my best.'

She led them into the flat and stood aside. 'Straight down the stairs, gentlemen,' she said, positioning herself squarely in front of a closed door from behind which, Steve was almost certain, issued the sound of snoring.

'They're in!' shouted Eddie Kander, and slammed the phone down. For a triumphant moment he surveyed the eager, upturned face of his researcher and occasional mistress Caroline as she waited for the word. He, Eddie Kander, was a player once again. He savoured the power.

'Kandid Productions is back in business! Let's have a meeting!'

Five minutes later, with coffee steaming in mugs on the boardroom table, Eddie was in full spate.

'Okay, I've godda get down to location. Caroline, put transport on your action points.' After years in the tv business, Eddie's mother tongue was overlaid by an impenetrable patina of jargon.

'What?'

'Call me a taxi, for God's sake.'

'Right.'

'And take a letter. Okay: to controllers and heads of acquisition at all the channels, on the new letterhead. Dear So and So, I'm giving you the chance, no, make that the exclusive chance, to be first British channel to bid for the new project from Kandid Productions, makers of bla bla bla. This time Kandid cameras – hmm, I like that, Kandid cameras, remind me to use that again – have gone where angels fear to tread, out on to the mean streets of south London, to uncover the flip side of the New Labour nightmare in a show that literally rips the lid off the establishment.'

'What does that mean?'

'Sorry?' Eddie did not like being interrupted in mid flow.

'Establishments don't have lids.'

'Oh for God's sake, Caroline, spare me the English degree.'

'And what's the New Labour nightmare?'

'It's an angle for God's sake. Continue. Bla bla bla, rips the lid off the establishment... This is the London that tourists never see, a twilit world of freaks, drug addicts and real-life perversion. So-called gays rub shoulders with anarchists, thugs and prostitutes. Are you getting this?

'Thugs and prostitutes. Yah. It's good.'

'Okay, then give them some old flannel in case they get nervous and think it's too kinky for mainstream audiences... And yet, in this modern urban hell, we see the first green shoots of renewal as funky young professionals move into an area of huge untapped resource, marking it out as London's next cooler-than-thou postcode. Don't miss out. Be a part of *Elephant and Castle* today. It's real life, but more so. Ends.'

'Ends.'

'Go and type it up, babe. And hey, while you're at it, try and find me some *nice* people in the area, for Christ's sake.'

Caroline, her buttocks still jutting skywards the way Eddie liked them, shambled out of the room in search of a notebook she hadn't seen for three days.

For the first time in over a year, Eddie felt the old Kander magic beginning to work. The vibes were right, the tide was turning. Mistakes had been forgotten, lessons learned. *Elephant and Castle* would put Kandid Productions back on the map.

Eddie made a name for himself at the BBC as the assistant producer, and subsequently producer, of a series of ground-breaking fly-on-the-wall series that culminated in the headline-grabbing *Sprayers*, the big success that gave him the leverage to leave the corporation and set up as an independent, selling back to the BBC at a vastly inflated price the kind of stuff that he'd churned out on a staff wage for so long.

At first it had gone well: the controllers came to him cap in hand as hit followed hit. Who could forget those *Beggars* and their heart-breaking cheerfulness in the face of adversity? Then there was *Prozzies*, a commission for Channel 5 that followed 'a group of feisty working girls in London's notorious Spitalfields area' and peaked with audience figures of over a million. The publicity that followed a Broadcasting Standards Authorities complaint only brought more work pouring in. For two years, Kandid Productions ruled the airwaves. No corner of British life was too murky for Eddie and his prying cameras. Audience figures stayed high for *Loonies*, peaked with *Other People's Pants* ('opening the door on the British laundrette' and giving the world another star in the mountainous shape of Doreen 'Dirty Bitches!' Dawson), but slid a little for *Steam!*, a 'tv first' look at the lives of the men who work in gay saunas. The critics turned hostile ('Sordid', 'Pointless', 'Desperate'), audiences stayed away and the schedulers at ITV, who had started the show in a 10pm slot, shunted it further and further into the night where it would be seen only by the elderly or the drunk.

Subsquent shows (*Abattoir, Babysnatcher!*) haemorrhaged viewers as Eddie scraped the barrel ever deeper in search of the elusive hit. His last series *Disposal Squad* ('ever wondered who empties the special bins in ladies' loos?') found itself without a broadcaster after *Watchdog* questioned the ethics of placing hidden cameras 'below the rim' in toilet pans.

But with *Elephant and Castle* he would make them all eat their words. It had it all: freshness, topicality, a strong cast of characters, a few laughs, a few tears. He could see the spin-offs already: the Christmas special, the personal appearances, the launches and lunches stretching ahead like an illuminated runway to paradise.

Caroline interrupted this happy flow by bursting noisily through the door in a way that said 'I'm important!', scratching her scalp with a pen and scowling at her notes.

'Okay, we've got... er... we've got a woman, Senna, is it? I'm sorry, I can't read my shorthand, I need some admin support on this one.'

'Serena. That's the one Steve's with now. She's my insurance. The only decent, hard-working heterosexual we've found in the whole area. Gotta keep her sweet.' He smacked his lips.

'Yah, Serena, sure, and the army bloke, begins with a J.'

'That's Jamie. Nice kid. Everyman sort. Not too bright. Photographs well. Go on.'

'And those poofs that keep ringing the office.'

'Characters, Caroline, characters! Not poofs! They're gold dust in this business, my darling. Gives people a glimpse of everything they fear. Parents of young boys will shit themselves. We're guaranteed coverage on those two.'

Caroline made a sour face. 'And you've got all the relevant documentation, I assume?' continued Eddie.

'What?'

'The releases, *par exemple*.' Eddie often made sarcastic use of French.

'Yah, it's all under control, I just need a bit more input on the office management side.'

'Have they actually been sent out?'

'Not as such.'

'Printed?'

'They're ready to go, really.'

'Written at all?'

'No.'

'Okay. You'll find standard all-rights release forms on my desk, I need names and addresses ready in an hour, understand? An hour.' Eddie sighed and pressed a wholly imaginary pain in his left temple. 'I guess I'll just have to do it myself.'

'I'm sorry.' Caroline looked as if she might burst into tears, a sight that Eddie always found intensely erotic.

*

In half an hour, Serena had shown Steve and Nicko around her pristine two-bedroom flat (all except one room which, she claimed, was 'a disgusting tip') and granted her first major to-camera interview in the garden, currently full of late spring flowers. The first crop of dark pink climbing roses matched the silk scarf at her throat; this was no coincidence.

'I've lived here for five years. It's very much home to me now. I never really thought twice about it, no, although friends and family said it wasn't the sort of area that a single woman should live. I suppose south London has a bad reputation, but, touch wood, I've always felt safe here. It's very busy, there's always someone around, and the neighbours are lovely. They say that Londoners are unfriendly' – she licked her lips and tilted her chin, like a professional model – 'but I've found the people round here to be absolutely gorgeous.'

Steve Soave's microphone picked up the sound of a toilet flushing inside the flat. Serena registered nothing.

'I like the fact that it's so close to town, and of course the transport's really wonderful,' she continued, just a little louder. 'I mean, the facilities round here aren't great, but it's a hop, skip and a jump up to the West End and there, of course, the world is your oyster.'

The microphone recorded the unmistakeable bang of the flat door, heavy feet stomping along the exterior passage to the street. Serena chattered blithely on.

'And that's important if you work as hard as I do. I mean, the agency is only 20 minutes away door to door on the bus, or I can walk it in 45 minutes, it's just up in Holborn, so it's a lovely stroll across the river and oh my goodness, look at the time, I'm sorry but I really must be off to work! I've got a presentation to do for a client today, a big new contract, so if you don't mind, gentlemen, I'll see you out.'

That upstairs door, so firmly closed when Steve and Nicko had arrived, now hung open, affording tantalising glimpses of a rumpled bed within.

'You're not filming now, are you?' asked Serena in a voice deeper and sterner than before. She bundled them both out of the flat, cleared her throat and resumed her poise. 'See you soon, then.' She had just enough self-possession to blow them a kiss.

Eddie was talking on his mobile in the back of a cab.

'What do you mean you just switch it on? That's exactly what I'm asking you how to do, for Christ's sake. Yah. Yah, I see it, okay, so where do I put that? Okay, right, I see. And then? Oh, okay. The button marked "on". Right. Well thanks a lot, I mean, I think you need to get your after-sales service sorted, actually.'

He switched the phone off and untangled himself from a web of thin black wires. The concealed camera was only delivered this morning; it was the first time that Eddie had used it. So: the bit that looks like a smartie, clips on to the lapel. The wire runs down inside the jacket to the black box 'that can be concealed either within a spacious pocket or, alternatively, a discreet briefcase'. He clicked his case shut, ensuring that the wires didn't show, and happily fingered the little button marked 'on' that dangled against his midriff.

'Where in the Elephant do you want, guv?' asked the taxi driver.

'I told you, Beckford House.'

'Where's that then?'

'You're the one with the knowledge.' Eddie mentally deducted 50p from the tip.

The taxi driver sighed, pulled over in front of a fags-and-mags kiosk and unwound the window.

''Scuse me mate, Beckford House?'

The news vendor, a retired footballer in a lime-green button-down Ben Sherman shirt, gestured across the road. 'You've found it. That fucking ugly monstrosity that's blocking my sun.'

Eddie craned his neck to see the building in all its glory. It was ideal: huge, brutal, forbidding, an architectural blight, a towering megalith of poverty a stone's throw from the Houses of Parliament.

'Yes, yes, yes, let me out!'

In his excitement, he forgot to wait for change from the proffered ten pound note, thus accidentally giving the driver a 75p tip (25p more than he had intended) and, more importantly, depriving himself of the receipt.

Beckford House. Built in 1962, the final insult heaped on an area still reeling from the Blitz and the slap-happy assault of the town planners. There it stood, all 20 storeys, filthy, crumbling, covered in graffiti, half its windows broken. The thud-thud-thud of music from an upper window the perfect soundtrack. Eddie shivered with pleasure and whipped out his dictaphone.

'Gedda wide-angle down here. Titles. Fantastic views of Beckford House. Find out cost of helicopter for aerials.'

He walked twice round Beckford House without finding the entrance. The nearest he had come in his life to a tower block was a visit to some wealthy friends of his former wife's who lived in an Erno Goldfinger building in Hampstead, where he was greeted at the door with a glass of chilled Orvieto. Here he saw nothing but a perspective of concrete stilts and dark empty spaces. He clutched his briefcase a little more tightly.

Rescue came in the shape of a haggard, whey-faced postman who trudged past Eddie and headed into the darkness. Eddie followed and, rounding a corner, was confronted with a 12-foot-high steel door. He stood behind the postman, waiting for something to happen.

'I don't carry money,' said the postman in a flat, hopeless voice, as if reading from a card, 'and I am not authorised to let you into the building.'

'I'm not a fucking mugger, pal,' said Eddie, bristling.

The postman slipped through the door. 'Paranoia, fear, violence, death stalks the mean streets, no I've said that already, the nether regions of London's forgotten something or other.' He replaced the dictaphone in his pocket and fumbled for a sheet of paper. There, freshly printed just before he left the office, was a list of names and addresses of all the people that Caroline had contacted in connection with the project. It was Eddie's mission this morning to seek their permission to use any film shot between the above dates, waiving all rights, bla bla bla, just a standard form, sign here. God knows, if you wanted something done, you were better off doing it yourself. This is the life, he thought. Down with the people, keeping it real on the streets. Even a major player like me needs to get his hands dirty.

He browsed the list. Serena Ward (AB advertising professional 35), 1 Spencer Street. Eddie knew from a conversation with Steve that she was already off to work. Daryn Handy (DE unemployed/single parent, benefits, 20), 3 Spencer Street. He could wait. Ah! Here it was. Jamie Lord (C2 personal trainer ex-army PT 22), Flat 44, Beckford House. Eddie's finger skated over the filthy buttons on the entryphone panel before gingerly pressing 44.

There was no response.

He tried again. From somewhere high overhead, a sudden silence replaced the industrial chug of music. A greasy window swung open and a face peered from the gloom.

'Who is it?'

Eddie stepped back into view.

'Eddie Kander.'

'Fourth floor.'

The window snapped shut, and within seconds the door was buzzing. Eddie was in.

Jamie Lord whipped off his T shirt and practised a few boxing moves in the hall mirror. It would take the bloke at least two minutes to get up to the fourth floor, five or more if he waited for a lift that would never come. Time to work up a little sweat. Left jab, right jab, right jab, dance back, straight punch left right left, dance forward, two low hooks to finish. The hands at face level, head tilted downwards, eyes looking up, brow furrowed. Half a centimetre of dark brown hair at the roots; the remaining centimetre white-blond. Tattoo on the left deltoid: peacock. Tattoo on the right deltoid: 'Paras', and a heart and dagger. Tattoo on the left pec: a black sun. Over the belly-button a line of Thai script that the tattooist, whom he'd encountered on a holiday in Phuket, assured him meant 'Peace, Strength, Life' but which, according to one of his mates, actually translated as 'Medium Green Curry with Chicken and Lime Leaves'. Out of sight, tucked inside his grungy grey sweat pants, his right buttock bore the legend 'When I Die I'll Go To Heaven Cause I've Done My Time In Hell – Bosnia 1995-6'.

He repeated the routine, surveyed with satisfaction the plumpness of his muscles, and ran a hand through the slightly damp hair on his stomach. Time for a minute with the skipping rope? No: halting footsteps at the end of the hall. Jamie stepped out and saw his visitor emerging from the stairwell, loosening his tie with exhaustion. So many of these middle-aged guys let themselves go. That would never happen to him.

'Down here, mate!' he shouted, smacking his left fist into his right palm in a routine familiar to Jamie's Beckford House neighbours since he had moved in on leaving the army. Many the well-polished pair of Oxfords that had climbed the stairs to the fourth floor since then...

Eddie took a deep breath and marched down the hall. He held one hand out in welcome; with the other, he found and pressed the 'on' button inside his jacket. The concealed camera, its lens on his lapel, went silently to work.

'Eddie Kander. You spoke to my researcher. Kandid Productions?'

Jamie beamed. 'Oh, right! The tv company!' He took Eddie's hand in a warm, two-fisted grip. 'Sorry, mate. I thought you were a... well, never mind. Come in. I was doing a spot of training.'

'Don't let me interrupt you. I just wanted to have a chat about the show, and what we're planning.'

'Right, as you were.' Jamie closed the door behind them and led Eddie into the front room, dominated by two huge speakers positioned at the window and a punchbag hanging from the ceiling. Around one saggy, smelly sofa were piles of CDs, 12-inch vinyl, discarded clothes.

'Okay, shoot.' Jamie aimed a couple of jabs at the bag. Eddie, he noticed, could not take his eyes off him. Perhaps, after all, the tv spiel, the calls from the researcher, were an elaborate bluff, the sort of thing that some men need to lend a gloss of legitimacy to their pleasures. Oh well, give him a show...

'Just a few formalities to get out the way first, legal stuff, nothing to worry about, if you could just sign this release form.'

'No problem. Oof oof oof!' Jamie gave the bag three vicious upper-cuts, took a pen from Eddie's hand and scrawled his name.

'So – ish! ish! ish! – what have you got in mind, mate?'

Eddie remained in a kneeling position, never once turning his back. Any minute now, thought Jamie, he'll start fiddling with himself, and I'll see what so-called Kandid Productions is really all about. Probably just wants to video me having a wank. No problem.

'Oh, you know, just a few hours spent with the cameras, we'll be around for a couple of months, get to know you, talk about your life and work. You, er, you work in a gym, I understand.'

'Well, not as such. I'm a personal trainer at the moment, you know, private clients.'

'Right.'

'Mostly they come to me.'

'I see. And is it a good living?'

'Not bad.' Jamie grinned, fetched the punchbag one final blow and dropped to the ground to execute 25 perfect press-ups. 'I charge – ungh! – sixty quid – ungh! – for the first hour – ungh! – and thirty – ungh! – for each hour – ungh! – after that.'

'I see. Well, of course we won't be paying you by an hourly rate.'

'Rates negotiable – ungh! – for overnight – ungh! – or long stay.'

Eddie had the impression that they were talking at cross purposes. 'What we generally offer is a flat fee on signing, if that's acceptable.'

Jamie jumped to his feet and started stretching. 'How much?'

Eddie swallowed. 'Would £800 be about right?'

Jamie's face lit up – he could buy a new PC for that money – then immediately clouded over. 'And what extras do I have to do?'

'As I say, that's the flat fee. Reasonable access for the cameras, a few legal things, it's all spelt out in the agreement that you've signed, I'll get my secretary to send you a copy.'

Jamie shrugged. 'Fair enough.' Perhaps, after all, the guy was genuine. Anyway, for £800 he wasn't going to split hairs. 'Mind if I have my shower?'

'Go ahead.'

Jamie left Eddie gazing down on the unrelieved vista of urban horror, and reappeared a minute later wrapped only in the shortest of white towels.

'Want to come and talk to me in the shower, mate?'

Eddie, disgusted by the idea of homosexuality, was journalist enough to know that naked flesh must never be turned down.

'Sure.' He followed Jamie down the sticky hall carpet and into the bathroom. 'I want to hear about *you*, Jamie. Your childhood, your hopes, your dreams, your ambitions. I want people to get to know you...' Jamie dropped the towel on the floor and stepped into the tub. 'As intimately as you know yourself.'

The showerhead sprang into action, drenching Jamie's body in an instant. Eddie felt a little queasy, but dared not turn away lest the lens miss a moment of ratings-boosting nudity. God, he thought, I hope he doesn't think I'm queer.

'Right. My hopes and dreams.' Eddie, Jamie noticed, seemed once again to be fumbling inside his jacket. He'd turn a blind eye.

'Well, Eddie, I guess you know I'm fresh from the army. Joined at 16. Wasn't much cop at school, good at sports, football, sprinting, javelin...' He let his hand linger in the suds at his crotch. 'So the army just seemed like the natural choice. I like the atmosphere, you know? All guys together. I mean, don't get me wrong, I'm not gay or nothing.'

You could have fooled me, thought Eddie, as he watched with horror the sinister elongation of Jamie's manhood. He focussed mentally on the commercial potential of an 'exclusive out-takes! What they couldn't show on tv!' video release.

'I'm young free and single now, the world's my oyster, as they say.' Jamie started drying himself down. Nothing had happened; perhaps the guy was genuine after all. He pulled on a towelling dressing gown from a hook on the bathroom door.

Eddie preceded him down the hall, walking backwards, making a mental note to find some way of holding the concealed camera that did not necessitate constantly facing the subject. ''Scuse me a moment,' said Jamie, diving into the bedroom where, to Eddie's surprise, the bed was neatly made – almost as if it had never been slept in... Jamie rooted around in a pile of clothes, picked out a pair of boxer shorts, shucked the dressing gown on the floor and pulled on a fresh T shirt.

'Right, I'm all yours. Where do you want to start?'

'Look out the window,' said Eddie. 'Tell me what you see.'

Two

Down the concrete walkway that provided the only public open space in the area, Mrs Margaret Renders was walking her Yorkshire terrier, Sid – or, to be precise, was pushing him along in a baby buggy which also contained her morning's shopping. She glanced up to the fourth floor, surprised at the unaccustomed silence, and saw Jamie at the window with another chap. She waved; he saluted back. He was a rascal, without a doubt, but not a bad lad. On occasion he helped her up the stairs with the buggy.

Mrs Renders – Peggy Renders, as she was known to audiences in the 40s and 50s – was used to seeing strangers around Beckford House and Spencer Street. In the 30 years that she'd lived as a retired widow in her fourth-floor flat she'd become a genial, cock-eyed mother hen to the waifs and strays of this unloved corner of London. They laughed at her behind her back – at her persistence in wearing, at the age of 70 plus, the elaborate Victory Roll hairstyle of her heyday, at the bangles, brooches and beads, the gold slippers that made up her theatrical wardrobe. But it was to her that they turned in times of trouble, confident of a sensible answer and absolute discretion. Thus Peggy Renders knew more about the inner life of Beckford House and Spencer Street than anyone.

When Steve Soave and Nicko McVitie, working on their hang-overs with styrofoam cups of hot brown water from The

CuppaChino next door to the tube station, first spotted Mrs Renders pushing her pram along the upper walkway, they looked at each other, nodded in unison and headed for the steps.

'Looks like we got ourselves a loony,' said Nicko, hoisting the camera on to one broad shoulder. Years in the service of Kandid Productions had equipped Nicko with muscles in pursuit of which others spent fruitless hours in gymnasia nationwide. Steve snapped on his headphones, hoping to get a little local colour. And who knows? He may even have discovered that Holy Grail of the docu-soap director – A Character.

'Excuse me, madam!'

Mrs Renders was a little deaf (a positive asset in noisy Beckford House) and sailed majestically on. Steve and Nicko ran to catch up with her.

'Watch out for Sid, young man.'

The terrier, roused from its geriatric slumbers, was eyeing the furry microphone with a psychotic glint in its gummy eye.

'Could we have a word?'

'With me? Whatever for? Is it an advert?'

Nicko aimed the camera at the battered gold slippers, the tan tights, the aquamarine mac with its gold chain-link belt.

'We're making a documentary about the Elephant and Castle,' said Steve, 'and we want to talk to people who really know the area.'

'Well, you've struck gold.'

'Really?'

'I've lived in this area all my life...'

Nicko zoomed in on Mrs Renders's face, the lipstick leaching along the wrinkles around her mouth, the blobs of blue on each eyelid, the tidemark around the neck where the powder stopped and old flesh began.

'Yes, I was born just over there, you can't see it any more, it was bombed in the war and they've built the college over it now. I worked in all the halls round the area, you know. You might have heard of us. Maxim and Peggy Renders. Max was my husband, he played the musical saw like an angel. I sang, of course. "I'm going to get lit up when the lights go on in London..."'

'What can you tell us about Serena Ward?'

Mrs Renders stopped in mid-phrase. Sid, out of vision, was audible as a low growl.

'Miss Ward at number one? What do you want with her?'

'Has she got a boyfriend?'

Mrs Renders's watery blue eye stared into the camera with undisguised contempt. 'Then of course by the time we retired we wanted to settle down, and Beckford House had been built, so we were grateful for a place.'

'Do you know her?'

'Who, young man?'

'Serena Ward.'

'Of course. She is a very good friend of mine. Now, I believe you wanted to know about the area?'

'And the people in the area, Mrs... Renders. It's the human stories that count.'

'Then I suggest you ask the young lady yourself.'

'She's at work.'

'And so should I be. Good morning.'

With their noses in the air, Mrs Renders and Sid continued their progress towards Beckford House.

Back at the Kandid Productions office, whither the morning's rushes had been biked in time for a 'viewing lunch', Caroline was removing the clingfilm from a plate of sandwiches, which made up for the sparsity of their filling with an over-abundance of garnish. The standard of catering was a reliable barometer of Eddie's professional standing. During the glory days of *Other People's Pants* Eddie entertained visitors with overwrought canapes from an Italian delicatessen in nearby Berwick Street. In the bitter aftermath of *Disposal Squad*, he issued a memo to 'all staff' – in effect just himself and Caroline, sole survivors of a 12-strong team who had once been 'the Kandid Kids' – urging them to bring in their own food. Caroline was even forced to cater the odd working lunch, a task to which she brought the utter lack of imagination that characterised all her professional life.

Now, however, sandwiches from the outside world were reappearing. This more than anything convinced Caroine that Eddie was serious about *Elephant and Castle.*

She opened the boardroom door with her elbow and reversed in with the sandwiches in one hand and a flask of coffee in the other. Eddie barely looked up from the screen.

'Here's lunch, Eddie.'

'Yah...'

She left him to it, dimly concerned by the fact that he was hunkered down over images of a semi-erect penis. As she closed the door, she heard a sigh of admiration.

'Awesome... who would have thought you could get something of that quality from such a small piece of equipment...'

Eddie, in fact, was enthusing not over the proportions of Jamie's genitalia, but over the pin-sharp clarity of the images he had gathered during the morning's trial run with the concealed camera. It was all there – the horror of Jamie's flat, the strip show, the shower, Jamie's unguarded monologue – in broadcast-quality pictures and sound on one tiny cassette, no bigger than a packet of fags.

'I've got plans,' he heard Jamie say. 'I'm not going to be stuck in this dump for long. I'll be a millionaire by the time I'm 25. I'm going to get a job at a gym, get some experience, open me own health club, build it up into a little chain, go in with one of the big companies, sell up at the right time, bingo! Yeah, then I'll be able to settle down. Not just any old scrubber. I want someone with a bit of class.' At that point Jamie had sighed and stared wistfully down on the terraced houses of Spencer Street, his eyes lingering on the door of number one.

Eddie chuckled in delight, removed the cassette from the machine and moved on to one of Steve and Nicko's, which he'd collected by courier at no little expense. Hang it! *Elephant and Castle* was going to be the biggest hit of his career.

Viewing the rushes, he got the old tingle in his palms. He'd felt it when he first saw footage of the ambulances drawing up outside the block of flats where Dave 'Missed It!' Merryweather's inaccuracy with a spray gun had cost a young London family their lives. He'd felt it the first time Doreen 'Dirty Bitches!' Dawson displayed a set of skid marks to the unblinking Kandid camera. And now, as he saw Serena Ward posed against the tumbling pink roses of her back garden, he felt it all over again. Without bothering to pick up the telephone or even open the door, he shouted at the top of his voice.

'Caroline!'

The door burst open and Caroline entered with her usual preoccupied air. 'I really need to talk to you about the access thing, the paperwork, I mean it's really not my job description –'

'Look at this,' said Eddie, not even pretending to listen. 'What do you think?'

Caroline, whose vanity prevented her from wearing glasses but who had only that morning torn one of her contact lenses and swallowed the other, squinted at the screen. 'Yah, she's a very attractive woman, who is she?'

'Who is she? She's our bloody meal ticket, that's who she is.'

'Right, the meals thing, I've spoken with the caterers and –'

'She's our new star.'

'Oh right. Yah.'

'Serena Ward.'

Caroline looked blank.

'Does the name mean anything to you?'

'Serena Ward. I think I went to school with her sister, or something.'

'*Pour l'amour de dieu, Caroline*' – Eddie pronounced it, as always in moments of stress, 'Caroleen' – 'you booked the bloody woman.'

Caroline, who had been expecting a bollocking for something or other, smiled in relief.

'Oh, right. The Serena woman. Absolutely. Is she great or is she great?'

'She's great all right. Christ, look at her!' Eddie traced a finger down the freeze-frame image on the screen. 'Great hair. Beautiful face. Lovely tits, nothing too big, just a nice little handful. Narrow hips. Long legs.' Caroline, who tipped the scales at ten and a half stone and could no longer fit into a size 14, grimaced. Eddie blundered on. 'That's the kind of woman we want. Someone with poise, elegance, a bit of style, a bit of fucking class for God's sake! What's a girl like that doing in a dump like Elephant and Castle? What's her secret, Caroline? Eh? Answer me that.'

'Well, right, I mean she's part of a new breed,' began Caroline, desperately trying to recall an article she'd read in *Marie Claire*, 'young single sexy and successful, moving back into the inner cities, the post-Islington generation, right, movers and shakers who can make the funkiest downtown area into tomorrow's must-have enclave.'

'Cutting edge stuff, Caroline. You've still got it.' Eddie ran a hand over Caroline's right buttock. For weeks he had scarcely touched her; now, she thought with relief, her position was secure.

'Okay, get me everything you've got on her. Make sure she's signed up, understand? Signed, sealed and delivered. I don't want anything going wrong with this one. Serena Ward. Serena. She's our star. The women will identify with her, look up to her. The men will want to shag her. They always criticise me for concentrating on low-life. Well now they'll have to eat our words, cos this one is class to the core. It's all in the name. Serrrrreeeena.'

He hit the play button.

'They say that Londoners are unfriendly, but I've found the people round here to be absolutely gorgeous.'

Even Caroline had to admit that Serena's voice sounded wonderful, like melting chocolate.

Steve and Nicko enjoyed a vegetarian curry (as much as you can eat for £3.95) in Durga's Curry Den, and a couple of pints under the wary eye of the regulars of the Princess of Wales public house, before the call came through from head office.

'Eddie says "Go, go, go!"' said Steve, replacing the phone in his pocket.

'Fuck,' said Nicko, a man of few words. 'Where now, then?'

It was at that point that Destiny, in the sagging shape of publican William Wicks, intervened.

'You the blokes from the telly?' he asked, collecting their glasses and wiping down the table. The regulars knew something special was happening: Wicks never wiped tables. The Princess of Wales was famous for its sticky surfaces. Steve and Nicko, however, took his question in the friendly spirit in which it was disguised.

'Yes, that's right,' said Steve, smoothing his short, dark beard. 'We're making a documentary about the Elephant and Castle. Perhaps you'd like to...'

'You know where you want to be, don't you?'

'No.'

'Down the school. Lovely kids. Smashing. St Agatha's, just along the frog and toad, can't miss it.'

'Oh right, thank you Mr...'

'Wicks. William Wicks. Your genial host.'

One of the regulars expelled beer through his nostrils. Wicks continued, lowering his voice as if a confidence was being wrung out of him.

'My little girl goes there... my little angel, my Debbie.'

'Oh yes.'

'Would you like to see a picture?' Wicks was already behind the bar, taking down a silver framed photograph from beside the dry roasted peanuts.

'That's her. That's my Debbie, on her 15th birthday. She's grown now. Nearly 16.'

He huffed on the glass, polished it with his cuff and handed the picture to Steve. There, in a white blouse open to the third button and tied up around the ribcage, the thin cotton straining over an unusually large bust unfettered by any form of bra, was a perfect English rose, blonde and pouting.

'Got that done professionally by one of those glamour studios,' said Wicks. 'Said they'd never seen a girl as lovely as my Debbie. Didn't need to do a thing to her.'

Nicko, who had a taste for gymslip, was studying the photograph in detail.

'And you say,' asked Steve, 'that she's at school just round the corner?'

'On my mother's life,' said Wicks, with unnecessary gravity. 'Go on. See for yourselves. St Agatha's. Can't miss it.'

Steve and Nicko, in their enthusiasm ignoring the call of nature prompted by all the curry they could eat and two pints of Wicks's notoriously gassy beer, shouldered their burdens and set forth.

Debbie Wicks and her best friend Shelley Smithers were walking around the perimeter of the school grounds, as was their habit during free time. Their friendship was a mystery to the pupils and staff of St Agatha's (school motto: 'Training Girls to Succeed', although one embittered alumna had scratched the words 'Condemning' and 'Failure' in the appropriate place). Debbie Wicks had it all – looks, personality, sporting ability and even the glimmerings of a modest intellect. Her beauty brought hordes of boys from St Agatha's brother school, Origen House, to gawp at the railings every lunch hour, and aroused Sapphic yearnings in even the most heterosexual mistress. It was Debbie who had been the innocent nemesis of the kindly old caretaker who, last year, lured her into his mop cupboard to 'show her a special pet' and left the next day.

Shelley Smithers, meanwhile, was squat, ugly, hopeless at games, rumoured to be a lesbian and bone idle in class. Debbie's parents were respected local figures; Shelley's mother was an impoverished single parent on one of the vast estates that ringed the area. Debbie was blonde and white, Shelley was black. Debbie passed exams; Shelley failed for 'lack of application', according to her report. Debbie had application, the *sine qua non* of a St Agatha's girl. To see her struggling over a page of Chaucer, her tongue moistening her beestung lips was, according to English teacher Mrs Brown, to see the soul awakening.

And yet for all their differences, they were inseperable. It had begun at the end of the fourth form when Debbie abandoned a promising career as The Most Popular Girl in the School, cut all her fair-weather friends and began turning down invitations to parties. She studied through the summer, and when she returned to the fifth form limited her social life to the daily round with Shelley Smithers, arm in arm as often as not. Before long the shouts of 'lesbians!' died away, and they were left alone.

Debbie, in Shelley's eyes, was nothing less than an angel sent down from heaven. When Shelley's family disowned her after her shoplifting summer, it was Debbie who held out a helping hand. It had been a hot August, not the best weather for stealing chocolate, and the wellington boots that Shelley had worn into the newsagents must, in retrospect, have aroused suspicion. The method had worked well before; pick up a couple of pens, a rubber or a ruler, drop one item into the top of the boot, replace the other on the shelf, walk out with wellies brimming with swag. Perhaps Shelley's decision to swipe chocolate in high summer – and not just any old chocolate, but Milky Bars – was, as Debbie later said, a cry for help. The white chocolate rapidly melted inside the boot, leaving Shelley with glaring evidence all up her calves and the shopkeeper's hand weighing heavily on her shoulder.

For a week, Shelley languished under house arrest until Debbie, who had learned of her disgrace, turned up at the door and announced, in a voice loud enough for the neighbours to hear, that 'I would like to play with Shelley please, Mrs Smithers.' Even when Shelley's mother bundled her inside and explained that she was not, in fact, *Mrs* Smithers as she and Shelley's father (now but a memory) had never married, Debbie did not condemn. And from that day on they were not parted.

This perplexed Shelley almost as much as the rest of the school, but after a while she simply came to accept the miracle. Debbie, it seemed, needed her just as much as Shelley needed Debbie. For all her looks and popularity, Debbie was by nature a shy child, thrust into the spotlight at the onset of adolescence by physical developments over which she had no control. By the age of 13 she had curves and 'a lot of promise' according to her father; by 15, when the framed portrait (which she loathed) was taken, she had achieved a 36DD. While other girls suffered from greasy hair and acne, Debbie awoke each morning with her skin clearer, her blonde locks bouncier than ever. This would have delighted most, but to Debbie, who just wanted to merge into the background, it was torture. Whenever she found herself the centre of attention – among a circle of her father's cronies at the pub for instance, dragged away from her homework to 'meet the gang' – she smiled sweetly and died inside. She developed a speech impediment, and by the time she reached the fifth form was a martyr to galloping spoonerism. It afflicted her every time she was obliged to speak in public. She could feel people's eyes burning into her. One day in assembly she had been forced, in front of the whole school, to read out a prize-winning essay on the subject of bird husbandry. She got no further than announcing 'Peeping Karrots by Webbie Dicks' when staff and students erupted in hysterics. The voice of Michaela Gittish – once

Debbie's best friend – rose high and clear above the hubbub.

'Webbie Dicks! It sounds like old men's willies!'

Debbie hung her head, the tears moistening her big blue eyes. That was the turning point. She became solitary and withdrawn, relying increasingly on Shelley as her one and only confidante.

Why Shelley? Perhaps because she was the only one who had never tried to suck up to her. Because she was an outsider, shunned by the rest of the school. In truth, Shelley had always longed to be Debbie's friend, and spent hours in class writing their conjoined names in the back of her rough book. It was only the certainty of rejection that kept her at bay. As far as Debbie was concerned, Shelley offered an escape from the attention that, she felt sure, would drive her to mental illness before she reached adulthood. With Shelley, she felt safe, unthreatened, judged only for her mind, not her body. Had she known that Shelley was tormented by sexual fantasies of the crudest sort every time they were together, she might have withdrawn her friendship. But Shelley kept her libido under lock and key.

When Steve and Nicko started cruising around the playground, there wasn't much to see. The younger girls were in lessons; most of the fifth form were sitting exams or at home revising. As luck would have it, Debbie and Shelley were the only two girls around. After a gruelling trial by English Lit in the morning, they were free for the afternoon. Debbie had no desire to go home to the Princess of Wales; it was impossible to revise with her father's constant interruptions. Shelley, who desperately needed to prepare for tomorrow's maths exam, was happy to sacrifice her future for a few hours of Debbie's company.

'That's her,' hissed Nicko, cantering across a hopscotch grid. 'Come on.'

To Debbie, the sight of a camera racing towards her was like something out of her worst nightmare. She froze in her tracks, her eyes wide and staring, sweat breaking out on her upper lip.

'Shelley...'

Shelley, shorter than Debbie but a good deal wider, stepped in front of her friend and lowered her head like a rhino about to charge. Nicko stopped and faced her. Steve, dragged along in Nicko's slipstream, smoothed his beard and attempted to charm.

'Hi ladies. We're making a programme about the Elephant and Castle area, and we'd really like to talk to you. It's Debbie, isn't it?'

Debbie blinked and panted, like an unfledged chick tumbled from its nest.

Shelley scowled and wiped her nose. 'Have you got permission to be here?'

'We're from the telly.'

'Does the headmistress know?'

'We're just making a programme. Can we have a word, Debbie?'

Steve, joined to Nicko's camera by an umbilical wire, was forced to trot round in circles while the slavering cameraman recorded Debbie from every angle.

'Debbie, have you ever considered a career as a model?'

'Leave her alone.'

'It's okay love, you run along, it's Debbie we want to talk to.'

'Shelley...'

'That's enough, mate. I'm warning you.' Shelley clenched her fists and glowered. Even Nicko backed off.

'All right! All right! Jesus, it's only a tv programme.'

'You'd better go and see the headmistress.'

'Okay! Christ.'

Steve and Nicko trudged obediently in the direction that Shelley was pointing. As they disappeared, she heard the word 'dyke'.

While Steve and Nicko were put through the third degree by the headmistress, Serena Ward was basking in the afterglow of an entirely successful presentation. The client – a publishing giant with plans for a lifestyle magazine aimed at 'tweenies' – made special mention of Serena to her boss, who took her out to lunch on the strength of it. 'You're a godsend,' he'd told her over fried courgette flowers and a bottle of mineral water. 'Don't leave us.'

'I have no intention of leaving. I'm happy at Rampling and Partners.'

'You deserve a raise.'

'Oh, Mr Rampling...'

'Please. Richard. Ricky, even.'

Were it not for the fact that Ricky Rampling was a known homosexual, Serena might have withdrawn her hand when his landed on top of it. As it was, she was delighted by the attention.

'Shall we have a drink? A real drink?'

'Oh, Mr Ramp... Ricky. I've got a lot to do this afternoon.'

'What?'

'A creative brief for the DofE job.'

'Leave it.'

'A report to write up for the BBC.'

'Oh for heaven's sake, woman. Let your hair down. Waiter!'

A very good looking young man was instantly at Ricky's elbow.

'Sir?'

'A bottle of Moët.'

'Yes sir.'

'Ricky, really!'

'You deserve it. And after we've drunk that, I shall take you into Soho and show you around some of my favourite haunts. I warn you, you might be a little shocked.'

'Oh yes?'

'Yeah. I run with a pretty fast crowd. Work hard, play hard, that's my motto. Are you game?'

If only he knew, thought Serena. If only he knew...

Three

While Serena was pretending to be shocked by the conversation of Ricky Rampling and his overgroomed friends in the Soho bars, a police car pulled up outside her house in Spencer Street. The net curtains at number three twitched once and were still. Before the bell could ring a second time Daryn Handy, 24-year-old father of Ben (6) had made a hasty exit over the back fence, landing heavily in Serena's lovingly-tended flowerbeds. Ben tore himself away from *Resident Evil XVI* and opened the door to uniformed officers.

'Lily Law at number three,' drawled Muriel, whose habit it was to look down on the comings and goings from his sixth-floor Beckford House window. His partner, Maureen, whizzed round the ornaments with a duster.

'Again?'

'Ye-e-es.' Muriel, who maintained the appearance of an ageing chorus boy thanks to a furious regime of potions and lotions, preserved the drawling accents of a refined background. Common Maureen, his tubby frame topped with a mop of shiny black corkscrew curls, executed a heavy *pas de chat* across the carpet to join his friend at the window. In black leggings and an apron adorned with the *Cats* logo, he looked like an inflated Wayne Sleep.

'That child will hang. Mark my words.'

'Oh Maureen, have some charity.'

'Bugger charity, dear, the little bastard called me a fat poof yesterday.'

'Well…' Muriel prided himself on the fact that he weighed not a pound more now than he did at 25. 'Out of the mouths of babes…'

'Look down there,' said Maureen, hastily changing the subject, 'that's those telly blokes that we're expecting.'

'Where?' Muriel scanned down his fine, aquiline nose.

'There. Trade with the camera, dear.'

'Ooh.' Muriel picked up the glasses that he wore on a chain around his neck. 'Oh yes. Very me.'

'Peggy says that they're shocking scandalmongers who practically offered her money to dish the dirt on Serena Ward.'

'Ye-e-es.'

'And as such we shouldn't have nothing to do with them.'

'Mmm.'

For a moment there was silence, save for the vocal stylings of Barbara Cook from the ancient hi-fi.

'Go on Mo, give 'em a toot.'

Maureen stuck two stubby fingers in his rosebud mouth and produced a piercing whistle which echoed off the walls beneath.

'I say!' trilled Muriel in a fruity coloratura. 'Up here! Gentlemen! Up here!'

Steve and Nicko were up the stairs before Muriel had time to 'glue', a fiddly process involving webbing, spirit gum, flesh-coloured pancake and a small toupée. Maureen opened the door on the chain.

'Just a moment, gents. She's still in her dressing room. Oi! Muriel! Visitors!'

Thus had Maureen dealt with stage-door johnnies in the old days at the clubs, Muriel as the bewigged, corseted, dragged-up star, Maureen his dresser.

'Are you decent, dear? Sorry, guys, but you wouldn't want to see her if she's not, take my word.'

Muriel burst out of the bathroom fully glued.

'Let the gentlemen in, Maureen. Oh for heaven's sake, take your fucking pinny off.'

While Maureen fumbled with his knots, Muriel, in a haze of Chanel, greeted his visitors. His face, pulled back tight over his skull, had the sheen of the long dead. His eyes slanted up in what he took to be a fascinating, Asiatic way. The large mole on his left cheekbone was touched up to the full Margaret Lockwood. A scarf with a brass ring at the throat completed the image.

'Make yourselves at home. Maureen, offer drinks.'

Maureen's eyes glinted maliciously from deep within their surrounding folds. 'Certainly, your majesty. Chaps. Coffee? Tea?'

'Or me?' supplied Muriel.

'Oh Muriel, you are an outrageous flirt!'

'I am. I am outrageous. I know it.' The hands – long, pale, Beardsleyesque – fluttered to the breast.

'Or something harder? Winnie Whisky? Vera Vodka? Or dear old stand-by Ginette?'

The pair of them goggled as Steve and Nicko struggled for words.

'Yeah,' said Nicko, coughing in the cloud of scent. 'I'll have a whisky, ta.'

'Ye-e-es, I took you for the whisky type. What's your name, Cameraman?'

'Nick McVitie.'

'McVitie. Mmmm… I like a bit of Scotch myself. And your… friend?'

The director, smoothing his beard with more than usual vigour, took the offered hands. 'Steve Soave.'

Maureen and Muriel turned to each other and nodded. 'Italian,' they chorused as one.

'*Che gelida manina*,' essayed Muriel, who prided himself on a gift for language based entirely on the lyrics of popular songs. 'Welcome to our bijou lattie, as we used to say in the theatre.

Ye-e-es, we're in the same profession as yourselves, gentlemen.'

'Don't be insulting, Mu.'

'Entertainment, I was going to say before my friend interrupted me.'

'She's in a much older profession than that, dear.'

Muriel rose above it. 'Come through and tell us what we can do for you. Bring your drinks and your... equipment.' Muriel's every word sounded like an invitation to sin.

'Now,' said Muriel, patting a cushion where Steve reluctantly sat (Nicko, 'for technical reasons,' preferred to perch on the windowsill), 'we really shouldn't have let you up here at all. We've been warned about you. We understand that you're very... very... naughty boys. Is that true? Mmm? Are you... naughty?'

'Well,' muttered Steve, blushing, 'I don't know about that.'

'What my friend is trying to say,' said Maureen, still dusting, 'is how much will you pay us for information. Let's not beat about the bush.'

'That's not really the sort of thing...'

'Oh come on,' said Muriel, all twinkling confidence. 'You want to know the gossip, don't you? I know what you boys are like. You come on with your charm and your good looks, all innocent, butter wouldn't melt, and win the trust of innocent souls like me...'

Maureen squealed.

'Then no sooner have you got us to open ourselves up than you toss us aside like so many... husks.'

'You tell 'em, Muriel. Husks. That's all we are to them. To be discarded when finished with.'

'I've seen it happen, dear. I know whereof I speak. You don't spend a lifetime in show business without learning a trick or two.'

'Turning a trick or two in your case.'

'So come on, gentlemen, we understand each other, do we not?' Muriel's lips and eyebrows executed a frantic gavotte around his face.

'Well,' said Steve, 'if you think you have information that might be of interest to us...'

'Information... Well yes,' hissed Muriel, 'that's one thing we've plenty of. We see things. We know things. We... observe, wouldn't you say, Maureen?'

'You spend the day with your lorgnettes trained on the street while I cook and scrub, if that's what you mean.'

'So *naturlich* we have a certain amount of *savoir faire.*'

'What about Serena Ward, for example?' tried Steve.

'Ooh, well –'

Muriel was about to deliver, but Maureen, dropping his duster, intervened. 'Just a second, gentlemen. We have to discuss terms, don't we? Nothing's free in this business. And you,' he added, turning to Nicko, 'turn that camera off and give me the tape. Now. I mean it. If we're going to work together, it's on our terms, understand?'

'Oh dear,' sighed Muriel, the sordid mention of business matters paining him deeply, 'I had better let you hammer it out with Maureen. He's the brains in this operation. I'm just the beauty.'

Half an hour and several whiskies later, Maureen had hammered out a muck/brass transaction satisfactory to all parties. The secrets of Serena Ward ('and anyone else you care to mention') would be laid bare in return for an agreed sum – enough, calculated Maureen, to enable him and Muriel to realise their cherished dream of reviving in south-east London the long dead variety circuit with a club of their own. Steve Soave, unable to contact Eddie Kander and therefore using his own executive powers, okayed the deal verbally. If push came to shove, they could always tell the old queens to fuck off.

The old queens, expansive in the afterglow of successful negotiation, allowed Nicko to switch his camera on and treated him to a trip down memory lane amply illustrated by albums of faded newspaper cuttings that they kept in a cupboard alongside a set of sherry glasses.

'Here's me backstage at Hanover Square with Danny. That was a fun night. Here's me performing "See What the Boys in the Backroom Will Have" on stage at the Royal Vauxhall Tavern in the late 60s. I was one of the first real stars of the place dear, course it's gone down something shocking now hasn't it Maureen?'

'Shocking.'

'Here's me interviewed in the *Express* in 1974 when we opened our own club in Bayswater, that was a smashing place wasn't it Mo?'

'Smashing.'

'Oh and here's me at my gala comeback night debuting the song that was in many ways to become my theme tune, "I Am What I Am", upstairs at the Apollo Club in Wardour Street, Francis Bacon was in the audience.'

'A dear friend.'

'He said I looked as pretty as a picture.'

'Yes. One of his,' whispered Maureen in Steve's ear.

'And here's my swansong at the Union Tavern, that last great bastion of the variety circuit, before all these so-called gays took it over with their disco music and their stripping and what not.'

'Not that we've got anything against the young.'

'*Au contraire*, we always say *vive la jeunesse* don't we Maureen?'

'We do. We take an interest in youth. We cultivate. We groom.'

'We *bring on*, Steve, if you get my meaning. Oh! And speak of the Devil!'

At that very moment there was a rattle of the letter box.

'That'll be our latest find. Our what's-it, Muriel?'

'Protégé.'

'Our protégé. Coming, love!'

Maureen flitted out to the passage, leaving Muriel to check his glue. He bent nearer Nicko's camera with a conspiratorial air.

'You'll like this one, dear. A very big talent. You could have something very special on your hands with this young man. I know I have.'

There was a brief, whispered conversation in the hall, then Maureen ushered the protégé into the room.

'Say hello, James.'

'Smile. You're on tv.'

Jamie furrowed his brow and nodded at the camera. His fists clenched, and he did a little nervous boxer's dance.

'James is a very promising young talent, a marvellous performer. Never fails in our experience. Now, James, what can we old timers do for you? Come for some advice, have you? We give the benefit to so many ambitious youngsters such as he.' Muriel wittered on while Jamie shifted from foot to foot.

'Spit it out, lad,' said Maureen.

'I don't like to.'

'Oh go on, whisper.'

Jamie bent down to Maureen and said a few words into the shiny corkscrew curls.

'I see. Come on then.' They left the room together.

'You see, so willing to give,' said Muriel, trying hard to maintain his poise. 'Possibly girlfriend trouble, common in many of the young talents we try to help. Or perhaps some uncertainty about conflicting job offers. We find with many of the artistes that we handle that jobs come in so thick and fast that they don't know which way to turn. The best we can give is advice based on years in the profession. Now, here's me at a private party in Gidea Park, wearing one of Maureen's finest creations...'

Next door, Maureen was giving the benefit. 'I told you, I've nothing for you. If a punter rings, I give the job to the first boy who picks up the phone. What have you been doing all day? Sleeping? Screwing that tart?'

'I had an interview.'

'Interview my arse, you'd get more sense out of it.'

'I'm really broke, Mo.'

'Tough. You should have kept your phone switched on. I told

you. What's the point of having a bloody mobile if you switch it off all the time?'

'It was the bloke from the telly. Offered me money.'

'What? Oh, and I suppose you took it, did you? Shame on you, selling other people's secrets for a few quid and the empty promise of tv stardom.'

'Yes, I did accept it, as it goes, but he ain't paid me nothing yet and I didn't tell him nothing about nobody.'

'Well. I'll see what I can do. I make no promises.'

'Go on, Mo. I need money now. I've got to get some new trainers. I'm seeing the manager of the gym tomorrow. I can't turn up for work looking like I don't mean business.'

'I see.' Maureen narrowed his eyes, insofar as this was possible given the amount of flesh that surrounded them. 'And how much do you need?'

'Forty quid.'

'Forty quid for a pair of shoes?'

'That's not even real good ones, it's just knock-off down the market.'

'God help us. Forty quid. All right then. The things I do for you. Just this once, then.'

'Thanks, Mo. I won't forget it.'

'Like the last time and the time before that.'

'If I get the job I swear I'll pay you back.'

'Don't say that. It's not a loan, remember. You earn it. Now, what does 40 quid get me?'

'You know the rates, Mo. Wank and a blow-job.'

'That's right, James,' said Maureen, gripping the front of Jamie's tracksuit bottoms. 'Wank and a blow-job.'

Maureen returned to the living room a quarter of an hour later, just as Muriel was trilling through the final chorus of 'Don't Rain on My Parade'. He dipped a pudgy hand into a colourful ginger jar, one of many ornaments cluttering the mantelpiece above the gas fire, and pulled out two £20 notes.

'What exactly are you doing?' demanded Muriel, switching from ingenue to harpy in the blink of an eye.

'He needs money.'

'Oh, and he's earned it, I suppose.'

Behind Muriel's back, Steve discreetly signalled to Nicko to keep the camera turning.

'What's it to you?'

'You don't use the housekeeping for trade. That's the rules, Maureen.'

'Oh fuck off, Muriel, and sing us another song.'

'The music would stick in my throat thinking about what you've been up to.'

'Just because it's many years since you've seen a live penis...'

'Put that money back.' Muriel made a swipe for the notes, missed as Maureen jumped back with an agility surprising in one so fat, and sprawled on the sofa.

Steve and Nicko crept silently from the flat, and followed Jamie down the stairs.

Debbie slipped into the Prince of Wales through the back door and raced upstairs to her room. Only then did she start to breathe normally again. The ordeal with the cameras in the playground had been a terrible setback.

'Pull yourself together, you silly girl,' she said. It was her habit to address herself as a strict but loving mother might admonish a wayward child. 'Sulking and skulking won't pass exams. Hard work! That's the ticket!'

With fresh determination, she sat at the desk and opened her folder. Quadratic equations danced before her, and once again she saw the monstrous eye of the camera looming up at her like a cyclops, ready to eat her alive. She breathed deeply.

'Snap out of it, you foolish child. Come along! Work work work!'

If she could just think a little faster... the quadratic equations tripped a few steps ahead of her, tantalisingly within reach. She picked up a pen and started jotting down the calculations that, this time, would surely lead her to the correct answer.

Yes... there it was... almost...

And then the heavy, familiar tread on the stairs, the soft knock on the door.

'Where's my little princess? Hiding yourself away in your bedroom on a beautiful afternoon like this? You'll ruin your eyes with all those sums.'

'I've got maths tomorrow, dad.'

'Come outside and get some fresh air.'

'I've got to revise.'

'Your Uncle Dudley's coming over this evening.'

'Please, Dad, just tonight, let me get on with it.'

'Don't be silly, Debbie. I'll send your mother up. You look peaky.'

'I'm fine, Daddy. I just need to work.'

'You? Work? You'll never need to work, Princess. Isn't that what I've always told you? You'll never need to work.'

William kissed the top of his daughter's head and left the room.

Less than half a mile away in Ringwood House, centrepiece of the notorious Ringwood Estate which featured so regularly on the front page of the local newspaper, Shelley Smithers was enjoying the complete peace and quiet of an empty flat. Her mother was out at work; her brother Steadman (named after the Five Star vocalist) came home only to eat and, occasionally, sleep. Shelley stared at the same quadratic equations but saw nothing. Her eyes bored through the paper to a world beyond maths exams, beyond St Agatha's, beyond Elephant and Castle, where she and Debbie could roam in eternal summer, untroubled by prying cameras, taunting schoolfellows or irate shopkeepers.

How long she stayed in this trance she could not tell. When she came to, conscious of her mother's key in the door, she found that she had doodled all over her revision. The name 'Debbie' appeared several times, alongside crude sketches of a blonde, naked woman, the breasts delineated so many times that the pen had gone through the paper and left ghostly tits on the page beneath.

Perhaps, thought Shelley, it's true what Michaela Gittish says. Perhaps I really am a lesbian.

'Uncle' Dudley Jenkins, an old army pal of William Wicks's and no relation at all, was a regular visitor to the Princess of Wales, particularly in the last year or so. It was he who had put into William's head the notion that Debbie was 'coming along nicely', who had arranged for her first sitting at the glamour studio and who was now at the bar persuading William and Theresa that their not-so-little girl had a great future literally in front of her.

'She's a natural. The agencies, they'd go mad for a girl like her. You could have her in every newspaper in the country, on telly, in *OK!* magazine...'

'*OK!* magazine?' breathed Theresa. 'You really think so?'

'Trust me. I know the glamour business. I've seen hundreds of tarts, no disrespect, with not an ounce of Debbie's talents, and they spread it pretty thin believe you me. But your little girl, she's something different. You're sitting on a goldmine there, if only you knew it.'

'I keep telling her!' said William. 'She says she doesn't want to be a model. She wants to pass her exams and train for something or other. Wants to be a vet. Can you believe it? Lovely girl like her with her hand up a cow's arse?'

'She should listen to her Dad.'

'No, but what if she doesn't want to?' said Theresa. 'She's a shy girl, really, my Debbie. She's not one to push herself forward.'

'She doesn't need to! That's just my point!' Dudley laughed into his beer. 'Or points, I should say, perhaps!'

'She'll do as she's told,' said William, refilling his friend's glass.

'She's got ideas of her own, love,' said Theresa. 'We shouldn't stand in her way.'

'The only thing that's standing in her way is that bloody Shelley Smithers that she hangs round with.'

'Well...'

'Bad influence.'

'Oh yes?' said Dudley. 'What's she look like, then? Nice girl, is she?'

William snorted. 'She's coloured.'

'Yeah, but some coloured birds are stunning, aren't they? The papers like them, bit of variety. Look at that Naomi Campbell. She's from Streatham.'

'Shelley Smithers ain't no Naomi Campbell. She's fat. Ask me, she's a lesbo.'

'Oh, William.' Theresa moved off down the bar.

'Yeah, ask me, that's what she is.'

'Really?' asked Dudley, staring meditatively into space. 'Well, there's potential there. A lot of potential.'

'What?'

'Girl-on-girl action. Very popular on the old websites.'

'Forget it. Not my Debbie.'

'It's where the money is. That's the future, my old son, you can't fight it. Or my name isn't Dudley Jenkins.'

Four

Every successful docusoap needs its tale of triumph over tragedy, of pluck and talent winning out against overwhelming odds – and if the person in question is hugely fat, it really helps.

And right on cue, careening around the corner into Spencer Street like a sofa on castors that has somehow slipped its moorings, comes local character Fat Alice, 'just dropping in' for the fourth time in two days on her 'lovely neighbour' Serena Ward, who so far had either been genuinely out or lucky enough to see her coming and retreat to a back room. But Alice was not easily deterred. She knew that there were cameras around, and she longed to hog them.

Fat Alice was the friendliest, and conversely the least popular, woman in the area. She made a big impact wherever she went, with her cut-glass voice, her floral-print dresses and her collection of 'fun' earrings. She ogled the world through the rainbow frames of big plastic glasses, but nobody looked back. Once the novelty had worn off, her offers of friendship seemed, even to the nicest neighbours, to smack of desperation. Her bright attire, intended to attract, served more effectively to repel.

What Alice lacked in height she more than made up for in girth – a fact which, against all reason, did not deter her from wearing skin-tight leggings which revealed every contour of her lower body. These and other sartorial affectations – berets, 'Keep It Live!' badges and even the occasional legwarmer – betrayed an affinity with the theatre that constituted Alice's sole, all-consuming passion in life. She went up to town at least three times a week, and had missed only four Saturday matinées of *Les Misérables* in the last eight years. She had done so many backstage tours of the Barbican Theatre that she knew the stage hands by name. She kept up her membership of Equity (gained in the 80s by a series of gruelling cabaret tours) even though she had not worked in the theatre since. She referred to her favourite actors by their first names (Rufus! Ralph! Derek!) as if they were on intimate terms – which, in her active fantasy life, they were. By day she worked for a charitable trust that forced scared children to take part in community plays; by night, she donned a shawl and swanned around foyers from Shaftesbury Avenue to the Strand. She referred to the Old Vic and the National Theatre as 'my locals', and would pop into the bar of one or the other just for the interval, to chat knowingly about shows she'd already seen twice, without the extra expense of another ticket.

In her spare time – on those evenings when she was not 'doing' a show – she managed the career of Miachail Miorphiagh, whom she'd 'spotted' ten years ago in *Troilus* at Stratford. She stalked him during the years of his success in tv medical drama *Surgeon General*, and now that the show had been axed in a welter of disastrous reviews (focusing mostly on Miorphiagh's complete lack of charisma) she represented his interests to an uninterested profession. Her unpaid efforts on Miorphiagh's behalf had resulted in occasional pantomime work, a series of charity workshops and a regular gig in police line-ups whenever the words 'short', 'weasel-faced' or 'shifty' appeared on the description. Now she was within a hair's breadth of getting him a job on *The Archers*. It would be, she predicted, a magnificent comeback.

Alice lived in Warfield Street, parallel to Spencer Street but outside *Elephant and Castle* as far as Kandid Productions were concerned. Alice was fast finding out that in tv terms her street, her house, her very self didn't exist. This, however, was a minor consideration to a woman who spent her life crashing situations where she was not wanted.

In theory, getting on the show should have been a piece of cake for Alice, with her theatrical connections and superabundant personality. Surely she had only to drop in on one of her dear friends while the cameras were there and she'd be noticed, 'discovered' and promoted to a starring role. Unfortunately, nobody in the area could stand the woman. Those foolish enough to allow her into their homes only got rid of her after two hours of unbearable monologue, leaving their ears ringing and their biscuit tins empty. In private Alice considered her neighbours to be 'terrible philistines' whose lack of refinement made for amusing tales on the coach to Stratford-upon-Avon. But now she cursed her isolation. Try as she might – decked in her loudest clothes, her wittiest accessories – she could not lure Steve and Nicko around the corner into Warfield Street. Without an entrée to Spencer Street or Beckford House she was doomed to languish in obscurity while others – how much less worthy! – basked in the sunlight of publicity.

Alice had always regarded Serena with a mixture of envy and contempt, but now, driven by her lust for publicity, she was prepared to review her personal feelings. She waited in the lee of the fags and mags kiosk until she saw Serena return from work – and then she pounced.

'Oo-ooh! Serena!'

Serena had her key in the lock, but was not quick enough to get inside the house before Alice – surprisingly fast for a woman of her dimensions – was beside her on the doorstep. She took in the apparition in one astonished flash, her aesthetic sense recoiling against the clashing palette of colours – the red Aids ribbon against the orange tartan shawl over the turquoise garment (what *was* it, exactly? A shirt? A dress?), the fuchsia earrings, the rainbow specs, the copper-coloured hair.

'If it's not convenient, oh well maybe just for a moment,' she said, squeezing past Serena and into the entrance hall.

'Why don't you come in?' said Serena with an irony completely lost on her guest.

'Oh well,' said Alice, looking at her 'fun' Betty Boop watch, 'maybe just for a second.'

An hour later, she was still in full spate.

'Of course, that's what Miachail calls me, a one-woman ICM, so I suppose I must be doing something right. We're trying to get together a convention for all the fans, he still gets a lot of mail from people who remember him in *Surgeon General*, some of it's quite kinky, well of course Miachail is a very attractive man, I don't have to tell *you* that do I?'

Alice fluttered her eyelashes in a 'just us girls' kind of way. Serena shook her head and tried to remember if, anywhere in the monologue, she'd explained who 'Miachail' was.

'But he's a one-man woman, I'm happy to say, gosh look at the time, I don't know whether I ought to be wearing this watch, it seems to aggravate my eczema, look.' She let the sleeve of the turquoise garment fall back to reveal a relief map of bumps and welts up her arm. 'I'm a medical marvel, what with that and the RSI, I'm still in negotiation with the union about that, they can't lay me off but they don't know what to do with me now that I can't work on screen any more, I mean I'm far too experienced to sit around stuffing envelopes but really I ought to be out in the field more often, I'm very much a people kind of a person, well we mostly are in the media, aren't we? Of course you're in advertising.'

Serena could not deny it.

'Well dear Miachail of course is so much in demand these days for voice-overs, you must have a chat with me about it some time, he has a marvellous voice, could sell Eskimos snow I always say, he's such a sweetie, I could eat him alive I really could.'

Looks like you have, thought Serena, pointedly removing Alice's coffee cup.

'So nice of you to ask me in, I'm so busy I rarely have a chance to chat,' said Alice, desperately trying to ignore her marching orders, 'but now the tv cameras are here I suppose we'll be in and out of each other's houses all the time. Have they approached you at all?'

Serena was holding the door. 'Yes.'

'How fascinating! I'm most amused by the way people are practically throwing themselves in front of the cameras. Good heavens, it's only telly. So what did they say?'

'They want me to talk to them about my life.'

'Isn't it strange, this obsession with real life, surely the medium is better suited to the portrayal of fiction, of fantasy, the element of magic that is missing from people's lives, we so badly need nourishing by the *living* arts, when exactly are they coming?'

'Tomorrow.'

'Poor you, what an invasion of your privacy that will be.'

'Goodbye, Alice.' Serena laid a firm hand on her arm to guide her out of the door.

'Ooh, mind my RSI! Ow! Oh dear, no harm done.'

With a little effort, Alice manoeuvred herself on to the street, savouring the knowledge that the cameras would be back tomorrow.

Jamie was by nature a confident young man. He'd survived, flourished even, during 6 years in the army in which time he'd risen to the rank of corporal. Unqualified for civilian life, adrift without the discipline of the forces, he made a living by entertaining 'friends' in his Beckford House flat. In the pubs and bars of south London and the West End, he could chat up any woman who took his fancy. But when it came to the prospect of a job interview, Jamie's confidence deserted him.

He woke up as limp as a lettuce. He sat over breakfast wondering if he was going to be sick. He trained for half an hour – skipping, press ups, ab crunches, bicep curls – but his muscles trembled and his breath was short. He showered, spent another half hour attempting to knot his regimental tie, and left home at ten o'clock with an hour to spare. The leisure centre, that Mecca towards which his every hope and dream tended, was only five minutes' walk away. Jamie spent the interval walking round the shopping centre, burying his nose in fitness magazines in the newsagent, shying away from anyone who knew him. He ran a finger around his neck, coughed and unconsciously flexed his muscles. The fey young man at the till blushed and looked away.

Finally, at ten to eleven, Jamie crossed the road by a labyrinth of subways and reported to the front desk of the leisure centre, where a bored, suspicious young woman picked up a phone.

'Rod. I've got a bloke here for you. What's your name?'

'Jamie Lord. I've got an interview.'

'Jamie Lord. Says he's got an interview. Okay. Sit down.'

Jamie sat in a decaying steel-framed chair, crossing and recross-ing his legs, staring at his nails. Ten minutes passed. Fifteen. He was about to remind someone of his existence when, suddenly, the sun seemed to darken and the room become smaller. Jamie looked up and there, towering above him, was a giant of a man extending a hand the size of a shovel.

'Jamie.' His voice rumbled somewhere below baritone.

Jamie sprang to his feet and fought an urge to stand to attention. The hand with which he was about to salute he forced downwards to return the greeting.

'Hi!' It came out far too high.

'I'm Rod. I'm the manager of this dump. Follow me.'

Rod turned and bounded up the stairs three at a time. Jamie fol-lowed, a terrier in the slipstream of a rottweiler. Rod's shoulders were almost as wide as the staircase.

At the top of the stairs, Rod kicked open a battered blue door with a round glass window. Jamie followed him into a small square room with a single overhead light, a table and two chairs. In the corner, a filing cabinet was bursting at the seams. On top lay a strange armoury of metal pincers, rubber hosing and cardboard tubes that Jamie recognised as the paraphernalia of the fitness professional.

'So, you want a job.'

'Yeah, I worked for four years as a PT instructor in the army and I've been training private clients since I left...'

'I've seen your CV. Why aren't you working?'

'I am, I told you, I'm personal training.'

'That's what they all say. Okay, put me through my paces.'

'Sorry?'

'Train me. Come on. Show me how you work.'

'Right.' Jamie's heart was beating too fast; he felt freezing cold, even in the overheated, airless office.

'Come on. I'm a punter. I want to get in shape. Tell me what to do.'

The word 'punter' worked like a charm. Jamie's mind snapped into focus and he stood up.

'Down on the floor. Now! Okay, give me ten press ups.'

Rod did as he was told.

'Come on, proper ones. Head up, chest all the way down to the floor. Ten more.'

Rod strained and obeyed. Jamie noticed that his arms, impressive enough when hanging inert at his sides, had doubled in girth, criss-crossed with a mesh of veins.

'Right, up on your feet. I want ten tuck jumps. No, knees higher than that. Up to my hand.' He held his hand at chest level. Rod was gratifyingly flushed and sweating, struggling to reach the target.

'Okay, down on the floor again. On yer back, on yer back.' The note of command returned to his voice – the voice that had middle-aged men grovelling around on the filthy carpets of Beckford

House. 'Right: crunches. Nice... and slow... One. Two. Keep your chin and your chest up towards the ceiling. Three. Keep your feet flat on the ground.' He moved round, placed a foot on top of Rod's trainers. 'Suck your gut in. That's it. Four. Hold it and pulse, pulse, pulse. Okay five, six, all the way, I said *all* the way up, and hold it there.'

Rod's red face hovered mere inches away from Jamie's groin. The erotic possibilities of the situation were lost on neither of them (Rod himself had, like so many 'trainers', filled in between jobs with a little casual prostitution), but to make the first move would be to lose face.

'Good, and seven-eight-nine-ten,' said Jamie hurriedly. 'You've worked well.'

Rod stood up, mopped his brow. 'Okay, hard man,' he said. 'You've got the job.' They exchanged a complicated handshake of knuckles and elbows then stood facing each other, their feet a yard apart, arms folded behind their backs, perfect mirrors. 'When can you start?'

'Right now!'

'And your... personal clients?'

'I can reschedule.' Jamie whipped the mobile from his jacket pocket and dialled. 'I'll get my assistant to make the arrangements.'

'Good man.'

On the sixth floor of Beckford House, where Maureen and Muriel perched, unglued, at the window, the phone rang.

The standard spiel about flat fees gained Eddie Kander entrance to 3 Spencer Street, where he was greeted at the doorstep by a pale, suspicious young man who asked him immediately if he was CID. When he assured him that he was not, that he was from a tv company and that he was here to discuss an idea greatly to his advantage, Daryn took the chain off the door and let Eddie into the hall, never once removing the scowl from his face. As Eddie's eyes adjusted to the gloom, taking in the peeling woodchip, the threadbare carpet, the empty light fitting hanging by flyblown wires from the ceiling, he fumbled with his 'on' button and hoped that the concealed camera's claim to operate in any light conditions was not exaggerated.

Daryn ushered Eddie into the front room, where a net curtain and several layers of soot protected them from prying eyes.

'Sit down,' he said, even though there was not a surface in the room uncluttered by toys, videos, empty cans or magazines. 'I've got to get Ben off to school. You'll have to wait.' He descended to the basement kitchen where six-year-old Ben was rounding off his breakfast with one of Daryn's cigarettes.

'Oh for fuck's sake,' Eddie heard, 'can't you buy your own?'

As voices screeched in well-rehearsed argument, Eddie strolled round the front room taking in every detail – the overflowing ashtrays, the empty pizza cartons, the stack of VCRs gathering dust in the corner – and mentally composed his voice-over. 'When politicians bleat about social exclusion, do they really know what they're talking about? This is reality for millions of Britons today – a life on the breadline, forced into crime, where every day children are caught in the crossfire of class war.'

The door slammed and Ben ambled down the road in the opposite direction from school.

'So, what's this programme you're making, then? Something about this lot round here? You must be mad.'

'Why do you say that?'

'Bunch of losers. Small time.'

'It's not them we're interested in, Daryn. It's the real power on the streets. The... playas.'

'Now you're talking.' Daryn wriggled in delight. 'This is my manor. Nobody does fuck all round here without my say so.'

'And that's why I want you in the show'

'Yeah...' Daryn looked shifty for a moment. 'But, I mean, tv and all that, won't it get me into trouble?'

Eddie laughed. 'No way! I always protect my talent,' he lied. 'Anything you might tell me is strictly in confidence.'

'I've seen these programmes,' said Daryn – and indeed he had, for he was an avid, undiscriminating tv watcher. 'They're good.'

'That's because I only work with the very best. People with real potential. People like yourself.'

Daryn frowned, trying to look as if he thought the whole thing was beneath his criminal dignity, while his mind span with visions of a glorious, golden future, a slavering media eating out of his hand, a small but acclaimed cameo in a London gangland film and then... Hollywood... Away from Elephant and Castle.

'I'll have to think about it.'

'I can't do it without you, Daryn. You're the Man.'

'Yeah,' said Daryn to himself. 'I'm the Man.'

It was time to get serious. Back in the office, Eddie picked up his battered filofax and looked under E for editors. He wanted the best.

'Caroline,' he shouted. Caroline, looking more than ever like a grazing animal, appeared at the door.

'Yes?'

'Get me Charlie Crook.'

'He's back at the Beeb.'

'Staff?'

'Think so.'

'Blow me. Okay, get me Wayne Thwaites.'

'No can do.'

'Why not?'

'He's dead.'

'Is he? Did we send?'

'Doubt it.'

'Bollocks. Okay, get me Pete Silverstone.'

'Are you sure?'

'Damn it, Caroleen, I know what I'm doing. He's the best in the business.'

'He's an alcoholic.'

'He's a *recovering* alcoholic.'

'When do you want him?'

'Like, *yesterday*, Caroline. We've got a *film* to edit.'

Five

Generally speaking, Mrs Renders ate for lunch whatever she'd bought that morning at the shops. But today, out of breath and out of sorts, she didn't feel equal to the stairs, subways and escalators of the shopping centre. Consequently there was no food in the house. She put on a house coat and her golden slippers and shuffled along the passage to Jamie's flat. He was a good boy; he'd said often enough that if she needed anything, she had only to knock.

But today he didn't answer.

Sid looked up at her, cocked an eyebrow and started to get up, anticipating a 'walk' in his pushchair.

'You stay where you are, Sid,' said Mrs Renders, locking the door behind her. 'Mum's going nowhere till she's feeling better.'

She opened a tin of Chum, emptied it into Sid's bowl and stood up. Colours whirled before her eyes.

'Dear me,' she muttered, half to the dog, half to herself. 'I don't know what's the matter with me.'

She shuffled back to the bedroom and collapsed with a sigh on the mattress.

Steve Soave and Nicko McVitie spent a successful morning with Serena, who allowed them to film her early-morning regime of make-up and toning exercises. She'd chatted in a perfectly relaxed fashion, wrapped only in a fluffy white towel, while Nicko's camera caressed her smooth, tanned legs, the statuesque curves of her shoulders, her collar bones, the nape of her neck where a few loose strands of hair hung down. Only when she was ready to step under the shower did she shoo them away.

'Come on, boys,' she cooed, 'it's not *that* sort of film, is it?'

By the time she was gussied up in her work gear – seamed stockings that conveyed just a hint of the kinky – Steve and Nicko were her slaves. She led them down into the subterranean car park where she kept her Peugeot, safe from the depredations of Ben and his gang of infant car thieves.

'Are you sure you can both squeeze into the back, with all that equipment? Why doesn't one of you come up front and keep me company.'

An undignified scramble ensued, from which Nicko emerged the victor. Steve sat in the back and asked questions while the cameraman struggled to keep his camera trained on Serena's face rather than her creamy thighs.

'I don't know what you expect me to say,' she said, pulling out of Spencer Street and slipping into the racing traffic with a dexterity that Nicko, a connoisseur of these things, had never seen in a woman driver before. 'My life is very ordinary. I get up, I go to work, I come home, I do a bit more work, sometimes I go for a drink with the girls, more often than not I collapse into bed.' She smirked into the lens. 'Alone, I might add.'

'Tell us about your childhood, Serena,' asked Steve from the back. A taxi cut in front of the Peugeot and Serena jammed the brakes on.

'Fucking wanker!' she boomed, then collected herself. 'Excuse me, gentlemen. You'll have to edit that bit out. Driving brings out the... worst in me. Not very ladylike.' Nicko, who liked a woman with a dirty mouth, felt funny in his stomach.

'What did you say, Steve? You asked me a question.'

'Yes. Your childhood. Tell us about that.'

A mist came over Serena's eyes and she bit her pink, plump lower lip. 'My childhood. Well, Steve, that was a long time ago...'

'Come on, you're young!'

'Bless you. Well, let me see. I had a very ordinary childhood. I grew up in... Chiswick. A very nice part of London. Perhaps I should drive you down there one day. Daddy's a civil servant. Mummy doesn't really work, she was a primary school teacher before we were born, that's me and my... er... brother, but of course she gave that up. I know it's very old fashioned, but I don't think children and careers really mix. Not that I'll ever have the chance to find out, by the look of it.'

I'll give her one, thought Nicko. A baby, that is.

'So, we had a very happy childhood, running around the woods, getting into all sorts of scrapes. I was a terrible tomboy. I loved sports at school, you couldn't get me off the... er... lacrosse pitch. Then of course I reached my teens and everything started to change, I discovered clothes and make-up and shopping and... boys.'

I bet you did, you horny little bitch, thought Nicko.

'And when did you start working?'

Serena jumped. 'Working?'

'Your current job, then.'

'Oh. I've been with Rampling and Partners for four years.'

'And you like your work?'

'Well, yes, most of the time. Of course, advertising is a high pressure job. And it's not easy being a woman in a man's world. You have to push, push, push. Sometimes it's hard to unwind. It's not as if I have a husband or a family to take my mind off it. I tend to eat, sleep and breathe work. I suppose my life might seem quite sad and lonely to a lot of people.'

Nicko, who was just formulating the thought that *he'd* give her something to take her mind off work, zoomed in on a tiny tear squeezing out of the corner of Serena's left eye.

Serena dropped Steve and Nicko outside her office in Holborn, leaving them to make their way back to Elephant and Castle on the bus. They sat in silence on the upper deck of a 171, Steve meditatively stroking his beard, Nicko shooting a few atmospherics out of the window, both of them daydreaming about Serena. They would have ridden all the way to Catford Garage had not Steve's mobile rung just in time.

'Shit! We're here!'

They sprang to their feet and lumbered down the stairs, Steve attempting to answer his phone at the same time, and practically fell out the doors.

It was Eddie on the phone.

'I've got a job for you two.'

'Shoot.'

'This afternoon, four o'clock. Split up. Take a hand-held and get out on the streets. One of you call round at number nine, you're joining Daryn on his rounds. The other one, up to Beckford House. You're escorting those two old poofs. Flip a coin to decide who's doing who. Call me to tell me it's all gone fine. I'm lunching a commissioning editor.'

'Fuck,' said Steve, digging into his pocket for a ten pence coin. 'Okay, your shout. Drugs or poofs?'

'That,' said Nicko, 'is what they call a no-win situation. Heads I do the queens.'

'Heads it is. Good luck, mate. Keep your back to the wall.'

The maths exam was a disaster. Debbie, knowing that an appointment with 'Uncle' Dudley Jenkins and his camera awaited her at home, was nervous and fretful, unable to concentrate on the meaningless signs and symbols on her paper. Shelley, sensing her friend's discomfort, suffered in sympathy (besides which she had spent two years daydreaming in lessons, and didn't have a clue what any of it was about). When the invigilating teacher told them to stop writing, Debbie rushed out of the room in tears.

'Go on,' hissed Michaela Gittish, confident that she'd acquitted herself rather well. 'Follow her.'

Shelley got up and stamped out of the room. Debbie was nowhere to be seen.

The first thing Debbie heard when she got home to the Princess of Wales was 'Uncle' Dudley's voice from the bar. It was unmistakeable, a mixture of asthmatic rattlings and nasal twang that contrived to be booming and insinuating at the same time. The flattened vowels of south-east London rendered it bland, sinister.

Debbie crept up the back stairs without a sound.

'Is that our little superstar?' Dudley's hearing was hideously acute. 'Come on in, my dear, we're all waiting for you.'

Debbie sighed and stopped on the stair. For a moment she screwed up her eyes, trying to summon fight or flight. But the rigours of the maths exam had left her drained and pliant. She walked into the bar like a zombie.

'Hello, Uncle Dudley.'

'Have you got a kiss for me my dear?'

'Of course.' She placed her lips on the smooth side of his face, avoiding the dry hanks of grey hair, the greasy spectacles.

'There's a good girl. Now, why don't you and your mother run along upstairs and get ready.'

'What for?'

'Uncle Dudley's come to take some pictures of you, Debbie,' said Theresa, 'remember?'

Of course she remembered; she had thought of nothing else all day.

'Isn't anyone going to ask me how my exam went?'

William, behind the bar, laughed. 'You don't need exams for the kind of work you'll be doing, Princess!'

'Run along then my dear,' said Dudley. 'Your mum'll show you what to do. William, may I borrow the ice bucket?'

*

The Elephant and Castle comes alive when the sun goes down. Those few residents with jobs are on their way home; those without are emerging from the long, uneventful coma of the day. In southern Europe, they call this twilight procession the *passeggiata*; in south-east London, they merely regard it as the pleasant prelude to another night's mayhem.

Daryn was a key player in these crepuscular wanderings. He emerged from 3 Spencer Street at six o'clock on the dot; his hunched figure, clad in stonewashed jeans and a windcheater, was as familiar to the neighbours as the postman. He ran down the steps on his stubby legs, a baseball cap pulled over his thinning brown hair, stuck his hands in his pockets and sauntered off, whistling as he went. It was a characteristic whistle: a piercing rendition of a phrase from 'You'll Never Walk Alone' that could be heard quite clearly in Warfield Street and at the top of Beckford House.

'I'm known for me whistle,' said Daryn to Steve Soave, trotting behind him with a portable camera. 'It's a bit like the chimes on an ice-cream van. Lets people know that I'm coming. That's what they call me round here: the Ice Cream Man. Cos I'm cool. And what I sell 'em's sweet.'

He was making all this up as he went along, thinking (quite rightly) that tv producers would respond to the *faux* gangland atmosphere.

'Time for a house call. I'm a bit like a doctor, doin' me rounds. Some of them round here call me Doctor Daryn, or just Doc.' It sounded good – better, perhaps, than the Ice Cream Man. 'Now remember,' he said, as they jogged up the stairs of Beckford House, 'I do the talking.'

They stopped outside a flat on the first floor, the door bearing the evidence of a recent fire. 'Put a bin outside his door, torched it,' said Daryn, improvising wildly. 'He's a silly boy. Got behind with his payments. A Very. Silly. Boy.' Daryn gave the whistle and waited. After a few minutes, the sound of shuffling feet was audible from inside.

'Who is it?' asked a tremulous voice.

'It's me. The Doc.'

'Who?'

'Daryn, you twat.'

'Oh, right. Thought you said something else.' The door opened, and a pair of watery eyes blinked in the gloom. 'Who's that with you?'

'It's all right, mate, it's the tv. They're making a film about me. You won't be shown, mate, Don't worry. They'll whatsit your face. What is it, Steve?'

'Pixellate.'

'That's the one. Hey, cool it.' The Very Silly Boy was panicking, attempting to close the door. Daryn pushed his way in.

'Right. You got the money?'

'What? What you talking about? You owe me –'

'The money, Colin, er, punk.'

'Fuck off, Daryn.'

'Hang on a sec, man,' said Daryn to Steve. 'Little problem.'

He led Colin into the living room and shut the door. Steve waited for the thuds and screams of pain. A few moments later Daryn and Colin emerged, both looking pleased with themselves.

'Honest, Doc,' said Colin, 'I ain't got no bread till next week, I told ya.'

'You slag,' said Daryn. 'You don't want another barbecue, do you?'

'No, mate. I promise I'll pay up. I've got to do a job tomorrow night on the flat upstairs, I'll fence the gear and you'll have the money by tea time. Please give me the stuff now. I beg you, Doc. I beg you!' Colin, getting carried away in his part, fell to his knees.

'All right, mate,' hissed Daryn, 'the film's about me, remember.' Then aloud: 'You fuckin' better not fuck me around, fucker. I'll be nice this time. But remember: the Doc ain't always in such a good mood.'

He tossed a paper wrap at the grovelling figure and aimed a soft kick into his stomach.

'Ow. That hurt.'

'Yeah, and that's just a taste of what you'll get if you mess wiv me.'

'You wanker, Daryn.'

Daryn ushered Steve out the door.

Their next port of call offered no such diversions. In Warfield Street, just a few doors up from Fat Alice's, Daryn's whistle brought a well-dressed young man, perhaps in his mid 20s, to the door.

'Hi Daryn!' He didn't notice Steve, who was standing on the other side of the street and using his zoom. 'Got the stuff? Good man.'

'Yeah, here it is. Two grams of cocaine you ordered, wasn't it?'

'That's right. I've got the money.'

'Right. Eighty quid we agreed, didn't we? Thank you very much. Twenty, forty, sixty, eighty. And here are the drugs that you're buying off me. Pleasure doing business with you.'

The deal was done, the money pocketed, the door shut. Daryn shot a thumbs-up across the street where Steve had captured every detail.

Maureen opened the door wearing nothing but a dressing gown which barely met around his tubby frame. 'Ooh, it's the Cameraman! And look at me! I'm not quite decent!' He did nothing to remedy the situation. Nicko prayed that the sheer fabric would not slide open. His prayers, sadly, were not answered. As Maureen stood there, his piggy eyes boring into Nicko's lens, the curtains parted and all was revealed. Or almost all: luckily for Nicko, and the viewing public of the future, Maureen's genitals were concealed by an overhanging apron of fat.

'Bollocks,' said Maureen, and scarpered into the dim recesses of the bijou lattie. Nicko tracked round the hall, taking in the beaded curtains, the signed photographs, the kitsch telephone table where names and numbers were scrawled in large, childish handwriting. From somewhere out of shot, a husky voice interrupted him.

'You like what you see?'

Nicko panned round to the lounge doorway where, backlit and half-concealed by cascading glass beads, stood Muriel in what could only be described as a negligée. One leg – slim, hairless – protruded from the diaphanous garment, the knee slightly bent, the toes pointed. Nicko took in the huge knuckle-duster rings on the fingers, the half-drunk martini held nonchalantly in one hand, the other clutching the door frame like a claw. Slowly he moved up the body – the narrow hips and waist, the flat chest, the turkey's neck – until he reached the head.

It was truly alarming.

Muriel had not trod the boards *en travestie* without learning a thing or two about beauty. Those basic principles – 'you can never have too much make-up' and 'when in doubt – pluck it out' – he had applied with gusto to his own small face which seemed, now, to be composed almost entirely of features. Over the eyes were two huge oval patches of shimmering white, bordered by dark pits of black. Where only yesterday were eyebrows, now there were none, thus leaving more room for cosmetics. Two arched brown lines had been drawn in an inch from the hairline, impersonating an expression of permanent surprise. Around the temples, under the cheekbones and jawline a heavy shading of burnt umber emphasised the skull beneath the skin. The tiny amount of flesh not yet accounted for was buffed to a perfect matte ivory. And then there was the mouth. Twice its normal size, a thick red band drawn a centimetre outside the natural lip line, the rest filled in with 'Vampire's Kiss', the brand to which Muriel had remained loyal since the 60s. Above all this, the

Margaret Lockwood beauty spot sailed like a sturdy little boat in a violent storm at sea.

In Muriel's mind, Nicko was struggling between professionalism and desire. Any minute now he would throw his camera aside, take him in his strong, tanned, hairy arms and carry him, as weightless as a butterfly, to the couch. In fact, Nicko was fighting down another ill-advised lunch at Durga's Curry Den.

'Yeah. Very nice. What happened to your hair?'

In the violence of his fantasy Muriel had forgotten his crowning glory, the wig that completed the illusion. He had appeared with his own hair concealed under a tight elastic bandage. His hands flew to his head.

'Oh fuck!'

With a jingle of jewellery, the vision was gone.

Just as Nicko was backing towards the door, already composing his letter of resignation to Eddie Kander, Maureen popped out of the bathroom like the little man on the weather house. This time he was safely covered from throat to ankle in an enormous black muu-muu. Beneath the loose fabric jiggled what to Nicko's eyes look distressingly like breasts, but was in fact only fat. Maureen's wet-look curls, his face and throat were all covered in a fine film of glitter which he'd just applied from a handy roll-on.

'Take two! Want a drink?'

'Yeah. Scotch.'

'Where's Muriel?'

'I'm gluing!' came a screech from the living room. 'Don't come in!'

'She won't be long. Come into the kitchen and let me tell you a story.' Nicko leaned against the fridge while Maureen poured three inches of whisky into a highball glass. 'You don't want water.'

'No.'

'Cheers, dear. Up yer hummus.'

'My what?'

'Hummus, dear. Hummus and pitta. Oh, work it out for your-self.'

Mrs Renders was awoken at six o'clock when Sid's sharp little claws pulled the counterpane off the bed. Her head was splitting. It took her a while to remember what had happened.

'Whatever's the matter with me?' She sat up; this time there were no swirling pits, just a vice-like pain across her forehead. She reached into the bedside table, found some aspirin and swallowed two. After half an hour, in which she'd listened to the dull thud-thud-thud of Jamie's music from along the corridor, the regular sirens and police helicopters in the outside world, she felt better. She realised with relief that she was hungry, and tottered out to the kitchen. There was five pounds in the tea caddy. Perhaps someone would run down to the chip shop for her...

No. This was not good enough. What would Max have said? He never complained, even after his leg went. He simply braced the saw against a bolster and carried on playing like an angel. Never cancelled a show, not even when he had pneumonia. He was made of sterner stuff, Maxie. Died with his boots on – well, his boot, he only needed the one. Simply collapsed half way through the Barcarolle. They drew the curtain, she went on and sang 'Danny Boy' and left them cheering while Max's lifeless form was loaded into the ambulance.

Mrs Renders pulled on her aqua mac, put Sid on the lead and made it as far as the corridor. With the fiver clutched tightly in one hand and Sid's lead in the other, she made her way to the stairwell.

One step at a time.

Twenty minutes later she was outside, Sid scampering ahead, frustrated by the unusual slowness of pace. She tottered on, smiling at her neighbours, stopping every few paces to lean against the rail-ings.

It took her another 20 minutes to get to the chip shop. Luckily for her, there was a wait for chips; she tethered Sid outside and took a chair.

Within the hour she was back in the flat, exhausted but triumphant. She ate the fish and chips – stone cold by now – straight from the paper.

In the upper room of the Princess of Wales (available for hire, functions, private parties) 'Uncle' Dudley had built a makeshift studio. Compared to the cramped conditions in which he usually worked (the living room of his own flat in Lewisham) this was luxury – plenty of space to hang the white paper backdrop, to position the wooden 'throne' on which the model would sit (and, hopefully, lie), plenty of room for lights and tripods. He rubbed his clammy hands and popped his knuckles.

'Shouldn't you be downstairs looking after the customers?' he asked William Wicks, who had followed him from the bar.

'No, wouldn't miss this for the world!'

'I think it might be better, on the whole. Don't want our little superstar getting nervous in front of dad, do we?'

'You don't think... oh dear... well, Dud, you know best.'

William plodded reluctantly back to the bar, where two old codgers sat inert, their pints untouched in front of them.

Dudley fiddled with his equipment for a few minutes, totting up in his mind the potential profits that the afternoon's work might bring. Single usage in a daily newspaper, maybe £2000... syndication and foreign rights another thousand... calendars and other merchandise, same again... private clients (for the more 'specialised' shots) – £3000, £4000, difficult to say. It all depended on how far Debbie was willing to go.

The future superstar appeared shivering at the door with her mother's hand digging into her shoulder, dressed in a white teddy, white stockings and a pair of red high heels. Her hair, which normally fell in natural blonde curls around her shoulders, had been anointed with a product which made it stand out from her face, emphasising her alarmed expression. Her face, usually devoid of make-up, boasted blue mascara, a reddish eyeshadow and blusher, and pearly pink lipstick that made Debbie look as if she had just been gnawing on a particularly greasy lamb chop.

'Perfect,' breathed Dudley, the word rattling somewhere in his thorax.

'Here she is,' said the proud mother, 'ready for her close-up.'

'Oh yes, my dear. Pretty as a picture.'

Debbie tottered an inch or two into the room, her eyes darting from door to window as if she might bolt at any moment. Despite the mildness of the evening, and the two-bar fire which Dudley had considerately switched on, she was shivering.

'Now, Debbie, let's get you warmed up.' He rubbed his clammy palms again; Debbie thought for one bilious moment that he was going to touch her. Instead he pressed a button on a portable stereo. Tinny synthesisers and a thudding drum beat preceded a Minnie Mouse voice.

> Ungh, touch me
> This is the night
> Ungh, touch me touch me touch me
> I wanna feel your body...

Theresa pushed her daughter forward and she teetered into the centre of the room on her red high heels.

'Come on, my dear, let's see a little dance, like you do with the boys down at the disco.'

Debbie, who had never set foot on a dance floor in her 16 years, shifted from one shoe to another like a child who wanted to go to the toilet – which, in fact, she did.

'Like this, love,' said Theresa, executing a wild rendition of the Pony.

Debbie, staring straight ahead, brought her hands up to shoulder level and attempted a few steps.

> Full moon in the city and the night was young
> I was hungry for love I was hungry for fun
> I was hunting you down and I was the bait
> When I saw you there I didn't need to hesitate

'Lovely, lovely,' exclaimed Dudley. 'Put some life into it. Let's see a bit of movement in the hair.'

Theresa stuck her thumbs in the elastic waistband of her leisure suit and started thrashing her head from side to side, like an ageing Iron Maiden fan. She encouraged her daughter to do likewise.

Debbie wanted to say something, to complain, but the words were jumbled up in her mouth. She could only obey, and nodded her head mechanically from side to side. A strand of soapy-tasting hair got caught on her greasy pink lipstick.

'That's it, my dear!' enthused Dudley.

> This is the night, this is the night
> This is the time we've got to get it right
> (This is the night)

> Touch me, touch me, I wanna feel your body
> Your heartbeat next to mine (this is the night)
> Touch me, touch me now

'You're nice and warm now, Debbie my dear. Quick, let's hop up on to the throne, shall we. That's it. Now, turn your back on me and look over your shoulder. Lovely. Lovely.'

Click. Click. Click.

'Lick your lip and let it hang. That's it. Like you're about to eat a lovely lolly. Mmm, delicious!'

Click. Click. Click.

'Mum…'

'You're doing brilliantly, love!' said Theresa, who was modelling for all she was worth just out of shot.

'I feel stupid.'

'Come on Debbie, hold your hair up with one hand, that's it, at the back of your head. Super.'

Click. Click. Click.'

'Now twizzle round to face me. That's it. Lean forward and head back.'

'It's embarrassing.'

'Don't worry love, Mum's here! Wooh! Wooh!'

> Quick as a flash you disappeared into the night
> Did I hurt you boy didn't I treat you right?
> You made me feel so good, made me feel myself
> Now I'm alone and you're with somebody else

Debbie could feel her face going red, her throat tightening, as if she was about to cry.

'Now, put a finger up on your mouth, like this.' Dudley demonstrated, looking like a retarded child trying to remember its address. Debbie obliged. In the corner, Theresa was practically gagging on her own fist by way of encouragement.

Click. Click. Click.

> Cold emotions confusing my brain
> I could not decide between pleasure and pain
> Like a tramp in the night I was begging for you
> To treat my body like you wanted to

'And bring the other hand up to your neck. Play with your beads, dear, that's it.' Theresa had kitted Debbie out with her best pearl necklace. 'Now let the hand rest on your boozie... Just the finger-tips, as if you're feeling yourself for the first time.'

Click. Click. Click.

> Ungh, ungh, ungh, ungh
> I was begging for you

'And spread the legs a little wider...'

> This is the night, this is the night
> This is the time we've got to get it right
> (This is the night)

Theresa wrapped her thighs round one of the pillars that held up the ceiling and thrashed her upper body from side to side. A photocopied sheet of A4, advertising 'Old-Fashioned Karaoke Upstairs at the Princess of Wales', worked loose from the pillar and sellotaped itself to her bust.

'Now, how about showing us a little bit more?'

'Mum...

> Touch me, touch me, I wanna feel your body
> Your heartbeat next to mine (this is the night)
> Touch me, touch me now

'Come on, dear, just unfasten the first few buttons at the top.'

'I'm not wearing anything underneath...'

'That's right.'

'Mum...'

Theresa, exceeding her acrobatic abilities, had fallen to the floor and was nursing a painful bruise on her coccyx.

'It's all right dear. You've got lovely boobs. Nothing to worry about.'

Touch me, touch me, touch me

Debbie could feel the panic rising in her chest. Dudley and his long lens took a step towards her, and another, and another.

'Do you need a hand, dear?'

'No...'

She wanted to explain, to tell him that she hated the whole idea of posing for the cameras, but the words spoonerised on her tongue like a mouthful of half-chewed food.

Cos I want your body all the time!
Ungh, ungh, ungh...

Dudley's hands were getting closer, closer. She had to say something, anything, to stop him.

Touch me, touch me, touch me

Debbie stood up, crossed her arms in front of her chest and screamed at the top of her voice.

'I AM NOT TOWING MY SHITS!'

A puzzled Dudley and Theresa scratched their heads as Debbie ran sobbing from the room.

Six

After a promising start, The Doc's drugs round petered out in an abortive attempt to sell cocaine to a handful of 12-year-olds playing football in the park.

'I could get Ben and a couple of his mates to buy some stuff off me, if you like,' said the obliging dealer. 'Obviously you'd have to lend them the money. I'd give it back to you after.'

'I don't think so.' Even Steve Soave, veteran of Kandid Productions' set-up techniques, foresaw problems with this one. 'What I need, Daryn, is something with a bit more drama. You know, a single mum, living in desperate squalor, looking like a zombie and going on the game to finance her heroin addiction. That would be ideal.'

'I'm sure one of my bitches would oblige.'

'What, you mean you've actually *got* a girlfriend?'

'Not as such, but...'

'It's okay,' said Steve. 'I've got the very person.'

Caroline Wragge, stupid and incompetent as she was, had no intention of remaining a lowly researcher forever. Show her a greasy pole and she was scaling it like a rat up a drainpipe. Her current work at Kandid Productions – contacting idiots who wanted to be on tv, sorting out paperwork, calling cabs for Eddie and occasionally sucking him off – did not satisfy her vaulting ambition. Filling in an expenses form may have been beyond her, but that was not going to stand in her way. Good contacts and an impressive CV (however fictional) were all that mattered.

What Caroline needed now was leverage. She'd been stuck in this job for months, awaiting the opportunity to prise herself out of her lowly rut – carefully assembling, plank by plank, her launch pad to glory. So when Steve Soave called the office with a routine request – no more outrageous or stupid than any other – Caroline, with a certain reptilian intelligence, recognised that opportunity had fallen into her lap.

'So you actually want me to appear in front of the cameras, yah? No, no, I'm not suggesting that I should get extra money for it. If it helps the production, obviously, that's what I'm here for... Right now if you like. I'll get a cab or something. What should I wear? Yah, yah, a drugged-up tart, I get the picture. I guess I'll think of something.'

Caroline looked in the mirror. This, she realised, was her big chance. She did not yearn for a career in front of the camera, had no illusions that her hamster cheeks, her strong, equine teeth, would propel her into the celebrity stratosphere. She dreamed of power without responsibility, of status without work – of being, in fact, a television producer. And how, without talent or other obvious qualifications, would she get there? By blackmail, of course. If Eddie Kander was stupid enough to allow this kind of thing to happen in the name of journalism, he would have to pay. And she would be the one to profit from it.

When Eddie thought of Caroline, he had an image of the top of her head bobbing in his lap. Little did he recognise that his manhood, his livelihood, his very career, were in the jaws of a practised Machiavelli.

Caroline prepared herself for her first location visit. She applied a haphazard blur of lipstick around her mouth. And then, for extra verisimilitude, she punched herself hard in the left eye. That should come up nicely in the course of a cab ride from W1 to SE1.

Such was Caroline Wragge's dedication to her career.

Nicko McVitie hadn't reached the age of 35 without dipping a toe, or so, into the murky waters of homosexuality. His appetite for sex was such that, in the right mood, he was more than happy to 'hop on the other bus' for a short ride down 'Bourneville Boulevard'. And while he was primarily a woman-lover, he recognised that there were certain things that only a man could (or would) do to another.

That said, he was less than eager to sample the treats on offer in the bijou lattie. By dint of hiding behind his camera, keeping the subjects in his viewfinder at all times, he escaped from Beckford House almost untouched. True, Muriel's fish-like hand rested once or twice on his hummus, while Maureen contrived every ten minutes to materialise at his side with yet another glass of neat scotch. But by the time they were in a cab heading towards Kennington he was still unravished, if not entirely sober.

They made a strange threesome. Even the cab driver, who had seen every variation on the human condition during 20 years of plying the London streets, raised an eyebrow when an ageing, skinny transvestite, a fat old poof in a tent and a skinhead with a camera lurched into view. All of them were drunk. Muriel tottered down the steps of Beckford House and headed for the nearest lamp post. He struck a pose and then, in a voice like a musical death-rattle, began to sing...

Vor der Kaserne
Vor dem groben Tor
Stand eine Laterne
Und steht sie noch davor...

Before he could reach the chorus, Maureen grabbed his skinny wrist and bundled him into the back of the cab, amidst much shrieking and kicking of stockinged legs. Nicko's camera caught a flash of reinforced gusset.

'Cheekies Wine Bar on Alexandra Square please driver,' slurred Maureen, trying to sound sober as Muriel shrieked through the next few lines of his song.

> *So woll'n wir da uns wiedersehn*
> *Bei der Laterne woll'n wir stehn...*

The cab disappeared into the gloaming while more respectable residents, accustomed to the 24-hour chorus of sirens and horns, detected an extra strident note in the urban cacophony.

> *Wie einst, Lili Marleen*
> *Wie einst, Lili Marleen...*

As one cab left with its strange cargo, another pulled up. Caroline Wragge, with a big black eye and a mouth so red it looked as if she'd been supping from a tomato ketchup bottle, stepped out on to Spencer Street. She paid the driver, pocketed her receipt and stood expectantly as the taxi drew away.

She was alone in Elephant and Castle, an unprotected female dressed like a prostitute in the most desolate setting she could imagine. Lesser women might have wavered for a moment – might have wondered if they were pursuing professional goals at the expense of their own self-respect. Not Caroline Wragge. Checking in a hand mirror that she looked utterly wretched, she set off in search of Steve.

She watched the world go by – a world so alien to her that she could hardly connect it with any clear and present danger to her own person. A child – it could barely have been more than six – hurried past her carrying a car stereo under its arm, the wires hanging out of the back like freshly torn ligaments. An over-painted school-girl in white underwear and one red high-heeled shoe ran sobbing out of the door of the Princess of Wales pub – perhaps a 'working girl'? A haggard, overweight young man in a baseball cap and stonewashed jeans eyed her from across the street. Caroline gripped her handbag and looked away.

When she looked back, he was still staring. She walked a few paces down the street; he shadowed her on the other side. Frightened for the first time, she vowed then and there that she would never, under any circumstances, no matter how successful her career, have anything to do with real people ever again.

She broke into a jog; the flap-flap-flap of trainers followed her. A piercing whistle broke through the evening air. Any second now, she thought, a gang of knife-wielding youths will descend on me.

Another pair of footsteps running towards her.

'That's her!'

She span to face her persecutors and was about to let rip with her famous bellow – scourge of the hockey pitch – when she recognised Steve Soave.

'God, what happened to your face?'

'What? Oh, it's make-up.'

'You look perfect. Right, this is Daryn.'

'All right, babe.'

'He's going to sell you some stuff, okay? And you're going to freak out. It's as simple as that. Got it?'

'Yah, no problem. So, what's my name? I need a name.'

'Do you?'

'Yah. Something really common, so I can get into character. What are people called round here? Doris or Flo or something, I suppose.'

'Nobody's been called Doris or Flo since the War,' said Steve.

'I wish I'd had time to research this more fully. I must have an identity.'

'Well mostly I'll be calling you bitch or ho,' said Daryn.

'I see,' said Caroline. 'Okay. Let's go for a take.'

'Look about you,' said Muriel, flinging a bony hand around the bar. 'Is this the best we can do? I think not.'

'Madam's on her high horse dear, pay no mind,' said Maureen, snuggling a little closer to Nicko who edged further down the red leather banquette.

'Look at these sad fuckers. My God, whatever happened to glamour?'

Muriel had a point. The few patrons of Cheekies Wine Bar desperate enough to be in there at this early hour were not a lively bunch. A small transvestite, trying to conceal her male-pattern alopecia with cleverly-sculpted bangs, sipped a coke at the bar, her legs twined round the stool like ivy. The barman, who looked barely old enough to drink in a pub, let alone work in one, alternately picked his face and wiped up glasses. A nervous straight couple, who had wandered in off the street, were hurrying through their drinks and glancing at the door.

'I remember the days of the great drag balls,' ranted Muriel, drawing himself up. 'People knew how to dress in those days. We spent weeks working on our costumes, wearing our eyes out with sewing, choosing our accessories, making sure that we looked fabulous. And now look!' He pointed an accusing figure at the wilting violet at the bar. 'Some of us can't even afford a fucking wig!'

The little trannie's hand fluttered up to her hair, touched it lightly at the temples and fell back into her lap. She sniffed, sipped her coke and turned her back on Muriel.

'Don't be savage, Muriel. Poor thing. She doesn't *realise*, you see. Fancy going out of the house looking like that...' Maureen shook his head in disbelief, the glitter on his wet-look curls and doughy, sweaty skin glinting in the dim pink lights of the bar.

'Well what do you expect,' said Muriel, grabbing Nicko's camera and turning it back on himself. 'They haven't got a clue, the fucking naffs who run this place. Only let it out to the queers to make a bit of money. Now when *we* have our club, dear, it'll be the talk of the town, I'm telling you. Oh yes. Bit of class. We're *known*, you see. We're *somebody*.'

'He'll tell you in a minute about how he nearly had a hit once,' whispered Muriel in Nicko's microphone.

'I nearly had a hit once, you know,' said Muriel. 'Oh yes. Went into the studio and cut the record and everything. It's a lovely little song, one that you might have heard, dear, called 'I Am What I Am', from a smashing show called *La cage aux folles*, well let me tell you I was the first singer in Britain to pick up on that song and I made it, I tell you, I simply *made* it my own until that *cunt* Gloria Gaynor came along and stole it from me.'

'Now now, we used to like Gloria Gaynor. First I was afraid, I was petrified...'

'And just because she had the backing of a big record company behind her fat arse, and just because she was a *real woman* she bloody had the hit with it and I was left with a stack of unsold 45s and no fucking record deal. It's so unfair.'

'Well dear, the business was very anti in those days, wasn't it? I mean, that was the 80s for you. They wouldn't touch you if you were the least bit unusual.'

'At least not until that fucking Boy George came along and stole all my ideas and watered them down and of course all of a sudden she's prancing around on *Top of the Pops* looking like a sack of fucking potatoes and where am I? Miming to Shirley Fucking Bassey at the Two Brewers, that's where.'

'Not that she's bitter...' murmured Maureen.

'But just you wait, when we open our own club we'll show them how it should be done. A bit of class, that's what we're going to bring back. A bit of real glamour. Not like these bloody poofs today, all they're interested in is cock, cock, cock and it makes me fucking sick, hanging around the toilets and showing no respect for an artiste.'

'Don't listen to her, she's just jealous cos she never gets any trade,' said Muriel, edging a little closer to Nicko.

'I've got it all worked out. New songs, new outfits, I've even made the tapes. All we need now is the club. Isn't it, Maureen? I leave the business side of things to my partner.'

'In more ways than one,' said Maureen, signalling to the barman to bring over another bottle of wine. 'If it wasn't for my enterprising ways, we'd be out on the streets. Not that madam would mind.'

Muriel rose above it.

'I mean you must have wondered, haven't you, how we maintain ourselves in the style?'

Nicko grunted an affirmative.

'We're still in show business,' confided Maureen. 'We manage the careers of a handful of very promising young stars, singers, models, actors, dancers, that sort of thing. We provide them with the contacts that they need from our extensive roster of clients and we leave the rest to them, taking only a small commission in return. I mean it's a hobby more than anything, we get great pleasure from watching these young talents, many of them untrained, develop into real professionals.'

'Some of us get more pleasure than others.'

'I shall ignore that remark, Muriel. Take young James Lord, for instance, a very very talented young man who's got a great deal to offer.' Maureen sounded like the MC at a working men's club. 'Now, he comes to us, fresh out of the army, head full of dreams, nothing in his pockets, and a lot of people would just turn their back on him.'

'You certainly did.'

'But not us. We're quick to spot the potential and to bring it out into the open.'

'Took you about 20 minutes.'

'And now he's working hard every day, learning to discipline himself...'

'And others...'

'Making the contacts that he'll need if he's going to succeed in a very competitive world. But like so many of these boys, he's easily distracted.'

'By pussy.'

'And when he should be working or practising he's out chasing any bit of skirt that takes his fancy.'

'And not just any ordinary tart, dear, oh no.'

'Oooh no. No indeed. Mm-mmm. No-o-o-o-o.' Maureen's face was distorted in its archness.

'Oh yeah? Who's that then?'

'Aaaaaah! Now that *would* be telling, wouldn't it?'

'Ye-e-e-e-s.' Muriel breathed vinous vapours on to Nicko's neck.

'You remember the deal, don't you dear?' said Maureen. 'You pay for information. And this one, my dear, is a peach.'

'Go on.'

'How much?'

'Two hundred.'

'Don't take the piss.'

'Five hundred?'

'Call it a round thousand and we'll talk.'

It's not my money, thought Nicko. He nodded.

'Well,' said Maureen, all dimples now that the money was as good as his, 'you'll never guess in a million years which of our delightful local ladies young James has set his sights on.'

Some poor cow with cobwebs up her fanny, thought Nicko.

'She lured him, the devious bitch. She lured him away from us,' hissed Muriel, his false eyelashes lowered in spite.

'Yes, it's *her*.'

'Who?'

'Her at number one. That slag.'

Nicko's heart jumped into his throat. 'You mean –?'

'Yes, dear. That surprised you, didn't it? Serena Ward.'

'Fuck me,' said Nicko.

'I thought you'd never ask,' cackled Muriel, grabbing Nicko's balls.

Eddie's lunch had already lasted seven hours, and it was not going well. The big cheese from Channel 6 was an old friend, an 'old mucker' in Eddie's parlance, they had propped up bars and even picket lines together in the 80s, but despite all that he gave Eddie's pitch a decidedly lukewarm reception.

'People are sick of that fly on the wall stuff, Eddie,' he said. 'They don't want to see some miserable bunch of queers fiddling the dole in a slum. Okay, there's a gay audience out there, but that's specialist stuff, Eddie. It's cable. It's just not mainstream.'

'But mate, this is public service television in the grand Reithian tradition,' said Eddie, filling their glasses from the umpteenth bottle. 'It's a state-of-the-nation zeitgeist thing. It'll take off, mate, it's got legs, it'll fly. We've got great characters, I promise you, real straight-down-the-line stars at the heart of the show and just a few... er... eccentrics round the edges to liven things up. Believe me, this is Appointment Television.'

'No it's not, Eddie, it's just a bunch of freaks who'd do anything to get their ugly mugs on screen.'

'I really respect your opinion, mate, and I want to give you the first chance to say yes to this, but I think sadly I'm going to have to take it to a competitor because I've already had...'

'What people want these days,' said the big cheese, with a visionary glint in his eye, 'is aspirational broadcasting. They want characters that they can identify with, people who go through the same hopes and fears as themselves. They don't want to look down the microscope at a bunch of little germs squirming around in the shit. This is what comes home to me time and time again out of the extensive focus groups that we've been running over the last four years. People want the old fashioned middle-class values. They want glamour.'

'We've got it!' said Eddie.

'They want lifestyle.'

'We've... er, we've got that too!'

'They want romance, Eddie. Romance. That's the key word for our infotainment programming over the next two years. Romance.'

Before Eddie could lie through his teeth any more, his phone rang. The big cheese signalled a grateful maître d' for the bill.

'Yah, Eddie Kander. Steve! Steve, my man, how's it going? Yah, yah, yah, yah, yah, yah, yah, yah, yah. No, I'll get this.' He threw a credit card over the bill like a desperate gambler playing his last chip. 'Steve. Yah. Yah. Yah. Yah. What? She's what? With...You're... wow, right, yah, that's fantastic, go for it, maximum resources, got it? A free hand. No can do mate, I'm tied up at the moment, you'll have to go it alone. Can do? Yah? Yah? Yah? Yah? Right!'

He put the mobile in his pocket and produced a Mont Blanc fountain pen. 'So, what were you saying, mate?'

'Romance, Eddie. That's what I want. Romance.'

'Romance, you say?'

'Yah. I mean yes.'

'You've got it.' Eddie signed the bill with a flourish. With a will-they-won't-they boy-girl love drama on his hands, he was home and dry. The peripheral queers and nutters could be explained away as 'colour'; now, he felt sure, Kandid Productions was assured its place in the sun.

By midnight, a large white van was parked at the end of Spencer Street. This in itself was nothing unusual: the residents were used to dodgy vehicles lurking around the place. One or two of them thought it was the detector van, and hauled their unlicensed tvs into the back kitchen to avoid discovery. Nobody else bothered much. It was just another illegally parked, probably stolen, possibly booby-trapped vehicle.

The interior of the van told a very different story. There, hunched over a control board bristling with knobs, gazing intently at four screens mounted to the rear of the driver's cab, sat Steve Soave and Nicko McVitie, bright-eyed with excitement.

They had found something that money can't buy: a 'real life' drama, the sort of affair that sweeps viewers up in its momentum and leads almost inevitably to a 60-minute wedding special. Hence director and cameraman were now sitting in a mobile outside broadcast unit waiting for something romantic to happen between the houses of Capulet and Montague, or 1 Spencer Street and 44 Beckford House.

They clocked every new arrival in the street with the precision of CID. '2305,' gabbled Steve into his dictaphone, 'Debbie Wicks enters Spencer Street for the fourth time this evening still dressed in underwear and one red high heeled shoe. Nicko for Christ's sake will you stop making the camera zoom in on her tits. Hello, who's this? Young black female enters from west end of street, it's that bloody girl from the school, she's running up behind Debbie, are you getting all this, Steve? Running up behind her, calling her name, remonstrating with her, putting her arm around her shoulders, stop grinding your teeth Nicko, and leading her away, repeat AWAY from the direction of the Princess of Wales public house, home of the aforementioned Wicks girl. 2308, subjects out of camera range. Note: install 360 degree remote-control cameras on all lamp posts in the vicinity for increased surveillance capacity. What's this? 2308 and a half, light goes on in front room of 44 Beckford House, Jamie is at home, repeat at home. No sign of anyone else in the flat. Light goes out in front room 2308 and a bit more.'

A quiet couple of minutes passed.

'Oh look Nicko, here come your two girlfriends. Cab pulls up outside Beckford House at 2314, two passengers alight, both clearly under the influence of alcohol, of uncertain gender although I'm sure my colleague with his greater experience of these things can fill us in on that one. Short fat one appears to be remonstrating with the cab driver, can you get some better sound on that one Nicko? Yeah? What's he saying? "Come upstairs and we'll have a nightcap." Okay, got that. Taxi drives off rapidly at 2316. Did you get that look of disgust on the driver's face? Fantastic. Okay. All quiet at 2318. Faintly audible sound of female voice singing loudly in distance to what sounds like... yes, I think definitely *is*, 'I Dreamed a Dream' from *Les Misérables*. Can't identify source of sound. Appears to be getting louder. 2319: small child approximately six years old letting itself into number three, carrying large hold-all.'

And so it continued, Steve and Nicko logging hours of useless footage of the night life of SE1. Far away in Warfield Street, Fat Alice lamented her continued failure to get in front of the cameras with ever louder, ever more maudlin selections from West End shows ('Midniiiiiight, not a sound from the streetliiiiiiight'). Jamie hovered at the window of 44 Beckford House, looking down on to the street for a moment before disappearing again. By half past midnight all was quiet, and the two intrepid reporters were thinking fondly of their beds.

Then suddenly, just as Nicko was nodding off over his monitor, Steve dug him sharply in the ribs.

'Wait! Look! What's that!' He scrabbled around for his dictaphone and clicked it on. 'It's, er, what, 0032, a light's just gone on in the window of number one, on and off, on and off. It's a signal. There again. Get that? Come on Nicko, get it for Christ's sake. Okay? There, again. On-off, on-off. And what's going on up there? Number 44's in darkness. Wait a minute. Wait a minute. Slowly but surely. Don't lose it... Remember, he's got all those stairs to get down... Keep it trained on the front door of Beckford House, Nicko. Come on, you bastard, come ON! We've got to get this... Come on!'

Nicko, aided by a night-vision eyepiece, shouted 'Yessss!' and punched the air. There, emerging into the dim orange darkness from his burrow in Beckford House, was Jamie Lord, dressed in T shirt and tracksuit bottoms and a brand new pair of trainers, carrying in his hand what was unmistakeably a sponge bag.

'Follow him, Nicko,' said Steve in agonised tones. 'Come on, baby, come on... He's coming down on to the street... He's looking straight at us...' Steve's voice dropped to a whisper. 'He's checking out his appearance in the wing mirror. Oh Christ, please don't let him try and nick the van... Are you getting this, Nicko?'

'Course.'

'Go on my son, go on... That's it. He's crossing the road. He's going up the stairs. The door's opening, he's expected... And he's in! He's in! Jamie Lord is inside Serena Ward's house, 0035 hours, we have entry, we have entry.'

'Romance,' said Nicko, turning off the camera. 'That's what he wanted.'

'Okay. First thing tomorrow you get in there and you fit the spy-cam in her bedroom. Let's go home.'

Seven

A week had passed.

The alarm clock went off, as usual, at 6.30 – plenty of time for Serena to bathe, dress and groom herself and to be at her desk by 8.30. This morning, however, she was less than eager to face the world. It was a damp, grey day – that much she could discern from the insipid light filtering through the bedroom window – and she hadn't slept well. She had so much on her mind...

She hit the snooze button and lay in silent thought, the duvet pulled up to her chin, eyes closed, mind racing. To go into work, after all that had happened in the last week, to face Ricky Rampling and an 'important new client', was too much to bear. She had never taken a day off sick in the four years that she had worked for Rampling and Partners, saving that drastic measure for a real emergency. Today, thought Serena, as her stomach turned in panic, was just such an emergency.

She picked up the phone and dialled the office, confident of getting through to the answering machine. Ricky's familiar sibilants greeted her. 'Hi, you're through to Rampling and Partners... after the beep.' Serena lowered her voice to the driest of husks. 'Hello Ricky, it's Serena. I'm really sorry to let you down but I'm feeling terrible. It's my period – you know what it can be like for us girls. I'll take a Nurofen and curl up with a hot water bottle for a couple of hours, and hopefully I'll be in by 11. Call me if you need anything,' she added, with a little extra pathos in her voice, confident that considerate Ricky (who himself took days off at the drop of a hat, particularly when his nightly trawls through Soho's high-end bars had borne fruit) would do no such thing. Jamie stirred beside her.

'Whassa time...'

'It's all right. It's only half past six.'

''kin' 'ell.'

The recumbent form hoisted itself, turned in mid-air and landed on the mattress with such force that Serena was almost jettisoned on to the floor. A hard, hairy thigh covered her smooth, silky one; warm, strong arms encircled her waist; something was prodding her buttock. Oh well, she was in no hurry. She returned the pressure with a thrust of her hips; within moments, Serena and a still-drowsy Jamie had kicked the covers to the floor and were copulating like animals as the first rays of sun penetrated the grimy window pane.

The doorbell rang at 7.30.

'Oh Christ,' said Jamie, wiping himself with a tissue, 'not again.'

'I'm afraid so.' Serena slipped on her dressing gown, a flimsy creation with a maribou trim, and fluffed up her hair in the mirror. 'Don't bother to dress, darling. You know what they're like.' She blew Jamie a kiss and slipped out of the bedroom.

'Good morning, ladies and gentlemen,' said Serena, her voice dripping with an irony that was entirely lost on the party standing on her doorstep. 'How nice of you to call. Won't you come in?'

Eddie Kander, Caroline Wragge, Steve Soave and Nicko McVitie trooped into the hall, the latter casting wistful glances at the parting of Serena's wrap where an inch or two of firm, tanned breast, so recently the plaything of Jamie Lord, was on display.

'I'm afraid we're still in bed, but I don't imagine that's a problem, is it?'

'Not at all, Serena,' boomed Eddie, whose first visit to the flat this was, although he was entirely familiar with its contents thanks to the hours of spycam footage that had been collected during the last seven days. 'In fact, that's exactly where I was hoping you'd be. I've brought my assistant producer with me, Serena Caroline, Caroline Serena.'

'The more the merrier. I've got no secrets, have I? Not any more.'

'We're not... interrupting, are we?' asked Steve, who, more than the others, kept up some semblance of politeness.

'You tell me,' said Serena. 'I'd say we'd just finished, wouldn't you? Nicko? I presume you were "on line", as it were?'

'Yeah,' gruffed Nicko, who had watched with a kind of tortured longing the live porn relay on his portable monitor.

'Come on in, then. This way!' trilled Serena like a cheery tour guide.

Jamie was lying on the bed, his hands behind his head, his gym muscles and tattoos on magnificent display, the duvet resting an inch above his pubic bone. He said nothing, but grinned. Serena sat herself beside him on the bed; the Kander crew arrayed themselves in a half-circle around them. Nicko hoisted a camera on to his shoulder, Steve dangled a microphone on a boom above their heads, Caroline fiddled with a clipboard and tried not to look at Jamie. Only Eddie was completely at ease; the man who had made *Abbatoir* was not to be put off his stroke by a little nudity.

'So, Serena, Jamie, as per our discussions of the last few days, we'll start right here and now with an exclusive on the relationship, how you met, your hopes and dreams for the future, your fears that class and professional barriers might affect the romance, that sort of stuff.'

'Just one thing, Eddie,' said Serena.

'Yah, surely.'

'The money, darling... Is it sorted?'

'Caroline?'

Caroline, who had been making unconsciously phallic doodles

on her clipboard, looked dimly around at the sound of her name.

'The money, Caroline. Is Serena's money sorted?'

'Right, absolutely.'

'We'll take that as a yes, then, shall we?' said Serena, conceiving an instant and implacable dislike of a woman who, for all that she looked like a dozy brood mare, still seemed to be getting the glad eye from Jamie.

'So, right, your hopes and fears...'

'And just one more little tiny detail, Eddie,' cooed Serena, wreathed in smiles and looking, thought Nicko, rather like Julie Christie.

'Yes, lovely?'

'The contract.'

'Caro?'

'Huh?'

'Take it as read, Serena.'

'With all the clauses we discussed, I trust? No footage of "intimate acts", I think those were the words that our solicitors agreed on, weren't they? Absolutely nothing of that sort to be shown at all.'

'Absolutely. Leave it to the solicitors.'

'Because,' purred Serena, fluffing her hair a little more, 'if anything should go wrong in that department, I can assure you that I'm retaining the services of a shit-hot show business lawyer who will sue your arse from here to eternity if you show so much as a nipple.'

'Understood, absolutely. Caroline? Action point, yah? Check re siduation with lawyer vis-à-vis the contract, okay?'

'Yah.' Caroline scribbled some rubbish on her pad and put a big tick mark beside it.

'Smashing,' said Serena, all warmth and intimacy. 'Fire away, then.'

'So, Serena, tell me how your romance with Jamie first began?'

'Well, Eddie...'

'Try not to use my name, love, remember that you're talking to Joe Public here.'

'Oh, of course. Well... now, let me see. How long ago was it, Jamie?'

Jamie was idly running a hand over his taut, hairy stomach, a gesture that made Caroline feel very strange and which, in truth, had even distracted Nicko's gaze from Serena's soft curves. 'Dunno. Six months?'

'Yes, it must have been about six months ago...' Serena looked off into the middle distance, presenting her right three-quarter view to the camera, making the best of the light like a true pro. Her voice took on a wistful, heavy quality that resonated in the balls of all four men in the room, and which set Caroline's large, equine teeth on edge.

'Six months... It was quite romantic, really. I had been living here for a while, my life wasn't what you'd call exciting. Up every morning, off to work, race through the day, home late at night, slump into bed... alone...' She allowed herself one theatrical glance at the camera. 'Then one day I was running a little late and hurrying up the road when I tripped on a loose paving stone... you know the council really ought to do something about the state of the pavements, if they're watching... and fell quite literally into the arms of this young man here.'

Jamie shifted his weight on to his side, turning to face Serena; the duvet, thus dislodged, exposed the Bosnia tattoo to the viewing millions. Eddie signalled nervously to Nicko, who reframed the shot to exclude the offending arse.

'And he, being the gallant young soldier that he so recently was, caught me up and prevented me from falling, asked if I was all right, saluted and went on his way. We might never have met again, I suppose, but I knew that I had found someone very special.'

Jamie buried his face in Serena's tanned flank, trying hard to suppress laughter at the memory of their actual first meeting in a bar in Brewer Street where the two of them, dismayed at the lack of trade, ended up drinking each other under the table.

'Life went on much as normal after that, but I suppose if I must be absolutely honest I was always half looking out for my handsome young cavalier for weeks after that. I saw him once or twice going out running, you know how important it is for someone in the fitness business to keep in training, but there was no further contact until one evening and... well, imagine my surprise when I answered a ring at the doorbell and there stood Jamie with a big bunch of red roses, asking me if I'd like to come out to dinner. And from then on it's been like a wonderful dream...'

Jamie, impressed as he was by Serena's powers of invention, remembered how they'd woken up the morning after their first date, spent the rest of the day screwing before she'd dropped the big one, after which he'd stormed out and avoided seeing her for three weeks until, with a severe case of the horn unassuaged by the fumbling ministrations of his regular clients, he'd woken her up in the middle of the night and announced that he didn't care whether she had once been a bloke, she was the best bit of pussy in the immediate vicinity and could he come in. Thenceforth he was uncertain who was using whom: he, to reassert his masculinity by having 'a bird' after all his male punters; she, to bolster her femininity by sexually enslaving the most virile young stud in the Elephant and Castle. Whatever the finer points of this delicate balance, over the months a tender feeling had grown between them – besides which, reflected Jamie, nobody on this earth gave head like a trannie. If ever the truth came out – that he, Jamie Lord, scourge of Serbian aggressors and champion shagger of his company, was shacking up with a queer, for that's the way his army pals would see it, surgery or no surgery – he would brain the person responsible. He sat up and scowled at the camera, and in doing so exposed himself completely to the assembled broadcast professionals.

'Cut!' shouted Eddie.

'No I ain't,' growled Jamie, hopping out of the bed and making a run for the bathroom, his manhood scything a path through the onlookers.

As soon as the torrential sound of his pissing had abated, Eddie was ready to roll again. 'Come on, Serena, you were doing beautifully, sweetheart. Nicko, come in close on her face.'

'I'd love to,' thought Nicko, manipulating his zoom.

'Now, where were we? Continuidy, Caro.'

'It's been like a wonderful dream,' read Caroline, torn between deciphering her shorthand and finding an excuse to follow Jamie to the toilet. It was many years since she'd had full sexual intercourse – her romantic adventures of late had mostly been conducted under Eddie's desk, and once in a cab to Waterloo – and she had emphatically selected Jamie as the man to restore her to functioning womanhood. If only she could get him out of the clutches of that tart...

'Yes, a wonderful dream,' continued Serena. 'I still can't really believe that it's all true.'

Every Friday morning the features staff of the *Newington News* was summoned to the editor's office for the weekly planning session. It was around this long, drawn-out meeting that the working life of the paper revolved; it was here that lists were made, promises freely given, excuses grudgingly offered, coups attempted and thwarted. The younger journalists wittered on about the great investigative campaigns they wanted to run; the older hacks sat around hoping that nothing would come between them and the pub. The editor, who had been in the post for 15 years, through three buy-outs and any number of resultant policy reviews, selected from the weekly haul of white-hot journalistic ideas those that he thought would a) get him in the least trouble with the current owners and b) actually get written in time to make one of the paper's twice-weekly editions. Currently he was listening with barely-concealed contempt to the features editor's proposals.

'So what I'd like to go with is the working mums thing,' she was saying. 'Women who try to do to much, who juggle their lives and end up dropping the baby. Are you spending too much time at work? Does your child love his nanny more than you? We're talk-ing about affection deficit, about the guilt trap, about women who work to pay the women who steal their children from them, it's absolutely aimed at the heartland reader.'

The editor took off his glasses and rubbed his eyes. 'Isn't this the feature that you pitched two weeks ago, Sally?'

'Yes, with the extra added value thing, talking to the mothers that social services have let down, best and worst mums in the area, Southwark's Most Hated Mum, a big pull-out sidebar on the future of parenting in the inner cities, that's really the big one for me.'

'Right. Anyone else?'

'Millwall at home this week.'

'Thank you, John. Philip. How about you?' All eyes in the room turned to a seat at the end of the table. 'In case any of you haven't yet met him, this is Philip Bray, who's joining us as Sally's new deputy. Phil comes to us from... where was it again?'

'The *Stoke Examiner*,' said Philip, a handsome black man in a charcoal suit and pink shirt with only a hint of a Potteries accent.

'Where he was editor.' The boss fixed Sally with a menacing glare. 'So, Philip, let's hear what you've got.'

'Okay,' said Philip in a voice that made everyone in the room want to be his best friend. 'First of all I have a question.'

'Fire away.'

'It's for Sally, really.'

'Right, all ears.'

'I just wanted to know what plans are in place for this big new fly-on-the-wall documentary series which is currently being shot around the Elephant and Castle and has just been definitely bought by Channel 6.'

'Right, well done, absolutely spot on for us of course with the local angle, and the docusoap trend, that's very much the kind of thing that we do.'

'So it's all in hand, then, is it?' asked Philip, confident (for he had made a few calls) that it was nothing of the sort.

'With the tv thing, I mean, that's more Jen's area. Jen?' Jen, or Jennifer to the vast majority who were not her friends, looked briefly up from a copy of *Tatler* and grunted.

'What?'

'The new documentary series that I gather is being shot on our very doorstep, although its the first I've heard of it,' said the editor.

'Christ, not another one,' said Jen, and returned to her reading.

'I take it, then, that none of you has done anything about this?' asked the editor.

Silence.

'I take it, in fact, that none of you had ever even heard about it before this morning?'

Further silence, in which a volley of imaginary daggers embedded themselves in Philip's broad back. He shrugged them off; the *Newington News* may be tough, but the *Stoke Examiner* was tougher.

'Very well then. Philip. The floor is yours.'

'Okay. I was speaking to some contacts at Channel 6 last night and of course they're very keen for publicity, albeit controlled publicity, so I said no way, we're going for the story that the people want to read, right? Behind the scenes, the truth not the lies, yeah? So I got in touch with DI Soanes down at Borough nick, I expect you all know him... well, whatever, he's the man with his eyes and ears on the street round here, took him out for a drink and he's already tipped me off, unofficially, protection of sources and all that, about some of the characters that are taking part in this film, so what I'd like to clear with you, if it's okay, is an allocation of resources to run a big special on it during the second week of tx when interest round here is going to be at tsunami level.'

'You've got it,' said the editor, feeling for a brief moment the frisson of excitement that, once upon a time, made him think that journalism was a worthwhile job. It was a frisson he had not felt now for many years. 'Any other business?' The rest of the staff sat around making fish mouths. Perhaps, thought the editor, it was time for a massive editorial reshuffle.

'And my mums?' asked Sally, as the editor headed for the door.

'Fuck 'em,' said the editor.

Eight

Philip Bray set about his new assignment with an alien vigour. His colleagues passed quickly from resentment to bemused tolerance; it was simply beyond their comprehension that anyone could bring such enthusiasm to their work. Philip's contacts in the local constabulary and council chamber were railroaded by his unstoppable charm into parting with secrets for which they usually demanded favours in return. And one by one, the stars of *Elephant and Castle* fell prey to his powers of persuasion. Nobody in the whole of southeast London had ever attacked a project with such certainty of success.

And Philip *was* certain, quite certain. Not for nothing had he chosen an obscure, unloved local newspaper with a dwindling circulation for his *entrée* into the charmed circle of London's media. On the *Stoke Examiner* he had risen swiftly from court reporting to news correspondent, to news editor, to features editor and finally, thanks to that lucky business about dope dealing in the local playgrounds ('Potteries Tots Gone To Pot'), editor. But glory in the provinces was not enough for Philip; no big fish in a small pond he. He wanted to feast with the sharks, and for that he had come to London with a professional agenda clearly mapped out before him.

Thus twin ambition beset the production of *Elephant and Castle*. On the one hand, Caroline Wragge, whose ascent up the greasy pole would be not so much through careful planning as an instinctive lurching from one opportunity to the next, scenting out the weak spots with unerring accuracy but never able, had she been asked, to tell anyone what she was doing or why. On the other hand, Philip Bray, who saw each triumph-over-tragedy in the *Newington News* as one more stepping stone to the Groucho Club, who would trample on widows, orphans and especially minor celebrities to get there. To both of them, *Elephant and Castle* represented the main chance; neither of them would ever dream of counting the human cost of their success.

Philip turned up at the bijou lattie with a blank cheque in his pocket, ready to spend almost any amount of money to secure the information he knew was locked within that overheated eyrie. A couple of phonecalls had got him thus far: one to his good friend DI Soanes at Borough nick, who told him 'if anyone knows the lowlife in that godforsaken area it's those two old vultures in Beckford House'; the other to the vultures themselves, who succumbed instantly to the old Bray magic ('Yeah! I *saw* you at Blackpool! You were *fantastic!*') and invited him round without further ado. Unlike his counterparts at Kandid Productions, Philip did his homework: he worked late into the night trawling through the *NN*'s cuttings library, finding out all he could (not much) about the glorious career of these two 'local entrepreneurs... who launch their latest cabaret club on Saturday night in ritzy Tooting' (1974), who 'brought back memories of a bygone era with a one-off comeback at the Union Tavern, Camberwell, on Tuesday night' (1986), and who had not been heard of since. Or had they? A small item from 1988 caught Philip's attention.

Male prostitution on our doorstep
Camberwell magistrates today fined Mr Roy Turner (50) and Mr Vernon Delgado (52) the sum of £1000 each for running a male sex ring from their home in Beckford House, Elephant

and Castle. The defendants both pleaded guilty to living off the earnings of prostitution of another man through an 'escort agency' which was closed by police earlier this year.

He made a note of the names, called his contact at the housing office and confirmed that they matched the address he'd been given by DI Soanes for 'those two vultures'. Had the vultures, so to speak, changed their spots? Philip, veteran of the Stoke-on-Trent magistrates' courts, thought not.

He dressed carefully for this visit: smart, attractive without looking too available – and, just before he rang the doorbell, he pocketed his wedding ring. No point in setting up barriers. There was a scuffling behind the spyhole, and a perfectly audible stage whisper ('Oh my God, Muriel, he's *black!*') before the door swished open and there, behind the dusty beaded curtain, loomed the familiar silhouettes of Maureen and Muriel, alias Roy Turner and Vernon Delgado, local showbiz legends and convicted ponces.

It was only lunchtime, but it was clear that preparations had been afoot in the bijou lattie since first light. Both the hosts (in 'man drag' for the occasion) were buffed and powdered to perfection, the ornaments and framed photographs were dusted and polished and the cuttings albums laid oh-so-casually on the coffee table. Delicately-cut sandwiches wilted on the sideboard; the decanters of Winnie Whisky, Vera Vodka and dear old standby Ginette, with appropriate mixers, were at the ready beside them.

'Welcome,' they chorused, their eyes darting in unison from Philip's face to his crotch and back up – noticeably wider – to his face. 'Do come in,' crooned Muriel. 'A drink?' asked Maureen, who had already had a few.

'Gin, please,' Philip shot back before Maureen had a chance to trot out the familiar litany. He was gratified to note that their eyebrows shot up. A gin drinker, he had correctly guessed, was so *simpatico*. 'Just a splash of tonic.'

'Yes. Don't want to drown it, do we?'

Maureen handed him the clinking glass, in which four fluid ounces of gin barely made acquaintance with a soupçon of flat tonic, and gestured towards the sofa where sphinx Muriel was already curled up. Philip took the drink and sat down with his arms extended along the padded backrest, thus drawing two pairs of eyes to the firm torso that his pink shirt did little to conceal. He waited for a count of five – long enough, he calculated, for them to fall in love – then leaned forward, all confidence.

'As I said on the phone, my editor's asked me to cover this new tv series that they're shooting around here, and so I'm planning to do a big feature profile on the two of you as the real stars of the show.'

'Oooh...'

'In fact, depending on how things go, it could be a two-parter.' He took a long swig on his gin; Philip had the journalist's ability to drink any amount of spirits and barely show it.

'Lovely.'

'And of course my editor has authorised me to arrange a deal whereby the *Newington News* gets the exclusive and all syndication rights in return for a fee to be agreed, payable to yourselves in two instalments, now and on publication.'

Maureen and Muriel, more accustomed to extorting money with threats from dissatisfied punters, had never encountered such up-front financial dealings before.

'How much?' rasped Maureen, one fat hand pressed to his womanly breast.

'Oh Maureen! Must you?'

'How much is Kander paying you?'

'That's a very personal question, young man.'

'Yes.'

'I... well... we haven't finished our negotiations yet...'

'Five hundred? Eight hundred?'

Maureen, who regarded himself as a hard-nosed negotiator, fell for the bait. 'Do you mind? We're not cheap. A thousand.'

'I'll double it.'

Maureen and Muriel gasped. £2000 closer to their dream...

'What do you want to know?'

'As I said,' breezed Philip, delighted that the sesame had opened with so little forcing, 'just an exclusive interview with your good selves, and perhaps a bit of expert insight into the locals.'

'Bloody hell dear, for two thousand quid I'll chuck in a night of passion with Muriel.'

'Or you could hire Maureen for a week, use him as a raft.'

'So,' said Philip, shorthand pad at the ready, 'perhaps we could start off by talking about your theatrical career. I'm most interested in the contribution you made to the great tradition of the variety stage.'

Muriel's claw-like hands grabbed the first album of cuttings like an insane *Jackanory* presenter, and the story began. 'Well, this is me on board HMS *Andes* in 1965, of course I had to lie about my age to enrol in the merchant navy, shut up Maureen, I was a mere child, and I swear to God that there were 150 queens on board that ship, we all had a fluffy sweater and a hairpiece tucked away in our cabins and we used to put on shows for the men, dear, so that was my first taste of the business... And this handsome young sailor here, dear, the one with his arm round my shoulders, can you guess who that is? Go on. Have a stab.'

'It's Maureen. He hasn't changed that much. Neither of you has.'

'Well... thank you... Hear that, Maureen?' Maureen was simpering behind the settee, refilling Philip's glass with another quarter pint of gin.

'Now here we are in mufti at a party at the Bridge House in Canning Town, that would be about 66, look at Maureen, her butch days were but a memory by then, and she's piling on the pounds, well you were dear, you were. That's us at the City Arms in Millwall, my first professional engagement, as "The Vernon Girl".' Muriel lowered his voice to a whisper. 'There's an exclusive for your readers, dear. That's my boy-name. Vernon. Can you imagine! I dyed it as soon as I could.'

'I'll make a note of that,' said Philip, whose shorthand translated as 'identity confirmed, Muriel = Vernon Delgado'.

'And here's me during my first residency at the Fifty Club in Frith Street, and still to this day there are people in Soho who remember it... Although the poor old Fifty Club has been taken over by the yuppies now dear, they've ruined it of course and you wouldn't believe that at one time all the legends trod the boards there... me, Phil Starr, Lorri Lee, Lee Sutton, Dodo Sweet, Terri Gardner...'

Philip continued to scribble, although his notes were less to do with this roster of stellar names than with the murkier details of the bijou lattie. 'Large desk diary with word "Rent" on front cover in black magic marker ... Post-it note stuck to phone reads "Call G re Sat nite no-show".'

It was good, but it was not enough. Philip was not leaving without getting his money's worth (half of the £2000 fee was from his own pocket – speculate to accumulate), and would endure any amount of dewy-eyed reminiscence for the one piece of hard evidence around which to base his exposé.

'Now we skip a couple of years and here's us again at one of the fabulous drag balls at the Porchester Hall, me in an outfit that Maureen wore her poor eyes out sewing, I've come as the little-known Hindu deity Lickme, with six arms because we had a lot of diamante trim and we needed somewhere to stick it. Oh Mo, you were a bloody genius dear, I have to hand it to you.'

For a moment, something like tenderness passed between the two of them. Then the phone rang. Maureen floated off on a cloud of gin to answer it, while Muriel carried on with his narrative. 'And here's me looking fabulous with Danny, dear, he said I was the only one apart from his self who'd raised drag out of the gutter, imagine...'

Philip was blessed with the ability, essential in his profession, to feign interest while listening to something entirely different. Thus, while he nodded and smiled at Muriel, his shorthand transcribed Muriel's business call.

'Hello, Gorge Guyz... Yes, that's right. Which of our guys were you interested in? Oh yes, a very popular choice, sir... This afternoon, no, I'm afraid Jamie is only available for evening and weekend work, long stays considered... Yes of course, sir... Well, let me see, there's Patrick, he's an *outstanding* young man in every respect, very talented and versatile, 21, straight acting... of course sir, all our guys are VWE or above, Patrick is – let me just see now – XXVWE, so I don't think you'll have any complaints in that department... Certainly. It's £80 for the first hour, £50 per hour or part of hour after that... No, I'm afraid not, no discount for pensioners or the disabled, sir. It's a flat rate... Okay, and if I could just have the address to pass on to Patrick... thank you... in about an hour, sir. No, thank you. Byee!'

'...which of course I was the first person to sing in this country, it was very much my theme tune, well as you'll probably remember I released it as a single with, I may say, a certain amount of success.'

'Pat? Wake up, love, I've got a job for you... Now. Come on, get your finger out dear... St John's Wood. Up to Waterloo on the Northern Line, dear, then change on to the Jubilee. Got a pen? Here's the address... He sounds posh, so play your cards right. As long as I get the usual cut, I don't care how much extras you make. And no thieving this time.'

'...as Lady Bracknell in *Importance*, an all-male dance-drama interpretation by a very gifted director friend of ours...'

'Indeed we do, sir, an exclusive portfolio of colour photographs of our most popular and *outstanding* guys, who exactly were you interested in? Ah yes, Jamie, well he certainly is flavour of the month at the moment, and will shortly be posing for our in-house lens artiste for private clients... Yes, that's £40 for a contact sheet of ten uninhibited poses, and then £10 for each luxury six-by-four enlargement of your favourite shot... Certainly, if you'd like to give me your name and number... No of course, I quite understand, then perhaps you'd like to call us back again in a fortnight to place your order. Thank *you*, sir. Byee!'

'...who of course stole all my ideas and watered them down for public consumption...'

'Jamie? Yes I know you're at work, I'll keep it short. Get round here tonight, soon as you finish. I've got a job for you... No, not that sort of job, it's modelling for snaps... I know! Exciting, isn't it! Who knows, you might be discovered by an agency, dear... Okay, seven o'clock, we'll be ready for you.'

Prostitution and pornography: it was enough. Philip jotted down a few trial headlines: Nest of Gay Filth. Local Boys for Sale. High-Rise Homo Harem.

'...which unfortunately closed after only two nights. Are you listening, dear?'

'Yes. Only two nights? That's shocking. So: tell me a bit about the other people who live round here. Your neighbours, for instance.'

'Well of course this is a very theatrical neighbourhood, now you come to ask,' said Muriel, pressing the tips of his fingers together and looking into the middle distance. 'Just downstairs there's a true star of the music hall era, none other than Peggy Renders.'

Even Philip couldn't pretend he'd heard of her.

'I don't suppose she was famous wherever it is you come from.'

'And he's young, dear, make allowances,' added Muriel, rejoining the conversation.

'But round these parts Maxim and Peggy Renders are still remembered as torchbearers of the variety tradition. I wonder if she'd agree to a comeback, Mo, when we get our club launched?'

'Your club?'

'Oh yes, Mr Bray, that's what we're building towards, and that's why any publicity that you might be kind enough to give us is so important. I can't stress this too much. We're opening a smart new *boîte de nuit* for today's generation. Time for the amateurs to stand aside and let the professionals show them how it's done.'

Oh yes, thought Philip, a legit front for the real business. Give them enough rope...

'That's a wonderful idea! Are you by any chance looking for investors? I'd be very interested.'

'I bet you would,' said Maureen. 'You know a sound business proposition when you see one. I know your sort, you just want a slice of the action, you see a surefire winner and you're keen, aren't you? Yes. Keen as mustard. Mmm.' He puckered up his tiny sphincter of a mouth in what he thought was an expression of inscrutable wisdom but looked, in fact, more like a cat's anus.

'I know it's a lot to ask, but I've been looking for just such a business in which to invest a recent inheritance...'

Two hours and several gins later, Philip emerged from the bijou lattie, his ears still ringing with the cacophonous rendition of Maureen and Muriel's night club act. He left them with a cheque for £2000; that could still, if necessary, be stopped. He'd promised them a further £10,000 towards the opening of the nightclub – a carrot that should keep them sweet until he had all the information that he needed. It was £10,000 that they would never see.

An elderly woman in an aquamarine mac with a chain belt and gold slippers was making slow progress across the walkway, leaning heavily on a shopping trolley, a small Yorkshire terrier tucked under her arm. Emboldened by drink, Philip wavered up to her in a pantomime of astonished recognition.

'Peggy... Renders? Is it really you? Of Maxim and Peggy Renders?'

The old woman's drawn, ashen face managed a smile. 'Why yes, that's me. And who are you?'

'Gosh... a fan, I suppose! My parents took me to see you when I was a child. I've never forgotten it! You were amazing.'

'Thank you, dear. That sort of thing means more than you can ever imagine to an old woman like me. I haven't got much left in life now; just little Sid here.' She waved the dog's straggle-haired paw at Philip. 'People forget so quickly. Since I lost Max... well, I'm not one to grumble. You've bucked me up no end.' And indeed, some colour returned to Mrs Renders's cheeks; she seemed for a moment to lean less heavily on the trolley.

'I don't suppose you could help me, could you, Mrs Renders?'

'Of course, young man. Anything for a fan.' She fluttered her eyelashes; Philip could discern the ruin of a once-great beauty.

'I'm looking for an old mate of mine. He lives round here, I believe. Jamie.' The first stab in the dark had worked; why not another?

'Who, dear, young Jamie Lord?'

'That's him. Lordy, we called him.'

'Army pals?'

'Wha... Yeah, that's it.' Philip made an attempt at military bearing – not easy with a skinful of London gin.

'You're in luck. Number 44. Wait a minute, though. You won't find him at home. He's working nowadays.' There was a note of maternal pride in Mrs Renders's voice. Of course: evenings and weekends only, thought Philip.

'Oh, that's good news!'

'Yes, and it's a decent, respectable job too, over at the sports centre.'

'Great. That's just what he was looking for.'

'Indeed. Well, you'll find him there, I expect. Now I must get on, dear; I've a doctor's appointment, and you know what they're like if you turn up late.'

'Of course. Can I give you a hand? These steps are so awkward.'

'Thank you, dear. How nice to meet with such kindness. So rare these days.'

Steve and Nicko were waiting, as arranged, in the surgery. 'I'm afraid it's not good news, Peggy,' said the doctor, who was coming up to retirement and had known Mrs Renders in her glory days. The camera zoomed in on her face. 'The results of the biopsy have come back from the lab, and there's evidence of some kind of malignancy in the soft tissue.'

'I've got cancer, haven't I, Ray?'

'Yes, Peggy.'

'Am I going to die, dear? It's all right, you know.'

'Not necessarily. With the right treatment, you could have a good ten years ahead of you.'

'Ooh... ten years... Well, I could do with that. Ten years. That would be lovely...'

'The only trouble is, Peggy, the NHS waiting lists are long.'

'I shall wait my turn like everyone else. I've never been one for pushing in.'

'But if you wait for too long, it may be...'

'Too late. I see.'

'There's one way of speeding things up.'

'Yes, dear?'

'I don't suppose you've got any private healthcare plans, have you?'

'Ray! What do you think Max would have said to that?'

'I know. Times have changed though, and these days...'

'Well I haven't, and that's that. I've got my pension and a nice little bit put by and that's it.'

'How much, Peggy?'

'Two thousand pounds.' She sounded proud.

'I'm afraid that's... not really enough.'

'Oh well. Not to worry, dear. You did what you could. I'm not afraid of death, you know. I've had a good run, but I'm tired and I want to go home to Maxie. As long as there's someone to look after little Sid...'

Nicko panned from the tear in Mrs Renders's eye to the pathetic little dog looking up at its mistress with adoration written all over its muzzle. Oh, yes. The money shot.

'Unless...' said the doctor, stroking his chin.

'Yes, dear?'

'Unless there was *somebody* who was willing to help you out.'

'I don't know any millionaires, dear, more's the pity.'

'But I think you do.' The doctor stared over the top of his half-moon glasses and straight into Nicko's camera.

Nine

The last day of exams was a cause for celebration at St Agatha's; not, however, for Shelley Smithers, who trudged out of the school gates after the rest of the girls had run screaming with joy to the nearest McDonalds. Shelley had nothing to celebrate. She knew she'd failed every single exam, just as the teachers said she would. That didn't bother her in itself; it was the fact that now school was over she no longer had the prospect of daily contact with Debbie Wicks to give her life meaning. Not that she'd seen much of her recently; in the last week Debbie had failed to turn up to all her exams, and the whole school was buzzing with tales of her pregnancy/sudden illness/secret marriage/fatal accident (depending on who you talked to). Michaela Gittish was the major advocate of the clandestine birth theory ('she went into labour behind the bar at the Princess of Wales; I know, a friend of my brother's was there') and even had a name for the baby (Ronan). Shelley refused to comment, pretending that her lips were sealed – but in truth she had no more idea of Debbie's whereabouts than the rest of them.

Since the events of that fateful night, the details of which tormented Shelley as she tried to concentrate on her exams, she hadn't heard a word from her once-best-friend. She had gone up to Spencer Street as usual, just to hang around the Princess of Wales; it was preferable to sitting at home with mum and Steadman smoking the place up. She lurked in the shadows of the bins, hoping to catch a glimpse of Debbie going to or from the bar – but on this occasion, there was nothing. She noticed lights and occasional flashes from the upper room; there must be a party in progress, she thought. What she didn't see – and perhaps this was just as well – was Debbie modelling for the prying lens of 'Uncle' Dudley Jenkins, her tearful exit from the room, the heads turning in blank amazement as she ran, in a white teddy, stockings and suspenders and one red high-heeled shoe, through the public bar and out into the street. William Wicks, who was changing a barrel at the time, missed the show; the regulars rubbed their eyes and sniffed suspiciously at their pints, wondering if the impurities in the beer had perhaps rendered it hallucinogenic. Debbie ran straight into the traffic (her white underwear saved her life); Shelley, unknowing at the rear of the building, maintained her misguided vigil until closing time.

Shelley was walking reluctantly back to Ringwood House when Debbie tottered into Spencer Street looking as if she'd escaped from a home for the glamorous but confused. Her over-processed hair looked like a haystack; her blue mascara had run down her face and merged with her pearly pink lipstick to form a purple slick around her chin. Her white tights were splashed with roadside filth; one foot was cut and bleeding. Only the surviving red high-heeled shoe remained unscuffed, a tribute to the durability of high-quality plastic.

No words were spoken. Debbie didn't seem to know what was going on when Shelley put her arm and then her jacket around her shoulders, under the discreet observation of Nicko and Steve in the outside broadcast unit.

Shelley took her back to Ringwood House, steered her though the living room (where mum and Steadman, respectively pissed and stoned, took no notice) and into her bedroom, where she closed the door and wedged a chair under the handle, not that anyone was likely to disturb her. Debbie was still staring ahead of her like a rabbit in headlights – and, indeed, with her hair falling down on either side of her head in flat, matted hanks, she looked not unlike a fancy lop-eared variety. She was shivering; even though it was a mild June evening, she had caught a chill wandering around the Elephant in her scanties. Shelley held her tight and gently rubbed her arms, hoping to impart a little body heat to that tortured frame. 'What have they done to you?' she murmured over and over again. 'What have they done to you?'

After half an hour of this, during which Debbie responded no more than a doll, she thawed a little and began to cry quietly. 'Oh Shelley, Shelley, I'm so ashamed... so ashamed...' And gradually the whole story emerged; 'Uncle' Dudley and his equipment, her 'glamour makeover' at the hands of her own mother, the 'session' itself, complete with Samantha Fox on the tape, her hysterical departure... 'I don't remember anything after that until you brought me here. Have I gone mad, Shelley?'

Shelley shook her head; she was too upset to speak. She clenched and unclenched her fists, wanting to go straight round to the Princess of Wales and sort the whole lot of them out, 'Uncle' Dudley and all. But she could not leave Debbie, not in this state, and besides, the pub would be closed. She would get her revenge another time; for now the most important thing was to make sure that Debbie was alright. She would stay here tonight, of course; there was no question of her going anywhere. She, Shelley, would sleep on the floor and protect her – unless, of course, Debbie got cold or frightened and wanted someone to hold her...

'Can I get out of these stupid clothes?'

'Yeah...' Shelley tossed her a dressing gown and turned her back as Debbie revealed those twin glories that she would not show to 'Uncle' Dudley's camera. She carried on chatting, quite happily now; this was no more intimidating to Debbie than a normal afternoon in the changing rooms after games. For Shelley, to whom the stupid clothes were unbearably erotic, it was torture;

she turned her back and stared hard at the wall.

'That's better,' said Debbie. Shelley turned around to see her friend swathed in grubby pink towelling, rubbing baby lotion into her face from a tub on the dressing table. The white underwear lay in a poignantly tiny heap on the floor; there was so little of it, and yet it had covered her just so... Shelley bundled it up and put it in the bin, whence it would later be retrieved and kept like a holy relic with the red high-heeled shoe in the bottom drawer.

'I need the loo...'

Shelley scouted the corridor, commando-style; mum and Steadman had either passed out in the living room or made it to bed. Either way, the flat was quiet. She beckoned to Debbie, and bundled her quickly into the bathroom, pushed her inside and heard the bolt being drawn behind her. Shelley waited in the passage, 'on guard' as she put it to herself. No further harm must come to her friend. She would protect her.

'Is the coast clear?' Debbie had a giggle in her voice. They were two best friends on a fantastic adventure together. They dashed back to the bedroom, wedged the door tight shut and collapsed on to the bed in giggles.

'I AM NOT TOWING MY SHITS!' said Debbie, almost screaming with laughter.

'My *shits*!' repeated Shelley, hysterical but still conscious of the fact that Debbie kept rolling against her, the dressing gown gaping dangerously.

'You should have seen his face! The disgusting old bastard!'

'I'd like to punch it for him,' said Shelley.

'Yeah, knock him for six! He's a bastard!'

'That's right. Bastard.'

Debbie was quieter now, more contemplative.

'All men are bastards, Shelley.'

'Yeah...'

'I hate them.'

'Me too.'

'I don't ever want to go home again.'

'You don't have to. You can stay here. We'll get a flat of our own. Don't worry, I'll look after you.'

'Thanks Shelley.' Debbie hugged her and planted a kiss on her cheek. 'Your the best friend I've ever had. Can we go to bed now, please? I'm really tired.'

She wouldn't hear of Shelley sleeping on the floor; the bed was big enough for both of them, and besides, it was comforting to have her there beside her...

Shelley lay rigid, fully clothed.

'Aren't you going to undress?' Debbie was laughing again.

'Yeah, course.' Shelley's voice was gruff now. 'I forgot.'

'You forgot! How funny!'

In her hurry to get out of trainers and jeans, Shelley lost her balance and sat down, hard, on the floor. This ony increased Debbie's mirth. Her laughter now was so high that it was beyond human audibility, but there was some mighty amused dogs in the area.

Shelley righted herself, quickly stripped off her shirt and bra, threw on a scruffy old t-shirt and hopped under the covers where Debbie was shivering, naked.

'I'm so cold... Can I snuggle up?'

Please God no...

'Yeah.'

'Ooh, that's better. This is lovely, Shelley.'

'Yeah. It's nice.'

'Thanks for everything. I'll never forget this.'

'Me neither.'

'Oh Shelley...'

'What?'

'I wish... I wish...'

'Yeah?' Shelley half turned towards Debbie, believing that, at any moment, their lips would meet in burning kisses.

'I wish you were a boy.' With which Debbie sighed, went limp against Shelley's body and slept like a baby.

Shelley spent the night rigid, not daring to move. When she awoke from a fitful slumber at 7am, Debbie was dressed in a selection from Shelley's wardrobe and was brushing the muck out of her hair.

'Good morning, lazybones!' she said, a little too chirpy for someone who, the previous night, had suffered some kind of nervous breakdown. 'Time I was up and about!'

'No... come back to bed. Stay here. It's too early...'

'No, I really must be off. Thanks awfully.'

'Okay...'

'Mum and dad will be worrying.'

Shelley sat up in bed. 'Your mum and dad? Those bastards!'

'Shelley, please. I'll see you later. Thanks again.'

And before Shelley could hold her back, Debbie was out of the door.

The moment she stepped into the street, strong arms grasped her from behind and she was frogmarched by William into the car where Theresa, with a face like thunder, was awaiting her.

'What the hell do you think you're playing at, young lady?'

'Ow! Get off! Dad, that hurts!'

'And there's a lot more where that came from. When I get you home I'm going to put you over my knee and give you such a spanking.'

'Oh, and I suppose you're going to get "Uncle" Dudley to take pictures, are you?'

'Don't be disgusting!' Theresa slapped her, hard, across the face. 'I'll teach you to cheek your father. And what have you been up to with that disgusting freak Shelley Smithers?'

Debbie burst into tears. 'What do you mean?'

'Did she make you do things? Tell me! TELL ME!'

'No... Shelley's my friend... she didn't... mouch te.'

'What?'

The car drove off into the dawn.

Debbie spent the next week under house arrest, forbidden to leave her room, prevented from sitting the rest of her GCSEs and under strict orders to 'think very hard about what you owe your mum and dad'. On the first evening, she attempted suicide by flinging herself from the first-floor window, only to get wedged half way through, her T shirt ripped and her breasts exposed to the firemen who were called out to rescue her. For the rest of the time she sat on her bed, rocking, until it was time for her next session with 'Uncle' Dudley. This time she was as docile and tractable as any photographer could wish.

And Shelley's problems, too, had only just begun. A few days later she was returning to another lonely evening at home when a man stepped out of the shadows beneath Ringwood House and accosted her. She had no fear of muggers; it occurred to her for a moment that this handsome black man might be her long-lost father (her mother had always excused her failure to marry either of her children's parents by saying 'but they were both very good looking').

'Shelley Smithers?'

'Who wants to know?'

He held out a hand. 'Philip Bray, *Newington News*.' Shelley kept her fists stuck in her jacket pockets.

'I told you people, I got nothing to say.'

'Which people.'

'Telly people.'

'I'm not working for the telly, Shelley. I'm from the newspaper. I want to tell the real story about what's going on behind the scenes.'

'Yeah?' Her chance, perhaps, to get back at the Wickses and 'Uncle' Dudley, to expose their cruelty and ruin them. So far her much-plotted revenge amounted to nothing more than a brick chucked at the pub's reinforced front window; it bounced off the glass and straight into Shelley's stomach, winding her.

'You're a friend of Debbie Wicks, aren't you?'

'I might be.'

'Do you know what's happened to her?'

'What?'

Got her, thought Philip. It was true what they'd said at the pub; this girl was in love with Debbie. 'Oh, I thought you knew... I had a call from a gentleman by the name of William Wicks. I see you know him.'

'Debbie's dad. Bastard.'

She's right there, thought Philip; what father in his right mind would phone the local press trying to sell nude photographs of his own 16-year-old daughter?

'Tell me about Debbie, Shelley.'

'She's very... confused.'

'What do you mean? About sex?'

'No...'

'Are you and her...'

'No!'

'And at school, is there much...'

'No! Fuck off out of my way.' Shelley pushed past him.

'Wait! I want to help your friend.'

'No you don't. You just want to use her, like everyone else.'

'Shelley, I want people to know the truth.'

'Good for you. Now get out of my way.'

'Won't you talk?'

'I said get out of my way.' Shelley lowered her head and pawed the ground, ready to charge.

'I take it that's a no.'

She clenched her fists and snorted.

'That's a great shame, Shelley. Because now I'm going to have to drag up all that boring stuff up about you.'

Shelley paused, cocked her head. 'What?'

'Well, I'm sure it was all a misunderstanding, believe me I know how ready the press can be to label all black people as criminals...'

'What are you talking about?'

Philip pulled out his wallet. 'Local girl caught shoplifting,' he read from a neatly-clipped newspaper cutting. 'St Agatha's school-girl Shelley Smithers was yesterday labelled a "compulsive thief" by Camberwell magistrates.'

Shelley made a grab for the paper; Philip held it above his head, way out of her reach.

'Fifteen year old Shelley was arrested after complaints by shop-keeper Wendy Potkiss of Pot Luck Greetings Cards on the Walworth Road...'

'That's lies.'

'What did you want with all that stuff, Shelley? Wedding invitations. Christening cards. Not for you, were they?'

'I don't know,' she mumbled.

'And it's best that everyone forgets it, I know. I want you to have a fresh start in life, Shelley, but if you don't help me, then people aren't going to get a chance to hear your side of the story, and then any old rubbish might get into circulation and you'll be back where you started, in the juvenile courts.'

Shelley's arms hung limp at her sides.

'Alright. What do you want?'

'I want your help, Shelley. That's all. Just your help.'

Another one down... and still time for another. Philip left Shelley to ponder her predicament and repaired to the Elephant and Castle Leisure Centre at nine o'clock, an hour before closing time. He asked the surly receptionist about joining, and was finally admitted to the gym where a couple of massive musclemen grunt-ed and strained on the machines while a handful of obvious homo-sexuals looked on, variously peddling on bikes or tugging on row-ers with evident lack of dedication. Philip stood at the desk and coughed. Six pairs of eyes looked swiftly up, assessed his physique and looked away.

From behind a door he could hear the sound of a lone male voice. 'I know... I know, but I've had to do the late shift... He's my boss, for God's sake, I can't, can I? All right, tomorrow, I promise Maureen... Yeah, yeah, I'll give you a freebie if you want, just get off my case. Good night!'

The door opened and there, in the uniform of fitness professionals the world over, stood the newly-employed Jamie Lord.

'All right, mate?' said Jamie. 'What can I do for you?'

'I'm interested in joining the gym, and I just want to know what's... on offer,' said Philip, deliberately glancing down at Jamie's groin.

'Right, well, as you can see we've got a full range of CV machines' – he gestured towards the broken down treadmill, rower and bike – 'as well as state-of-the-art resistance equipment. Qualified instructors, that's me and Rod, to put you through your paces, what more could you want?' What was the meaning of that raised eyebrow?

'Sounds good. Very good. And what are the facilities like?'

'I'll show you.'

Philip followed him into the changing rooms, redolent of deodorant and socks, and gestured magnanimously around him. 'There you go, sir. Lockers, showers, sauna.' They were all there, in various stages of disrepair. 'Get changed, and I'll show you round the... equipment.'

'Okay,' said Philip. 'And after I've worked out, I usually like to get a massage. Do you have a qualified masseur here?'

Jamie grinned. 'Yeah. Me.'

'I'll make an appointment.'

'That's all right. I'm, like, freelance.'

'Fine. So I'll do a workout, have a shower...'

'And a sauna, if you like...'

'And then maybe you could sort me out with a massage afterwards?'

'Only thing is, we close at ten... but if you don't mind waiting till I've locked up, I can give you my undivided attention.'

'No, that's fine. And how much do you charge?'

'Basic's 40 quid,' said Jamie, delighted to think of earning this extra money without having to hand over the usual 50% to Maureen.

'Basic?'

'Yeah, then it's... up to you, you know...'

'We'll discuss that later.' Philip began to get changed. 'See you in a minute.'

Jamie's patter as he led Philip around the gym was impressive; there was no doubting his aptitude for the work. After 30 minutes, during which time he'd run, rowed, cycled and struggled through a variety of painful and humiliating exercises (all of which Jamie demonstrated with a sickening ease) Philip was actually beginning to think that it might not be such a bad idea to join a gym.

Ten o'clock came and went as Philip sweated the pain away in the sauna, trying to ignore the plaintive looks of two persistent visitors. Finally they were dressed and gone, and the gym was empty, save for Philip and Jamie.

He ladelled more water on the hot stones and closed his eyes, enjoying the heat on his muscles. The door clicked open, and there was Jamie wrapped in a towel bearing the legend 'Property of Southwark Council'. He whistled, rubbed his bleached head and sat down beside Philip, allowing the towel to fall open (Philip's remained chastely wrapped around his waist).

'Hot enough for you?' said Philip.

'Yeah... Lovely.' Jamie ran his hands down his body; he was certainly in shape. Five silent minutes passed.

'Okay, ready for yer rubdown, mate?'

'Oh... yes.'

'Come on out into the gym. We won't be disturbed.'

There was one light burning at the desk; the rest of the room was in seductive semi-darkness. Jamie gestured towards one of the benches. The black vinyl covering was ripped and the yellow foam rubber stuffing was breaking up. 'Make yourself comfortable on that, mate.'

Jamie padded over to the desk and picked up a bottle of oil.

'You won't be needing this,' he said, pulling Philip's towel aside. The journalist lay naked on the bench while Jamie oiled his hands up.

'You cold?'

'N-no.'

'You're shaking. This your first time?'

'Yeah.'

'You married?'

'Yeah.'

'It's okay...' Jamie's hands made contact with Philip's chest. 'Just relax. I'm in charge now. Relax...'

Torn between revulsion, desire and the sharper appetite for a story, Philip forced himself to lie still. He closed his eyes and thought of the headlines, the glory, Mrs Bray's gratitude... Jamie certainly had a sure touch. He was kneading away the aches and pains in Philip's arms, his shoulders, his thighs...

'Turn over.'

Philip was relieved to do so; he was only flesh and blood, and was responding as flesh and blood will when baby oil is liberally applied.

'Gonna work on your back.'

Jamie stationed himself at Philip's head and began to work his way down the spine in great sweeping movements that ended at his buttocks. Again and again he pushed, kneaded and stroked; Philip could feel the tension easing away. That was not all he could feel; *something* had just nudged him in the forehead. He jerked his head up, his mouth open in horror.

'Ah-ah,' said Jamie, waving himself with one oily hand. 'That's where the extras begin.'

That was when Philip leapt to his feet, feeling for the first time in his life that a Pulitzer prize wasn't, after all, the most important thing in the world.

'What's the matter?' shouted Jamie. 'Don't you like me?'

'No, no,' jabbered Philip, racing into the changing rooms. 'It's not that. I just feel so... guilty.'

'Yeah, looks like it,' said Jamie, casting a glance at Philip's inexplicable arousal.

'Well, I'm... er... sorry. Here.' He pressed a £50 note into Jamie's hand. 'It's okay. I'm... I'm...'

'You know where I am,' said Jamie, taking the money. 'You'll be back.'

'Thanks for everything. Keep the change.'

'I will.'

And so Philip dressed swiftly, ran from the leisure centre and straight into the welcome anonymity of a cab.

There was a hold-up at the junction of Warfield Street and the main road; Philip saw the blue flashing light of an ambulance, and a small crowd gathered around the prone figure of a woman. A car, its front end seriously dented, stood at an awkard angle to the pavement.

'She jumped in front of me, I swear to God.' sobbed the driver. 'Didn't you see it?'

'Yeah, yeah, it's all right, we got it all on film.'

'And you are?' asked the policeman.

'Steve Soave. We're making a film round here. We've got remote cameras round the streets. One of them's pointed at exactly the spot where the accident took place.'

'And you say that she walked into the road, madam?'

'Yes! I was just coming off the traffic lights. I'd seen her standing there; I mean, she's so large, you couldn't really miss her, could you?'

'Not in that outfit,' said Nicko, who was filming the entire scene on hand-held video.

'I wasn't going very fast, hardly 30,' said the shaken driver. 'Suddenly she just threw her arms in the air and jumped in front of me. Will she live?'

'She'll be fine,' said the policewoman. 'To be honest, I think your car's sustained more damage than she has.'

'Oh God,' sobbed the driver, who was led away with a blanket round her shoulders.

Fat Alice, barely conscious, was being loaded on to a stretcher.

'Wha... where am I?'

'It's all right, love,' said the paramedic. 'You've had a bit of an accident. Lie still now.'

Alice was looking wildly around, her face a mask of panic.

'It often takes them like this,' said the paramedic to the policeman. 'It's the shock.'

'Where is it?'

'What, love?'

'The camera! Where is the camera!'

Nicko stepped forward into view. Alice saw him, smiled weakly, and fell back on to the stretcher with a contented sigh.

'Could you... could you give us a hand, lads?' asked the paramedic, tottering under the weight.

And so Steve, the policeman and a couple of kindly onlookers loaded Alice into the back of the ambulance under the all-seeing eye of Nicko's camera.

At last she was in the show.

Part Two

The Launch

One

For the press launch of *Elephant and Castle*, Eddie pushed the boat out and hired the upper room of the Ivy. This was not the original plan; he'd intended something a little cleverer than that, and to hold the event in the world-famous Elephant and Castle shopping centre, suitably equipped for the occasion with giant tv monitors playing back to local people their own lives in the very heart of the community. This, he told Caroline, would be 'post-modern'. The big cheese at Channel 6, who had been persuaded to buy the series when Eddie showed him rushes of the 'romance' footage, thought otherwise. 'You won't get proper journalists going south of the river,' he said. 'Do it at the Ivy like everyone else.' Eddie quickly changed his tune, and began talking about the 'cachet' of a West End launch, while privately working up a line about the Channel 6 controllers' 'inability to connect with working-class audiences', should he need to leak it to *Broadcast* magazine.

Throughout August, the Kandid office in D'Arblay Street witnessed a frenzy of activity unparalleled in the company's history. Caroline was transformed from a witless incompetent into a paragon of ruthless efficiency. At last she could get her teeth into something that had meaning and substance for her, something that was both within her scope and truly worthwhile – party planning. She harangued the Ivy management on a daily basis, 'keeping them on their toes,' ignoring their assurances that they catered this sort of function several times a week. She plagued a handful of local limousine-hire services, calling them up for competitive quotations until one of them agreed to give her its entire fleet for practically nothing. She engaged the services of 'a really talented graphic designer' (her brother) to produce the invitations, which were the subject of several time-consuming meetings as Caroline forced Eddie to debate every last detail of font and leading. She threatened violence in the Kwik-Z-U-Like printing bureau on Berwick Street when the order was not completed within 24 hours as promised, and managed to reduce the invoice so that it actually cost the printers money to do the job.

And then there was the guest list. Who to invite? Who not to invite? Who to play like a fish on a line, witholding the actual invitation until they had as good as promised front covers? Rather than handing the whole business over to the Channel 6 publicity department (who, after all, had a budget to do this very job) Caroline witheld all information and decided that the launch should be controlled 'in house'. She went to a newsagent on Wardour Street and wrote down the names of all the papers and magazines who ought to cover the programme. She spent a happy morning bullying directory enquiries into giving her the numbers, followed by a delirious three-day ring-round.

'Hi, this is Caroline Wragge of Kandid Productions. Put me through to your senior editorial person ... Wragge, W-R-A-G-G-E. No, I don't want voicemail, this is important... I don't care. What's your name? Right. I've made a note of that ... Well get them to call me back.'

On the rare occasions when she did actually manage to speak to a member of the editorial staff, Caroline was magnificent.

'Yah, hi, Caroline-Wragge-Kandid-Productions. It's about the E 'n' C launch ... Didn't you receive the advance press release? Okay, could you check in your in-tray now, please?... I'm just doing a final call before I cross you off the list... No, you can't just see how it goes on the day, admission is strictly by invitation only... I don't care about that, I'll be glad to have a spare ticket, *The Times* is begging for another one... No, I shan't be taking any further calls on this one. Right. Right. Right. Good. Good. Good. Yah, bye.'

Thus she secured the definite attendance of most of the women's weeklies, the tv weeklies, the down-market fashion and lifestyle monthlies and a host of special interest magazines who were thrilled to be invited to anything, and forever alienated all the dailies and Sundays. When the Channel 6 publicists mentioned *Elephant and Castle* to their regular contacts, they were taken aback by the naked hostility they encountered.

Even more mercurial were Caroline's invitations to the stars themselves. She invited Jamie by a personal phonecall followed up by a bottle of champagne; Maureen and Muriel, however, she omitted to ask altogether. She would have left Serena off the list as well – she, like Maureen and Muriel, was a 'bad influence' on Jamie, to be discouraged whenever possible. But Eddie beat her to it and pressed an invitation into Serena's hand during a 'research visit'-cum-dinner-*à-deux* at the Ivy. 'I only want what's best for the show,' Caroline told the mirror, but what she really wanted was Jamie all for herself. Ever since that afternoon when she watched him lolling naked in Serena's bed, Caroline had nursed an unconscious longing in the secret centre of her womanhood. She never seriously considered Jamie as a partner – this was not the sort of boy that one could take home to meet mummy and daddy – but that didn't matter to her lower self. And it was Caroline's lower self that wore the trousers.

Her final list read as follows:

Jamie Lord YES ✓✓✓ ❤
Serena Ward ~~NO~~ yes dammit Eddie invited ✓
Maureen and Muriel yuk no disgusting ✗

Alice, Warfield Street YES jolly ✓
Mrs Renders yes triumph-over-tragedy ✓
Daryn and Ben YES family values thing ✓
Debbie Wicks YES definitely star in the making ✓
Shelley Smithers no way told me to f*** off ✗

Luckily for Caroline, Eddie Kander was too busy to pay much attention to the guest list; he spent the entire summer in a cutting room with editor and recovering alcoholic Pete Silverstone, a relic of the 80s whose career Eddie was singlehandedly resurrecting at very reasonable rates. Silverstone's hands shook too much to do the more delicate work, hence Eddie's daily presence in the subterranean edit suite where the two men staved off the craving for alcohol with hourly lines of cocaine. Cries of 'yes! yes! that's it!' occasionally echoed up to the street above them, but that was all.

The date was set for the first Tuesday in September: early enough to catch the monthlies' November editions (which of course came out on the first of October), close enough to the tx date at the end of the month. RSVPs were demanded, limousines despatched, last-minute invitations biked around the city, and finally the big day arrived.

Caroline spent the night in the office making futile phonecalls to people's answering machines, and sparked out at 6am muttering 'yah' and 'no way' in her sleep. She snapped, bullied and cajoled; she wheedled, flattered and kissed arse. She arrived at the Ivy at 10am – the launch was not until midday – and 'supervised' every last detail, from the hoovering to the flowers at the front desk. She descended on the nervous Channel 6 publicity contingent like a wolf upon the fold, and would have meeted-and-greeted herself had not she overheard the arts editor from *The Times* asking 'where is the awful bitch who's been phoning me every day for the last six weeks?'. After this warning shot, Caroline retired into the main room and prepared to grease the wheels of media relations.

By 12.30 they were well and truly greasy. Despite Caroline's best efforts, a good percentage of the major publications were represented. The assembled journalists pitched straight into the drinks and cast about for some canapes with which to soak them up. They were out of luck: Fat Alice, bigger than ever after a month in a hospital bed and supported by two Daliesque crutches, had positioned herself at the strategic point where the waiters entered the room and was siphoning off each *bonne bouche* as it came within the reach of her pudgy hands. With her mouth full of flaky pastry she collared every passing guest and asked them if they knew of any other observational documentaries in the offing. 'Something about the victims of road traffic accidents, for instance, I could be in that,' she said, 'or a behind-the-scenes look at the West End theatre. Or something about fat people?'

Mrs Renders, bright-eyed and pink-cheeked, found herself surrounded by a group of adoring young journalists, who listened attentively to her tales of music hall triumphs. Among them was Philip Bray, who occasionally prompted her with a question.

'That's fascinating, Mrs Renders... So, is it true that Kandid Productions are paying for your private health care?'

'Oh yes, dear, Eddie's been wonderful. I thought such generosity had died out in the Blitz.'

'So in fact he's paying you to take part in the series.'

'Don't be silly. I won't have a word said against Eddie.'

'Would you have agreed to take part if he hadn't paid for treatment?'

'Young man, I wouldn't be alive to care one way or another. I know you from somewhere, don't I? Now excuse me. Sid's got his eye on a sausage roll.'

Daryn swaggered around, speaking an impenetrable drug patois and envisaging himself as a loveable rogue of the Charlie Kray/Howard Marks type. Little Ben attempted to unscrew the monitors from their wall mounts. Debbie Wicks chatted happily to the older gentlemen of the press and occasionally touched the bottle of Prozac in her handbag for reassurance. Her first set of photos was due to appear in a national newspaper during the week of transmission. It was true what her dad had said all along: a girl like her would never need qualifications. Just as well, as she'd left school without a single GCSE to her name.

And what of Serena and Jamie? They glided into the Ivy at one o'clock, she in a plain coffee-coloured wool dress with discreetly expensive accessories, he in black Hugo Boss and a new set of highlights. He held the door open for her, and they stood thus framed until every pair of eyes was focused on them (apart from those belonging to a soon-to-retire tabloid editor who spent the entire afternoon addressing Debbie Wicks's poitrine). The more astute among them noticed that Serena was sporting a diamond solitaire on her wedding finger. There was a moment's silence before they were besieged.

'No questions, please, no questions until after the screening,' said Eddie Kander, parting the crowds and leading Serena and Jamie to the seats of honour. At a signal from his mighty hand, the lights were dimmed and the monitors flickered into life.

Eddie's voice boomed from the PA. 'Ladies and gentlemen, welcome to *Elephant and Castle*,' it said, over aerial footage of the shopping centre, the traffic system, the architectural mêlée. 'What you are about to see is a short assemblage introducing you to this major new six-part series from Kandid Productions. The stars and producers will be available for interview in a few minutes. Thank you.'

To the strains of a specially-commissioned soundtrack, a reggae-handbag version of *Maybe It's Because I'm a Londoner*, the showreel got under way. Images flashed past... Serena among the roses... Fat Alice looking brave in a hospital bed... topless Jamie executing perfect press-ups in the gym... Debbie in deep *décolletage* posing for photographs... Mrs Renders taking Sid for a walk along the river... Daryn preparing his wraps, little masterpieces of origami... and finally, to the hearty laughter of the assembled company, Maureen and Muriel in grotesque semi-drag performing selections from their nightclub act. A caption came up promising 'All will be revealed… 30 September', and the tape was over. There was applause; not just Caroline's hysterical clapping and screaming, but genuine, unprompted applause, from the press. The stars were beaming.

Eddie stepped up to the microphone with swaggering assurance. 'I'm Eddie Kander… but I expect you all know that. Good to see so many old friends here. Nice of you to come. Where were you for *Disposal Squad* you bastards? Hah, just kidding! Now, before we get down to the serious business of lunch, we have an announcement to make.'

A hush fell upon the room.

'Serena, Jamie… if you'd like to step up for a moment?'

The sheepish couple joined him at the mike.

'All yours, Serena.'

Serena moistened her lips and smiled at the company; Jamie hovered protectively behind her.

'Thanks Eddie, and thanks to everyone for turning up.' There was something not quite right about Serena's nervous cheeriness, thought Nicko. She's lost her poise.

'I won't take up much of your time. I just wanted you all to be the first to know.'

Pens hovered above notepads.

'Well, it's nothing much I suppose… just that… Jamie has asked me to marry him.' She held up her left had, where the diamond glinted. 'And I've accepted!'

The journalists, sentimental softies at heart, cheered. All of them, that is, except Philip Bray. His nostrils flared as he scented possibly the biggest story of his career.

'Married?' he muttered under his breath. 'Oh no. I think not. Not under British law.'

*

Whatever his information, Philip was sitting on it until the time was right. No point in announcing to the world in general that Serena Ward, gorgeous star of Channel 6's forthcoming docu-soap *Elephant and Castle*, is in fact not a woman at all but a man named Sean, a biological fact which neither surgery nor deed-poll can change. No point in demonstrating his impeccable research, the personal testimonies of a variety of witnesses, the documentation... not at this juncture. Shocking revelations about a nobody are not news; they would raise barely a ho-hum among readers of the *Newington News*, that twice-weekly catalogue of aberrant behaviour. But the merest peccadillo of a public figure, someone who is actually on telly, is money in the bank. And now Philip had something on just about everybody in *Elephant and Castle* – juicy little stories that he would trot out when the market for his wares was high. Daryn's drug dealing was a start. The scandal of Mrs Renders's health-care was even better. And then, the Turner-Delgado prostitution racket, implicating bridegroom-in-waiting and gym-gigolo Jamie Lord.

But best of all was the news about Serena. It had all fallen into place like a dream. Acidic remarks by Muriel ('she's not all she appears, dear, oh no. She's got a tale to tell... Well, my lips are sealed...') were sweetened by another down-payment on the club. Maureen was more forthcoming. 'She was a bloke. You don't believe me, do you? Go and ask in the Worcester Arms in Blackheath. They remember her. Oh yes.' So he had. And they did. And he had even found Serena's mother...

Post-production on the first episode of *Elephant and Castle* carried on up to the day of transmission; no preview tapes were sent out to the papers because none were ready, although that was not what Eddie Kander told the world. 'This is something I want people to come to fresh, without the half-digested views of the critics rammed down their throats,' he told anyone who asked. In fact, the cocaine hell of the edit suite was such that Eddie and Pete Silverstone were spending whole days fussing over tiny details, while the bigger issue of actually delivering finished programmes to Channel 6 went over-looked.

However, by some miracle the tape arrived at Channel House the afternoon before transmission, leaving Eddie and Pete with only five more to produce over the next five weeks. Steve and Nicko, meanwhile, were still out on the streets garnering more material. 'We've got the first one right,' said Eddie. 'Now we've just got to give the public what they want. Go with the flow. Chop us one out, Pete.' Their dealer moved into the edit suite on a semi-permanent basis, saving expensive couriers to and from his Muswell Hill flat.

And at 9.30pm on Thursday 30 September the viewing public sat down to meet, as the continuity announcer had it, 'the colourful residents of London's Elephant and Castle, where strong language and adult situations are a part of everyday life.' The nauseating sig-nature tune burbled over a frenzied montage of clips, demonstrat-ing such enthusiastic use of the edit suite's effects buttons that it was hard to make out much at all. (This was what the drug-addled editor called 'a Silverstone special'.)

At length the nasty video scrim melted away and resolved itself into a clear image: a naked youth in a shower. Pale young men in suburban homes across the land sat up and took notice.

'I'm fresh from the army. Joined at 16. Wasn't much cop at school, good at sports, football, sprinting, javelin...' The naked youth turned round and started soaping his front parts – which had been pixellated at the eleventh hour by nervous hands at Channel 6.

Jamie, watching at home with Serena, furrowed his brow. ''Ere,' he said, 'I don't remember filming that bit. What's going on?'

'So the army just seemed like the natural choice,' continued his voice on the tv. 'I like the atmosphere, you know? All guys togeth-er. I mean, don't get me wrong. I'm not gay or anything.'

Maureen and Muriel, although officially in a huff with Kandid Productions about the launch, goggled at the screen. 'They ought to run a little announcement at this point,' said Maureen. '"If you wish to see more of this young man's genitals, phone the following number". Think of the trade, Muriel.'

'The whole thing disgusts me,' sniffed Muriel, half-closing his eyes to counteract the pixellation.

'I'm young free and single now,' said the on-screen Jamie.

Serena hit him with a cushion then snuggled up a little closer on the couch. Perhaps one good thing had come out of all this nonsense, she thought, feeling Jamie's bicep through his tracksuit top.

The scene faded. 'The world's my oyster, as they say.'

Caroline Wragge, watching in the deserted D'Arblay Street office, kissed the screen where Jamie's bum was now but a ghost...

Some scene-setting shots followed, with a grim commentary intoned by an ex-*EastEnder*.

'They should have given Miachail that job,' moaned Fat Alice to her dozing cat. 'I sent them all his details. He can do cockney. He was wonderful in *East*. Steven said so. You know, Steven Berkoff. He's such a love...'

She stuffed another slice of Marks and Spencer's tarte tatin into her mouth.

'... Paranoia, fear, violence, death stalks the mean streets of south-east London, where a brave frontier community walks the line between survival and disaster...'

The camera panned down from the aerial view to an arterial road clogged with traffic, then cut to the interior of Serena's car.

'Mmm, nicely cheated,' said Pete Silverstone, watching the broadcast with one eye and cutting the next episode with the other.

Serena looked beautiful, dewy-fresh as ever, just a hint of strictness as she scowled at the traffic. 'And not a hint of an adam's apple,' she thought with satisfaction, touching her neck where the scars were no longer visible.

'It's not as if I have a husband or a family to take my mind off it,' said her voice from the tv speakers – soft, low perhaps, but not in a *masculine* way. 'I tend to eat, sleep and breathe work.'

'Oh yes,' snarled Muriel high up in Beckford House, 'she was always a working girl. Ask the customers of the Worcester Arms in Blackheath.'

'I suppose my life might seem quite sad and lonely to a lot of people…'

'Lonely!' spluttered Fat Alice, sending fragments of delicious golden pastry flying around the room. 'What does she know about loneliness? Oh God this is enough to make me sick!' Tears fell on the last remaining slice of patisserie as Alice knelt on the floor to get nearer to the box.

Over the road, Sid cocked an ear at the sound of his mistress's voice. He checked the armchair: no, there she was as normal, barely moving, her breathing laboured. The voice was not coming from her. It was coming from the box in the corner, from a huge close-up of the familiar face, focusing hard on the blue blobs of eyeshadow, the tidemark around the neck.

'I've lived in this area all my life. Yes, I was born just over there, you can't see it any more, it was bombed in the war.'

Sid looked quizzically between the screen and the human figure slumped in the armchair. She waved a weak hand at him, patted her lap. 'Come on Sidney. Up you hop.' The little dog scrabbled his way on to Mrs Renders's knee. She tried to focus on the screen, but it was too much effort. Perhaps this medication was too strong for her…

'We ought to pop down and see how the poor old thing is,' said Maureen. 'I've not seen her for a while.'

Mrs Renders slipped into unconsciousness.

'Oh, she's fine, don't you worry about her,' said Muriel. 'Fit as a fiddle these days. Why haven't *we* been on yet?'

In the Princess of Wales on the corner of Spencer Street, much the same question was being asked. 'Why hasn't my little angel been on yet?' boomed William Wicks from behind the bar. The pub was packed; he'd look a fool if, after all his big talk, Debbie had been dropped from the series. Old friends that he hadn't seen for decades had been hunted down and invited to the pub with a vague promise of free beer; he wanted as many people as possible to share with him the excitement of becoming a showbiz father. 'He'd better not of cut her out,' he said to the fags-and-mags vendor, who had changed his lime-green button-down Ben Sherman shirt for a similar model in purple.

But no: here was the familiar tarmac of St Agatha's playground, and here was Debbie hovering nervously into view.

'Debbie Wicks is only 16,' said the voiceover; the rest of the sentence was drowned out by an almighty 'phwoar' from the assembled multitude in the Princess of Wales. '...her GCSEs. But Debbie has other ambitions. She wants to be a topless model.'

'I got eight A grades,' said Debbie in a scene shot only two days ago, 'but I don't think university is for me. Who needs qualifications when you've got big breasts?'

'THAT'S MY LITTLE ANGEL!' shouted William Wicks, the veins standing out in his neck.

Debbie, upstairs in her room, heard the uproar and took another Prozac. Tomorrow, she knew, the pictures would appear in the *Daily Beacon*...

And there was more: Jamie standing at the window of Beckford House, talking about his ambitions... Serena amidst the roses in Spencer Street, talking about how lovely the neighbours were... Mrs Renders with the doctor, receiving her cancer diagnosis... Debbie being made up by Theresa for 'her first professional session with glamour photographer Dudley Jenkins'. 'Find out what happens next week in the second part of *Elephant and Castle*...' The jingle-jangle of the theme music, the credits rolling...

Assistant producer: Caroline Wragge
Director of photography: Nick McVitie
Director: Steve Soave
Producer: Edward Kander
A Kandid Production for Channel 6

'Where the fuck were we?' screamed Muriel.

'Where am I?' sobbed Fat Alice into her damp cat.

'I'll kill the cunt,' spat Daryn.

'And meet some more of the colourful residents of *Elephant and Castle* at the same time next week. And now it's time for *Lose Your Furniture...*'

Caroline was alone at the office the following morning. While Eddie and Pete had a celebratory gramme (each) at the edit suite, Caroline fielded calls. The answering machine had gone into meltdown; she simply extracted the tape and dropped it in the bin.

'Don't speak to me like that. You're a criminal. You'll be in the programme next week and maybe then you won't be quite so rude. Fuck off yourself.'

'Could you spell that for me? M-U-R-I-E-L. Isn't that a woman's name? But you're a man, surely, aren't you? Okay, I'll make sure he calls you. What? Why weren't you in it? Probably because the censors at Channel 6 got to it first, goodbye.'

'Oh Serena, hi, can I just put you on hold?' Slam.

'Eddie, hi! Have I seen the papers? Yah, of course I've seen the papers! We're on the front page of every single one.'

Two

The morning after tx, Jamie and Serena were shopping for their special day and tasting for the first time the terrifying aftermath of being on television. Normally, Serena wouldn't be seen dead in the Elephant and Castle shopping centre; Sean may have come from Blackheath, but Serena was strictly a West End girl. But Eddie had insisted. They would go over to the shopping centre with Steve and Nicko to buy their trousseau, and they would meet their public.

The first shock came before they'd even got as far as the underpass. A placard outside the news kiosk proclaimed in bold black letters 'TV's SERENA TO WED'. Serena stopped dead in her Patrick Cox shoes (size seven: plenty of women had size seven feet...). TV Serena? TRANSVESTITE SERENA? How had they found out? She was gripped by a sudden urge to flee, but fear paralysed her. She dug her nails into Jamie's arm.

'Ow! What's the matter?'

'I'm not a TV, I'm a woman...'

She saw the news vendor, still in yesterday's purple shirt, grinning as if he knew every detail of hormones and surgery... But all he said was 'Congratulations, love! I'm made up for you!'

And then it dawned. She was no longer her own property. She was television's Serena. Not TV Serena. Not yet...

Steve and Nicko stood at the mouth of the underpass beckoning them down into the darkness, through tunnels stinking of piss where 12-year-old derelicts held out trembling hands, repeating their spare-some-change mantra with no hope of success... garish murals of jungle animals, the anti-graffiti coating peeling off in great yellowing flaps, stared from either side... Thank God she was wearing her shades. The camera would never see the fear in her eyes.

'Come on, Serena, pull yourself together.' Thank God for Jamie, she thought. The engagement may be a sham, a stunt pulled for the show, just another part of the deal, but she knew she couldn't make it through the next few weeks without a strong young man at her side.

They emerged into the purlieus of the shopping centre, where an encampment of rickety market stalls flogged pirated sportswear, cheap household goods and dodgy videos. Serena had never seen the like. For all her talk of the lovely, friendly neighbourhood, she always directed her footsteps north into town, never south. But all around her were smiling faces, proud faces.

'It's them!'

'It's her off the telly!'

'Look, mum!' A three-year-old child stopped and pointed, and was beaten soundly around the ear for inconveniencing its mother – until she too saw Serena and Jamie and joined the ecstatic throng, while her offspring howled in pain and despair.

'Here, love,' said the grizzled old florist, pressing a bunch of dyed carnations into Serena's hand. 'We're all dead proud of you. You've put us on the map. You're a lucky fella,' he said, nudging Jamie in the ribs. I am, thought Jamie. As long as nothing goes wrong... He remembered for a panicked moment the photographs that Maureen and Muriel had taken, now available on the net to anyone with an AdultCheck ID... But surely nobody would put two and two together...

They went to WH Smith to look at wedding stationery; within five minutes the shop was besieged with curious thrill-seekers. Word reached St Agatha's where the students and staff, already near-hysterical by their close association to one of the stars, descended like maenads on the shopping centre, hoping for a glimpse, a touch, a shred of clothing...

'Jamie!' they squealed. 'Jaaaaaaaay-meeeeeeee!'

Steve and Nicko went around vox-popping for all they were worth.

'It's like Beatlemania,' said one of the security guards.

'In't she lovely?' said the checkout girl at Tesco. 'Just like that Lady Diana.'

Debbie Wicks was tasting fame of a different sort. Long before opening time, she was summoned to a meeting in the public bar with William, Theresa and a beaming 'Uncle' Dudley. A pile of the morning's *Beacon* stood by the door, ready to be handed out to each and every customer; page three had already been framed and hung above the bar. The paper was open on the table. Everywhere Debbie looked as she entered the room were images of her naked self.

A round of applause greeted her.

'There she is! "The biggest thing on telly", and I quote!' said her father.

'We're so proud of you love,' said her mother. Debbie was cold and unresponsive in her embrace.

'We've got business to discuss,' said 'Uncle' Dudley, beckoning her to the table. 'Now, me and your mum and dad have agreed that we're going to manage everything for you, cos we don't want you to have a single thing to worry about. Answer the phone, Theresa.'

'It's not stopped ringing! Hello... yes, this is her moth– er, manager speaking...'

'See?' said Dudley. 'It's happening just as I said it would, my dear. You're literally an overnight sensation. It says so here. "Delightful Debbie is an overnight sensation, but with her looks and intelligence (she left school this summer with eight GCSEs) she's definitely here to stay. We say: forget the studying and concentrate on the *bare essentials* Debs!"'

'Get it, Debbie? *Bare essentials*? Good, isn't it?'

'That was *Razzle* magazine!' said a breathless Theresa. 'They've offered £5000 pounds for an exclusive shoot.'

'Fuck me,' said William.

'Five thousand? We can do better than that. Cheap bastards,' said Dudley who, only a year ago, had been begging *Razzle* to run a set of photographs of a protégée from Weston-super-Mare. 'Anyway, we're not ready to do held-open poses yet.'

'What?' said Debbie.

'Got to build up the mainstream profile. I'm thinking big here. Very, very big.'

'How big, Dud?' asked William.

'Melinda Messenger big,' said Dudley.

'Coo.'

'That's when the money will start coming in. We've got to be pre-pared to work for nothing at first,' said Dudley, who had already pocketed £2000 from the *Beacon* without telling his fellow-managers. 'Got to get the image right. Now Debbie, I want you to pretend that you're on tv, okay? Not like you were last night, you didn't make the most of yourself if I may say so. I want a big smile! Come into the room and say "Hiya, I'm Debbie Wicks!"'

Debbie's Prozac was strong enough to enable her to do these things; it had not, however, cured her rampant spoonerism.

'Hiya,' she said, stumbling back into the bar. 'I'm Webbie Dicks.'

'No love, try again,' said Theresa.

'Webbie Dicks.'

'Not Webbie Dicks, for God's sake,' said William, his knuckles turning white, 'Debbie Wicks! Debbie Wicks! DEBBIE WICKS! Just say it, girl!'

'Hiya. My name's Webbie Dicks.'

'It's no good,' said Dudley, after half an hour of fruitless effort.

'She just can't hack it. Sit down, Debbie, my dear, and let "Uncle" Dudley think.'

Dudley sat and scratched his head, and a shower of dandruff settled on page three like light snow.

'I've got it!' he said, the gleam of inspiration struggling through his thick, greasy spectacles. 'You need a new name!'

'What?' said Debbie.

'A name that's easy to say. A name that you can never get muddled up with. An alliterative name.'

'Ooh, Dudley,' said Theresa, who was impressed by anything over three syllables.

'Like Debbie Dallaglio' said William, who was glancing at the sports page.

'Or Debbie Dangerfield,' said Theresa, in homage to her favourite show.

'I have it,' said Dudley, getting to his feet. 'I have it!'

'What?' said Debbie.

'A name that will go up in lights and down in history. A real star's name!'

'Come on!' said William.

'Well, what's Debbie famous for? Apart from her brains, that is,' said Dudley, chucking her under the chin.

'Her tits,' said William.

'Correct,' said Dudley. 'And what size are her tits?'

'36DD,' said Theresa, who had taken Debbie shopping for bras only last week.

'Correct. 36DD,' said Dudley, savouring the words. 'Thirty six double dee. So there you have it. Ladies and gentlemen, I give you...'

'Yes? Yes?'

'Miss Debbie Doubledee!'

'Oh Dudley! You're so clever!'

'Say it, Debbie,' shouted William, punching the air. 'Say it!'

'What?'

'Say Debbie Doubledee!' the three adults chorused as one.

Debbie frowned, opened her mouth, closed it again, licked her lips and concentrated.

'Debbie... Doubledee.'

The cheering was audible in the street, where a few thirsty punters waited in the late summer sun for the first pint of the day.

Fat Alice was leafing through the broadsheet reviews.

'Hmm, let's see... "Serena Ward has natural star quality..." – what utter nonsense. "Semi-cretinous schoolgirl Debbie Wicks and her sinister Svengali..." No... Ah! Here we are. "But the heaviest censure must fall on the producers' exploitation of the mentally ill. A massively overweight woman whose life has clearly been completely destroyed by this invasion of privacy was shown throwing herself under a car, bleeding in the back of an ambulance, undergoing a painful skin graft and, later, being cut out of her casts, all the while simpering for the cameras like a grotesque Shirley Temple." Look at that!' she showed the cat. 'Nearly ten lines! That's more than anyone else got! I wonder if they'd like an interview.'

'Go on dear, log on.'

'It's peak rate, Muriel, the phone bills will ruin us!'

'I don't care, I've got to know.'

'Oh, you're a bitch possessed, you really are. Come on then.' Whining and gibbering noises filled the front room.

'Here we are.'

'Get it up, Maureen, get it up!'

'Many years since you said that to me, dear.'

'Don't be stupid, I mean the site.'

'Thank God for that. Possess your soul in patience.'

'It's so slow!'

'Here it comes.'

The screen went black for a minute, then burst into life. Maureen and Muriel gasped afresh at the wonder of it all.

'Welcome to Gorge Guyz,' announced the legend in black on red, 'London's premiere service for discerning men. Enter your AdultCheck ID for access to the listings.'

'Go straight to the doings, Mo, go on!'

'I'm going, I'm going!' Maureen tapped in a code and waited.

'Directory of Guyz,' said the heading on page 2. 'Click on the thumbnails for details and more pics.' There followed a list, each name illustrated with a postage-stamp sized shot of a naked torso, the faces cropped or obscured. Patrick, Simon, John, Mykel, Fletcher, Tim, Daniel... and Jamie.

'Hit Jamie! Hit him!'

Maureen clicked on the thumbnail, and the screen went black again. And then, line by line, came the familiar torso, the tattoos – 'Paras', a heart and dagger, a peacock, a black sun, medium green curry with chicken and lime leaves. Again, no head – but in this shot you could see what Channel 6 had chosen to obscure.

'Bona,' they said in unison.

'Go down!' rasped Muriel.

'I –'

'Spare me the wit, dear, just do it.'

A second picture appeared, a rear shot. 'When I Die I'll Go To Heaven Cause I've Done My time In Hell Bosnia 1995-6'.

'Fabulous! Go on, further!'

'Jamie, 22, ex-army PT instructor, offers full escort service, ACTIVE ONLY, in/out calls, most scenes catered for, cp a speciality.'

And then, in huge dayglo green letters: AS SEEN ON TV.

'Further! I want to see the counters!'

Maureen click-click-clicked in the right-hand margin and screamed. 'Over four thousand!'

'Ah!' shrieked Muriel. 'It worked!'

*

Way out east at Channel House, the daily emergency meeting was getting under way.

'What were the ratings?' screamed the controller. 'I can't say anything until I've seen the overnights!'

A secretary burst into the room with all the drama of Greek tragedy, waving in her hand a still-warm fax.

A pause, during which several employees mentally reviewed their pension plans. And then, from the controller, a sigh of relief.

'It's okay. We did two million.'

'That's very good. I mean, against *Car Crash Kids* on ITV that's really great. You know, a result...' burbled the big cheese who had signed the cheques. 'It's a slow burner, this one. Wait till they get to know the characters, then when the romance kicks in in week two...'

'What does the research say?' asked the controller.

'The focus groups are happening as we speak,' said the big cheese.

'I want growth on this one,' said the controller. 'Clear, demonstrable, week-on-week growth. Can you deliver it?'

'You bet, I mean what people respond to is romance, human stories...'

'I don't care a stuff about romance. I just want ratings. You've got to give the people what they want. Get those research results and treat them as your bible.'

'I have every confidence in the creative team on this show. I don't think they need to be dictated to by focus groups...'

The controller flinched in her chair as if she'd been slapped. 'You get that research,' she said in a voice of deadly *froideur*, 'and you follow it to the letter. Do you understand me?'

'You bet. I'll call them now.'

'Good. And now, ladies and gentlemen, to the disastrous performance of *Pets with Cancer*...'

*

On the streets of Woking, employees of Random Research Limited were combing the crowds for likely candidates.

'Excuse me madam, I'm doing independent research into people's viewing and listening habits. Did you watch tv last night? You did. And can you remember what you watched? Not at all? Not even a little bit? Thank you madam, you've been most helpful.'

'Excuse me sir, I'm doing independent research into people's viewing and listening habits. Did you watch tv last night? You did. And can you remember what you watched? *Car Crash Kids*. And would you say you enjoyed it very much, quite a lot, not very much or not at all? Very much, great. And finally, could you just tell me your age? And what you do for a living? That's great. No, there's no payment, sorry.'

'Excuse me madam, I'm doing independent research into people's viewing and listening habits. Did you watch tv last night? You did. And can you remember what you watched? A programme about London. Right. And can you remember anything more about it? A fat girl in hospital. Okay, that would be *Elephant and Castle* on Channel 6, wouldn't it? And would you say you enjoyed it very much, quite a lot, not very much or not at all? Not at all. That's great...'

'Excuse me, sir, I'm doing independent research into people's viewing and listening habits. Did you watch TV last night? You did. And can you remember what you watched? Oh, right, *Elephant and Castle*! And you thought it was fabulous! Great, that was completely unprompted... And would you be interested in taking part in further interviews about this programme? Well, at lunch time today, actually. You would? Oh that's fantastic! Thank you so much!'

And so the focus group that took place in Random Research's plush interview suite consisted of one excessively camp young man, a couple of old ladies who thought they might have had the telly on last night, and a middle-aged gentleman who kept trying to steer the conversation round to his prostate problem. The two old ladies were so confused by the questions that they said 'yes' to everything. The older man talked about anything but the show, and was eventually asked to leave when he started shouting. This left the camp young man with the floor to himself.

Given that there was only time to run the one group, the research executive felt quite at liberty to attribute the usable quotes to a number of different respondents, thus making the final report look more worth the money. By nine o'clock at night she was putting the finishing touches to the fancy perspex binding, and the research was ready to go.

Copies landed simultaneously on the desks of Eddie Kander and the big cheese at Channel 6. Eddie took one look at his and dumped it without ceremony in the bin. He was a television professional of the old school: research, ratings and appreciation indexes to him were so much red tape holding back the creative freedom of the visionary documentary maker. The big cheese, however, held his in trembling hands, touching the cover with reverence. He told his secretary to cancel all meetings, and opened the sacred pages. There were the tables, the bullet-points, the graphs, the quotes... He bent over them like a druidic priest studying the runes, trying, through meditation and prayer, to extract the kernel of meaning from the gnomic mystery of the message.

'I'm sending you a fax,' he told Eddie at lunchtime. 'I suggest you make it your constant study over the weekend. Don't disappoint me, Eddie.'

Eddie, to whom fax machines were still, somehow, agents of the devil, shouted at Caroline on his way out of the office, and spent the rest of the day in a drug-fuelled frenzy.

The fax when it came through read thus.

to: Eddie Kander
from: Head of Factual Entertainment, Channel 6
re: *Elephant and Castle*

Congratulations on an excellent first tx. I've now had a chance to look through the research findings, and I think there's room for some tweaking. Please ensure that you take on board the following points:

The show has developed a strong gay cult following. Please emphasise the role of 'Maureen' and 'Muriel', get more of Jamie on show, and give prominence to the three characters identified in research as 'camp icons' viz Serena, Mrs Renders and 'Fat' Alice.

Strong narrative drive is essential. Viewers reported that they were 'confused' by some of the characters and wanted it to be 'more like *EastEnders*'. Develop fewer, cleaner ongoing storylines with cliffhangers wherever possible.

Many viewers felt that there was a failure to engage with serious male health issues eg prostate problems (see last month's memo on Channel 6 Infotainment and the Health Education Agenda for a reminder of your responsibilities in this area).

Watch your language! General concern from older viewers about profanity and sexual references.

Ensure fair and demographically-accurate representation of all minority groups *especially homosexuals*.

Please bear in mind at all times that your core audience is male, 25-35, unemployed but living in AB household with major wage earner 35-45, picking up significant fringe support from female C2DE 65+ and a maverick factor of C1 males 45-55 and the mentally ill. These demographic targets are *absolutely crucial* to the success of the show – and, I might add, to any question of a recommission.

Caroline picked the fax off the machine, nodded sagely and put it in Eddie's overflowing in-tray, where it was almost immediately buried by messages of congratulation from former colleagues desperate to jump aboard the gravy train.

Three

It was too late to save the second episode of *Elephant and Castle*; apart from anything else, it was another four days before the big cheese at the Channel 6 managed to force Eddie to sit down and actually read the research report. Eddie made a few feeble noises about journalistic integrity and the Reithian tradition, then caved in completely and agreed to make 'some exciting changes', which in effect meant sacking Steve Soave. Something had to be seen to be done.

Without Steve to mop up the day-to-day problems of filming, a dangerous vacuum developed at the heart of the production. Something had to fill it – and come the hour, come the woman... Step forward Caroline Wragge: director. The moment Steve Soave walked, Caroline was on location. Nobody asked her to go, but nobody told her not to; Eddie Kander was now so chemically dependent that it was impossible to get a straight answer about anything. Thus another great media career was born.

Caroline's first move was to install a unit base on a bombsite just behind the leisure centre. Early one morning a fleet of winnebagos drove through a gap in the corrugated iron fence, and by lunchtime they were fully operational offices. Caroline ensconced herself in the largest and most luxurious (with flush toilet) and stuck a notice on the door reading 'Strictly No Unauthorised Entry'. She installed her brother and a couple of old schoolfriends as assistant and runners; the caravan next to hers was dedicated solely to the comfort of Jamie Lord. She put a star on the door and a bunch of lilies on the table – hoping that, in the weeks to come, this would become their mobile love nest. Security at the gates were given strict instructions to allow nobody except those with official Kandid laminates on to the unit base – and, apart from Caroline's immediate family and friends, and, very grudgingly, Nicko McVitie, the only person to be issued with one was Jamie.

Caroline was not a 'hands-on' director; since her experience at the hands of Daryn, she was determined never actually to speak to any of the freaks and lowlifes that populated this doomed project except, possibly, at awards ceremonies. She regarded Random Research as a kind of Delphic oracle, and pored for hours over the report, admiring the neatness of the tables, the cuteness of the little talking-head illustrations – thinking, quite rightly, that if she hadn't made a go of television she would have been peculiarly well suited to a career in market research. Her creed, taped to the fridge door so that she would be sure to see it, was simple and direct.

More poofs
Cut characters
Stronger stories
No swearing

But before Caroline's streamlined, viewer-friendly *Elephant and Castle* could come on line, there was the very major hurdle of Episode Two to be negotiated and, if at all possible, disowned.

What Eddie and Pete Silverstone had delivered to Channel 6 could not have been further from the Random Research vision of things to come. It opened well enough, with a view from Maureen and Muriel's front room, but proceeded to cut rapidly between shots of Jamie pumping iron at the gym, Debbie preparing for a shoot with 'Uncle' Dudley and Daryn packing up the day's deliveries in neatly-folded gramme wraps. It was what Silverstone called a 'montage', but with no scene lasting for more than five seconds it was difficult, nay impossible, for the core audience to engage. True, there were flashes aplenty of Jamie's upper body, but what of the narrative drive?

There followed a long (and, to Caroline, nauseating) sequence of Maureen and Muriel reminiscing over their scrapbooks, with lengthy pauses and mumbled asides in which the only audible words were 'cock' or 'trade'. The camera dwelt not on the characters themselves, but on what Pete Silverstone called 'the telling detail' – the buckle on a shoe, the ring on a finger, a framed picture of a kitten, a dusty decanter. The voices themselves nattered on like the disembodied *dramatis personae* of a Beckett play.

The rest was no better. Fat Alice may have been a camp icon, but the sight of her slumped drunk against the railings of her house propositioning passers-by was, perhaps, just a little *too* Judy Garland. Candid footage of Serena and Jamie's love-tussles may have improved the viewing figures, but did nothing for the show's profile.

But they'd saved the worst till last. The scenes that followed Daryn on his drugs round were right up Pete Silverstone's street; he fancied himself as a cutting-edge *verité* film-maker, besides which he'd already pegged Daryn as a supplementary dealer and wanted to butter him up with extra screen time. And there it all was, in glorious, grainy, underlit colour – an evening in the life of 'Doctor' Daryn. Several half-hearted sequences – Daryn pretending to threaten his neighbour, Daryn failing to sell speed to children, Daryn beating up his 'bitch' (Caroline herself), Daryn making a substantial sale to a yuppie in Warfield Street – had been edited in such a way as to make Daryn look, in his own words, like a 'playa'. 'Amphetamines are the lifeblood of south London,' claimed the narrator. 'They serve as currency, as sustenance, as religion. The Doc is a king in this drug-addled underworld, where life is cheap and speed kills.' It meant nothing, but the viewers swallowed it hook, line and sinker. As did Daryn.

And at Borough Police Station, DI Soanes was watching too.

*

Reviews for the second episode were scant and even less flattering than before. *Ladz* magazine, quick off the mark as ever, ran some of the milder shots of Jamie from his Gorge Guyz shoot and dubbed him 'the hottest piece of spunkmeat on television'. (The editor, a regular of the Worcester Arms in Blackheath and occasional patron of the Gorge Guyz escort service, started dining out on his 'unprintable' stories about the 'outrageous' new series on Channel 6...) The tabloids made Debbie Doubledee into a star, but barely mentioned her involvement in *Elephant and Castle*. What little interest there was in the show focused almost entirely on the forthcoming wedding.

At the Channel 6 emergency meeting, the big cheese was sweating. 'I have every confidence in the new creative team,' he said. 'Just give them one more week to turn it around. I admit they were wrong at first...' Maoist denunciation was good for the soul. 'But I know we're on the right lines now. Please don't shunt us into the graveyard slot.'

The show was given a week's grace. Caroline, waiting outside in the corridor, received the news with relief. 'I won't let you down,' she promised the big cheese, and returned to unit base to kick arse.

And where, during all this, was Eddie Kander? Frying his brains with drugs in a Soho basement, that much we do know – but why was he content to allow Caroline Wragge, whose very career he could snuff out with one phonecall should he so wish, to steal his thunder? The answer was simple: blackmail. Caroline, despite appearances, was no fool: she had amassed over the weeks of filming a sizeable dossier of Eddie's personal and professional misdemeanours, everything from the creative accountancy that allowed him to pay his coke dealer out of the Channel 6 co-production budget to the much more serious matter of falsifying 'documentary' footage. He knew, she knew, the big cheese knew that this was nothing unusual – why, without it, there would be no 'infotainment' – but in the light of yet another scandal (this time concerning a completely fraudulent documentary about sexual abuse in a boys' public school) it paid to be discreet. The makers of *To Sir: with Love?* had been fined over £1 million – a sum that neither Eddie nor the channel could afford to gamble. For Eddie, whose reputation in this area was precarious enough already, it would mean curtains.

When Eddie discovered that Caroline was running a schismatic production office, he arrived at the unit base with blood in his eye. The first check came in the shape of two massive security guards, recruited from the large local Kosovar community. 'Do you realise who I am?' Eddie snorted, his inflamed nasal membrane producing unnatural amounts of mucus. A walkie-talkie crackled into life.

'Is there a problem?'

'We got an intruder, Miss Wragge.'

'I'll be right there.'

'Miss Wragge? *Miss* Wragge? What the fuck is going on here?'

'Mind your manners, sir,' said the more psychotic-looking of the two.

Caroline picked her way across the rubble and craters of the unit base.

'Eddie, hi.'

'Carol-een, what do you think you're playing at?'

'I'm running the show now.'

'You... I...'

'Come into my office. It's okay guys. I'll deal with it.'

An hour later, a car took Mr Kander back to the edit suite in Soho, his position in his own company a good deal clearer to him. He would remain as 'series producer' while Caroline became 'producer'; he would 'oversee' the finished tapes, which would now be edited by a friend of Caroline's brother. Pete Silverstone, who was at that very moment putting together a montage of scenes so brief that their impact could only be registered on a subliminal level, would be retained on the understanding that he would be paid directly out of Eddie's personal account, not by Elephantine Productions Limited, the independent company that was being incorporated just then by an old school friend who had married a lawyer. The closing credits for the show would now read 'An Elephantine Production for Kandid Productions for Channel 6'.

Caroline picked up the phone. 'Rachel? Get Nicko McVitie here now. I don't care where he is. Get him.'

She dialled again.

'Hi, Jamie, it's Caroline Wragge... Yah, I know you're at work, but I want to take you out for lunch... Oh, somewhere nice. I'm paying, of course... No, no, it's good news... Good, good, good, good, good, well just think of an excuse. Come round to unit base in half an hour.'

Half an hour: more than enough time to do the necessary.

'Come in, Nicko. Rachel: take minutes.'

The frightened lensman sat gingerly on a piece of newspaper that protected Caroline's soft furnishings.

'What's the problem, Caroline?'

Caroline looked down her nose at him. To think – once she had been in awe of professionals like Nicko McVitie. Now she had him in the palm of her hand. It felt good.

'A very good question, Nicko. Have you seen the reviews?'

'No, I've been...'

'I just want to get a couple of things clear. From now on, you report to me. Not to Mr Kander – do you understand?'

'Yeah.'

'And I've got a few changes to run through with you.'

'Go for it.'

'First, no more footage of those two disgusting freaks in Beckford House.'

'What, Maureen and Muriel?'

'Whatever you want to call them. They're out of the show from now on.'

'I thought we were meant to have more poofs in the show.'

'They're the wrong sort of poofs. Second, build up Jamie Lord.'

'What did you have in mind?'

'The stag night.'

'Is there going to be one?'

'Of course there is – if you organise it. Third: more Fat Alice.'

'She's back in hospital.'

'What happened?'

'She joined Jamie's gym and had an accident on one of the running machines while we were filming in there. The whole thing just collapsed. It was really weird; afterwards they discovered that someone had deliberately cut through the belt...'

'Okay. Get cameras to the hospital. And make sure she doesn't die on us.'

'What about the others?'

'More Mrs Renders. I don't care how ill she is: just get it. More Debbie Doubledee. She's famous now, we've got to cash in on her success. And find me some more homosexuals. I want to show gay men putting on a happy face for the cameras, hiding a secret sorrow, probably drinking too much and possibly making some kind of suicide attempt. I do not, I repeat NOT, want any more of those nauseating drag queens that you gave us before.'

'That's what Eddie wanted...'

'Stuff Eddie,' spat Caroline. 'I'm the producer now. I want my gay men lonely but brave, do you understand me?'

'Yes, boss.'

Caroline studied Nicko's face: the merest hint of sarcasm and he would join his friend Steve Soave in the job centre.

'Go on then. Don't waste any more of my time'

'Just one more thing.'

'Yes?'

'What about the wedding? What about Serena?'

'Oh,' said Caroline, checking her watch, 'you leave Serena to me.'

Caroline's courtship of Jamie Lord was unsubtle but effective. She took him to posh restaurants and plied him with the best wine. She took him shopping in Jermyn Street. She told him in no uncertain terms that he was the star of the show and that her next project would be built entirely around him, possibly as a chat show host. On top of all that, she gave him large amounts of cash. Jamie, who was easily bought by either sex, would have gone for a lot less. He didn't fancy Caroline – she was overweight and looked like a horse – but that was never a problem. Jamie didn't fancy 90% of his punters, but he could always perform for them. It mattered little who else was there as long as they reflected back to Jamie an image of himself as a desirable stud. In his own way, he loved Serena and fully intended to marry her – but Caroline, with her open wallet, was an offer he couldn't refuse.

Jamie's caravan on the unit base became the venue for almost daily copulations. The rest of the team dubbed it 'the Honey Wagon' and, in a misguided spirit of raillery, sellotaped a notice to the door reading 'If the Trailer's Rocking, Don't Come Knocking'. Miss Wragge was not amused, and nearly sacked her own brother. Jamie didn't care who knew about it; he was making on average £200 a day out of Caroline – a very considerable advance on his income from Gorge Guyz and the gym, and with no tax, national insurance or agency fees to deduct.

But even for a fit young 22-year-old, the pressures were building up. Caroline took a lot of satisfying; her appetite, both for food and sex, was prodigious. Jamie regarded sex with her as exercise – unpleasant while you were doing it and you need a shower afterwards, but beneficial in the long term. Sex with Serena was an altogether more pleasurable experience: she understood what a man liked – probably, reflected Jamie, because she had been one herself. Jamie's subconscious found this fact extremely exciting, but he preferred not to analyse it too much, concentrating instead on the overwhelming pleasure of their nightly liaisons. On top of this were his commitments to Gorge Guyz which he was obliged to honour thanks to the crude persuasions of Maureen and Muriel. 'Play the game or we go public,' was their bottom line, and given the amount of evidence that they could produce Jamie had little choice but to service three or four 'platinum' clients a week. He had ambitions now beyond the world of prostitution – and, while public opinion was certainly getting more liberal, Jamie doubted whether the world was ready for a chat show host with a recent past as a rent boy and porn model. At least, not on terrestrial tv.

Little wonder that Jamie was turning up for work every day looking exhausted. 'The missus kept you up all night again then did she?' Rod would say as his whey-faced deputy nodded off at the desk – but privately the boss was becoming concerned. Jamie was a good instructor, an asset to the gym – why, since his appearance on tv the uptake on membership had doubled. One evening Rod closed up the gym and ordered Jamie to come out for a drink with him; Jamie, unused to overtures of disinterested friendship, burst into tears over the first pint and blurted out selected highlights of his sorry tale to his wide-eyed employer.

'What, mate, you mean you go with blokes as well as birds? And you with that gorgeous girlfriend at home? I don't know, some guys have all the luck.' Rod gulped his pint rather too quickly; the idea of Jamie as a sexually available younger brother was making him nervous. 'Come on, Jay, let's go and unwind in the sauna...' And so to the burdens already piled on Jamie's shoulders was added the considerable weight of a lovestruck boss whose sudden emergence as a practising bisexual surprised nobody more than himself. Jamie would have quit his job at the gym in order to escape this extra pressure, but Caroline wouldn't let him. 'It's important that the public sees you as a hard-working young man,' she said, ignorant of the fact that much of his work now went on behind closed doors with an amorous giant.

Even with Jamie's extraordinary powers of recovery (and the large amounts of Vitamin E that he was now guzzling on a daily basis) there was a limit to the number of times that he could actually come in 24 hours. On a 'quiet' day, when he only had to perform once apiece for Caroline and Serena, when he could take the lady's part with Rod, and when there were no Gorge Guyz clients to accommodate, Jamie was fine. But sometimes, he was called on to produce up to five orgasms – a feat which he could just about manage, but with severely diminishing returns. He began to fake it with the women, disposing of the unfilled condom before they could get a look at it. He thought up dozens of little tricks to make Rod finish before he did – and his apparent enthusiasm in this field only had the effect of making the boss think that Jamie loved his 'work' more, perhaps, than he really did. The regular punters were the most demanding; they had been sold the full package, and there was no getting away with half measures. Jamie's schedule became a nightmare of calculations, exercise and dietary supplements. With the added pressure of the impending wedding, something had to give.

Maureen and Muriel noticed that their star turn was looking underweight and haggard, but ascribed it to the sinister ministrations of 'that bitch Serena' and thought nothing more of it. 'You look like shit, Jamie,' said Maureen. 'Get a fucking sunbed or something.'

Besides, Maureen and Muriel had more important things on their minds. They had discovered from a reluctant Nicko that they'd been dropped from the series – an insult which, coming on top of the debacle of the launch turned them into a pair of implacable gorgons. They beat their brazen wings high on Beckford House, waved their snakey locks and cast around with deadly eyes for victims of their wrath. Had they known that the author of their downfall was hidden away in a luxury winnebago just five minutes' walk from their front door, things might have turned out very differently – but this was another detail that Jamie had chosen to keep quiet, lest they discover the extent to which Caroline was supplementing his income. Instead, they dragged themselves up in their suits and ties (usually reserved for court appearances) and took a bus into the West End.

After ringing for several minutes, during which time Eddie and Pete hid their stash in the toilet cistern, Maureen and Muriel finally gained admission to the edit suite.

'Kander, you bastard,' spat Maureen, 'we want a word.' Muriel hovered in the background, the very image of a classical fury.

'It's okay, Ed,' said wide-eyed Pete, 'it ain't the law.'

The room was in darkness; an insane jigsaw of images glowed on the monitors. Maureen flipped the light on.

'My God, what's happened here?' asked Maureen, momentarily cowed by their mad, hollow faces and the disgusting smell of unwashed drug addict that pervaded the room. The floor was scattered with burnt scraps of silver foil, evidence of the dealer's successful attempt to wean his clients on to heroin ('a seriously creative drug'). Thanks to heroin, Eddie didn't worry that he was no longer in charge of his own company; Pete could churn out his deranged work and never register the fact that none of it was broadcast. They could even face the terrifying sight of Maureen and Muriel in man-drag with a certain degree of equanimity.

Maureen got straight to the point. 'You dropped us, you bastard.'

'Dropped you... right...' Eddie was having trouble with his words.

'You promised us a starring role and money for our club and now I hear that you're trying to get rid of us. Well it won't be that easy.' For a moment it was possible to discern beneath the rolls of fat and the effeminate exterior the tough little guttersnipe who used to beat up and rob his tricks. 'We have a tendency to stick.'

'Stick it where you like,' said Eddie, laughing too hard.

'Now listen, Kander,' said Maureen, feeling in his pocket for a knife, 'either you honour your obligations or things round here could get very, very nasty.'

'What you going to do?' asked Eddie, 'cut my hair?'

'There's no point talking to that one, Mo,' said Muriel. 'He's off his fucking rocker.'

'You listen to me good, Kander.' Maureen grabbed Eddie's collar and pulled him to a half-standing position. 'You get us back into your poxy tv show or we will bring you down, do you hear me? We know things and we're prepared to talk. And that wouldn't look too good for you, would it?'

'Say what you want, fucker,' spat Eddie. 'I don't give a toss.'

'I don't think you fully understand my friend,' hissed Muriel. 'We know about Serena... *all* about Serena... and we know about Jamie too...'

'Well bully for you, you sad old queer.'

Maureen and Muriel were not used to resistance. Their vicious routine usually reduced even the butchest of numbers to jelly. Maureen vacillated for a moment, and all was lost.

'You put us back in your programme or we'll...'

'You'll what? Slap our wrists? Go on, fuck off back to the obscurity you so richly deserve you pig-faced old whoopsie.'

With a final flicker of forked tongues, they retired to lick their wounds over a restorative gin in a small private members' club off Leicester Square.

'Right,' said Maureen, 'he's had it now.'

'We offered the hand, Mo, and he spurned it.'

'He'll be sorry. Oh yes. Just let him wait and see.'

Hell hath no fury like a drag queen scorned, and for the rest of the week the slighted besoms of Beckford House stewed in their own sour juices. Out of this noisome cauldron emerged a plan so outrageous, so simple, that it surprised even Maureen and Muriel. It was just... perfect. It would avenge them on Kander, on Channel 6, on those snot-nosed boys and tight-fisted punters, on every mother's son who had stood in their way over the years – and it would put money in their pockets into the bargain. Oh yes, it was perfect all right. So perfect in its malice and wickedness that it would bring revenge showering like fire and brimstone on the Elephant and Castle. Would the bijou lattie itself be safe from the coming storm?

Four

And so, amidst much fanfare from the tv magazines, we reach the week of the wedding.

Six months had passed since Kandid cameras first took to the mean streets of south-east London; a mere five weeks since the first tx brought the wrath of Channel 6 down on the head of Eddie Kander and sidelined him into smacked-out obsolescence while a well-shagged Caroline Wragge usurped his throne. During the last month, Caroline's determination to make the perfect docusoap put such a squeeze on production schedules that poor Nicko McVitie couldn't supply footage fast enough. And so the last show in the series – the all important wedding special – was going to have to go out largely live.

This was a shame for all concerned, as it unleashed the chaos that had been waiting to burst over *Elephant and Castle* all along. It couldn't have happened at a worse time, as the main events of the final episode, heavily trailed the previous week and previewed at great length in the weeklies and dailies, were Jamie's stag party, Serena's hen night and the wedding itself. The potential for disaster was unlimited.

Nicko left Caroline's office with instructions to organise Jamie's stag night ringing in his ears. It was not the sort of thing at which Nicko excelled: his idea of a good time was several beers in a congenial public house, then whatever it took to get a shag. Parties, launches and all such functions were not his cup of tea. So it was with intense relief that he learned that matters were already well in hand.

'What you doing for your last night of freedom, then?' he asked Jamie while preparing one of the lengthy and transparently false set-ups that now dominated the show.

'All taken care of, mate,' said Jamie. 'Big party. It's gonna be wicked. You coming?'

'Course, if I'm invited.'

'Bring yer friend.' Jamie jerked his head towards the camera.

'Never go anywhere without it,' said Nicko.

There were no further discussions about the stag night; Caroline had simply specified that she wanted 15 minutes of 'unforgettable footage' ready for transmission on the Thursday evening. Caroline herself decided not to attend; she knew that a couple of drinks would strip her of her dignity and see her chewing Jamie's trousers on prime-time television. Perhaps if she had been a little more in control of her libido, all might yet have been well... but, without Caroline's chilling presence, plans for the party rolled ahead unchecked.

It will surprise nobody to learn that the hosts of Jamie's stag night were none other than those two well-known entertainers Turner and Delgado, who hired Cheekies Wine Bar in Kennington for what was to become the most talked-about party of the year. This they had done not out of the kindness of their hearts; the invitations were nothing less than the teeth of a vicious mantrap set to spring round the unwary feet of any who might stray within its jaws. They asked Jamie, of course, and the rest of the Gorge Guyz (might as well get their mugs on tv while they were at it) with strict instructions to drink heavily before arriving and to shed their clothing as soon as possible.

And the guest of honour at Jamie's stag night, of course, was

Philip Bray. The readers of the *Newington News* had not heard a great deal about *Elephant and Castle* in recent weeks – nothing, in fact, that they could not have gleaned from the national press. At the weekly planning meetings, the editor badgered Philip for 'this bloody exclusive you promised us,' and was met with a seraphic smile. For five weeks, the features editor filled the paper with inconsequential drivel about working women, the family and how to look fabulous for a fiver, until she too was practically begging her deputy to come up with the goods. 'When the time is right,' said Philip, inscrutable as ever. He wondered if they would be so eager when he revealed to the world that Serena Ward, the nation's sweetheart, was nothing less than an ex-man. This he planned to do on live television.

On Wednesday afternoon, Maureen and Muriel loaded half a dozen suitcases into the back of a cab outside Beckford House. 'When we throw a party,' they told Philip, 'we like to do it properly' – and to that end they had three changes of costume apiece, a selection of their favourite records – including a generous stack of Muriel's 45rpm of 'I Am What I Am' to give away as party favours.

When the first guests arrived at 8pm, Maureen and Muriel had already taken their own advice and downed the best part of a bottle of vodka between them. The rest they poured down the throat of the under-age barman, confident that in his fuddled state he would forget to charge for drinks and may even win his spurs as a future Gorge Guy. Jamie arrived on the arm of Rod, who was not used to alcohol and, after two glasses of wine, was declaring his love on camera and agreeing to an in-depth interview with Philip Bray. Jamie, who knew Philip only as the nervous punter who had bolted at the crucial moment from his after-hours massage, was delighted to see him in cahoots with Rod, hoping that they might reach a mutual understanding and thus lighten Jamie's sexual burdens. Little did he know that the slurred details of their afternoon sessions, even down to that bit of improvised bondage with the skipping rope, would soon be delighting breakfast tables across south-east London.

By 9pm the joint was jumping. The Gorge Guyz, true to their word, were pissed and dancing topless on the tables. Nicko, unable to capture all the business with just one camera, put in an emergency call to Steve Soave who swallowed his pride and hurried down to Cheekies with his apparatus.

At 10pm the entertainment began. Maureen was hoisted on to the stage by a couple of his burlier employees, and took to the microphone like the old pro he was. He had dressed for the occasion in a boiler suit hand-stitched from heliotrope organza.

'Gentlemen! Can we have some hush, please!'

Barbra Streisand was cut off in mid flow.

'As you all know, we're gathered here today for a very special young man, he's like a son to me and my partner, so we'd like to wish him all the best in his forthcoming marriage to the lovely Serena...' Maureen's teeth were clenched so tightly that the name was barely audible. 'I'm sure he's going to make her very, very happy. Let's face it, we all know what she's getting, don't we?'

A coarse laugh from the floor where, indeed, 75% of the guests had enjoyed quasi-marital relations with the young groom.

'Now, as is customary at this sort of event we have some very special entertainment for you. It wouldn't be a stag night without a stripper, but this isn't just any old tart getting her minge out for a packet of pork scratchings. No, gentlemen, this evening I'm very proud to present for you an exclusive one-night-only performance by the Gorge Guyz All-Male Burlesque Revue! Take it away, guys!'

Maureen winked at Nicko, the lights went down and the DJ span 'Love to Love You Baby'. Just as Donna's toothache was beginning to kick in, the lights went up and revealed four Gorge Guyz dressed in jockstraps, boots, white socks and motorcycle helmets, gyrating wildly in time to the music. The crowd (exclusively male) cheered and jostled for position at the front of the stage. Money was handed across the footlights to be tucked into socks and pants. One by one the boys took the spotlight to perform a 360-degree turn, ending with a backwards bow that revealed their hidden assets to a slavering crowd.

The chants of 'get 'em off' were becoming deafening when Maureen stepped once more on to the stage. 'Not you, dear, you can keep 'em on!' hollered one inebriated guest.

'Thank you, thank you. And now, gentlemen, it's the moment you've all been waiting for, the star of the show, the biggest thing on tv (and I speak from experience), I give you... Jamie Lord!'

The four Gorge Guyz knelt and extended arms towards the wings (or, rather, the door of the under-employed ladies' loo). A couple of fireworks exploded at the front of the stage, leaving one guest with minor burns, and Jamie burst out in full military uniform – a khaki sweater, combat trousers, boots, puttees, a webbing belt and, to top it all, a jaunty beret. Jamie was not an intelligent boy; he had been easily persuaded by Maureen and Muriel that a 'show' at his own stag night would not only be good for trade, but would also enable him to impress 'the right people' with his qualities as an all-round entertainer. Of course, by the time quantities of liquor and cocaine had disappeared down throat and up nose, Jamie was hot to trot. He was a natural exhibitionist, and an audience of one at a time was no longer enough.

Donna by now was writhing in the dentist's chair; Jamie leapt into the spotlight and began thrusting his groin in time with the music. No adept of the ancient art of ecdysis he: there was no tease in his act, just plenty of strip. With one tug at his trousers (specially modified by the skilful needle of Maureen) Jamie's legs and Y-fronts were exposed; another quick yank and the sweater and belt joined the trousers in a khaki pile on the floor. The groom-to-be was now dressed only in white pants and vest, with the military accoutrements on head and feet still in place. He hooked his thumbs into the bottom of this vest and began to pull it up, exposing the hairy, muscular stomach that had played such a crucial role in his rise to stardom. A little more 'dancing' (stomping from boot to boot and thrusting his pelvis) and the vest, too, was off. The audience was enjoying the performance. So was Jamie – that much was clearly visible.

The Y-fronts came down an inch or two, revealing more hair and then, to the punters' astonishment, evidence of a further set of underwear yet skimpier than the last. Eager hands left Jamie's modesty protected only by half an ounce of red lycra.

Donna Summer segued into Boney M (the wholly inappropriate 'Brown Girl in the Ring') to which Jamie danced with equal enthusiasm. The focus of his act was now quite plainly the contents of that over-stretched scrap of red fabric, which was being vigorously palpated and variously rearranged for the edification of the audience (and, of course, the cameras). Finally it could contain Jamie no longer and was pulled aside for the final great revelation.

The act was meant to stop there; give them a quick show, wave it around a bit and leave them wanting more, had been Muriel's instructions. But Jamie was by now so carried away that there was no getting him off the stage. He paraded along the front row, allowing fingertips to brush against him before stepping gingerly back to a safe distance. He grabbed one of the Gorge Guyz and joined him in an improvised samba. He lay on his back and writhed around in ecstasy, while frustrated onlookers craned to get a better look.

This was too much for the MC, who stepped back on to the stage and announced, undeterred by a volley of booing and bottles, 'Thank you, gentlemen, now would you please welcome on to the stage the very fabulous, the one and only, she's very talented and I know you're going to give her a big hand, Muriel!'

Boney M were replaced by Muriel lip-synching to 'I Am What I Am', waving at imaginary friends in the crowd and generally playing the diva for all he was worth. Jamie, who had no intention of surrendering the spotlight to this tatty old hen, stood up and did a convincing impression of a helicopter preparing for take-off.

Maureen launched himself across the stage, slipped in a puddle of beer and tumbled down on to a table, upsetting glasses and rendering one of the guests unconscious with the impact. This was the signal for all hell to break loose. The Gorge Guyz, aroused by the situation to an erotic frenzy, started having sex with each other heedless of onlookers. Rod, roused from an alcoholic stupor by Maureen's crash landing, realised that his little brother was being molested on stage, and, with a bovine bellow, charged through the room to rescue him. He reached the stage just as Jamie had reached the point of no return, finishing himself off in a pint mug that had been handed up from the audience. Muriel, undeterred, continued to regale the audience with selections from his night club act. In his own mind he was headlining at a Royal Variety Performance.

Maureen, stunned and bloody, decided to cut his losses. He crawled through the crowd, his boiler suit torn from midriff to exit, and bolted the doors.

Philip didn't go home that night. Instead, he walked the mile and a half from Cheekies Wine Bar in Kennington to the *Newington News* offices to clear his head. The security guard greeted him on the door, and soon Philip was seated at his terminal. He rustled up a strong black coffee, cracked his knuckles and began to write.

'Local man Jamie Lord (22), star of television's *Elephant and Castle* documentary series, has a raunchy double life as a male stripper, it was revealed last night. And that's not all...'

Nicko and Steve didn't go home either. After drinking their fill at Cheekies, they decamped with their video footage to the Soho office, did a quick edit and delivered the results to the unit base at 8am. 'Stag night stuff ready for tx,' read the note from Nicko. 'Any problems, call me on the mobile. I'll be setting up at the wedding.' Both of them knew that Caroline would pass the footage straight on to Channel 6 without viewing it.

Jamie, who had passed out at about 5am, woke up on the morning of his wedding in Rod's bed, his giant host slumbering contentedly beside him.

Serena went to bed at 10pm. She wanted to look her best for her big day.

The registry office usually closed at 6pm, but on Thursday evening they had been persuaded to stay open until 10.30pm by the entirely fatuous suggestion that Elephantine Productions were 'in development' of a new fly on the wall series about Southwark Town Hall. The wedding was scheduled to take place on live television between 9.45pm and 10pm. Serena was ready by eight, filming a few last-minute clips in the hairdresser's chair, lying about the fun she'd had on her hen-night and betraying a few rather endearing nerves. Jamie was filmed in the shower at the gym, desperately trying to shake off his hangover. Crowds of teenage girls gathered on the town hall steps; by the time the show went on air at 9.30pm, traffic on Peckham Road had come to a standstill.

The Friday edition of the *Newington News* rolled off the presses an hour earlier. Philip had persuaded the editor to impose a strict embargo on his feature; nothing must prevent the final broadcast. Just as the continuity announcer was saying '...a right royal knees-up at the *Elephant and Castle*', just as the ghastly opening music tinkled for the last time, the first copy of tomorrow's *Newington News* was delivered to the front desk of Channel House by Philip Bray himself, marked 'for the urgent attention of the controller'.

'Sorry, sir,' said the receptionist, 'we don't take packages at reception. You'll have to take it round to despatch.'

But Philip had already disappeared, racing back to Peckham to be in time for the ceremony. The receptionist added the envelope to a pile of unsorted mail.

The familiar title sequence faded to black, and there was a moment of silence before the nation's screens were slashed across with a couple of jagged lines and a burst of white noise. What had gone wrong? But no: all was well. An image – dark, blurred – flickered into life. A man's head was dimly discernible in silhouette against a livid greenish light that occasionally flared from behind the skull. The profile, for regular audiences of *Elephant and Castle*, was unmistakeably Muriel's.

'There's a special surprise in store for you tonight, viewers,' came the familiar voice. 'You'll be seeing Jamie in an entirely new light. Stay tuned, now!'

Caroline, who was watching on a monitor down at the town hall, jerked upright in her chair.

'Where is Nicko McVitie!'

'He's filming, Caro...'

'I don't care. Bring him to me NOW! I told him no more of those two. NO MORE! I told him –'

One of the runners thrust a copy of tomorrow's *Newington News* into her hand.

'I think you ought to see this, Miss Wragge.'

There, in 48point helvetica was the headline:

CASTLE OF FILTH

Alongside it ran a picture of Jamie in his boots, beret and red lycra posing pouch. Caroline screamed and ran towards the registry office, where the young couple were undergoing some preliminary instruction.

'I'm sorry, miss, you can't go in there,' said the security guard.

'I'm the fucking producer, for Christ's sake.'

'I'm sorry, I'm under strict instructions to let nobody through these doors.'

'I'll have you sacked for this you bastard.'

'As far as I'm concerned, miss,' said the security guarded, leaning confidentially towards Caroline's ear, 'you can swivel on it.'

Meanwhile, homes across the country were being treated to a show that redefined the meaning of post-watershed television. The grapevine sprang into action. Viewing figures shot up dramatically, leaving the *Car Crash Kids* pile-up special to languish unobserved.

A red light flashed outside the registry office, which was packed for the occasion with friends and family of the happy couple, as well as all their co-stars and neighbours from the series. Fat Alice took up two seats in the front row, with Miachail Miorphiagh at her side. Daryn took Jamie aside for a reviving line before the cameras started to roll. Debbie Doubledee, as bridesmaid, looked blank in a white lace boob tube. Only Serena was composed: flawless, emotionless, a Sphinx...

'Three, two, one, and we're on air,' said Nicko.

The registrar began the solemn rites.

At Channel House, the controller was close to a heart attack. 'Why wasn't I warned?' she cried, clutching her left shoulder. 'Why...'

'What should we do?' asked the big cheese.

It was several minutes before the controller could find the breath to reply.

'OK lads, he's there,' said DI Soanes, pointing to Daryn's image on the screen. 'Go, go, go!'

Three panda cars peeled away from Borough police station, their blue lights flashing.

'We are gathered here today to join Serena and Jamie in marriage...'

At the back of the hall, Philip tried to remain calm. He concentrated on his breathing. He closed his eyes and visualised himself and Mrs Bray dining with a few close media friends at the Groucho...

'Pull...' gasped the controller of Channel 6.

'What?' asked the big cheese, unable to grasp her meaning.

In Beckford House, the gorgons licked their lips and smiled.

'If there is anyone here present who knows of any reason why this man and this woman should not be joined in wedlock...'

Stay calm, thought Philip. Stay calm.

'Pull... pull...'

'Pull what?'

Three panda cars screamed to a halt outside the town hall, and six uniformed officers began to push their way through the crowds.

'...or forever hold your peace.'

Philip stood up at the back of the hall and cleared his throat.

'Yes, I do.'

'Sir?'

Philip stepped into the aisle and moved purposefully towards the front of the room. All eyes in the room – across the viewing nation – were on him.

'I know a reason why they cannot marry.'

'Sir?'

Philip paused for effect just a moment too long.

'She's... a...'

The doors burst open and six uniformed officers invaded the hall. The congregation screamed.

'A man!' shouted Philip above the hubbub. 'Serena Ward is a man! A man! A MAN!' But he could scarcely be heard.

Daryn vaulted the registrar's desk and stood at bay in the corner of the hall. The police closed in around him.

Nicko's camera zoomed like the eye of a drunk on to Serena's tear-stained face.

In Channel House, the controller mumbled through bluish lips. 'Pull... the... fucking... plug...'

The screen went blank.

Part Three

Mixed Reviews

One

Six months had elapsed, and a clean, sober Eddie Kander found himself once again in the inner sanctum of Channel House.

'The bottom line,' said the big cheese, 'is that we've got to find something to compete with *Police Vet* on ITV.'

'So that's it,' said Eddie. 'You tell us we're axed, you drag my name through the shit for the last six months, then as soon as you get the wind up you come crawling back cap in hand. That's about the size of it, isn't it?'

'The thing is,' said the big cheese, who had undergone some kind of nervous breakdown over Christmas, 'you can't argue with the viewing figures.'

'So all that stuff that the controller said about putting our house in order, about raising standards of documentary journalism, and, I quote, "being more selective about our choice of independent producers", was bollocks.'

'Of course not,' said the big cheese, who could no longer look anyone straight in the eye. 'We're looking for a new improved *Elephant and Castle*, something that reflects the core values of Channel 6, that addresses issues of citizenship as well as providing entertainment.'

'So no more tits and bum?'

'If you look at the appreciation index figures, you'll see that what people are responding to is a strong character-driven story...'

'Bullshit. They want sex, and you know it. The moment they started taking their clothes off in the final episode the viewing figures rocketed so much that there was a dip on the national grid.'

'That's as may be.'

'So, mate, what I'm asking you...' Eddie fixed the big cheese with a gimlet eye. 'What I'm asking you is: do we have a recommission?'

'On the understanding that within the parameters of certain guidelines...'

'Yes or no?'

'The thing is, Eddie, you lied to us. You told us that we had, and I quote, "straight down-the-line stars", people that the mainstream audience could relate to. And we discovered, one by one, that they were sex changes or prostitutes or criminals. What kind of message does that put across about the channel's brand proposition?'

'Bollocks to that, mate. People love us and you need us.'

'But you see within the context of a portfolio of new programmes for the summer season...'

'...?'

The big cheese cowered under Eddie's psychotic glare. Since that fateful night when the blue-faced controller had collapsed over a blank, fizzing monitor, the big cheese had been unable to withstand pressure.

'Yes.'

'Okay. So we're looking for a new series, I think you mentioned something about a 13-week run, obviously that means improved budget and resources, high production values, nothing less, in fact, than the full Kandid Productions treatment. *N'est-ce pas*?' Oh yes, Eddie was back on form.

'Y-yes,' said the big cheese. 'Can you deliver?'

Eddie sat back in his chair and folded his arms. 'Don't ask me, mate. I'm just the *series producer.*' He sneered down the table. 'Let's ask the woman in charge. Caro-leen?'

Caroline, who had been trying out the various ring options on her mobile phone, jumped at the sound of her name.

'Yah, absolutely, good.'

'There speaks a major force in British broadcasting. God help us.'

It had not been a good six months for Caroline Wragge. The fall-out from series one landed squarely in her lap – and there was no denying the fact, squirm as she might, that she was responsible. She tried to pass the buck to Eddie, to Nicko, to anyone at Channel 6, but it kept bouncing back. 'You are, are you not, the producer?' asked the man from the Broadcasting Standards Authority after a special post-mortem screening. Caroline's mouth had already framed the word 'no' when her name appeared on screen. Producer: Caroline Wragge. She thought for one insane moment of blaming the man who had done the titles.

Elephantine Productions did not survive the post-transmission purge; its demise was reported in gleeful detail in the pages of *Broadcast*, the Monday *Guardian* and, of course, the *Newington News*. Kandid, on the other hand, emerged smelling of roses.

Why, then, did Eddie not get rid of Caroline there and then? The blackmail threats had been defused; any accusations of falsifying documentary footage looked like a parking violation compared to the mass carnage of Caroline's own tv misdemeanours. And it was not as if the show couldn't survive without her, despite her claims that 'If I go, Jamie goes'. Eddie set less store than Caroline by her relationship with young Jamie Lord. In private discussions, the two men agreed that Jamie would go with the money – and Caroline, with no job and no access to 'expenses', would be powerless to stop him.

No: it was not her threats that kept Caroline in Kander's employ. It was the fact that, in Eddie's opinion, she was worth the money. Privately, he took his hat off to her. He reluctantly admitted, but only to himself, that episode six of *Elephant and Castle* was one of the finest pieces of television he had ever seen.

Viewers agreed with him. The figures, which held steady around the two million mark through episodes two to five, were hiked dramatically by episode six. Twelve million witnessed the stag night, the will-they-won't-they wedding cliffhanger and the arrest. Floods of letters demanded to know what had happened to Serena, Jamie and Daryn. Channel 6 played its cards close to its chest, announcing in a tight-lipped press release that 'no decision has yet been made on the future of *Elephant and Castle*'. 'Never,' said the controller, 'will those bastards work for us again.'

And then came *Police Vet*.

It started out small, a regional opt-out on HTV. But then it grew bigger. Watchful eyes at Network Centre could no longer ignore the fact that it was out-performing almost all other ITV output in terms of audience percentage. They took a gamble, and networked it for a trial period after the 11 o'clock news. After three weeks a trickle of letters from insomniac pensioners had grown into a flood of fan mail from across the demographic spectrum. The schedulers brought it forward to 9.30pm and announced that the initial six-week run had been extended indefinitely.

So what, exactly, was the secret of *Police Vet*? Heads were scratched long and hard at Channel 6 over this very question. There was nothing original about the formula – so that was obviously a point in its favour. This was back-to-basics fly-on-the-wall television: a couple of cameras, some cute animals in distress, nice scenery and one central character. But *what* a central character. Barry Llannelly was a uniformed policeman, a trained vet and a warm, compassionate character. At the end of a hard, rewarding day rescuing stranded sheep in the Clocaenog Forest or breaking up illegal dogfighting dens in Ruthin, he relaxed at home in Wrexham with only his cat, Cher, for company. The majority of viewers wanted to mother him or marry him – anything that involved cooking a lot of meals, basically. Those with a little more insight wanted to shag him or shoot him. Either way, people tuned in in their millions. When Barry burst into tears over a beached halibut at Talacre, the figures topped ten million.

'No competition,' said Eddie, putting his feet up on the table. 'We'll piss all over them. What's *Police Vet* got that we haven't?'

'Well,' said the big cheese, 'what viewers seem to be responding to is the fact that Barry Llannelly is a really nice person.'

'Nice? *Nice?*' roared Eddie. 'People don't want nice! They want a freak show! That's the only reason people watch *Police Vet*, because they enjoy laughing at that skinny Welsh pansy.'

'I don't think...'

'Anyway, *Elephant and Castle* is full of nice people.'

'No it's not, Eddie,' said the big cheese, 'and that's just the trouble. It's full of monsters. Viewers want someone they can identify with, someone with hopes and dreams and disappointments like their own.'

'God, have people really so little imagination?'

'I'm afraid so.'

'Whatever happened to realism? To *satire*, for Christ's sake? It's all lovey-dovey wishy-washy navel gazing these days, isn't it? What a decadent, bourgeois culture we're creating, when the only thing people are interested in is sanitised, tarted-up reflections of their own pitiful little lives. Where's the fun in that?'

'If *Elephant and Castle* is to be recommissioned... and that's still a very big "if" at this stage, then we have to put some sympathetic, likeable characters centre stage.'

'No problem.' Eddie was willing to compromise his ideals 100% in order to make a sale.

'So, who would you suggest?'

'We've got Serena.'

'Serena Ward, I need hardly remind you, is a transsexual who attempted to break the law by marrying another biological male. Hardly a major point of reference for Middle England.'

'Fair point. Well, there's Debbie. She's a lovely girl.'

'Debbie's a topless model.'

'So?'

'So she's *dirty*, Eddie, can't you see that? And don't bother telling me that's there's nothing wrong with girls showing their breasts in the papers, or that sex is a natural and beautiful thing, because I've heard it all before.'

'Okay. Jamie? No, fair enough. Shelley? No, she's black, never good for ratings. And Daryn's in prison. What about Fat Alice?'

'Christ, Eddie, we've seen that woman crawling down Spencer Street on her hands and knees begging some poor unfortunate tramp to come back to her flat. We've seen her with abrasions down either side of her face caused by zippers. She's nearly 20 stone. I'm sorry, it's just not on.'

'Mrs Renders?'

'Research shows that she failed to connect with over 60% of viewers who either found her "not very interesting", "not at all interesting" or "downright depressing".'

'Oh bloody hell,' said Eddie, 'I could have saved all that money and just let the old bird die. Hey, Caroline! Remind me to stop payments to that private clinic, okay? Maybe the viewers will regret their callous rejection of a sick old woman when they've killed her off.'

'Yah, right.'

'So what would you suggest, Eddie?' asked the big cheese. 'I'm assuming that you want a second series?'

'Of course. Let me see. Caroline, any ideas?'

'We could get some new characters in.'

'Have you actually met anyone nice in the Elephant and Castle, Caroline?'

'No, that's true... Well, how about getting an actor in to play somebody.'

'Hmmm, not bad, not bad at all. Who did you have in mind?'

'Well, I've been looking at the CV of an actor called Miachial Miorphiagh...'

'Miachial Miorphiagh?' roared the big cheese. 'Are you insane? He was officially declared "ratings poison" after we axed *Surgeon General*.'

'Anyway,' sneered Eddie, 'using actors instead of real people would hardly be in keeping with the controller's tough new line on documentary journalism, would it?'

'Can't we get one of our friends to move into the area?' said Caroline. 'Maybe if we bought a flat for my brother or someone...'

Eddie and the big cheese ignored this remark.

'There's nothing for it,' said Eddie. 'We'll just have to transform one of our existing stars. I mean, come on – these people got 12 mill in the last series. We must be doing something right.'

'But nice, Eddie. They've got to be nice. We're talking mainstream here, not cult.'

'It's okay. We do nice. Serena can be nice. Debbie can be nice. We'll clean them up, make them repent, turn them into stars.'

'Do you think,' asked the big cheese, staring down at the carpet, 'that either of them is actually psychologically capable of handling that, Eddie?'

'What?'

'I mean, you're putting two very unstable people into a potentially damaging situation here.'

'Stuff that,' said Eddie. 'Do you want ratings, or don't you?'

Philip Bray called Serena every single day after the interrupted wedding.

'I want to help you, Serena. I want to give you a chance to tell your side of the story. I've got all the evidence, but I'm a believer in fair play. I don't want the world to think of you as some kind of freak. I know you better than that. I see the struggles, the fears, the hopes, the courage in your story. But that's because I'm a sensitive kind of guy. To the average newspaper reader, you're just a drag queen who's been pulling the wool over the public's eyes and they'll eat up every last sordid little detail that they can get their hands on. And if you don't help me, there's nothing I can do to stop those details getting into the wrong hands.'

Usually, Serena put the phone down before Philip got to the 'some kind of freak' bit. She was a cool customer, he had to admit: most people crumbled in the first two weeks. He didn't want to throw his material away on an unsubstantiated story – that would consign him to local newspapers for the rest of his life. He wanted the big exclusive, the one-to-one interview that nobody else could get, that he would then flog to the highest bidder among the nationals and leave *Newington News* to the tender mercies of Sally and 'Career vs family: are your kids losing out?'. But so far, Serena wasn't taking the bait.

Philip tried blackmail, he tried money, but nothing worked. Serena, unlike most of the cases he dealt with, had a decent job, no immediate need of cash and no stupid ideas that tabloid fame would lead to lasting prosperity. Neither did she believe the 'I want to help you' line; it was Philip, after all, who had 'exposed' her in the first place. She was, it seemed, impregnable. Philip probed and prodded to find her weak place. He took advice from Maureen and Muriel, from Serena's mother (only too happy to oblige – at a price), from former friends and associates of Sean Ward. Nothing worked. And then he thought of Jamie.

Jamie was the one person who would not dish the dirt on Serena. He had co-operated with Philip on the coverage of his own murky deeds, giving an exclusive interview on 'My escort hell' and even posing for photographs looking adorably repentant. But on the subject of his relationship with Serena he would not be drawn – not even for ready money.

It begun to dawn in Philip's benighted mind that there was, after all, some spark of genuine human feeling between these two young people. Perhaps, underneath all the hype and the bullshit sur-rounding the series, they actually did care for each other – cared for each other more than they cared for fame or profit. It took Philip a long time to come to this conclusion; it was his first ever brush with such a phenomenon, and at first he was unwilling to believe in anything so outlandish. But eventually he admitted the possibility that Jamie and Serena were actually in love.

'Before you put the phone down on me this time, Serena, I want to talk to you about Jamie.'

Silence; not the too-familiar click-buzz of disconnection.

'Are you still there?'

'I'm here.'

'How much exactly do you know about Jamie?'

'As much as the entire newspaper-reading public, thanks to you.'

'Ah, but there's more than that, isn't there?'

'What do you mean?'

'Well, we both know that it's not just a little bit of casual whoring here and there, don't we? There's all the kinky stuff, the S&M – I didn't put that in.'

'Oh come on, as if the public cares.'

'And then there's that bloke he works with down the sports centre.'

A short silence, the sound of swallowing.

'You did *know* about Jamie and Rod, didn't you, Serena?'

'Yes. He told me about it. It's over now. Why would you want to ruin yet another life?'

'Oh, I don't want to. That's just what I'm saying. There's no need for any of this to come out.'

'I see. Provided that I give you an interview.'

'Precisely.'

'That's all then. Goodbye.'

'No, don't hang up. There's more.'

'I know there is. Go ahead and tell the world that I used to be a rent boy, that I used to wank off married men in the bogs of Blackheath, that I used to hang around truck drivers' cafés and get shagged for five quid. Do you really think I care? You've done enough. People won't believe half of it anyway.'

'Oh no, Serena, we're not talking about you now. No. It's Jamie I'm interested in.'

'What about Jamie?' At last: the true note of defensiveness.

'I'm interested, for instance, in where he was getting his money from last year.'

'Money! He's never had any money.'

'That's funny. He was chucking it around when I saw him just before the wedding. Lots and lots of the stuff. Didn't he tell you?'

'No...'

'Where do you think he was getting it from?'

'Punters, I suppose.'

'I don't think Jamie would regard Caroline as a punter, exactly.'

'Caroline? What's she got to do with anything?'

She didn't know.

'Oh, I'm sorry, I just assumed that you knew all about Jamie's relationship with Caroline. I mean, you must have done. After all, he spent the best part of the summer hopping straight from her bed to yours. Surely you must have *smelled* her...'

On the day after Channel 6 announced details of its forthcoming spring/summer season, including a second series of the surprise hit *Elephant and Castle*, the *Daily Beacon* published an in-depth interview with sexy Serena Ward, the new he-she star of British television, talking for the first time about her past, her relationship with Jamie Lord and her hopes for the future. She talked about everything except her gender dysphoria and her surgery. Details of that, however, were supplied by Philip's meticulous research. It was 'a Philip Bray *Beacon* exclusive' – the first of many.

Serena found herself unable to go into work for a few weeks. She couldn't get out of bed in the morning, spent hour after hour crying uncontrollably. She loved Jamie, certainly – but this much?

There had been others – many others – about whom she'd felt the same. Jamie was a simple soul, affectionate, occasionally unkind, led by his dick. So why was she so upset?

Of course, it wasn't just Jamie. It wasn't the fact that her 'secret' was out at last; she'd known that it would happen one day, if not perhaps on such a grand scale. It wasn't even the fact that her mother had betrayed her, revealed secrets and told lies for money. Serena and her mother had not been friends for years. So if it was not over Jamie that she was crying, not over her mother, not even over Serena, then what? Why this debilitating pain, day after day? Perhaps, she thought, reading over the double-page feature once again – the family photographs, the pictures of little Sean in his shorts, at cubs, at a birthday party – it was for her own childhood that she was grieving.

After a fortnight of this, Serena took herself to the doctor's surgery and left with a prescription for temazepan. That, at least, would allow her to get some sleep...

She returned to work a shadow of her former self, lacking confidence with clients, unable to take the merest hint of pressure. Ricky Rampling and all her colleagues bent over backwards to make allowances for her; they would give her time, they would cover up her mistakes. Whatever Serena's personal circumstances, Ricky didn't want to let her go. But after a disastrous debrief which had resulted in Rampling and Partners losing one of their most prestigious contracts, he agreed, sadly but with certainty, to accept Serena's resignation.

'Never mind,' Eddie told her over dinner a couple of nights later. 'You're a star now. You don't need a job. Do as I say and the world is your oyster.'

'I just want things to be normal,' said Serena.

'Normal? When every other fucker is desperate to escape from the drudgery of "normal" life, you have to be the one who wants to stay put. You must be mad! Who wants to work for a living when they can just sit back, look beautiful and count their money?'

'I do.'

'You're out of your mind.'

'All I ever wanted was a normal life. That's why I went through all the crap of my childhood, being thrown out by my parents, living off what I could earn, then surgery. You don't endure the surgeon's knife just to look pretty.'

'Yeah, but the thing is, you *do* look great and you might as well capitalise on it. It's payback time.'

'I just wanted to be an ordinary woman.'

'Well it's too late for that, love, because now you're famous.'

'Yes…'

'So what do you say? Are we going to work together on this?'

'I don't have much choice, do I? I've lost my job, I've lost my boyfriend…'

'No you haven't. He's just a lad, he's been playing around. It's you he loves.'

'I may be a weak and feeble woman, Eddie,' said Serena, with a hint of the tough-as-nails south-east London queen she had once been, 'but I'm not entirely stupid. Jamie doesn't care about anybody. He doesn't even care about himself. He's not a bad boy. But that's it: he's just a boy. Pussy and money. That's all he wants. My misfortune to fall in love with him.'

'It's over between him and Caroline, you know.'

'So he tells me.'

'I mean, God, what man in his right mind would choose her instead of you?' I certainly wouldn't, thought Eddie, one of the many men whose interest was piqued rather than dampened by Serena's unconventional road to womanhood.

'Let's get down to business,' said Serena, to whom compliments from Eddie were anathema. 'I need to earn a living. I have no desire to lose my flat, and if I don't get some money coming in this month

I'll get behind on the mortgage. So: what are we going to do?'

'We're going to fight this thing together.'

'Meaning?'

'You're going to marry Jamie, you're going to star in our next series, and you're going to live the life of riley.'

'I can't marry Jamie. That much has been made abundantly clear.'

'Why not?'

'Because, as you well know, in the eyes of the law I am still male.'

'So what? You're a star. You can do what you want.'

'I can't rewrite history.'

'That's where you're wrong. You can do precisely that. Fling their accusations back in their face. Tell them it's bullshit, that you've always been a woman.'

'I gave Philip Bray an interview, for goodness' sake.'

'Disown it.'

'It's too late for that.'

'Okay: tell the truth.'

'But what he printed was the truth.'

'Whose side are you on, Serena?'

'I don't know...'

'Look, it's perfectly simple. We tell them our side of the story. We make Bray look like the second-rate provincial scandalmonger he is. We defy anyone to believe him.'

'But he interviewed my mother.'

'Who cares? She's nobody. We can discredit her. Just say she was doing it for the money. He will have paid her.'

'But there are so many other witnesses.'

'Like who?'

'Those two old harpies in Beckford House, for starters.'

'You've got to understand two things, Serena. First of all, people believe what they want to believe, and nobody wants to believe that you're not a real woman. Secondly, we've got budget. We can *buy* the truth. You wait: within a couple of months people will be wondering what all the fuss was about. Within six months they'll have forgotten it altogether.'

'But what about my birth certificate? There's proof, Eddie.'

'I don't think we need to worry about minor details like that. Nobody will believe it, not when we've finished the job.'

'And what, precisely, is that?' asked Serena, a note of severe misgiving in her voice.

'May I ask you a very personal question?' said Eddie. Serena raised her eyebrows. 'I mean, you are... you are *all complete*, aren't you? Collar and cuffs to match, as it were?'

'Of course. But what's that got to do with anything?'

'Serena, I'm going to save your life, I'm going to make you very wealthy, but you're going to have to trust me. Do you trust me?'

'Do I have a choice?'

'Not really.'

'So?'

'We're going on to the offensive. We're going to prove to the great British public that Serena Ward is, was and always will be a woman.'

'And how do you propose to do that?'

'We're going to *show them*.'

Two

At the Princess of Wales public house, now redecorated and rechristened The Double Dee, William Wicks was in excellent spirits. Since Debbie's first appearance on tv and in the tabloids, his life had been transformed. The pub, once dying on its feet, was full every night with curious drinkers hoping for a rare glimpse of 'London's twin treasures'. Even at lunchtime they came, but Debbie was never there – her days now were one long round of personal appearances, photo shoots, chat shows, openings. She sailed through them all with grace and equanimity, carrying her best assets before her. The terrified, mumbling schoolgirl had been left far behind. Debbie Doubledee, thanks to a little chemical assistance about which William Wicks knew nothing, could face the world and smile.

Fame had its benefits. She had more money now than she'd ever dreamed of – a generous allowance from her parents of £200 per week. The rest of her earnings (and she had no idea how much they were) went straight into 'the business' – Debbie was not to be troubled by that side of things. Whenever she wanted new clothes, she had only to ask and they would be given, free of charge, by manufacturers grateful for the publicity. To have Debbie Doubledee turning up at a film premiere wearing your latest creation was worth thousands in free advertising. There was even talk of a down-market retailer producing a 'DD' line of branded clothing – 'for girls with a lot of front'. Meals, cabs, hairdressers were all taken care of. The only thing she really needed money for was drugs.

That side of things was neatly arranged by her PA – whom the reader will recognise as former shoplifter Shelley Smithers. The last time we saw Shelley, she was repining in the chilly shadow of Debbie's new-found success, unable to contact her friend, besieged by predatory journalists. Tempted as she was to spill the beans, Shelley refused to betray a trust that she still regarded as sacred. Perhaps Debbie would never know of her loyalty – but she, Shelley, would know, and that was enough. She spent her days at home, dreaming over her growing collection of Debbie Doubledee pin-ups, leaving the flat only to sign on.

But Fate smiled on Shelley. No sooner had she resigned herself to a life of loneliness and poverty than the phone rang.

It was Debbie.

Within a week, Shelley was on a £500-a-month salary as Debbie's personal assistant, and Philip Bray was left making snide remarks in the *Beacon* about 'an unknown gal-pal'. At first her duties amounted to little more than accompanying Debbie to shoots, holding her hand, giving her confidence and a shoulder to cry on. But then, as Debbie's diary filled up, Shelley became secretary as well as companion, she was equipped with a mobile phone, she vetted and liaised with stylists and photographers, she even talked to the art directors who wanted Debbie's pictures. She had a flair for the work. Theresa and William Wicks, who strenuously opposed the appointment at first, eventually admitted that they were getting a great job for next to no money. They increased Shelley's salary to £600 and stayed home counting their profits.

Success came fast. Over Christmas and into the spring, Debbie was everywhere, in newspapers, on calendars, advertising everything from bras to ISAs ('for maximum growth...'). Prozac kept her happy at first, but there were only so many repeat prescriptions that the doctor was willing to hand out – besides which Debbie felt the need for something to lift her up as well as calm her down. And so Shelley, who had not grown up on the Ringwood Estate (where her brother Steadman put 'Doctor' Daryn in the shade) for nothing, became Debbie's dealer as well as her PA. She started off providing the odd line of coke: nothing too serious, just a little something to perk Debbie up in the morning and make her sparkle at photo shoots. But soon she needed more and more – and, inevitably, she had trouble sleeping. So Shelley procured valium. The combination of coke and valium seemed to her not only dangerous but also costly, and so, on Steadman's advice, she introduced Debbie to smack.

It was just what the doctor ordered. Of course, Debbie never injected; it wouldn't do to spoil her lily-white arms with unsightly track marks. Instead she smoked. It was wonderful to behold... the day's troubles slipped away... Debbie became relaxed, happy, compliant... She never took so much that she nodded out, not in front of the cameras at any rate.

Shelley herself never touched the stuff, but slaked her appetites on a series of stylists and photographer's assistants whom she picked up in studios.

Philip Bray had never liked Shelley Smithers; few men did. He ascertained that she was indiscreet in her sex life – that she picked up women, 'had' them and then dropped them just like a man. He hired an 'actress' of his acquaintance, a pneumatic blonde who looked like a cheaper, older Debbie, and simply tossed her in Shelley's way at a launch. The bait was good, and Shelley swallowed it whole.

What started out as a personal vendetta against a bolshy little dyke became a full-scale and utterly motiveless campaign against the entire Debbie Doubledee phenomenon. The deeper Philip dug, the more he unearthed. Drugs, lesbianism, and to cap it all the sordid past of 'Uncle' Dudley Jenkins, more than an uncle to the dozens of under-age 'models' he had photographed for various European publications, *much* more than an uncle to the hapless charges of a children's home in Lambeth back in the 70s... The empire was under siege.

Philip bearded Shelley at the press launch for series two of *Elephant and Castle*, a lavish affair at the Soho House paid for entirely by Channel 6. (Nothing was too good for Kandid Productions, upon whom they pinned all their hopes in the spring/summer ratings war.) Debbie was seated at a table, surrounded by a dozen journalists, all thrusting dictaphones towards her cleavage, as if her breasts themselves might speak. Shelley was leaning against a nearby pillar, ready to intervene.

'Hello, Shelley.'

'Hi. Oh, it's you. If you want to talk to Debbie you'll have to wait your turn.'

'No, not today. I'm not really very interested in her any more.'

'Aren't you, indeed. That's why you've been phoning up every day to beg for an interview, I suppose.'

'Well, I think for the readers of my newspaper Debbie is – how shall I put this? – old news. They see her as a bit... tacky.'

'Right you are.' Shelley was wondering how she could get Philip chucked out.

'No,' he continued, 'it's not Debbie I'm after. It's you.'

'Here we go again. Why don't you just fuck off back to Stoke, coconut?'

'I just want a little chat.'

'Look, pal, last time we had a little chat you blackmailed me with a load of crap about my criminal past. Well, big deal. Go ahead and publish them. "Schoolgirl nicks chocolate bar." That's about your level, isn't it?'

'I wouldn't dream of it. I believe in letting bygones be bygones. I mean, why would the readers of a major national newspaper care what you get up to in your personal life? You're absolutely right, Shelley, nobody could really give a shit.'

'Just piss off, Bray.'

'Right.' He turned as if to leave, stopped in a doorway. 'By the way, how's Sonia?'

That got her attention. 'What?'

'Oh, didn't she tell you? Sonia's a good friend of mine. A very good friend. I'm surprised she didn't mention it to you.'

'What do you mean, fucker?'

'Strange that *you* should call *me* that...'

'What's she said?'

'Oh, nothing much. She didn't need to. You see, I have the photographs.'

'You're full of shit.'

'What would Debbie think if she found out that her best friend, the woman who sees her undressing five times a day, was a lesbian?'

Shelley was speechless.

'She wouldn't be too pleased, would she? The very person who's supposed to be protecting her is in fact just waiting for an opportunity to pounce.'

'I wouldn't touch her...'

'Oh really? I thought you liked them blonde and busty. That's what you told Sonia. In some detail.'

Shelley stood awhile in thought. She had two options: compliance, or violence.

She chose the latter.

Philip left the Soho House with blood streaming down the front of his shirt. But the photographs, which he carried in his breast pocket, were unsullied.

The *Daily Beacon* ran the story the following Tuesday, with a front page photograph of Debbie and Shelley under the headline 'Beauty and the Beast'. No detail of Shelley's 'sinister hold' over Debbie was unexposed, from her 'cool, calculating scheme' to plunge Debbie into 'the hell of heroin addiction', to her 'sordid lesbian love games' with top model Sonia, who described her 'kinky video evenings' (they'd rented *Desert Hearts*) at the hands of 'woman-eater Smithers'. The thought of that 'intersexed freak' getting her 'stubby fingers with bitten nails' on (or possibly in) the nation's darling was too much for the readers.

No mention was made of Dudley Jenkins, who, that very morning, clinched a five-figure contract for Debbie's first held-open poses with a Harlow-based periodical, *Reluctant Teens*. No mention was made of the fact that Debbie was locked in an upstairs room at Theresa's sister's house, where she was undergoing unsupervised cold turkey and screaming constantly for Shelley. Philip Bray knew, or suspected, these things, but was too good a journalist to let them stand in the way of his story. Let the competition worry about that. His were the laurels.

Shelley's salary was stopped, her mobile phone confiscated, her company credit card ripped from her wallet and chopped up in front of her eyes. 'Come near my daughter again, dyke,' said a trembling William Wicks, 'and I'll fucking rip your head off, do you understand me?' And thus, with righteous indignation, did the doughty publican defend his daughter's purity.

Two days later, in a studio in Harlow, with a small camera crew from Kandid Productions in attendance, Debbie was listlessly moving a selection of fresh vegetables in and out of her vagina. 'Can't you turn the heating up a bit, love?' moaned Theresa, whose every effort to cover her daughter's goose-flesh with layers of pancake had failed. 'Look at her, she's freezing!' The photographer's assistant turned on another bar fire; Nicko McVitie, already red-faced and sweating in the studio's sauna-like heat, pulled off his shirt.

'That's it, Debbie my dear,' said Dudley Jenkins, who was art directing the shoot, allowing a professional glamour photographer to zoom in for the money shot, 'try to stop trembling, just hold it still for me. Close your eyes, lick your lips... Theresa, can we put a bit more gloss on her lips? They still look dry and chapped to me...

No, dear, the other ones. That's it. Lovely. Now then Debbie, sit up and look surprised at what you've done, come on, do it for me... Debbie... Debbie? DEBBIE! Oh for Christ's sake Theresa, wake her up again. She's dribbling on her bustier.'

Debbie was not the only star of *Elephant and Castle* to plumb the lower depths in the wake of the first series. Daryn 'The Doc' Handy paid a high price for his flirtation with serious crime and found himself facing up to five years' imprisonment subsequent to his arrest at the registry office. As he was dragged away from the dock, he yelled 'I'll get you, Eddie Kander', and appeared in the papers the next day making a clenched fist salute as he was bundled into the back of a large black van. The pill was sweetened when he discovered, on arrival at a prison on the Kent marshes, that he had real respect from his fellow convicts. 'You showed the cunts,' said his cell-mate, who shared the general admiration. 'They stitched you up.'

Encouraged by such hero worship, Daryn played the big man more successfully than ever in the real world, massaging his tales of inner-city dealing to such inflated heights that he found himself elevated to the ranks of prison royalty. Anything he wanted, within reason, was his for the asking. Cigarettes, decent food, drugs, extra visits – anything except a woman. 'It don't bother me,' said Daryn, who claimed to have 'a kennel full of bitches' on the outside. 'Gives me a rest, know what I mean?' Occasionally, prompted by his cellmate's desire to please, he allowed himself to be sucked off, and found it more pleasurable – because less effort – than any sex he'd ever had in his life. Daryn's stock rose. Playa, star, stud – even the governor couldn't touch him.

Happy as he was in prison, Daryn nursed a grievance. He had, after all, been taken for a ride. True, the destination suited him well, but it was not a journey of his own choosing. Someone, he felt, had got the better of him. He sent threatening letters to Eddie Kander, implying that he would 'get' him, demanding that Kander should pay for an expensive appeal or, at least, send a camera crew in to record Daryn's new pre-eminence within the prison system. Revenge and stardom hovered before him, just out of reach. The adulation of his peers was not enough; the world, Daryn felt, owed him more. Increasingly, as the weeks inside stretched to months, he began to talk about 'the hit'.

Back in Beckford House, Peggy Renders faced certain death with grace. Since the day when she was turned away from her weekly chemotherapy appointment by an embarrassed receptionist, she realised that her stay of execution had been revoked. To Eddie's relief, she didn't call the office to complain. She simply reviewed her humble insurance policies, arranged with her niece to take care of Sid, and waited for the end. One morning she found herself unable to get out of bed; she phoned the ambulance, was admitted to hospital and died in a sedated sleep a week later.

'Fuck,' said Eddie Kander, slamming the phone down after the ward sister had rung him with the bad news. 'I think we slipped up on this one, Caroline. We should have kept tags on her, found out when she was getting sick, arranged for someone to go to the hospital. As it is the old cow died *off camera*.'

'What a waste,' said Caroline, who instructed Nicko McVitie to cover the funeral.

Without Shelley to guide her, Debbie slipped into a passivity that frightened even her parents. 'She looks... subnormal,' said the editor of *Reluctant Teens*. 'Great tits, but is she all there up top? Not that our readers care. They like 'em stupid.'

'What's the matter, love?' said Theresa, spoon-feeding Debbie as if she were a baby. 'You're off your food. Tell me, darling. Come on. You can tell your mum.' Debbie spat out the yoghurt and rolled on to her side, hugging her knees.

'We've got to do something,' Theresa said to William. 'She's losing weight. If we don't get her sorted out, something terrible's going to happen. Like... her tits might shrink.'

William stared at his wife, awestruck.

'You're right, darling,' he said, with true paternal concern. 'This has gone far enough.'

The very best treatment, William informed the doctor at the private clinic, was not too good for his little girl, money was no object, they just wanted her on her feet and back at work. It took the consultant less than the allotted hour to diagnose severe depression, malnutrition and an immune system ravaged by heroin withdrawal. He prescribed methadone, and within a week Debbie was back to her usual bouncy self, charming her way through the daily round of launches and lunches. Theresa and William persuaded Dudley to postpone her first video shoot, and concentrated instead on a harmless schedule of personal appearances. A young gay entrepreneur believed she had potential in the clubs, and took her into the studio to record a speeded-up version of 'Big Girls Don't Cry'. Debbie focused her energies on her debut appearance at G.A.Y. and happily agreed to a Kandid crew following her through rehearsals and vocal training.

During her absence at the studios in Acton, Nicko and Eddie slipped into Debbie's bedroom at the Double Dee and fitted a small closed-circuit tv camera in the pelmet. 'Don't worry,' Eddie told Theresa, who fussed around the foot of the ladder, 'it won't leave a mark on the curtain. You'll never know it was there.' 'If you say so,' said Theresa, her voice trembling with emotion. 'I've only just had the place decorated, and I don't want the fabric spoiled.'

While one crew recorded Debbie's enthusiastic efforts at simple dance routines ('No darling it's kick step step kick step ball change! Try again!'), another team watched the presses roll at a small printers' out near Camberley. William Wicks and Dudley Jenkins pored over the chromolins. 'She looks lovely,' said William. 'I'm so proud.'

'Can we adjust the cyan?' said Dudley. 'The courgette doesn't look green enough.'

Two new publications were delivered to the Elephant and Castle fags-and-mags kiosk on the following Thursday. One was *The Stage*, of which the ex-footballer ordered a single weekly copy for Fat Alice. A small front-page headline mourned 'Death of Variety Legend' and continued 'Green room gossip suggests that Peggy Renders's untimely demise – she was only 75 years young – could have been hastened by the fact that she'd been dropped from the cast of Channel 6 docusoap *Elephant and Castle*. No memorial service has yet been announced.' (The story ended with a cross reference in bold type: 'So you want to be a reality tv star? See page three for Ten Tips to success'.) The other new publication that morning was *Reluctant Teens* volume 8, with a close-cropped portrait of Debbie on the cover and a single coverline in garish yellow type: DEBBIE GOES VEGGIE. Both periodicals – 25 of one, one of the other – sold out within an hour of delivery.

Debbie knew nothing of her public intimacy with fresh produce until her dancers arrived at rehearsal later that morning. She'd been in the studio since 8.30am, practising her routines over and over again until she could execute them with a certain elephantine efficiency; Debbie was not naturally light on her feet. Now all she had to do was lip-synch the words at the same time, and she was home and dry...

'Hi Debs,' snapped Troy, a skinny queen who had spent so long in the gym that he looked like a string of sausages wrapped round a lamp post. 'What's fresh today?'

'I beg your pardon?'

'You know, down the greengrocers. Haven't you seen?'

'What are you talking about, Troy?'

'Come on, darling. It doesn't bother me. I think it's fabulous. You know, I've stuck a few veg where the sun don't shine, although I assure you I didn't stop at a courgette, I mean I was with this really hot guy who wanted to put a whole pound of potatoes up me one by one, and I ain't talking new potatoes, no, I'm talking full-size baking spuds, King Edwards they were, and so of course, I took them all and then...'

Something was stirring vaguely in a dark corner of Debbie's mind.

'Cour... courgettes?'

'Yes my darling. You know, little baby marrows. Suitable for beginners...'

'Troy...'

'Yes darling?'

'Have I... done something?'

'Ask Zak,' he said, bending himself in two for the first big stretch of the day. 'He bought a copy.'

The other dancer, a handsome young man with short dreads, had just slouched into the room.

'All right, Debs.' Debbie didn't entirely like the grin on his face.

'Hi Zak.'

'She ain't seen it.'

'You're kidding me.'

'Go on. Show her.'

'Debs, ain't you checked it? Fucking hell, babe, I had no idea you was so dirty.'

Debbie was trying to speak, trying to ask what they were talking about, but the words stuck, as if she had a mouth full of chewing gum.

Zak pulled an A5-sized magazine out of his pocket and slapped it down on the table, picked up a bottle of Evian and strolled off to roll a joint. Debbie stared up at herself from the glossy cover.

A memory was hurtling through her subconscious like a steam train... She felt sick. Her knees were shaking.

'What have I... done...'

'Well, there's a fabulous one here, look, you're sucking on it like it was a real dick, that's very convincing, look at the way your eyes are closed, that one really got Zak going, I mean I think he's interested in me too actually, because when I said to him that I could do it better than that he kind of laughed in that way that means "Hey, you can show me any time, big boy", well, I mean in this profession they may start straight dear but they don't stay that way for long, there's precious few of them who won't get into it with another guy if the mood's right, and once they've tried it then... God, darling, what's the matter?'

Debbie had fallen into a faint on the floor. Her head hit the table and a small trickle of blood was collecting in her hair.

Within 20 seconds of her collapse, Troy was on the phone to Eddie Kander.

'Hi, Mr Kander? Troy Helpmann here... That's right. Well, you said to call you if anything was to happen... Yeah, she's just seen it and she's collapsed ... What? I don't fucking know, I'm a dancer, not a doctor ... No I haven't rung 999, I called you first, like you said ... Okay, how long will you be? ... No, she's breathing all right, I think she's just fainted, and cut her head. Nothing serious. Okay, well get here as quick as you can. See ya.'

Zak was bending over Debbie's prone form, blowing cannabis smoke into her face.

'God, she's freaked out.'

'Yeah, looks like it. So: what did you think of those pictures, Zak? Do they turn you on?'

'Course they do, it's porn innit?'

'So would you be equally turned on by seeing pictures of guys doing that?'

'Fuck off Troy, I told ya, I ain't gay.'

'But if you looked at those pictures, and got turned on, I mean, it wouldn't really matter who was touching you, would it, not if it felt good.'

When Eddie arrived half an hour later, the two dancers were

nowhere to be seen. Little did they know that a camera installed in the bathroom, intended to capture candid footage of Debbie changing, was now recording Zak's first (he said) tentative steps on the road to Sodom.

Eddie carried Debbie to the car; the fresh air woke her from her swoon, but she seemed to have slipped back into the darkness of previous weeks.

'It's all right, Debbie,' he said. 'I'm taking you home. You've had a funny turn. Your mum will look after you.'

'Shelley...' moaned Debbie, 'Shelley...'

Debbie was tucked up in bed, her window and door securely locked. Not that she intended to escape; in the cloudy part of her brain that was still functioning, she intended only ever to leave the room in a pine box...

Downstairs, the anxious parents were in emergency session with Dudley Jenkins.

'What's happened to her, Dudley? You said everything would be fine. If anything goes wrong...'

'It won't go wrong, William, trust me. She'll pull through. She's a fit young girl. She's just... tired.'

'We've already borrowed a huge amount of money to have this place done up on the strength of that video deal.'

'Don't worry. It's all in the bag.'

'But what if she refuses to do it? What if she starts causing trouble? She took one look at them pictures and she passed out. You said she was all right. What happens if she sues us?'

'Sues you? Don't be ridiculous. Whoever heard of a nice girl like that suing her own parents?'

'That Sammy Fox did it,' said Theresa.

'Look,' said Dudley, covering his justifiable nervousness with an authoritative bluster, 'Debbie's signed model release forms. She can't go back on it now. If all you're worried about is the money, then you're fine. Personally, I'm more concerned with the little lady upstairs...'

William and Theresa looked ashamed, and slunk off to open the pub. Dudley, taking advantage of their temporary absence, slipped away.

Debbie didn't touch her food all day; Theresa removed each tray from her room exactly as it went in. She looked down at her sleeping child, and gently pulled back the covers. Could it be? Were her breasts not just a tiny bit smaller than normal? Theresa, seeing her dream castles collapsing, buried her face in her hands.

'Look at that, Nicko,' said Eddie, watching the scene unfold in real time on the monitors back at unit base. 'Real remorse. This is fantastic stuff. See her touching her own daughter's breasts. Tenderness, pathos. Channel 6 will crap themselves with joy.'

Twelve hours later, while Nicko dozed over the remains of a nasty kebab, another drama was unfolding on the unobserved monitor. Debbie, wide awake, pale and sweating, was pacing around her tiny room, hugging herself, muttering, occasionally pulling her hair. If Nicko had been paying attention he would have been delighted by the way that the spycam installed so unobtrusively in the pelmet captured her every move; its tiny lens left no corner of the room to hide in. She paced, she muttered, she sat on the bed, jumped up again, paced, cried.

Half an hour later she was crouching at the foot of the bed staring in front of her. Nicko, waking up for long enough to sink a bottle of coke, wondered dimly what she was doing and went back into a deep sleep.

Debbie was seized by a sudden demon of activity. She pulled the covers off her bed; she lifted the mattress and threw it against the window, causing the picture on the monitor to judder and flicker. She seemed to be looking for something; something that had been removed.

She screamed for her mother, who kept Debbie's works locked up in the bathroom cabinet, to administer only when the doctor said.

She ransacked her bedside table for pain killers, hoping that an overdose might kill her, but all she could find were contraceptive pills. She swallowed the lot anyway.

Eventually, finding no other means of self-harm, she twisted her bedsheet into an impromptu noose and attempted the hang herself from the hook on the back of the wardrobe door.

Just as the deadly linen was tightening around Debbie's snowy-white throat, there was a tinkle of broken glass from the public bar of the Double Dee, and a gloved hand reached through the pane to manipulate the lock. A stealthy figure, its outline shrouded by the darkness, crept silently across the beer-stained carpet, clambered over the bar and took the stairs quietly, two at a time.

Upstairs on the landing it stopped, listened, waited...

'Debbie... Debbie... it's me...'

Nothing.

Again, a little louder, risking detection. 'Debbie! Where are you! It's me!'

From the other side of the door, where she was now struggling and swinging at the end of the remorseless noose, Debbie heard her friend's voice and wanted to live. But she could not speak.

'Debbie, please let me in... I'm sorry for everything.'

With one last desperate act of will, the dying girl jerked her leg and kicked against the door. The thump took Shelley by surprise.

'What's going on in there?' she shouted, no longer caring if she woke the household. 'Debbie, stand back... I'm coming in to get you!'

With one kick of her Doctor Marten shoe, Shelley sent the door smashing into the suspended form of her friend, knocking out a front tooth and almost breaking her nose.

Lucky for the Wicks family that Shelley, contrary to police guidelines, always carried a knife. She had Debbie cut down and gasping for breath in a trice, as the enraged parents thundered up the landing behind her.

'Get away from her, lesbian!' boomed William, who assumed

that the crouching form was some kind of succubus. Theresa, in pink and grey 'slumberwear', looked as if she was about to pounce.

'Don't touch me, fuckers,' spat Shelley. 'She's coming with me.'

Ten minutes later, the two girls sped towards St Thomas's Hospital in an ambulance, accompanied by a bleary-eyed Nicko and his camera.

'They did this to you,' Shelley said, holding Debbie's hand. 'I swear to God that I will get my revenge on those tv bastards. I will. I swear to God that I will kill somebody for this.'

Three

One week before the second series of *Elephant and Castle* was due to go on air the press war over the series entered a new and more violent phase. The *Citizen,* the *Daily Beacon's* main rival, carried a double-page profile of Serena accompanied by photographs which left no room to doubt that she was now, and always had been, a woman. Nobody, from boardroom to building site, could believe that that long, slender neck, those delicate wrists, and most of all those adorable little breasts, were the work of anyone other than Mother Nature in her most beneficent mood. Serena posed naked against a window, hair up to reveal her soft nape, the sunlight catching the top of her heartbreaking little muff... No, said the suits and ties on the trains. No, said teachers in common rooms, porters in hospitals, customers waiting in barber's shops. No, said the builders, van drivers, plasterers, carpenters and electricians who pored over every curve and detail... that was never, never a man. She couldn't have been. With the unanswerable logic of the sexually aroused, they translated Serena's attractiveness as proof of her gender. Why, anyone who said that she was a bloke was calling them, the men of Britain, a bunch of poofs. And that was neither true nor right.

The *Beacon* was on the ropes. Philip Bray's story was true, of course, but it lacked credibility. To little avail he trotted out his sources in a follow-up feature the next day. My heartbreak over a son who became a daughter, by Serena's mum. We let scumbag Serena use our flat for gay sex, by former friends Vernon Delgado and Roy Turner, with a snap from the albums of an obviously male young thing in semi-drag, adam's apple visible beneath a chiffon scarf. The display quote, thought Philip, would clinch it. 'For a member of the oldest profession, she was a complete f***ing amateur' – Maureen at his poisonous best.

The *Citizen* declined to respond for two days, leaving its front page clear to re-establish its caring credentials with a story about cot death. Then on the day before transmission they delivered the whammy. Serena photographed yesterday with twin brother Sean. 'It's me who's been causing all the trouble,' admits long-lost looka-like. 'Serena tried to cover up for me and keep me out of prison. I can't let her suffer because of what I've done.'

Thanks to some clever work in the make-up department, dancer Troy Helpmann had been made to look like a more or less male version of Serena. 'Now perhaps I can get on with my life,' said lovely Serena, who was appealing against a high court judgement preventing her from marrying the man of her choice. 'I hope in future that people will be less quick to judge those in the public eye.'

The *Beacon* retired hurt, and devoted next day's issue to an exclusive profile of Barry Llannelly, star of *Police Vet*, a new series of which started at nine o'clock that night – at exactly the same time as *Elephant and Castle*. Llannelly was old news, his popularity seriously dented over the summer by an incident in a sauna outside Chester – but at least a boost for *Police Vet* could damage the opposition. 'I'm so, so sorry for what I've done,' lied Llannelly to the *Beacon* journalist, whom he later entertained in his Wrexham bachelor pad, familiar turf to a high percentage of the sexually active men of the north west.

On the morning before tx, Eddie Kander had a lot to celebrate. Not only was *Elephant and Castle* ahead in the opinion polls (a phone vote in the *Sun* gave 'sexy Serena' a 40% lead over 'bad-boy Barry'), not only were the broadsheets giving serious coverage to the 'Kandid phenomenon' – he'd also regained his own company from the Wragge interregnum, and was once again in control of his destiny. Heroin addiction was a thing of the past (editor Pete Silverstone, however, was now a hopeless, unemployable junkie). The Kander coffers were full, thanks to a golden handcuffs deal with Channel 6. And to top it all, the newly pliant Serena Ward agreed to have dinner with him.

Eddie booked a *chambre privée* at the Soho House, and installed a couple of small portable televisions so that he and his companion could watch while they ate. The waiters fawned over Serena, who looked fragile and more beautiful than ever in a black silk Yamamoto trouser suit. She picked delicately at her rocket salad as the repulsive theme tune assaulted the airwaves once again...

The show opened with a montage of images from the last series. Serena and Jamie walking hand-in-hand through the shopping centre... Fat Alice waddling into the path of an oncoming vehicle... Maureen and Muriel preening themselves for a night on the town. And then the fateful wedding, the arrest of Daryn Handy, a flashing blue light dominating the screen...

'Nice,' said Eddie through a mouthful of fusilli, which protruded from his lips like snaggle teeth. 'Watch this, now.'

The police car crossed the screen from left to right; the flashing blue light of an ambulance arrived from right to left.

'It's another dramatic night in south London's Elephant and Castle,' announced the narrator. 'Schoolgirl supermodel Debbie Doubledee has found the pressure of fame too much to take...'

Cut to the interior of Debbie's bedroom, where the confused child is tying her bedsheet to a hook on the back of the wardrobe door. Cut to William and Theresa hurrying down the corridor and kicking the door open, in a scene shot some days after the actual event. Shot of the door opening from inside, smashing the hanging

Debbie in the face. Cut to Theresa and William's faces, twin masks of horror. Cut to Debbie being loaded into the ambulance, the concerned parents holding each other on the pavement, waving farewell. No sign of Shelley.

'Brilliant!' shouted Eddie, launching a fragment of half-chewed pasta across the table and into Serena's salad. 'That's what I call editing!'

'That's what I call fake.'

'You know that. I know that. Joe Public won't notice a thing.'

'But it was raining on the night Debbie tried to kill herself. It was dry when you shot Theresa and William in the street. It's all wrong.'

'Don't worry about details like that,' blustered Eddie. 'That's just technical stuff. People believe what they want to believe, Serena. You of all people should know that.'

He reached under the table and gave her knee a squeeze. Serena suffered his hand to rest there awhile before recrossing her legs and bending his fingers painfully in the process.

'But Eddie, you said in the publicity material that *Elephant and Castle* is, I quote, "the most searingly honest portrayal of how real people live their lives in the modern urban jungle", did you not?'

'Yeah, good that, wasn't it,' said Eddie into his glass.

'And it's all a pack of lies.'

'No more so than anything else.'

'I've gone on the record claiming to have been born a woman. Jamie's denied ever having been on the game. You said that Debbie's parents saved her life, that little Ben, Daryn's son, has gone into care...'

'Oh yeah. What has happened to him, incidentally?'

'Well since you ask he has his breakfast and tea at my house and he goes to school, in theory, but I imagine he's following in daddy's footsteps and keeping the business ticking over until he gets out. Nice of you to care.'

'I do care, I do,' said Eddie. 'We'll make sure he's looked after...

Yeah, kid doing the drug run, it's got legs... Hold it now, this is a good bit, watch this...'

'It's up bright and early for Maureen and Muriel,' said the voice-over, 'who have got their work cut out transforming a run-down pub into what they hope will be a major addition to the south London cabaret circuit.'

'My God,' said Serena, who had more reason than ever to hate her 'former friends', 'I thought you'd dropped them.'

'Dropped them? No way, babe. Okay, they're a couple of slimy old bastards but they are, you have to admit it, very watchable.'

Muriel perched on top of a ladder, his legs intertwined, while Maureen, in a perky bandana and boiler suit, laid about him with a roller full of emulsion.

'What on earth are they up to?'

'Listen and learn, Serena.'

'We'll be attracting a very select clientele, I mean obviously we're not appealing to the hoi polloi,' said Muriel. 'We're professionals, you see. We wouldn't want to be accused of cashing in our success on the telly. No, this is strictly a members only club, with an *intime* atmosphere, *une vraie boîte de nuit*, if you know what I mean. Very Weimar. Very Christopher Isherwood.'

'Nisht the polari and pass me a fucking cloth, dear,' said Maureen.

'You mean to say,' asked Serena, 'that you've actually put money into their business, Eddie?'

'A little. Don't know where they got the rest from. Course it's going to be a disaster, but that'll make good tv. The public loves to hate them. They'll have a taste of success, get the freak vote, then they'll blow it and end up back in the dock. It's all good, baby.'

'Oh Eddie,' said Serena, gazing across the table in admiration, 'you really are the pits.'

'Yeah,' said Eddie, leaning back in his chair so that his stomach rested on the table, 'and you fucking love it.'

'Someone should stop you.'

'Who can touch me? I'm top of the world.'

'Pride before a fall, Eddie. I'd watch my back if I were you.'

'Is that a threat, my unorthodox darling?'

'A threat? From a weak and feeble woman like me? No, Eddie, I shan't touch you. I need you. I lost my job, you'll recall. But someone will do something.'

'And I don't suppose you'd shed many tears, would you?'

'Not a sniffle, my dear.'

'We understand each other, you and I,' said Eddie, pressing his leg against Serena's thigh.

'Touch me again,' said Serena, dabbing her mouth with a napkin, 'and I will rip your bollocks off and stuff them up your nose.'

'I don't doubt it,' said Eddie. 'Once a vicious little queer, always a vicious little queer. Now shut up and let me watch some classic fucking television.'

Eddie's high opinion of his own work was borne out by the critics, who hailed series two of *Elephant and Castle* as 'zeitgeist television' and wasted several column miles fretting over what it said about the state of the nation. 'The show that dares to blow the whistle on the so-called permissive society' ranted the *Express*, identifying the fate of Jamie Lord as 'a dire warning to those who seek to put homosexuality on the curriculum in primary schools'. Fat Alice was acclaimed in the highbrow women's pages as 'a positive role model for over-eaters everywhere', and her on-screen announcement that she was available to childless couples as a surrogate mother was greeted with fervid approval. 'My womb's untenanted,' she told the camera, 'and my life's too fulfilled and busy to look after a child. But I'd like to do something for people less fortunate than myself.' (Privately Alice saw this as a good way of getting sex, and of securing all the medical attention that a complicated, painful pregnancy and labour would give her.)

Dissenting voices there were few. *The Times* wondered, vaguely, whether Debbie Doubledee's best interests were being served by her parents, but seeing as its sister paper the *Sun* was running topless shots the day after ('these are the only shots we were ALLOWED to print: the others are just TOO DARN HOT!') didn't dwell on the matter. Shelley wrote to the papers revealing the truth about Debbie's suicide attempt and her parents' refusal to let her see a psychiatrist, but nobody was interested. Editors everywhere looked forward to Debbie's 'acting debut', which was hinted at towards the end of the episode.

Eddie called a press conference to announce Serena's decision to go ahead with her marriage plans despite 'adverse publicity and a cheap smear campaign' orchestrated by 'rival broadcasters'. 'Wear something skimpy,' he instructed his protégée, counting on the fact that male journalists would be more sympathetic if they could see some tit.

Five minutes before they were due to take their seats in the Channel 6 conference room, Serena had still not turned up.

'No problem,' Eddie assured the publicist, glancing nervously at his watch and dialling Serena's number for the tenth time in as many minutes. 'She's a professional. She'll be here.'

Five minutes later, and the hacks were getting restless.

'Don't worry,' said Eddie, hanging back in the toilets with the publicist, 'I know my talent. She's just doing this for effect. She's a natural star. You have to make allowances.'

Ten minutes later, and he was making excuses about the traffic.

A quarter of an hour after start time, the publicist pushed Eddie into a room full of now-hostile journalists.

'Hi guys, thanks for coming, good to see so many familiar faces here... Hi Andy... Frank... Geoff...'

'Where's Serena?'

'She's on her way, guys. You can't rush a legend...'

'Eddie, is it true that you're going ahead with the marriage?'

'Yes, Frank, Serena and Jamie will be tying the knot at the end of the series.'

'But it's true, isn't it, that Serena is still legally speaking a man?'

'Christ, they let you in did they?'

Philip Bray sat at the back of the room, with empty chairs all around him. 'And unless there's a change in British law, there can be no marriage.'

'Listen, I've said this a million times, and the public know that we're not pulling a fast one here, I don't know where these ridiculous rumours come from, but if you knew Serena as well as I do you'd be in absolutely no doubt about the fact that she's all woman.'

'And that, in fact, any attempt to marry another biological male is a criminal offence.'

There was an approving murmur from the throng, who admired Philip's cool persistence and thought they might try it on as well.

'Do we have to waste time with these side issues, gentlemen? Anyway, Serena will be here herself in a moment so if any of you has the guts you can ask the lady herself.'

Walk through the door, he prayed, walk through the door.

'Mr Kander. We're all waiting for some answers. Our readers need to know the truth.'

'The truth, gentlemen...' Eddie was sweating. He'd kill the bitch. Without her disarming physical presence, his story looked threadbare. 'You'll just have to stay tuned for that one. Keep writing about us! It's all good publicity, whatever you try to do! Thanks for your interest.' He glanced towards the door one final time, hoping for a miracle. 'No, that's it. Thanks for coming.'

Eddie hurried out of the door, leaving the press to draw their own conclusions.

She disappeared as completely as if she had never been. Little Ben rang the doorbell in vain, and went without breakfast. Jamie spent

sleepless nights watching her window from his darkened flat, rue-
fully rubbing his crotch which, for the first time in months, was
denied regular attention. His relationship with Caroline was over,
and in Serena's sudden absence he found that he didn't want to give
it to anyone else, paying or otherwise. From another window in
Beckford House, Maureen and Muriel scanned the horizon in vain.
Eddie conducted a door-to-door search, with Nicko at his elbow
filming every conversation, but nobody had seen Serena. Ricky
Rampling had nothing to add. Serena's mum hinted that she knew
something, even accepted money, but couldn't help. As the days
turned into weeks, and series two rumbled along without its star,
Eddie began to panic.

He sat in his office, unshaven and drinking heavily, jumping
every time the phone rang. He fielded the growing hostility of the
press, who had been ready to take his unorthodox new star to their
bosom but now, cheated of their game, turned on *Elephant and
Castle* with a vengeance.

'You're playing this all wrong,' said Caroline, who found Eddie
with his head down the toilet bowl retching dryly. 'You should be
making a virtue out of necessity.'

'What do you mean, you stupid cow? If I'd taken your advice we
wouldn't have a show at all, Serena or no Serena.'

'Look, yah, I made mistakes, I'm big enough to admit that, and
I've learned from them. But if you won't listen...'

'No, don't go. I'm listening.'

'Good. Wipe your chin.' Caroline handed Eddie some wadded-
up toilet roll. 'Better. Okay. You've lost Serena. I don't know what
you did to frighten her away, but I can imagine...'

'I didn't fuck her.'

'Well that's something to be grateful for. But whatever the reasons, she's gone and it's your fault. The press is turning against you.
The viewers are switching off. You've lost it, Eddie, and what are
you doing about it?'

'What can I do? She's fucked off. Without her there's no show.'

'Au contraire. You've got the biggest story you've ever had. But you're sitting on it.'

'I don't understand.'

'You've got a missing star. She's somewhere, right? And everyone knows what she looks like.'

'Yeah...'

'And you're doing nothing about it. You should be getting the people involved. Getting them to search for her. Following up leads, sending out camera crews, putting it all in the show.'

'You mean like... actually hunting her on air?'

'Yah.'

'Caroline,' said Eddie, fumbling around in his pants, 'you've earned this. Come to Daddy.'

'Eddie...'

'Yeah, baby?'

'You still have puke on your teeth. Shall we say – my office, ten minutes? And you can leave *that*' – she dug his crotch with her toe – 'where it is.'

The next episode of *Elephant and Castle* began with a shot of Little Ben sitting on Serena's doorstep.

'My Daddy's been taken away,' he lisped, 'and now the lady that looked after me has gone and left me all alone. I'm hungry and I'm frightened.'

After the shot, Ben ran down to McDonald's with the £20 note Eddie had given him, agreeing to be back on the doorstep at the same time the next morning.

'Have you seen Serena Ward?' asked the narrator over a long shot of 1 Spencer Street. 'It's two weeks now since she disappeared from her flat, and neighbours are worried.'

'She's such a dear friend,' blubbed Maureen, the tears weaving through clumps of fat before dispersing in a moist delta around his chins. 'I just hope to God she's got someone to look after her. Serena, love, please come home. Everyone misses you.'

'Someone somewhere knows where she is,' continued the narrator. 'But so far, even her family are mystified.' Troy Helpmann, Serena's 'brother', was seen walking away from the camera, his hand shielding his face. 'Have you seen her? We want to know.'

A telephone number flashed up at the foot of the screen.

'If you have any information, however trivial, let our operations room know without delay. We'll be updating you in a special programme after the 11 o'clock news...'

The hunt was on.

Serena watched the broadcast in the front room of the small cottage she'd rented in Hastings. The curtains were drawn; in the last few days she'd not shown herself in public, she hadn't drunk in a bar or eaten in a café. She'd been for long walks along the coastal path, avoiding strangers, sticking to the less frequented tracks through quiet woods, dodging on the windward side of the thick, aromatic gorse bushes that lined the cliffs. She wore a headscarf and sunglasses, a thick sweater, jeans and walking boots. She was unrecognisable.

When the show was over, she drank the last few gills from a bottle of whisky and sat tight. If it was going to happen, she thought, it would happen tonight. If the knock came, she could nip out the back, lie low in the woods for a couple of hours before hoofing it to the station for the first train back to London, and anonymity...

Ten minutes passed, half an hour, an hour. Nothing.

She was safe for another night.

Four

After a working lifetime spent creating drama out of reality, Eddie Kander himself became the biggest drama of them all. It was, everyone agreed, a shame that he didn't live long enough to see it. But somebody killed him first.

There were mutterings in dark corners of West End bars that Eddie's death was the last in a long line of insane publicity stunts designed to boost the flagging popularity of his diabolical fly-on-the-wall shows. No surely, said some, even Eddie Kander wouldn't go that far... Others sucked in their cheeks, raised an eyebrow and looked knowing. Even if Eddie hadn't contrived his own death, there were plenty in the company who would... plenty of valued colleagues who knew that Eddie's death would render *Elephant and Castle* untouchable, beyond criticism, a fixture in the primetime schedules. 'We're carrying on as normal,' sobbed Caroline Wragge, acting chief executive of Kandid Productions, at a press conference the day Eddie's body was found in a black bin liner underneath the Westway. 'It's what he would have wanted. Eddie Kander was the finest professional it's ever been my privilege to work with, and like me he believed that the show must go on.'

Caroline Wragge was prime suspect in the case, even though she had a cast-iron alibi for the time of Eddie's death. She had been on location in Kent for three days, filming inside the prison where

Daryn Handy was serving his sentence for drug-dealing. She flew back to London the moment Eddie's disappearance began to concern the police, and had been under constant surveillance from that point onwards.

And if not her, whom? So many people had both motive and opportunity. Serena Ward, on the day she was dragged kicking and screaming back to her abandoned flat in Spencer Street, announced to the viewing public that she hated the fame *Elephant and Castle* had given her and 'would do almost anything to turn the clock back'. Anything? Including murder?

Jamie Lord, an ex-soldier, was automatically suspect... as Serena's accomplice, he'd have the skills and training to take human life without risk of detection. And hadn't Maureen and Muriel threatened violence just a few months before? It would be like them to hold a grudge, to enjoy their revenge served cold.

And then, of course, there was Debbie Doubledee, a teenage girl with severe mental problems, a drug habit and an unwanted career in hardcore pornography thanks almost entirely to Eddie Kander. Perhaps she was incapable of homicide herself, but she had friends... that Shelley Smithers, for instance, who had grown up on south London's notorious Ringwood Estate, had been heard on many occasions to threaten those who crossed her. 'I swear to God that I will kill somebody for this' – were not those her very words?

Never had the police known a man with so many enemies. Everyone whose life he had touched had good cause to kill Eddie Kander. Perhaps, in a bizarre homage to *Murder on the Orient Express*, they had all had a hand in the crime... The further the investigation went, the more skeletons came rattling out of closets, shaking their fleshless fists for revenge. Doreen 'Dirty Bitches!' Dawson, the mountainous star of *Other People's Pants*, still nursed a grudge from Eddie's refusal to bankroll her recording career. Dave 'Missed It!' Merryweather had petitioned unsuccessfully for a second series of *Sprayers*. Pete Silverstone, picked up wandering the streets of

Finsbury Park, had Eddie's bloodstained business card in his pocket. Had he really used it to shovel amphetamines into a gash on his arm after his nasal membranes had dropped out? Or was there a more sinister explanation?

And the police didn't restrict their investigations to the human realm. Mrs Renders's niece received a call from a WPC who wanted to know if she could account for Sid the dog's whereabouts on the date in question. Was it not possible that Sid, crazed with grief for his lost mistress, had found his way back to his old home, cornered Eddie and somehow... gummed him to death?

'We are ruling nothing out at the moment, however far-fetched,' said the officer in charge of the enquiry to the massed news-gatherers (among them a Kandid crew who were following the investigation as part of *Elephant and Castle*). There was only one name they could definitely cross off the list: Daryn Handy had been incarcerated long before, during and after the crime. Little Ben was in the frame, but his father, for once, was beyond suspicion.

'What we've got here,' said Caroline Wragge at a meeting with the head of Channel 6, 'is something that defies categorisation. It's a cross-genre phenomenon. It's more than a documentary, it's more than a drama, it's more than reality tv... this is life imitating art. This is tv transcending reality. It's a whodunnit, a *Crimewatch*, a *Poirot*, but it's better than all those things, and that's why I believe, no, I demand, that you should extend our run.'

Caroline was a changed woman. Not only was her vocabulary improved – she had emerged from the chrysalis of lowly researcherdom to the glorious final instar of fully-fledged tv producer. She had lost weight. Her bone structure had gained a razor-sharp definition. Her mouth and teeth were more prominent, her hair glossier and more abundant. She still looked like a horse, but a glossy thoroughbred rather than a brewer's nag. Through the deft choice of a capsule wardrobe, she could dominate situations that had hitherto left her mumbling and confused. In Eddie's death, Caroline was reborn. The fact that people suspected her of having a hand in the crime excited her. Of course, she knew that her alibi was good – but in the aftermath of the tragedy she was delighted that it had happened.

The new controller of Channel 6 (once the big cheese in Infotainment) slumped further into his chair. 'Thing is, Caroline, we're absolutely committed to running *Kill Me Slowly* in that slot.'

'What? A poxy drama series that you've had sitting on the shelf for two years? You must be out of your mind!'

'We committed a lot of resources to the show...'

'And it's crap! Everybody knows!'

'There are budgetary considerations...'

'In other words, you want me to drop my prices. No way.'

'Your latest demands are insane, Caroline.'

'Fine. We'll take *Elephant and Castle* to a proper television channel, and 6 will go down the pan at last. We're the only show you've got that anyone's watching.'

'Look, I can't make a decision just like that. I have to run this by the board of directors...'

'You've got 48 hours. If you don't sign the contract by lunchtime on Friday, I'm taking the show to the BBC. I warn you.'

It goes without saying that Caroline had spoken to nobody at the BBC, nor had the Corporation the slightest desire to buy *Elephant and Castle* – but the very mention of its name worked like a charm on the terrified controller of Channel 6. Caroline left Channel House with a spring in her step. The ratings were still climbing, putting on nearly a million a week. The police had no new leads in the Kander murder. She was in clover. And if push came to shove, there was always her trump card, the ace that she would play when she was in extremis... For Caroline, innocent as she was herself of Eddie Kander's death, knew perfectly well where the blame lay.

Now all that remained was to tailor the series to her vision, to erase any elements that might undermine her authority... and for Caroline, that meant just one thing. She must sack Serena.

Serena? The most popular character in the show? A tv creation to rate alongside the immortals: Jeremy out of *Airport*, Maureen out of *Driving School*, Darius out of *Pop Idol*? Yes... time to get rid of her. They did it in soap all the time: take the most popular, beautiful and charismatic character and send her flying over the bonnet of a speeding car to a sticky end against a kerbstone... Serena, she would tell the press, was leaving to pursue a stage career... She would hint that tv stardom had gone to her head, that she despised the great British public who had made her, that she had ideas above her station. Serena and Jamie would split up, cheating the viewers of their longed-for wedding, and they would turn against her. Serena would soon be nothing but a memory.

'Why's she never at home?' Caroline asked Jamie, whom she'd summoned to the office for a 'consultation'. 'Doesn't she have a mobile?'

'She's unemployed at the moment, you'll remember.'

'Well she should get a job!'

'She's tried. Nobody will take her seriously. You've really fucked her up good and proper.'

'Me? I think not. It was Eddie. Eddie did all the bad stuff. He forced her to make a fool of herself in public. I always advised against it, but Serena wouldn't listen to me. She's got a very high opinion of herself, hasn't she, Jamie?'

Jamie furrowed his brow and looked adorably stupid. 'You're talking about the woman I'm going to marry here...' But it lacked conviction. Just lately, since her return from Hastings, Serena had been moody and argumentative. Worst of all, she'd gone off sex.

Caroline tinkled with girlish laughter. 'Oh, that old story! Come on, Jamie, we're in the real world now, not on the telly. That's all make-believe. You really must learn to distinguish between them... darling.'

'What do you mean?'

'You don't seriously think you can marry Serena, do you?'

'Why not? I love her.'

'Jamie, don't you read the papers? She's a man.'

'No she ain't, and anyone who says she is...'

'In the eyes of the law she's a man.'

'But Eddie said...'

'Eddie's dead, Jamie. A great man, certainly, but with strange ideas about the truth. Eddie thought that truth is defined by what you can make people believe. We know better than that, don't we?'

Jamie was struggling. 'But even if we can't get married in a church, like, we can get a blessing.'

'Oh dear. It's rather sweet I suppose. Perhaps in your own way you really do care for Serena...'

'Yeah.'

'And are you willing to put her before your career?'

'What's my job got to do with anything?'

'I said your career, not your job. You don't have to slave away in that grotty little gym, you know. You can do a lot better than that.'

'They've been good to me.'

'That's one way of looking at it...'

'Anyway, I like the work. It's what I'm good at. I'm not cut out for this telly stuff. It's all bollocks anyway.'

'Good. Now we're getting somewhere. It is, as you say, bollocks, but it just happens to be incredibly lucrative bollocks. Jamie, you don't seem to realise a fundamental fact about your situation.'

'What's that?'

'You're a star.'

'Oh come off it, Caroline.'

'You are. Millions of people know you. You're in their homes once a week, you're in the papers every day. Have you any idea what that means? You're up there with the pop stars, the footballers. You're *on the telly*.'

'But the programme's shit.'

'That's beside the point. It's made you famous. The papers can say whatever they like about you – as long as you're in there.'

'They tell lies. That's bad.'

'No it's not. You know the truth. As long as they're printing your picture that's money in the bank. Don't you want to be rich, Jamie?'

'Course I do, but –'

'Then you must listen to me. You must break it off with Serena.'

'Why?'

'Because as long as you've got her hanging round your neck the public are going to think of you as a freak. They like Serena today, because they feel sorry for her, but they'll go off her when they realise what she really is. I'm sorry, but that's the truth. You and I both know the situation. Eddie tried to turn things round, but you can't alter facts. As long as you're with Serena, people are going to say you're... queer.'

'I ain't.'

'I know, Jamie. Who better?' Caroline allowed herself a girlish blush. 'But the viewing public have seen you in bed with a known transsexual. They've seen you selling your body to men. Nobody minds a few youthful indiscretions, as long as you turn your back on them, clean up your act and say that you're sorry. You've got to do that now. Your time is running out.'

'That's crap, Caroline. You just want me for yourself.'

'I beg your pardon?'

'You want this.' He clutched his groin through his tracksuit bottoms. Caroline had forgotten just how blessed he was in that department.

'How dare you?'

'It's the truth...'

'You think I'm doing all this just because I want you back in my bed, is that it?'

'You tell me.'

'Right. That's enough. Get out. I don't know why I bothered. They were right: you're just a cheap rent-boy and trannie-fucker. I thought there was something more to you, Jamie. I thought I'd seen real potential beneath that rough exterior. But this is one of the rare occasions when I'm wrong. I admit it now. I shall learn from my mistakes and move on. Are you still here? I asked you to go.'

'No, but wait...'

'It's too late.'

'What do you mean?'

'You're out of the show and out of my life.'

'I didn't mean that...'

'What did you mean, then?'

'I thought you were coming on to me, honest I did... Please, give me another chance. I know I can work with you. I just want to prove that there's more to me than what the public's seen.'

'Well...'

'You won't regret it, I promise you.'

'I must be mad.'

'Thanks, Caroline!' Jamie bounded across the desk and planted a kiss on her powdered cheek.

'But you'll have to do what I told you. Drop Serena.'

'Oh, that...' He scowled.

'Drop Serena or we have no deal.'

Jamie shuffled out of the office, clutching his forehead in thought. Caroline had won. Closing the door after him, she stuck her hands down her pants and squealed with delight.

Ever since the spectacular success of Jamie's stag night, Maureen and Muriel had been greatly in demand. Small-time pimping was no longer enough to contain their ambitions. They were destined for greater things, as well they knew. Lack of funds was the only thing that had ever barred them from the big time – and they lacked no longer. Thanks to the enthusiastic investment of a handful of major 'names' – wealthy businessmen and industrialists with a taste for rough trade – Maureen and Muriel were well on their way. The club, of which they had spoken for so long, would open soon. They had capital, they had backers – and, as long as Channel 6 continued to run *Elephant and Castle*, they had a guaranteed free advert once a week.

Time was when they would have been satisfied with a regular cabaret spot in a gay pub – sling on the drag, make up a new tape to mime to, dust down a few ancient blue jokes, what could be nicer? But now their horizons had expanded. 'It's surprising to think that your horizons could be stretched any further, dear,' Maureen said to Muriel, 'but there they are, wider still and wider.'

The premises were situated in a strange adjunct to the world-famous shopping centre, a sort of lean-to or afterthought rendered in breezeblock and concrete. As The Castle Arms it had enjoyed sporadic patronage in the sixties; it reopened in the seventies as a bistro and rapidly closed; its last incarnation, in the eighties, was as an unlicensed post-rave chill-out 'space'. Since the final raid in 1990 it stood empty and decaying.

'It's a bit drab,' sniffed Muriel when they were shown round by a desperate estate agent.

'Damp, if you ask me,' said Maureen, stepping through a puddle of brackish water.

'Well, gentlemen, if I may say so, the... er... lack of decorative finish is reflected in the asking price.'

'Which is?'

'Two hundred thousand.'

Maureen hooted. 'You'll be bloody lucky, sunshine. I wouldn't breed dogs in a skip like this.'

'Come, Maureen. We're wasting our time.'

'But the vendor is open to offers...'

They turned as one. 'One sixty. That's as high as we'll go.'

'I don't think...'

'Not a penny more. Come on, no other fucker's going to buy it and you know it.'

'I'm not authorised...'

'A hundred and sixty grand. Take it or leave it. Just give us a bell, sweetheart.'

The bell was forthcoming, and the property theirs (they'd even knocked off another five thousand for 'subsidence'). Happily for Maureen and Muriel, a close personal friend of theirs was a dominatrix in Clapham and provided a labour force free of charge: within a month of purchase the damp, stinking shell had been transformed into a chic little *boîte de nuit*. The walls were painted black (nothing else would cover the stains) and hung with red velvet, bought for a snip from an old theatrical suppliers; tables and chairs were covered in gay gingham, and the ceiling glowed with an eccentric assortment of light fittings. When finished, it looked like a homosexual smuggler's cave.

'Ooh, fabulous!' simpered Muriel, pacing up and down the new stage. 'At last, a home of one's own. Somewhere one can... shine!'

'And no landlord to chuck us out. No mortgage, either.'

'So elegantly appointed.'

'Yes, dear. The office at the back is very snug. And the upper rooms are everything we could desire. Just the thing for your tired businessman to relax in after a busy day.'

'I leave that side of the business to you, Mo.'

'Yeah, cos you're too old to do it yourself. Time was, my dear, when you'd have been up there flat on your back six nights a week entertaining.'

'That's no way to speak to an artiste.'

'You concentrate on front of house, dear, and leave the trade to me. Remember, we open in three weeks. So if madam would like to climb off her trapeze and join the rest of us clowns down here in the sawdust, we might actually be ready in time.'

The opening night of the Las Vegas Showbar was a smashing

success: how could it be otherwise, when the entire viewing nation had watched the transformation from sordid health-hazard to 'south London's answer to the Crazy Horse,' as Muriel claimed? Tickets were strictly limited: all the investors, naturally, had ringside seats and priority booking on any extra services they might require. The rest of the 250-strong crowd was made up of close personal friends, agents, broadcasters and the winners of an ill-advised Channel 6 competition. Muriel had assembled a roster of first-rate talent to regale the 'seated trade', while Maureen's troops were ready to provide more intimate entertainment in the upper rooms, each of which was fitted with a miniature camera linked to a bank of monitors in Maureen's office. Just at present he was investigating the lucrative potential of live pay-per-view webcam broadcasts featuring the less inhibited boys, and was ever mindful of the limitless blackmail material should the legit side of the business go belly-up.

The Las Vegas Showbar opened for business six weeks into the second series, while Caroline was busily renegotiating with Channel 6 for the run to be extended indefinitely. It was the biggest showbiz event south of the river since the collapse of the music hall circuit after the War: for once, the press corps crossed the Thames, searchlights raked the skies, adding considerably to the light pollution, and traffic came to a standstill. The venue was located right on the central roundabout, 'the ganglion of roads from Kent and Surrey ... the far-famed Elephant' (Charles Dickens, *Bleak House*), in the shadow of the equally famous shopping centre – and every passing vehicle slowed down to take a look until the whole of south London, and thus Kent and Surrey, was brought to a standstill.

Neon lettering spelt out the club's name against a background of tiny shimmering metal disks, completely outshining the once-magnificent Coronation Bingo sign (now erratically flashing 'Coro t on in o') and bathing the streets and subways in an infernal crimson glow. A red carpet, quickly soaked with reeking water, led up to a velvet rope across the door; a burly bouncer – none other than Jamie's lovestruck employer, Rod from the gym – demanded to see invitations.

Once inside, the lucky initiate passed through an obscure tunnel, its black walls illuminated by a single UV bulb, before emerging into the foyer, a triumph of taste over budget. Gold lamé hung in ruches around the circular walls; strings of lights were embedded into the floor to lead the eye and foot inexorably towards the *grande salle*. A couple of perky drag queens sold cigarettes; a bottle-blond boy worked for tips at the cloakroom (he would later receive much bigger tips upstairs). A plain black door marked PRIVATE led to Maureen's dominions. But on the ground floor, 'this little palace of varieties', Muriel was queen.

The privileged guests, and whatever celebrities Muriel was able to rustle up, arrived between nine and ten, enjoyed a glass of complimentary cava and milled around for the photographers who were allowed into the foyer in groups of no more than three. In truth, A-list was thin on the ground, but the Kandid crowd was well represented (Dave Merryweather, Doreen Dawson, alongside more recent stars) as well as Barry Llannelly, whose attendance sparked speculation about a possible defection from *Police Vet* to the more fertile pastures of *Elephant and Castle*. 'I love London,' he told journalists, 'although, as you know, I'm a country boy at heart. I miss my furred and feathered friends...' Just at that moment Muriel swept by in a creation quivering with dyed plumes... 'But I like to see the bright lights once in a while.' In fact, Barry had already negotiated an hour with Jack, a new recruit to the Gorge Guyz stable, a much pierced and inked young man with a red mohawk and a vaunted aptitude for fisting.

After an hour of chinning and ginning, Muriel and her attendant fairies ushered the glitterati into the main auditorium, where the overture (a CD of *Sunset Boulevard*) was already playing. The house was hushed, Muriel was in the wings giving her glue one final check, the lights were dimmed...

'Good evening ladies and gentlemen!' Muriel burst on to the stage in a cloud of shed feathers, waving at imaginary friends at the back of the auditorium – a trick she'd picked up from an old queen at the Bridge House in Canning Town, who claimed it lent intimacy to the performance. 'Nice to see so many famous faces here tonight. All the stars of *Elephant and Castle*...'

Not quite all. At home in Spencer Street, Serena sat in the dark drinking wine. Earlier that evening, she had given Jamie an ultimatum: stay with her, don't go to the opening, or they were through. In response he had cuffed her round the ear and said 'Listen, mate' in an all-too-masculine way, before informing her that she was too late, he was already seeing somebody else and that their sham of a relationship was over. 'It's time you woke up to yourself, Serena,' he sneered. 'You're going nowhere.'

And on that note he left her.

Debbie, too, was unable to attend, but for different reasons. She was holed up in a studio in West Norwood 'making movie history', as screenwriter Dudley Jenkins kept telling her. 'I'm not comfortable in this corset,' she whined, wriggling inside the over-tight leather carapace that nipped in her waist and pushed her breasts up to comic heights.

'It won't be for long, my dear,' chuckled Dudley. 'Come on, you're doing ever so well.'

And she was. As soon as the cameras turned over, Debbie was transformed. She was a vixen, a cruel mistress, handing out punishment to her girl slaves... All the fear, the misery in her eyes, disappeared the moment she was on.

'And... action!'

Debbie stomped three paces forward in her spiked thigh boots. 'I'm going to punish your little boobs, my dear.' The camera, down at floor level to represent the querulous gaze of her lesbo love slave, zoomed in on Debbie's sneering face. 'You've been a birty little ditch.'

'Cut! Try again, love. Say it with me. You've been a dirty little bitch. Come on. Do it for me, Debbie...'

'Where's Shelley?'

'I'm here, Debbie. It's okay.'

'Thanks... All right, I'm ready now.'

The camera turned, and Debbie snapped into character. 'I'm going to punish your little boobs, my dear. You've been a dirty little bitch.'

A big thumbs up from the director, and the scene progressed.

Back at the Las Vegas Showbar, Muriel was into his seventh minute. 'And so the Pope turned round and said "Nanty the drag, dear – vada the bijoux!" Thank you very much!' Maureen was making throat-cutting signs from the wings. 'Anyway, enough of my polari, let's get down to the business in hand, as the rent boy said to the bishop...' Maureen rolled his eyes to heaven. The audience was getting restless. He slipped a tape into the deck and pressed play. Cheesy middle-eastern music flooded the hall.

'May I present to you,' said Muriel, shouting to make himself heard above the din, 'all the way from sunny Spain, a very special lady, I know you're going to give her a big Las Vegas welcome, the one and only, I love her to bits, turn that fucking music down Maureen you bitch, ladies and gentlemen I give you... Two-Ton Carmen!'

An obese, dark-haired woman gyrated on from the wings and gave Muriel a bump to the hip that sent him sprawling. The audience, assuming it was part of the act, roared its approval.

'She's sacked, the fat sow,' hissed Muriel in the wings, frantically regluing.

'*Au contraire*, my dear, she's going down a storm, which is more than can be said for some of tonight's turns.'

'What do you mean, there's only been me.'

'Je reste ma valise.'

'Trust you to spoil my big night.'

'Don't get huffy with me, dear. Just keep it short and sweet and let them marvel at your unnatural beauty. Listen! They love her!'

Out on stage, Two-Ton Carmen was peeling off layer after layer of an ingenious costume made out of chiffon scarves which she'd picked up for less than a fiver at East Street market. Muriel peeped out to see her expose her billowing midriff; the audience shrieked in delight.

Not everyone was delighted, however. 'My God, look at her!' snapped Fat Alice from the 'stalls'. 'I don't see anything very special about *her*. I mean she's what – 15 stone? I'm fatter than her. Much fatter! I should be up there! Look at her!' She sniffed. 'Amateur!'

Two-Ton Carmen ended her spot with a triumphant juggling act involving two eggs, a flaming baton and a frying pan. They flew simultaneously into the air, she caught the baton between her naked breasts, the frying pan landed on top of it and the eggs, hurtling down from the flies, broke into the pan and were cooked.

The cheering was clearly audible in Spencer Street, where Serena was throwing a few necessaries into a bag.

'Thank you thank you thank you, the lovely, the one and only Two-Ton Carmen, isn't she great ladies and gentlemen! And now without further ado I'd like to introduce you to some very special friends of mine, they've been delighting audiences all over Southwark for many years now and I know you're going to give a really big Las Vegas welcome to, here they are, the one and only Kay and Jay!'

Two elderly transvestites dressed as nuns took to the stage and berated the audience's carnal wickedness for a few minutes before one of them whipped a ukelele from the folds of his habit and warbled a selection of hits from the 1920s.

*

Down in West Norwood, where Debbie had just finished shaving her captive's nether regions, there was a loud pounding at the door. Dudley Jenkins blanched.

'Are we expecting anyone?' he asked the director.

'No, Dud. You'd better go. Girls, cover yourselves.'

'Good evening officers,' simpered Dudley to three uniformed policemen. 'We're just having a little private party here.'

The officers marched straight past him and, to his astonishment and delight, straight past the lights, the cameras and the girls, who trembled in dirty dressing gowns.

'Shelley Smithers?' said one of them.

'Yes...' answered Shelley, staring pugnaciously from beneath her baseball cap.

'I am arresting you on suspicion of murder. You have a right to remain silent...'

As Shelley was frogmarched from the premises, Debbie fell into a deep swoon from which no amount of persuasion could rouse her.

'Thank you, thank you, the unforgettable Kay and Jay.' Muriel had been obliged to whip them off after the second chorus of 'Today I Feel So Happy'; he could see the audience getting restless. 'And now what you've all been waiting for, *musique maestro s'il-vous plaît*, I give you the one and only, I know you're going to love them a lot, here they are, the Las Vegas Showboys!'

Six athletic young men took the stage to the strains of 'Eye of the Tiger'.

There was a ring at the door of 1 Spencer Street.

'Hang on, Ben darling, I'm coming!'

But it was not Little Ben come round for his bedtime story. When Serena opened the door, there stood Philip Bray.

She was calm. 'You've got a lot of nerve, I'll give you that much.'

'I know you hate me. I need to talk to you.'

'I don't think there's very much to say. I'm leaving. For good this time. You won't find me, no matter how many telephone lines you run in your filthy newspaper. Where I'm going, nobody can find me. There. That's an exclusive for you, Philip. Now please go. I'm packing.'

Philip didn't move.

'Just go. Please. Do you want to see me cry?'

'Serena,' he said, his rich, deep voice perfectly controlled, 'do you have any idea who killed Eddie Kander?'

'What?' It flashed across Serena's mind that she was about to be framed for a crime she did not commit, applaud it as she may.

'I just wondered. Because an arrest has been made.'

'Oh, thank God.'

'And I don't believe it's the right person.'

'Why are you telling me this?'

'Because I want you to help me.'

'Again? That didn't get me very far last time, did it?'

'I want to bring the killer to justice, Serena. Is that such a bad thing to do?'

'You want to get the credit for solving the mystery, that's all.'

'Maybe. Well, if you can't help, you can't. An innocent woman will go to the dogs...'

'Who have they got?'

'Shelley Smithers. You won't know her. Debbie Doubledee's girl-friend.'

'Of course I know her. Oh no. She didn't kill Eddie. I'm sure of that.'

'Why?'

'I've met killers. Been out with a few of them, as a matter of fact, when I was a boy, but I'm sure you know that already. Shelley's not the type.'

'That's what I think. That's why I want you to help me.'

'Be your partner?'

'If you like.'

'Like on the telly, Philip? A mismatched pair team up to catch a killer? Is that the sort of thing you had in mind? You should get out more, dear. Now if you'll excuse me, I have a train to catch.'

'If you reconsider...' He handed her a card with his mobile number.

'You're not by any remote chance trying to get me into bed, are you? Because I am, as you'll doubtless be aware, single again.'

'What about Jamie?'

'He's dumped me. Thank you for caring.'

'I didn't know.'

'And basically, my dear, I hold you responsible. So forget your *Sapphire and Steel* fantasy and get out of my way.'

She slammed the door in Philip's face. He walked away, defeated.

On the stage of the Las Vegas Showbar, jockstraps joined helmets, jackets and boots in a pile on the floor as Muriel, joining the Las Vegas Showboys on stage for the finale, 'I'm one of the girls who's one of the boys...'

Five

Whither now for Serena Ward? Hounded from her job, ridiculed in the streets she'd called home, brutally sundered from the one man who could bring her happiness, her secrets exposed for the world to share... She had, when Philip Bray came to call, seriously been considering suicide. A few days in a hot country where nobody knew her... Italy, maybe, they liked trannies there, she had heard... and if she couldn't find a safe haven there, then... death. Immortality of a kind, as a footnote to television history, one of those names and faces who are remembered in a dozen tasteless jokes, the currency of the public house and building site. And then, gradually, forgotten, laid to rest. Perhaps someone would write a book one day, she thought, fondly stroking the cover of her diary. The truth! That would raise a few eyebrows. But who would ever believe it? And who was Serena, after a lifetime of evasion and disguise, suddenly to emerge as a champion of honesty?

But for all that, she couldn't go. She sat on the bed after Philip's departure utterly incapable of moving, as if lead weights pinned her down. She had felt this way once before, as the anaesthetic kicked in just before her surgery.

There was nothing to keep her here. If she died intestate, everything would go to her mother – a bitter irony which Serena rather relished. She had no lover, no friends, no children. Little Ben might miss her, but she could hardly count herself responsible for Daryn's by-blows. Let social services do their worst. She'd survived it; he would too.

So why wasn't she leaving? The bag was packed, the passport ready... all she had to do was drift along to Heathrow and find the cheapest flight available.

Her hand rested on the mock-leather cover of an old diary that she'd pulled at random from her bookshelves. 1988 – the year before she emerged from her masculine disguise. What a year it had been... hustling for money, fighting with doctors, facing the wrath of her family and the occasional punter who took exception to the 'something extra' between her legs (most of them were delighted). She flicked through the volume... there, today's date. What was she doing all those years ago?

Finally kicked the punter out at 6am and got some sleep. He was a noisy bastard, demanding a refund because I wouldn't fuck him. Good job I'd stashed the money where he wouldn't find it, behind the baked beans in the kitchen. He looked everywhere else, including the toilet cistern, the ugly twat. If he'd been better looking I would have said yes. Still I got £60 out of him which isn't bad. Another step nearer to WOMANHOOD. This had better be worthwhile. When I'm a woman I will be HAPPY HAPPY HAPPY because let's face it I've sunk pretty low in order to get there.

She flicked forward a couple of days.

Walking down Lewisham High Street a woman came up to me and punched me in the face for no reason at all that I could see, apart from the fact that she 'read' me. She looked so indignant and righteous, as if she'd done her duty. I felt like turning round and waving my dick at her, but instead I ran crying into the nearest shop where they were very kind. When I am a woman I will never, ever let anybody walk over me in this way. Went down to the Worcester and had a couple of Pernods to straighten myself out. Picked up a nice HGV driver I've seen down there before, went back to his place and he gave me £30. Not my usual rate but he was sweet. Slept all afternoon then got ready to go up to the Piano Bar...

There it was in black and white: three, sometimes four tricks a day, the money carefully put by, living on the most frugal fare, making do and mending her tiny hooker's wardrobe, focusing on the day when she would check into that private clinic on the south coast. God, she had been a tough little customer in those days. Hard as nails. She had purpose in life, a driving anger that kept her going even in her darkest hour. And for what? To allow a bunch of cheap bastards from a tv company, so cheap that they didn't even pay for her services in the way that the meanest punter had, to drive her to suicide. Was it for this that she'd suffered and degraded herself throughout her teens and twenties? Was it for this that she'd spent the summer of her youth in dark, damp toilets redolent of piss and disinfectant? That she'd hauled her tired body from pub to bar, back home in a minicab if the punter was generous, on the night bus if not? To be defeated, finally, by Caroline Wragge? A woman unworthy of her biological gender? Who had lured Jamie away with nothing more than a fat wallet and a 'real' pussy?

Oh no. That was not good enough. If she left now, to exile or death, Caroline would have won, Jamie would forget her, and to cap it all her bitch of a mother would get the flat.

Serena slammed the diary shut and hugged it to her bosom. No, she would not betray her younger self by giving up now. Back then she would have fought tooth and nail for what she wanted; she would have burst into Caroline's office and flayed her face off. She would have lied, cheated, stolen, to get Jamie back. And she would get every single fucker who had ever made her feel bad about herself. Had the intervening years of womanhood mellowed her so much that she was anyone's meek, obliging doormat? She thought not.

But now there was some quick thinking to be done. The first priority was money; if she didn't do something about her three-month mortgage arrears pretty damn quick, she'd be out on the street again – not a prospect which, at her age and with her notoriety, she relished. So, once again, the eternal problem of putting money in her handbag. She thought at first of going back on the game; not in the old way, hanging around bars and corners literally pulling the punters off the street. No, there were better ways now, thanks to great leaps forward in telecom technology. All she needed was a mobile phone, a packet of sticky labels and some coloured felt pens and she could rejoin the regiment of sex workers. And, being something of a celebrity, she could push her prices up.

But that would hardly be a great step forward, would it? Twelve years on, and still on the game? A successful, hard-won career in advertising cast aside? Self respect all gone? Well, perhaps one day she would get back to work, when all this had died down... but at the present moment, she was professionally untouchable and she knew it. And even if she started a new job tomorrow, that didn't solve the immediate problem of the building society, whose letters had gone from friendly concern to open threats in the space of a few weeks.

There was only one option left, as far as she could see. She was desperate, and she was famous. The solution was obvious. She would go on stage.

And so our three female protagonists find themselves embracing unexpected careers in the performing arts. Debbie Doubledee was wildly successful as a vicious lesbian dominatrix in a series of videos which sold all over the world and brought her offers of work from the big boys in Hollywood, who were looking for a new star to front up their *XXXTreme Fisting Sluts* brand. Fat Alice spent her days practising a song-and-strip routine based around some of her favourite numbers from the West End shows, shamefully neglecting the career of Miachail Miorphiagh (that call from *The Archers* had still not been forthcoming). And Serena... Serena, who had vowed that she would never cash in on her tv fame, entered the Las Vegas Showbar one sunny afternoon and asked the cloakroom twink if she could see 'Mr Turner'.

'Who, dear?'

'You know... Maureen.'

'Oh, why didn't you say? By the way, I think you're fabulous. I'm thinking of doing hormones myself. What do you think? Wouldn't I make a gorgeous woman?'

'I wouldn't advise it.'

'Hmmph. It worked for you, though, didn't it? What's the matter, Serena? Worried about the competition? There's a new generation coming up behind you dear, and we're going to steal your trade.'

'Spare me the *All About Eve* routine and find Maureen, there's a good boy,' said Serena, whipping off her graduated shades and quelling the twink with a gimlet eye. 'Tell him it's business.'

'I don't doubt it,' huffed the twink, flouncing through the door marked PRIVATE. Give me a pair of scissors, thought Serena, and I'll geld the little pony myself.

Maureen was appropriately high and mighty, enjoying the spectacle of Serena being brought down a peg or two. She'd always had ideas above her station, that one, and had indeed declined to work for various branches of the Turner-Delgado showbusiness/prostitution empire before. Now the slingback was on the other foot.

'Well the thing is, Sean... sorry dear, I was forgetting, Serena, the thing is we're only employing professional entertainers here, but funnily enough Muriel was thinking of starting an amateur night, Legends of Tomorrow she was going to call it, so maybe if you wanted to work up a little number for that we could fit you in among the other hopefuls.'

'If I appear at your club,' said Serena, refusing to rise to the bait, 'you'll be full every night.'

'We are already dear. We're doing rather well, in case you hadn't noticed.'

'I could do a lot for you.'

'It's not really a question of what you can do for us. It's more what we might do for you. I'm sorry, but that's the way it is. Ask any agent: their books are full of semi-pro drag queens who come on and lip-sync to hits from the shows.'

Like Muriel, thought Serena, but bit her tongue just in time.

'I was thinking of something a little more original than that, Maureen.'

'Oh yes? What? Speciality strip?'

'I'm not going to wave my operation scars around on stage, if that's what you're hoping for.'

'Shame. That would have been worth seeing.'

'It's more of a one-woman show. The story of my life. The truth.'

'Oh my dear, that sounds a bit dismal. I mean, it's hardly a bundle of laughs, is it? Alcoholic old bitch of a mother, cottaging from the age of 11, on the game at 15... Well, I'd enjoy it of course, but then I'm simpatico, aren't I? But for your average punter, it's all a bit... sordid.'

Seldom had the pot's accusations of blackness been less justified.

'Oh no, I shan't dwell on the sordid side, as you so kindly put it Maureen. I shall stress the upbeat, the positive. I'll make 'em laugh, I promise you. And if you really think it would help, I'll show a bit of tit. Not that I've much to show.'

She bunched up a little handful of natural, hormonally-induced breast. Not for her the perils of implants. Jamie liked them small.

Maureen's own dugs, the result of many years of over-eating, were a good deal larger.

'We could always provide opera glasses so that the back rows could get a vada.'

'You mean you'll give me a chance?'

'It won't be much money, dear, you understand that.'

'How much?'

'Let's say... two spots a night, mind... fifty quid a night?'

'I won't do it for less than £150.'

'Seventy-five?'

'A hundred, and that's as low as I'll go. Two spots, tits out for the second curtain. Take it or leave it.'

'Well...' pondered Maureen, delighted that he'd secured a sure-fire hit at such modest prices, 'I'll give you a try. No, don't thank me dear. I'm not doing you a favour. You'll earn every penny of that money, if I decide to pay you at all. You do a freebie on Friday night. After that, if they like you, we'll talk business.'

'I knew you'd see sense.'

'I warn you though, dear. The Friday crowd can be rough.'

Rough? thought Serena. I'll take every mother's son of them.

While Serena was swallowing her pride and starting again at the bottom of the ladder, Jamie was tasting the high life. Caroline made good her promise and showered him with every useless gift that money could buy, until his flat in Beckford House resembled a branch of Curry's and his person scintillated with jewellery. Life is sweet, he thought, walking down Moulton Street with a bag in each hand, the Kandid credit card nestling comfortably in a new pigskin wallet in his new Ralph Lauren leather jacket. Caroline didn't ask for much: a shag a day, two at the most, and his company at launches and lunches, where he was required to do little more than eat, drink and occasionally flex a muscle. No more nagging from Serena, no more punters, no more of Rod's painful attentions in the back office... and to fill his cup of happiness to the brim, the new exercise studio in which he would personally train a handful of wealthy clients was even then receiving the finishing touches from a team of builders and decorators. All of this went through the company books: Caroline put it down as 'capital allowances' and thought nothing more of it. Jamie had more screen time than ever in the weekly episodes of *Elephant and Castle*, and there was talk of further projects when the series took its summer break: presenting a daytime fitness show, perhaps, or even an acting role in a gritty south London crime drama. Yes, reflected Jamie, life is sweet. If all went according to plan, he would move out of Beckford House within a month (he could barely walk the streets now without being mobbed) and take up residence in the Kandid penthouse, a recently-converted suite of rooms upstairs from the office in D'Arblay Street, which Caroline was renting out (theoretically as a 'conference facility'). From there it would be no hardship to take a chauffeured car to 'work' every day, to pretend that he was still living in the Elephant and Castle but to leave every evening.

All would have been well in Jamie's simple universe but for one nagging question. It began one afternoon, when he was sitting in Caroline's office admiring a new pair of trainers and cleaning his teeth with a hallmarked silver dental pick she'd just given him after noticing his tendency to root around in his cavities with a spent match. Caroline was hard at work, wheeling and dealing over the phone – securing him a comfortable future, which was all that mattered to Jamie. Later on they were going to a drinks reception, then a movie premiere... Jamie's presence at these events was much in demand. Perhaps he'd be photographed with a former *Big Brother* contestant. And later... maybe he'd go off to a club for a dance, see what the night held in store. It was the music at Heaven that attracted him, not the men, he told himself...

He was just losing himself in an agreeable fantasy of what he might do with another fit young bloke like himself, not gay but up for it, versatile, when a string of words unexpectedly jarred on his semi-consciousness.

'... to make a full confession in front of a camera crew ...'

A confession? Whose confession, wondered Jamie. Was someone else stealing his screen time?

'... complete legal indemnity for us and a major plea-bargaining option for your client. If he confesses to the murder ...'

Murder? Jamie's ears pricked up. He carried on languidly picking his teeth and staring at his shoe, but now, despite appearances, he was tuned in to every word.

Caroline was uncharacteristically indiscreet. 'Well that's your job,' she was saying. 'You're Daryn's lawyer, you figure it out. He can confess to planning Eddie's murder himself, we'll use it when the time is right, when it could actually do him some good, or you leave it with me and I'll tell the police when it suits me. That way Daryn gets a shitload of negative publicity and a life sentence. If he plays it my way, you might be able to turn it round for him. Either way, he's fucked, but there are degrees of fuckedness.'

A voice gabbled on the other end of the phone.

'You think I haven't worked that one out?' sneered Caroline. 'It wasn't difficult. He's banged up with a prison full of assorted criminals – it can't have been hard to find a hit man to carry out his wishes. The only thing I don't understand about the whole sorry business is why the police didn't cotton on. It was so obviously a professional job.'

Again, the voice chattered ferociously away.

'Yes, I've known for a long time, but we'll keep that quiet, shall we? We all have secrets, don't we? Even lawyers like yourself ... Well, I leave the ball in your court. The police have their suspect. Shelley Smithers goes on trial next month. Now, if Daryn doesn't play ball I'll stand up in the courtroom and say four words. Daryn. Handy. Did. It ... And that's curtains for Daryn. Or, if he's smart, he'll talk to the camera, tell the world that he took out the contract and –'

Suddenly, Caroline noticed that Jamie was listening.

'Yeah,' she said, changing her tone, 'the contract for the second series, that's right, he hasn't signed it, and he stands to make a "killing" or even a "murder" as we call it in tv, that's right, he would be a real "hit, man" … Okay, bye, gotta go.' She slammed the phone down and laughed too loud. 'Well, big boy, enough of that boring negotiation with a contract lawyer, which is what I've been doing for the last ten minutes, sorting out very dull business to do with the series, God it was uninteresting. What's the time? Shouldn't we do some shopping before we go out tonight? Or maybe you'd like me to give you a blow-job?' That usually calmed him down, Caroline thought…

'No,' said Jamie, 'let's shop.' His mind was too busy to feign excitement. 'I could do with a widescreen telly.'

And so Jamie's life went from good to better. He knew something about Caroline – something that could land her in prison and put paid to her ambitions of media clout. She not only knew who was responsible for Eddie's murder, she was prepared to withold information from the police in order to serve her own ends. She may also have conspired with Daryn in the murder – 'I've known for a long time,' those were here words, were they not? Known for how long? Since before the crime? Since discussing it with Daryn, perhaps, on one of her many prison visits? Daryn was not a bright spark, and for all his talk of getting back at Eddie Kander it may not have been within his intellectual ambit to source a professional killer, arrange and pay for the hit. Caroline, however, was just the sort of person to find the creep for the job.

Jamie didn't let on that he knew; he didn't need to. All he had to do was look Caroline straight in the eye, and she understood. It was a civilised agreement. He'd play dumb, keep things sweet, and she'd be a little more generous. Hitherto she'd tried to keep a lid on his spending; now, if she started to demur at some needless extravagance, he gave her the eyeball and the matter was settled. He enjoyed the power. He became greedy, careless. If Jamie didn't feel like boffing Caroline – and in truth he never really did – he turned her down. Sometimes she was useful in that department – she was willing to do things that most real women weren't – but most of the time he kept himself for others. He dated a string of young lovelies of both sexes, all of them eager to break into television. He appeared in public with a succession of glamorous women, and in private with equal numbers of glamorous men. Rumours swept around the West End after Jamie was seen disappearing upstairs in the Soho House with a hotly-tipped young English actor, poised to make his international mark in a major independent film... The actor's PR people denied all the rumours, but they were true nonetheless. Jamie brought out the dirty little slut that lurks within men and women alike. That, he found, was the advantage of a working class background, a spell in the army, a fit muscular tattooed body and a large, ever-ready endowment. He was everybody's bit of rough. He had never had it so good.

The health studio opened, but the glossy state-of-the-art fitness equipment remained untried. Every so often Jamie would entertain a new friend there, finding that the mirrored walls added greatly to his enjoyment of certain sexual positions, but as a business venture it was a dud. He kept himself in shape, reasoning rightly that his body was his fortune. He sweated and grunted in private, then sweated and grunted for slightly different reasons with his manifold partners.

Caroline asked no questions and began to think of ways of getting rid of him. But for as long as she needed to keep Daryn's guilt under wraps, a card to be played only when all others were out, she had to buy Jamie's silence. She was prepared to gamble. She swallowed all his insults, his greed, even his demands for money to pay off the trash he picked up in the clubs. She paid without demur. But somewhere in the chilly, reptilian part of her brain, each offence was logged.

Most entertainers of note have more than 72 hours in which to for-mulate the act that will launch them into the showbiz stratosphere – but then again, most entertainers do not have the same vast pool as Serena in which to fish for material. As she worked her way through her diaries, she remembered incidents and anecdotes that seemed now fraught with interest and significance, episodes that would illuminate her journey to womanhood and keep audiences on the edge of their seats. She honed her delivery, she practised her gestures in front of the mirror, she repeatedly interrupted rehearsals to assure the importunate hireling from the building society that the first instalment of the overdue payments would be paid in on Monday morning. She selected a couple of songs that, she thought, she could carry off in a smoky, supperclub diseuse sort of way – songs made famous by other vocally-challenged divas: Marlene Dietrich, Lotte Lenya, Amanda Lear… She even chose the music to which, if necessary, she would make the stipulated revelation of her breasts. No bump and grind for her, but a beautiful piece by Ravel. If she must stoop, at least she would do it in style.

While Serena smooched smokily in Spencer Street, Fat Alice wob-bled wildly in Warfield Street, stomping naked around her front room to a tape of Queen's 'Fat Bottomed Girls'. Juggling had been tried and rejected – she didn't want to be branded as a Two-Ton Carmen copyist, besides which she couldn't even keep two oranges in the air at the same time. Neither was dancing her forte. Best to remain rooted to the spot and shake it: that, as the mirror revealed, created an extrordinary sensation which would be clearly visible from the back of the largest auditorium. But true to her theatrical training, Alice realised that she had to have a gimmick. Once she'd got her clothes off (and this, she calculated, would take less than two minutes) she had to do something to keep the audience's attention.

Dramatic recitals? Mime? She had done a workshop in the eighties with Lindsay Kemp, who told her that she was fabulous and even hinted, later that night in the bar, that he might have a role for her in his ambitious new production of *Die Walküre*. Alas, funding had not been forthcoming, or he would surely have called...

But mime, yes, that could be the thing. The plate of glass. The dog on a lead. High wind at the bus stop. If only she could make her flesh *move*. She gathered up two handfuls of stomach, twisted and poked them to resemble a cottage loaf.

Then inspiration struck. That was it! Of course! Contortions!

Caroline now weighed two stone less than she had when *Elephant and Castle* launched. She felt happy with her new bony silhouette, but much more of this and she would end up making herself ill. By the middle of May, she was looking forward to the show's summer break. By dint of some brilliant negotiation, she had secured an uninterrupted run for the forthcoming autumn/winter season, right through from September to February, with a ludicrously large budget from Channel 6. Viewing figures stayed high, and advertisers were in fierce competition to sell their goods during the breaks. *Elephant and Castle* was a cash cow for all concerned, funding, incidentally, a crop of daytime DIY and lifestyle shows one of which may provide a handy retirement home for Jamie Lord if and when she had to sack him from the series. Things were going well: better than she could ever have dreamed. But with success came unforeseen pressures: Jamie's subtle blackmail, her anxiety relating to Daryn, a tangle of legal complications. Little wonder that Caroline could neither eat nor sleep.

At least the second series would finish with a bang. Channel 6 had been happy enough when the hunt for Serena brought them viewing figures in excess of eight million – but Caroline knew she could improve on that. The series would end with a double whammy: the debut of Serena and Fat Alice at the Las Vegas Showbar (lowlife comedy) and the trial of Shelley Smithers for the murder of Eddie Kander – drama most thrilling. If only she could keep everyone quiet, keep the lid on the Daryn Handy situation, all would be well. Daryn wasn't happy. He was going around the prison telling anyone who would listen that he had done the job, hired the hitman, wiped out Eddie Kander – that he was a murderer, and thus prison royalty. But nobody would listen. Little man talking big, they said, and he went down in their estimation. His cocksucking cellmate moved on to bigger, badder inmates.

But despite the governor's assurances, Caroline was not happy with the situation. In a tense meeting, he told her that prisons were full of men boasting about crimes they'd never committed, that Daryn was just another sad Billy Liar trying to claw his way up the pecking order. If she ignored him, all would be well. But Caroline wisely took precautions. She persuaded the governor to put Daryn into solitary confinement – something the governor was unwilling to do until the prospect of a fly-on-the-wall documentary series set in his prison was dangled before him.

If Daryn could be kept quiet for long enough to convict Shelley, all would be well, the third series would be dynamite (the retrial) and Caroline would join the British broadcasting elite, a woman whose name alone assured success, a producer bigger than any tv channel, any star, any market research. A brand in her own right. She was thinking Esther. Bigger than Esther. Oprah.

But Daryn would not keep quiet. With time on his hands in solitary, he kept up an insane correspondence. 'Dear Caroline,' ran one of his regular threatening letters,

You know what happened to Eddie Kander well be careful because I might decide to do the same to you. Eddie stitched me up he said that I was cool with the drugs thing on tv but that was not as the case turned out to be the police said I had been taken for a ride and nobody takes The Doc for a ride NOBODY. Now you are pushing youre luck and you better be careful cos I have made some very nasty friends here if you know what I mean and I think you do. People who are going to be on the outside soon and looking for a job. I have money so don't think I don't I can pay them if I have to although theres some that would rub you out just cos of what you done to me you better believe it I will kill you bitch. Now about that tv special you talked about I had loads of ideas for a programme about my life and where I come from and how Im the boss of this prison, it would be a big success and you got to make it, get the cameras down here and we will show them a thing or two...

Just like everyone else, thought Caroline, Daryn would do anything, swallow any amount of shit, for his moment in the limelight. And thus she had stumbled upon the brilliant expedient of filming Daryn's confession, convincing him that he was going to be the star of a big tv show in his own right, buying his temporary silence and equipping herself with the biggest bit of leverage that had ever come her way. The pundits were saying that *Elephant and Castle* was yesterday's news, that despite its massive ratings it couldn't sustain that level of interest, that it was all played out. Let them wait, thought Caroline. I'll show them – when it suits me.

But first for the twin climax of series two: the trial and the nightclub show. In the final weeks of the run, Caroline devoted more and more screen time to the build-up of these two stories. She showed Serena and Fat Alice rehearsing their acts; she showed Shelley going over her evidence with her brief. Perverting the course of justice! cried the papers, who knew that they could add substantially to the day's sales by running any old crap about *Elephant and Castle*. But it was true: Caroline was, in theory, on very thin legal ice. But nobody was stopping her. The papers complained, but only to whip up more interest. At first she lost sleep worrying about solicitor's letters that never came.

The other stars of the show were sidelined. Debbie Doubledee was in Los Angeles, shooting *XXXTreme Fisting Sluts 1: Up to the Wrist* with co-star Mellodee Jones, a local girl and loyal shopping companion.

Maureen and Muriel were busy with the business, appearing occasionally to offer a few words of queenly wisdom but content with their lot; their greed, at least, had been satisfied. They had no ambitions left to fulfil.

Daryn was in prison, looking forward to greater fame and the resumption of his daily servicing. Little Ben, never more than a peripheral character, was in care.

Jamie made sporadic appearances when he could be bothered to turn up on location. Caroline thought it best to keep him at some distance from the two main storylines.

Everyone else was dead.

Caroline focused all her energies on Serena, Alice and Shelley. All of them would go down, one way or another. She would see to it. It would be sensational television, the stuff of legend.

And then she could sleep again.

Six

The opening sequence of the penultimate episode of the second series of *Elephant and Castle* was a classic. It started with an aerial shot of the locale – the familiar jumble of high-rise and mid-Victorian, the roads carving through it like rivers, the sky a dirty white; but this week, instead of zooming down towards Beckford House and Spencer Street for another half hour of bugs under the microscope, the camera scanned the skies, latched on to an aeroplane starting its descent towards Gatwick and followed it into the clouds as the title music faded and the voice-over began.

'We haven't seen Debbie Wicks, or Debbie Doubledee as she's better known to fans all over the world, since she left for California two months ago. In a few short weeks she's become a star of the adult film industry, but now she's coming home where friends and family need her...'

Cut to the arrivals gate at Gatwick airport, where photographers, newsmen and a couple of dozen elderly fans waited to hail Debbie's homecoming, all observed by a Kandid crew.

'She's made us so proud,' said Theresa Wicks, clutching one end of a hastily-painted banner ('Welcome Home Debbie'). 'We always knew she had it in her,' said William at the other end. He had not yet seen any of the *XXXTreme Fisting Sluts* series (Debbie and Mellodee had just completed volume five: *Handball Heaven*) or he would have known that Debbie, as a femme dom top, never 'had it in her' but, rather, put it in others. Some of the fans clutched copies of their favourite selections from the Doubledee oeuvre; the Kandid cameras tried to avoid them.

'Here she comes now!' screamed Theresa, as a volley of flash-guns exploded around her. The doors opened, and Debbie emerged tanned, relaxed and blonder than ever, her eyes concealed behind ray-bans, the epitome of west coast celebrity. She smiled, even stopped for a few poses and a chat with the news gatherers. 'It feels great to be back. London will always be very special to me ... Oh yes, I've had an amazing time, and we've got some very exciting projects lined up when I go back, a big movie role ... Just a few personal visits, friends and family ... No comment on that one, I'm afraid. Thanks, guys.'

Could this be the same Debbie Wicks who, just a few short months ago, would have hopelessly spoonerised every word and wet her knickers at the sight of a flash gun? The same little girl who tried to hang herself from her wardrobe door when she'd been caught in flagrante with a vegetable? The twitching, slavering junkie who couldn't get up in the morning without her fix? There she stood, in her designer slut wardrobe, her hair a perfect halo of candy floss, her glorious breasts pushed up to her chin... and simply radiated health, confidence and happiness. Could hard-core pornography really have been her salvation?

The viewers had little time to ponder this transformation, as there was high drama just around the corner. Theresa and William Wicks burst through the lines of press, shaking their still-wet banner, and held their arms wide for the ecstatic reunion. The camera caught their joyful, expectant faces. Cut to Debbie – smiling, cool, impassive. Back to the parents, almost hysterical with anticipation. Cut to Debbie whispering to an aide (ponytail, rhino-hide tan). Cut to the parents, the smiles freezing on their faces, their eyes widening. Long shot of Debbie turning on her snakeskin heels and walking in the opposite direction, Theresa and William rooted to the spot with horror.

'Debbie... my little angel...' muttered William, but she was gone.

'Has stardom spoiled Debbie Doubledee?' asked Kandid's on-the-spot reporter. Time for some vox-pops as the confused parents stumbled back towards the railway station. They had envisaged a triumphant return to Elephant and Castle in a limousine; public transport was the final ignominy.

'She's a lovely girl,' said one middle-aged gentleman, pocketing his copy of *XXXTreme Fisting Sluts 3: PussyBusters!*. 'I'm sure she's just tired after her journey.'

'I didn't like the look of that bloke she was with,' said the Kandid runner, posing as an Ordinary Member of the Public. 'He looked well dodgy. I expect she's picked up some weird ideas out there in Californ-eye-aye.'

Debbie, meanwhile, was zooming out of Gatwick in the limousine that her parents had missed, accompanied by a middle-aged man and an eight-year-old girl. The former – her aide, manager and constant companion – took off his shades and rubbed his watery grey eyes. Debbie reached over and brushed some dandruff off his black Nehru-style jacket.

'We made it, baby,' he said in a low, bland American accent.

'Yes,' said Debbie, her voice betraying the nerves she'd concealed at arrivals. The limo's windows were opaque from outside; no chance of prying lenses now. (As a precaution, she'd ordered a security sweep of all transport and hotel rooms for hidden cameras.) 'Home at last.'

'Yeah... home sweet home.' There was something in his tone of voice that Debbie didn't like – as if they were never leaving again.

The little girl set up a whine. 'I need a pee-peeeeeeeeeeeeeee.'

'Okay honey,' said Debbie, 'we'll stop at the next service station.'

So who are they, this strange new family unit? The gentleman with the greying ponytail, the rhino-hide tan and the vaguely

Indian wardrobe was, until recently, a studio hireling, 'working out some bad karma' in the porn industry until something better came along. That something was Debbie Doubledee, a woman desperately in need of a mentor, who fell for his second-rate swami act, allowed him to move into her Hollywood condo and even agreed to call him 'Bodhi' (real name: Brian). Bodhi did not travel alone: he dragged around with him more tangible evidence of bad karma in the shape of his daughter, a limp little creature named Goa (where her father had reached enlightenment on a backpacking holiday in the mid eighties). Bodhi and Goa travelled to England on tourist visas, but Bodhi had no intention of leaving in a hurry. It was, he told Debbie, 'karmically appropriate' for him to get out of California for a while. He almost succeeded in losing Goa at Los Angeles International airport; it was only due to Debbie's vigilance that she'd made it this far. She was truculent and incontinent for the whole journey; already the limo was redolent of stale piss.

Bodhi refused to be drawn on the subject of Goa's mother, preferring a guru-like smile and some gnostic waffle on 'Gaia, our universal mother'. In fact Goa was the result of a short-lived ashram that Bodhi had established in suburban Los Angeles, where he surrounded himself with pliant young female disciples all of whom were required to practise strict birth control precautions. One of them, a stoned little rich girl from Encino, broke the rules and gave birth to Goa shortly before being found wandering in the middle of the freeway. Her revelations during 'deprogramming' were enough to disperse the ashram and send Bodhi into hiding, literally holding the baby. Subsequent attempts to disembarrass himself – the most recent at LAX – had all failed. Now he was hoping that he could establish himself in London, that Debbie (or 'Dharma' as he called her, and she was learning to call herself) would take Goa back to America, and that his special gifts could be brought to a nation in desperate need of enlightenment. Why, he thought, if they could make Debbie a tv personality, there was surely a great future for him here...

None of this, however, was of any interest – yet – to the ten million viewers of *Elephant and Castle*, who were engrossed in preparations for the trial. And it was primarily for this that Debbie Doubledee had timed her visit to Britain.

Shelley Smithers, as we all know, was entirely innocent of any involvement in the Eddie Kander slaying, despite her indiscreet pronouncements to the contrary. He was not the first man she'd threatened to kill, castrate or generally mutilate; Philip Bray knew that all too well. It was unfortunate for Shelley, however, that she'd been caught on camera making certain threats which had been broadcast to the nation and therefore received the stamp of truth, however scanty the rest of the evidence. Her arrest was based largely on the fact that the sole witness to Kander's final hours, a nervous businessman who had been cruising the White City area in the vague hope of a pick-up, had seen 'a figure in a baseball cap and a bomber jacket' running from the spot where Kander's body was found. Shelley had no reasonable alibi, she had a professed motive and, as the police discovered when they raided her flat, her wardrobe comprised little else but baseball caps and bomber jackets.

Everyone wanted her to be guilty, and Shelley did herself no favours by refusing to co-operate with the investigation. Even her own solicitor found her an unsympathetic client, disliked her brand of sulky arrogance, and decided it would be better all round if she took the rap and the case was closed.

But why was Shelley not protesting her own innocence? Whatever she may have heard of the tribadic delights of women's prisons, surely she didn't want to be punished for a crime she did not commit? What perverse motive lay behind her non-co-operation, her grunted replies to all questions, her general air of criminal guilt?

Love was the motive. She hadn't killed Eddie Kander, but she would have done – should have done, she told herself, for what he'd done to Debbie. Debbie, beautiful Debbie, her only friend, the star around which her humble satellite revolved, taken away from her, all because of what Eddie Kander did. Perhaps if Debbie could be persuaded that Shelley had indeed killed for her sake – if she could give a good performance in the witness box, and explain herself in terms of quiet, dignified passion – then at last Debbie would wake up to the truth of Shelley's love. A doomed love – if she succeeded, she failed, for a guilty verdict would separate them forever – but love, at least, acknowledged.

Kandid cameras caught the morning's papers whizzing off the presses, the crowds gathering outside the Old Bailey, Shelley being bundled out of a prison van, cool, collected, devoid of the customary blanket over the head. Ten minutes into the show, the viewing nation was on the edge of its seats. Debbie's sensational snubbing of her parents was a tasty starter to the main course of the evening. Not for nothing had Caroline Wragge persuaded Channel 6 to run daily updates on the trial throughout the week; now, on *Elephant and Castle*, she would show the heartbreak behind the headlines.

Caroline negotiated long and hard for the right to bring cameras into the courtroom, and when she was turned down for the umpteenth time retaliated by attempting to gain access by main force.

'But we go on air at nine o'clock tonight, cretin,' she boomed at the police officer who barred her way. 'How can I give the British public a trial special if you won't let the cameras in?'

'I'm sorry, madam,' said the officer, clearing his throat and holding in his stomach, conscious that the camera was on him, 'I have my orders. No further than this.'

'And so British justice continues to operate in an atmosphere of secrecy and concealment,' claimed the hastily-added voiceover. 'Will there be justice for the killers of Eddie Kander? We will never know.'

Caroline left Nicko McVitie in charge 'front of house', and concentrated on nobbling potential jurors in the waiting room, to which she gained access with a forged letter. 'I think it's shocking that they've allowed it to come this far,' she said to one bored looking old man who'd been waiting for eight days to set foot inside a courtroom. 'She's obviously guilty, isn't she?'

'Yeah,' said the juror, unaware that Caroline's ugly metal lapel brooch concealed a tiny camera. 'She looks like a villain. Black and that.'

'I say it was a lovers' tiff,' said a tired-looking woman in a charity-shop overcoat. 'I mean, it says here' – she was reading the *Daily Beacon* – 'that she was having an affair with that blonde girl off the telly, her with the big you-know-whats. I expect that's what it's all about. They're mostly killers, those lesbian types. Comes of not having babies.'

Cut to the swearing-in of the jury – and there, to Caroline's delight, were the two who had provided such obliging soundbites earlier in the day. Justice for Shelley Smithers! That would be her new campaign – provided that the guilty verdict came down. Caroline Wragge, crusader for truth – a role she could not resist. She would tirelessly maintain Shelley's innocence while allowing her to go to prison, then, when the time was right, new evidence would come to light in the shape of Daryn's taped confession, guaranteeing a sensational third series and journalistic immortality.

Viewers had to be content with exterior shots of the Old Bailey and occasional whispered interviews with bribed clerks; the lack of solid courtroom footage forced Caroline to give more screen time to Serena and Alice's preparations for the show.

'While Shelley Smithers battles for her life,' said the voice-over, 'Serena Ward is battling for her livelihood. But has she got what it takes to sing for her supper?'

Serena, nervous as a kitten, was rehearsing her one-woman show in the deserted Las Vegas Showbar, with only a half-cut Maureen as audience.

'And so I decided that the time had come to finish what I'd started. I looked like a woman, I felt like a woman, but I knew that I wasn't a woman. It was a big step to take, but it was right for me. There's a song that meant a lot to me at the time, and I'd like to share it with you now. Maestro, please.'

She trotted to the wings and pressed the play button on her portable stereo. The introduction to 'Natural Woman' filtered through the room as Serena bowed her head, closed her eyes and prepared to give it her all.

Cut to Fat Alice's front room, where the overweight contortionist executed a series of balletic movements to the strains of Def Leppard. She dipped, she pliéd, she lunged. She scooped up two handfuls of her enormous bared stomach, wound them round each other like modelling clay and then, with a jerk of the hips, sent them spinning free while the rest of her trunk wobbled in sympathy. As the music reached its climax she attempted her grand finale, a complex contortion she referred to as 'the last sausage in the shop' which involved putting her knees behind her ears and propelling a cylinder of fat through her thighs. She smiled sweetly, and there was a nasty clicking, stretching noise. The smile froze.

'Could you help me?' she said, straight to camera. 'I think I've injured myself quite badly.'

'Will Alice be fit for tomorrow night's performance? Will Serena get over her rehearsal nerves?' demanded the voice-over, as the shot dissolved to footage of Serena downing a large Southern Comfort at the Las Vegas Showbar.

Debbie Doubledee arranged a surprise press conference on the first morning of the trial. A Kandid crew, of course, was there, getting footage for the closing minutes of the show.

Debbie, in fringed leather jacket, a black stetson, stretch jeans and brown cowboy boots, sashayed into the lobby of myhotel at 11am. Bodhi, in his black Nehru jacket and shades, was at her side.

'Thank you for coming, ladies and gentlemen of the press,' said Bodhi, enjoying the power. 'Miss Doubledee will make a short statement, and then there's time for a few questions. Thank you, Debbie.'

Debbie stood up and smiled. 'Is she anorexic?' scribbled Philip Bray in his notepad – and, indeed, there was a good deal less of Debbie than there used to be.

'Hi everyone, it's great to see so many familiar faces. Hope you've all been enjoying my movies...' She giggled. Many of the assembled hacks were indeed familiar with her work. 'Now, down to business.' She read from a typed sheet. 'It is with great regret that I have to announce that as from today I will no longer be represented by my former managers, Dudley Jenkins and William and Theresa Wicks. Henceforth I will be represented solely by Bodhi Image Enterprises.' She gestured vaguely towards Bodhi, who smiled beatifically. 'They have lined up a number of exciting new projects for me including a meditation video, a self-help book and a lecture tour around the UK. We'll have more details for you in a couple of weeks. Thanks for listening. That's it!'

There was a moment of silence, and then uproar.

'Debbie! Debbie! Does that mean you've given up porn?'

'Debbie, over here! Why have you sacked your own parents? Has there been a big bust-up?'

'Debbie, is he your boyfriend as well as your manager?'

'Debbie, is it true that you'll be giving evidence in the Eddie Kander murder trial?'

'Debbie, can I ask you who does your hair and make-up?'

'Certainly you may,' said Debbie. 'It's all my own work.'

'Any further questions?' said Bodhi, looming threateningly.

'Debbie, are you actually a lesbian?'

'Debbie, are you still using heroin?'

'Debbie, are you aware that your videos are illegal in this country and that anyone caught selling them is liable to a prison sentence?'

'Debbie, what's your favourite thing about Los Angeles?'

'Oh my goodness, I guess the climate and the people,' she said. 'I love the sunshine and the friendly open attitude out there.'

'Debbie, is it true that you're leaving England for good?'

'Debbie, do you know who killed Eddie Kander?'

'And I guess that just about wraps it up, folks. Thanks so much for coming. We'll be seeing ya!' said Bodhi, steering Debbie from the room.

'Obviously, we're gutted,' said Dudley Jenkins, denied entry to the press conference but watching on a monitor in the lobby. 'We made little Debbie into a star and now she's turning her back on us. It's the same old story: Marlene Dietrich, Samantha Fox, Charlotte Church. They've all regretted it. Debbie's been brainwashed. You mark my words'

'Bodhi, is it true that you face extradition to the US?' asked Kandid's on-the-spot reporter as Bodhi and Debbie slammed the doors of their car and zoomed off into the lunchtime traffic.

And that was the end of the episode.

'Don't miss next week's final visit to Elephant and Castle for the sensational conclusion to the trial, and a big night out at the Las Vegas Showbar, here on Channel 6,' said the announcer, before three minutes of top-dollar adverts.

Caroline Wragge sat back with a temporary glow of satisfaction. At least there was one corner of her life that was working. If nothing else, she could say that she had done a bloody good job on the show. Okay, Jamie was running amok, forcing her into the role of procuress – he couldn't even be bothered to go out and get his own tricks any more. Okay, she'd alienated most of her old friends. Her social life revolved around work and work alone. There was no relaxation for Caroline Wragge. This, she thought with grim pleasure, is what success feels like. I work hard all day, I give pleasure to millions, I campaign tirelessly for justice in an unjust world, and I go home alone... She rather liked the image. She even worked up a tiny tear at the corner of one eye.

She picked up the phone and speed-dialled Channel 6.

'Thanks. Yah, I know. A triumph. That's what I think as well. Yes...' She sighed. 'I do my best to please. Okay, just one thing? I want a total reporting black-out on all my stories for the rest of the week, do you understand? That's right: no news coverage on Channel 6, no co-operation with print media, gag them as much as possible. Yah, I do know what I'm doing. You're gonna have to trust me on this one.' She put the phone down, the taste of power like metal in her mouth.

And she was right: a sudden interruption of the hitherto blanket coverage of the Kander murder trial was just enough to send public interest in *Elephant and Castle* into the stratosphere. Starved of their daily fix of salacious details, people started to make special trips to SE1 to sniff around for clues of their own. Spencer Street was barricaded at either end, the residents supplied with Channel 6 laminates to get them in and out of their homes. No additional filming took place: camera crews were concentrated on the Old Bailey and the Las Vegas Showbar. Their footage would make up the whole of the special extended final episode of series two.

The Double Dee applied for and was granted a late licence, and did enough business to soften the blow of William and Theresa's filial desertion. Fat Alice took advantage of the increased human traffic by sitting on her front steps and engaging passers-by in conversation, showing off her injured back (she was strapped into a body brace for a prolapsed disk) and hauling any remotely interested males into the flat to show them more. The Las Vegas Showbar employed extra security to keep the riff-raff away, increased its annual membership to £300 (it had been

£20 before) and watered down the spirits even further.

Only Serena stayed out of the limelight, a prisoner in her own home, unable to walk the streets for fear of recognition. She demanded a car and driver to be on call 24 hours a day; Caroline obliged, knowing that as soon as the final episode was in the bag she would leave Serena to rot. The car sat immobile in Spencer Street for 23 hours out of the 24, accruing a drift of parking tickets and only moving when the clampers (themselves the stars of a fly-on-the-wall documentary series) were out and about.

Far away in Holloway Prison, Shelley Smithers waited out the unforgiving hours alone. The first day of the trial had gone well enough: the charges had been read, she'd pleaded 'not guilty' in tones of quiet dignity, and the prosecuting barrister launched into his case. It seemed cut and dried. The jury nodded approvingly at each veiled racial sneer, each covert homophobic pleasantry. The judge looked bewildered. A courtroom sketch artist rendered Shelley's baseball cap and bomber jacket in telling detail. Would he, she wondered, simply add a touch of blood to her hands and be done with it?

The court adjourned that first day before Shelley was called upon to give evidence. Tomorrow – Friday – the prosecution would conclude his case; it was unlikely that Shelley would do anything but listen until Monday. The judge directed all and sundry to take their time, and looked forward to a forthcoming profile in the *Sunday Telegraph*. If he could spin things out a little longer he might get on to the tv news.

What he heard that day was routine stuff. The body of Eddie Kander, said the police officer under oath, had been found in a black plastic bin liner under the Westway flyover on Wood Lane. There were severe contusions on the head and shoulders, suggesting that he had been beaten repeatedly with a heavy object, probably a plank. Post-mortem examination revealed that he had consumed a large amount of alcohol and cocaine in the hours prior to his death. Supplementary injuries – two broken arms, a broken leg and a ruptured spleen – were thought to be the result of the now-dead body being dropped from the flyover to the road beneath, a fall of some 30 feet. And there was another thing: the pathologist also found evidence of recent sexual activity.

'And so,' said the prosecuting barrister, 'it seems that Mr Kander was approached in one of his regular West End watering holes, rendered insensible with a cocktail of drink and drugs, lured out to a waiting car by a young woman, who distracted him with sexual favours while he was driven to the scene of the crime where he was bludgeoned around the head, stuffed into a bin liner like so much human detritus and flung over the side. I ask you to remember that there was a dustmen's strike in the area at the time, and that his body landed among hundreds of similar bags of rubbish. Such was the killer's contempt for her victim that she simply threw his life away like so much used toilet roll.'

Shelley sat tight and waited for her moment. Tomorrow, she knew, she would be martyred. The interviewing officer had caught her in belligerent mood, and it was all on tape, every last grunt and profanity, for the jury to relish. Prosecution witnesses – the Wickses, Dudley Jenkins, a string of jilted ex-girlfriends – were straining at the leash to assassinate her character. The jury, trained by years of watching television to swallow anything they were told as long as it was expressed with conviction, would believe every word. It didn't matter; that's what Shelley wanted them to do. Already she was looking forward with suppressed excitement to her late guilty plea next week. Perhaps she would go with the flow for another day or two... Monday, Tuesday, then drop the big one on Wednesday. Yes: that would guarantee maximum impact.

Even Shelley Smithers, who professed loathing and contempt for the media, whose very freedom was in the balance, had begun to think like a television producer.

Seven

Let us leave Shelley Smithers to stew in her own bittersweet juices and turn to happier things. At the Las Vegas Showbar the excitement was mounting. Muriel, in anticipation of a full house and over ten million viewers at home, had zhoozhed up the stage with a backdrop of sparkly strips of tinfoil. Hire companies had been raided (and told to invoice Kandid Productions) for supplementary lighting; Muriel was determined that no detail of Friday night's performance would go unnoticed. Upstairs, Maureen instructed the boys to abstain from sexual activity for a minimum of 24 hours before the show, thus ensuring maximum stamina for the increased volume of premium-rate punters. A five-star bill of fare was in preparation for the regular house (and the viewers at home), culminating in the Las Vegas Showbar World Debut of Fat Alice and Serena Ward.

Alice was all readiness; she contacted every agent in town, including a few who specialised in freaks, and invited them to 'my opening'. Miachail Miorphiagh, whose star Alice now threatened to eclipse, was prepared to audition at the drop of a hat. Several of Alice's admirers, who had already enjoyed X-rated previews in the privacy of Warfield Street, had their names on the door for 'comps'. So what if it was Southwark rather than Stratford, cellulite instead of Shakespeare? It was Alice's big night.

She had conveniently forgotten the fact that Serena Ward was going on last, that her own act was merely a grotesque *amuse-gueule* before the main dish. Be that as it may, where Alice was all confidence, Serena was coming unstuck. Dismayed at her utter lack of vocal ability, and the dismal response to rehearsals, Serena had no choice but to buoy her resolve with copious amounts of alcohol. Terrified of the siege around her flat, she spent more and more time in the Las Vegas Showbar, rehearsing and drinking. Maureen and Muriel watched her descent into alcoholism without compassion.

'She can't go on like that,' said Muriel, ensuring that a camera was at hand to catch the exchange. 'She can barely stand.'

'Who cares?' snapped Maureen. 'It's so Neely O'Hara.'

Serena watched her dismal performance in the penultimate episode of the series through a blur of Southern Comfort. She had a little over 24 hours in which to get it right, or she might as well kiss her home, her independence, her self-respect goodbye.

There was time for one more run-through before the theatre opened for business. Alice wobbled and writhed for all she was worth, the flesh cascading over her body-brace like dough through a baker's fingers. Occasionally she screamed in pain, but never stopped smiling.

'You'll do, dear,' said Maureen, as Alice wrapped a dressing gown around herself and joined him in the auditorium. 'Come on, Serena. Try and remember the fucking words this time, dear...'

Serena staggered on to the stage and launched into an a capella rendition of 'Over the Rainbow'.

'Very funny, dear. Save it for Carnegie Hall. Now if you wouldn't mind, take it from the top, just so we can get some vague idea of lighting cues.'

Serena hiccuped and prepared to launch into her autobiography. 'I was born...' The temptation was too great. 'I was booooorn in a trunk in the Princess Theatre in Pocatello Idahoooooooooo...'

'Fuck me,' said Muriel. Maureen rubbed his hands in glee.

Blinded as she was by the stage lights, Serena could dimly discern a familiar figure slouching in the doorway, picked out from the darkness by an occasional glint of chunky gold jewellery.

Jamie.

She had not seen him for weeks, and the knowledge that he was in the club witnessing her disintegration made her stomach turn over. She belched, and clamped a hand over her mouth to contain the flood of sour bile. The euphoria of drunkenness was wiped out by an instant, painful sobriety.

'I'm sorry,' she whispered into the microphone. 'I'll be fine tomorrow. I'll have to call it a day...'

She ran off stage and fled to what Muriel laughingly referred to as her dressing room, a small cupboard that housed the central heating controls.

She sat in front of the mirror propped up on top of the boiler. The room was unbearably hot, the light from a single unshaded bulb harsh and sinister. But at least here she could have a breakdown in private.

She was just at the uncontrollable weeping stage, wondering vaguely if she was going to faint, when the door opened and there he stood. Serena froze in mid sob.

'All right, Serena.'

Her make-up had slid down to her chin in a slick of tears and snot; her eyes were wet and puffy.

'Yes, fine. And you?'

Jamie scowled. 'Yeah.'

Serena took a handful of tissues and repaired herself. 'To what do I owe the pleasure?' she said, suddenly aware that she'd managed to pull one set of false eyelashes off. They lay like a glamorous spider amidst the mucus and foundation of her sodden kleenex.

'I was just passing.'

'It's nice to see you.'

Jamie's frown deepened. Somewhere within that simian psyche there was turmoil.

'Don't get any ideas,' he mumbled. 'It's not like I want to get back together or nothing.'

'Oh, no,' said Serena, brightly. 'Just friends.'

'Yeah. That's right. I've got an image to consider.'

'So, how are things going, Jamie?'

'Good, yeah. I've got a lot of projects in development right now.'

'So I hear. How's the private health club?' Tales had reached Serena's ears of the kind of training that took place amidst the gleaming barbells and leather-cushioned resistance machines.

'Going well, actually.'

'Got a lot of… customers?' She couldn't quite keep the sarcasm out of her voice. Jamie was immediately on the defensive.

'I'm not doing that stuff any more. I'm a professional now.'

'I'm sure you are.'

'Look, Serena, I got nothing to prove to you or to anyone, I'm my own boss, right, and the world's my oyster.'

'So why are you standing there looking like a child that's lost its dummy?'

'I ain't… Fuck off, Serena, you're always nagging at me. Fucking hell, why can't everybody just let me get on with my life without making things so fucking complicated all the time?' Serena sat through this, and five minutes more of the same, with a look of kindly concern. Something was clearly very wrong in Jamie's simple world.

'… when all I want to do is make an honest living and not get dragged into a load of dodgy business with the police.'

There was a pause, filled only by the hum and gurgle of the boiler.

'So, Jamie, what's on your mind?'

She caught and held his gaze. There was pleading in his eyes. Whatever it was he wanted to tell her, it wasn't going to come easily.

'Nothing.'

'Is it Caroline?'

'No, Caroline's great, but...'

'Well if not Caroline, what? Are you in trouble?'

'Give us a chance. Fucking hell, everyone always trying to tell me what to think.' And he was off again on another monologue of unfocused grievances. Give him time...

'... cos in my position I can't afford to get mixed up with any kind of crime, right, I mean I've got an image to protect.'

Crime. Police. A pattern was begin to form in Serena's mind. If only she was a little less fuddled with drink.

'Something's happened, hasn't it, Jamie? Something bad.'

'Yeah, I think it might have done.'

'Is it to do with Eddie?'

'Might be.'

'Do you know something, Jamie?'

'I'm not sure.'

Serena suddenly felt very, very sober. 'Because if you do, you'll have to go to the police right now.'

'I can't do that.'

'Shelley's on trial. She'll get life if they find her guilty.'

'She probably deserves it. I never liked her.'

'She didn't do it, did she?'

'I don't...'

'You know something, don't you? You know something that proves Shelley's innocence.'

'I...'

His brow was furrowed, his hands buried deep in his designer tracksuit pockets. Serena knew from expert knowledge of the type that he was about to make his big confession.

'I...'

Suddenly, the door burst open and there stood Caroline Wragge. She surveyed the scene with a quick, appraising eye. For a moment, the cold-blooded reptile within her peeped out for the world to see. And then in a flash, realising that the worst had not been done, she was all professional bonhomie.

'Jamie! There you are! My two big stars together! Catching up on old times? You look great tonight, Serena, it's going to be a wonderful show. Big opportunity for you. Well we mustn't disturb Serena any longer, James, I'm sure she's got a lot to think about.'

'Serena's all right.'

'I'm sure she is. But we've got work to do, young man! We haven't filmed any of your scenes for the final episode. Don't forget: every commissioning editor in the business will be watching! We don't want to miss our big chance for a daytime presenting job, do we?'

Caroline had somehow interposed herself between the former lovers; now she was edging Jamie out of the door.

'All the best for tomorrow, Serena darling,' she said. 'Try and sleep it off. The camera's not kind to drinkers. Ciao.'

Serena smiled sweetly as the door slammed behind them.

I must speak to him, she thought. More than my personal happiness depends on it.

A big Friday ahead, then, for our fun-loving stars. For Shelley, another day enduring the venom of the prosecution witnesses. For Debbie Doubledee, a round of interviews and castings and an agonising decision over whether or not to present herself as a witness in the Kander case. For Fat Alice, a day spent 'preparing' in the Las Vegas Showbar while the rest of the denizens were asleep. She jumped around, she guzzled high-fat snacks and occasionally, when she was sure of being unobserved, she made certain discreet adjustments to the stage arrangements... And for Serena, struggling through her Southern Comfort hangover, the twin horrors of performing in the Las Vegas Showbar and somehow confronting Jamie over his clumsy dressing-room revelations of the night before. And while these life-or-death issues were being resolved, Caroline Wragge finalised the details of what she hoped – knew – would be the highlight of her career to date.

Short of placing Jamie under house arrest (which she considered), the most effective way of ensuring his silence was to keep him busy. To that end she biked five grams of top quality cocaine round to the flat, fixed a lunch date with two young female hopefuls who would keep him occupied well into the weekend, then arranged a 'fashion shoot' with a rising young photographer well known for persuading his subjects (all of them athletic males) into revealing their all. Fuel Jamie's narcissism, his libido and his drug habit, and he was sweet as pie. That sad sack Serena wouldn't get a look in.

Next she swamped the streets of SE1 with camera crews to whip up a frenzy of anticipation about the show. The resulting footage ('Yeah, I think it's great that we're on the telly', 'Who?' and 'Get that camera out of my face, bitch') was mostly unusable, but it had the desired effect of causing a crowd to collect outside the Las Vegas Showbar by tea time. Deliberately enraged by maverick security staff (a group of young Kosovar refugees whom Caroline found hanging around in the park), the crowd turned, blocked the traffic and ensured coverage on the nine o'clock news. 'And finally, mob scenes on a scale not witnessed since the height of Beatlemania greeted the stage debut tonight of Serena Ward, star of tv docusoap *Elephant and Castle...*' Fat Alice, watching in her dressing room, went immediately into a huff and would have spoken harshly to her manager, if she'd had one.

At ten o'clock, the doors opened. The revellers were greeted by scantily-clad showboys who hung around the lobby ungraciously handing out drinks. From within the venue came the strains of Muriel's favourite records, a selection of Broadway classics interspersed with his own unforgettable rendition of 'I Am What I Am'. Lifesize cardboard cut-outs of Fat Alice, Serena, Debbie and Jamie added a touch of the surreal. Caroline, who had just heard from her team at the Old Bailey that the prosecution case appeared water-tight, sat in the office and clinked glasses with Maureen.

'A pleasure doing business with you, I'm sure,' said the fat old queen, unnerved by Caroline's generosity in the gin department.

'Tonight,' said Caroline, drinking deeply, 'we walk into the history books. And the beauty of it is...' she smacked her lips and put her feet on the desk, 'nothing can go wrong.'

In her dressing room, Serena was sweating and heaving, pale as dough under her make-up, her eyes bloodshot from a sleepless night. In less than an hour she would be on stage, exposed to final humiliation, living out a nightmare that had plagued her since childhood of appearing in public without knowing her lines, without clothes. But what else could she do? At least if she showed her tits she'd get paid, she'd keep the flat... And then she had to get to Jamie. Repeated calls to his mobile phone yielded nothing: she had no option but to slip away after the show and find him.

The hubbub in the lobby subsided, and to her horror Serena heard the first bars of Fat Alice's overture, 'Don't Want to Bump No More with No Big Fat Woman'. She closed her eyes and held her hands above her head, hoping to regain some of the composure that, in happier days, made her such a killer in the boardroom. But now all she could see were swirling, exploding balls of colour. Her hands, drained of blood, began to buzz with pins and needles. She doubled up and retched drily into the bin. She tried to remember a few words of her carefully-prepared monologue, but all that came were fragments, jokes without punchlines, punchlines without jokes... 'And ever since then I've taken a keen interest in football...' 'And let me tell you, there's more than one Queen in Buckingham Palace...' '...because at the end of the day, a married man's got more than one ring...' She stared into the mirror in a paroxysm of self-disgust. Better, surely, to flee now, to lose everything and start again in a new place where nobody knew her. Or if that failed, to die.

A tap on the door recalled her to the degradation of her situation.

'What?'

'Can I come in?'

The door inched open. Jamie again, and the sound of Fat Alice's act in full swing.

'You haven't come to wish me good luck, I suppose.'

'Serena, I've got to talk to you.'

'Shut the door then.'

'I shouldn't be here.'

'She got you under observation, then?'

'Might as well. Had to do a bit of duckin' and divin'.'

'So, what's the big emergency? Caroline not giving you what you want in the downstairs department?'

'No. I mean yes. As a matter of fact I turned down a very tasty proposition to come and see you tonight.'

'Flattered, I'm sure.'

'There you go, nag nag nag again.'

'Jamie, I am going on stage in ten minutes to destroy the last tiny fragments of my self-respect. If you've come here to rub my nose in it, I assure you it's far too late. So if you've nothing else to say, please leave.'

'But I have, Serena. You've got to listen to me.'

Feet sounded in the corridor outside; both held their breath. The footsteps passed.

'Is Caroline here?'

'Of course she is, Jamie. This is her big night. We all jump through her hoops tonight, don't we.'

'She mustn't know I'm seeing you.'

'All this secrecy. It's terribly exciting, of course, but I really have other things on my mind.'

'Serena...' She could see that the climax had arrived.

'Go on. I'm listening.'

'It's just that... I heard Caroline talking to someone... about –'

A deafening cheer resounded down the corridors, followed by scream, a crunch and a roar of applause.

'Sounds like Fat Alice is going down well.'

'Yeah. But listen...'

'Oh my God, please hurry up.'

'She was talking to someone on the phone, about –'

Suddenly, a bang on the door.

'Serena!' It was Muriel's voice.

'Oh Christ!' said Jamie. 'You've got to hide me!'

'Quick. In the mop cupboard. Hello! Who is it!'

'You've got to get out there now, right now, darling.'

'I'm not on for ten minutes.'

The door flew open and there stood Muriel, his wig awry, blood dripping from his arm.

'What happened to you?'

'The silly bitch destroyed my stage and brought the DJ booth crashing into the first few rows of the audience.'

'Is everyone okay?'

'I don't fucking know, dear. There's a riot going on. The fat cow is buried underneath a pile of timber. Now get out there and save the show. I beg you.'

'Well, I never thought the day would come. I shall be delighted, Muriel, to do what little I can to salvage your reputation. Leave everything entirely to me.' And, ushering Muriel ahead of her, she swept towards her debut.

The auditorium, as Muriel foretold, was in pandemonium. Injured punters were crawling from beneath shattered tables; blood mingled with red wine on the carpets. Fat Alice's naked, dimpled leg protruded from beneath a twisted scaffolding pole. Those untouched by the disaster were making for the doors, their exit blocked by the Kosovar security boys posted by Caroline to ensure that nobody left before the show was over. Panic was rising – and the cameras captured every detail.

Serena stepped on to the stage and surveyed the wreckage. Well, she thought, this time you really brought the house down.

'Ladies and gentlemen,' she improvised, 'I was going to tell you the story of my life this evening, interspersed with jokes and songs, but under the circumstances I hardly think that would be appropriate. And so instead, if I could just have a moment's hush... thank you so much... instead, I'd just like to dedicate one song to a dear friend of ours, currently on trial for a crime that I know, and one or two of you out there know, that she did not commit. Shelley, this one's for you.'

Serena was about to launch into an *a cappella* rendition of 'I Shall Be Released' when she caught sight of Caroline Wragge, hair awry and sleeves rolled up, whispering into the ear of a particularly fit looking security guard. She drew breath to sing the first note, and saw him hurtling down the room towards her. She froze.

A split second before he leapt across the mêlée of broken furniture and injured punters, Serena felt strong arms around her waist propelling her to the wings. The security guard caught air and landed with a thud, bringing yet more heavy timber down on top of Fat Alice, pinioned but still conscious beneath.

As Jamie carried Serena through the maze of tunnels to the goods entrance at the back of the Las Vegas Showbar, the police arrived at the front.

A cursory inspection of the disaster scene revealed that the scaffolding supporting the stage had been loosened, and the main wooden supports sawed through.

Sabotage!

But who would do such a thing?

Emerging at the top of Walworth Road, out of sight of the still-milling crowds, Jamie flagged down a cab.

'Where to, guv?'

'Soho.'

'Traffic's terrible. I'll have to go backroads.'

'Don't worry,' said Jamie, 'I've got the money.'

''Ere,' said the driver, looking in his rear-view mirror, 'you're them off the telly, ain't you?'

'No. Just drive.'

Serena, freezing cold in her tiny sequinned dress, huddled close to Jamie in the back of the vehicle. He opened his tracksuit top, pulled her against him and warmed her chilled shoulders against his torso.

'Where are we going?'

'The flat. We've got to pick up the money before she gets there.'

'Money...?'

'I've got a bit put by. We'll need it. We're going on the run.'

'Jamie,' said Serena through still-chattering teeth, 'you're full of surprises. You're so... organised.'

'Once a soldier always a soldier,' he said, flexing a bicep.

The cab driver, conscious that his fare was too engrossed to notice, took the most expensively circuitous route he could think of, arriving in D'Arblay Street nearly 40 minutes (and £30) later. Serena could not help goggling when Jamie peeled three tenners off a fat wad of bills in an engraved silver clip. If he had this kind of money...

We will not eavesdrop on the conversation that took place in the flat. Suffice to say that the lovers resumed tender relations, and that Jamie told Serena all he knew about Caroline's involvement with Daryn Handy and the killing of Eddie Kander.

'Where to now?' she asked when they emerged into the Soho night, carrying a few changes of clothes and every last coin or credit card that Jamie could lay his hands on.

'Dunno. We've got to get away from here. She'll turn up any minute. Any suggestions?'

'Yes. Philip Bray. He'll know what to do.'

'That scumbag?' Jamie had still not fully forgiven Philip for running out on his 'massage'.

'It's either him or the police.'

They exchanged a look, pondered, then shook their heads in unison.

'Philip Bray it is, then,' said Serena. 'The *Beacon's* offices are in Holborn. Come on, we can walk. Save our resources.'

'I'm loaded, Serena. Honestly.'

'My darling boy,' said Serena, squeezing Jamie's arm, 'if only you knew how happy I am to hear that...'

And so, for the weekend, animation was suspended. Shelley rested in her cell, having heard herself described as 'a textbook psychopath' by a doctor she had never met before, and 'a dirty black dyke' by a former girlfriend (now on the Kandid payroll, although the court didn't know that). Witnesses had claimed under oath that she was at the scene of the crime. Her own confession, which she planned for Monday, would surprise nobody.

Jamie and Serena holed up chez Philip Bray and planned their strategy, while Mrs Bray provided hearty meals and endless pots of tea.

Caroline Wragge sat with her head in her hands for the best part of 48 hours, wondering whether the editor existed who could get her out of this one smelling of roses.

Debbie Doubledee decided, or rather Bodhi decided on her behalf, that it would be better not to get involved in the Smithers/Kander case, but to concentrate instead on promoting her as-yet-unmade meditation video.

Maureen and Muriel spent the weekend frightening the life out of a young investigator from the insurance company, and on Sunday evening celebrated what they were certain would be an enormous pay-out with a small supper party for friends at the bijou lattie.

Fat Alice lay in a hospital bed, a variety of metal pins holding her shattered limbs together, and spoke to invited press about her plans for a comeback. 'I've already been offered a recording contract,' she lied, but the news spread quickly and soon she found herself the object of a bidding war between rival labels. A police officer asked her if she had any enemies who might have sabotaged the stage. Alice had no idea. 'I suppose some people are jealous of my success,' she sighed, confident that she'd disposed safely of the hacksaw and monkey wrench with which she made those near-fatal adjustments.

Part Four

The Difficult Third Series

One

The show took its summer break after a final episode that sent viewing figures over 15 million and drew an avalanche of complaints the like of which Channel 6 had never seen before. The closing images – Shelley's impassive face as the judge handed down a sentence of life imprisonment, Fat Alice gurning and waving from a hospital trolley as she was wheeled into theatre – were grotesque and unforgettable. The controller of Channel 6 faced an official enquiry, while Caroline Wragge checked into a private health club for an extended stay. Whatever their private misfortunes, both basked in the glow that only a ratings smash can give.

But Fate is a capricious mistress, and it was just at the height of its fortunes that *Elephant and Castle* took a nosedive. With the defection of Serena and Jamie, and the heavy censure attracted by Fat Alice's galloping Munchausen's syndrome, the series was left without storylines. Debbie Doubledee got her own self-help show on cable, and was tied up in a contract that prevented any further appearances in the programme that made her famous. Daryn languished in prison, fretting at the delay in his own tv vehicle, a fiction that Caroline could barely be bothered to maintain. Of the original stars that left only Maureen and Muriel still able and willing to appear. But even Channel 6 recognised that a series based entirely around transvestism and male prostitution had little chance of mainstream appeal.

But, as Caroline told the controller the week after she checked out of the health farm, the Elephant and Castle was an area with a population of approximately 500,000, among whom there must be at least a handful of presentable characters. Unfortunately, nobody could be bothered to go through the gruesome preliminaries of sourcing them – that would mean talking to real people, something that Caroline had long ago forsworn. Thus the only option left was to buy in new talent.

Barry Llannelly, after a summer of intense media speculation, agreed to leave the rural charms of *Police Vet* for the dubious delights of the metropolis. He would move into a flat in Beckford House (vacated by the late Peggy Renders) and would adopt bereaved terrier Sid, a ploy guaranteed to win audience sympathy. (His cat, Cher, was less happy with the arrangement.) Working on the principle that familiarity breeds success, Caroline also drafted Dave 'Missed It!' Merryweather and Doreen 'Dirty Bitches!' Dawson, if only to put an end to their constant begging phonecalls. And in a desperate bid to attract female viewers, she cast the permanently available Miachail Miorphiagh as a new doctor at the local practice, despite the fact that his only medical qualification was regular attendance at the GUM clinic.

'Then half-way through the series we're going to introduce a new boy band that we'll recruit from the estates, they'll be very real, with problems and lives of their own, none of them over 18, and by the end of the series we're guaranteed a recording contract, such is the power of the brand,' waffled Caroline over an expensive expenses lunch. 'Then of course I've got the ace up my sleeve that I was telling you about earlier...'

'What exactly is that, Caroline?' asked the controller.

'Shh,' said Caroline. 'Least said soonest mended. Walls have ears.' She cocked an eyebrow towards a bored waiter who, had he known whom he was serving, would have been auditioning for all he was worth.

'The trouble with your characters, Caroline, and I'm not saying this as a criticism of the show but merely as an observation, is that we can never sympathise with them.'

'So why do millions tune in every week?'

'They love to watch disasters.'

'So? It works.'

'But what I'd really like, if I dare suggest it, to take *Elephant and Castle* forward as a brand and assure its longevity, is some characters that we can really get to know as people, rather than the two-dimensional freaks that we've had so far. We want warm, human people with lives and aspirations just like ours.'

'Yah, I hear what you're saying, but if you want nice people you're going to have to commission a new series set north of the river, say in Highgate or Fulham or somewhere.'

'But surely your research has found some nice people in SE1. Everyone you show is selfish, greedy, or mentally ill. Where are the decent, ordinary folk?'

'I've yet to meet them,' spat Caroline, washing her mouth out with mineral water.

'I don't think you have a very deep understanding of human nature, Caroline, and that limits the scope of your work.'

'Oh fuck off and pay the bill,' said Caroline. 'I've got work to do.'

This was a mistake. The controller of Channel 6 didn't like being told to fuck off by a woman so entirely in his debt. At that moment he determined in his meek, nervous heart to destroy *Elephant and Castle*.

This, however, was a process that needed little outside encouragement. Caroline's essential laziness had brought to the show a handful of profoundly unstable new stars, lunatics who made the previous incumbents look like model citizens in comparison. As Nicko brought in less and less useable footage, Caroline was obliged to bank all her hopes on that ace up her sleeve – Daryn Handy's on-video confession. But that was one ace she may not be allowed to play. Legal advisors revealed that her failure to produce the evidence during the Shelley Smithers trial rendered Caroline herself guilty of perverting the course of justice, and liable to a criminal prosecution. Thus she was faced with a stark choice of saving her show, or saving her skin. Naturally, she chose the latter option, and began to look for ways of wriggling out of *Elephant and Castle* before it collapsed around her.

The controller of Channel 6, hearing from his spies that *Elephant and Castle* was in trouble, initiated a course of action that he privately referred to as 'death by a thousand cuts'. He bombarded Caroline with petty, irritating memos, guaranteed to waste her time and further sabotage the series. 'Government directives on metrocentricity in the media demand that we change the name of the show from *Elephant and Castle* to *"London's Elephant and Castle"*. Suggest you produce new title sequence to reflect this,' ran the most effective of these irritants. 'New guidelines on institutionalised racism in broadcasting necessitates a 25% quota of non-white characters across all our output. Please action immediately,' ran another. Caroline delegated these tasks to a newly-employed executive producer (her brother again) and set about a punishing round of meetings with commissioning editors outside Channel 6 whom she tried to interest in 'a raft of exciting new projects currently in development' by her brand new independent production company, WraggeTime Television. Astonishingly, her pitch for a major new 13-part adaptation of Anthony Trollope's *Barsetshire Chronicles* (all of them) was green-lit by the BBC.

The third series of *Elephant and Castle*, sorry, *London's Elephant and Castle*, was a damp squib. The critics were keen to find fault: it had been far too successful to date, and they wanted to flex their muscle. They didn't have to look too far for holes to pick. After a flurry of pre-publicity promising exciting new storylines, the biggest drama was a scrap between Sid the dog and Cher the cat. Doreen Dawson waxed philosophical over her new washer-drier, and Dave Merryweather made a fruitless trip to the shopping centre in search of a pair of socks.

Serena and Jamie, watching at home, indulged themselves in a little gloating. 'We're well out of it,' said Jamie, snuggling up to his beloved on the couch. It was the only piece of furniture they had left in the front room – everything else had been sold to pacify creditors. But they had done it, reflected Serena with satisfaction. They'd swallowed their pride, soldiered on at the Las Vegas Showbar, suffered every fresh humiliation with a stoic smile and survived with a roof over their heads and a new sense of commitment. Jamie, cut off from the Kandid purse-strings, had no option but to beg Maureen and Muriel for a job; the money that he'd taken from his former protector just about paid off Serena's mortgage arrears. Maureen, ever on the look out for an opportunity to cut people down to size, vada'd him with a frosty eye. 'Well obviously, dear, you're too old and knackered to work upstairs. But I expect we could find a space for you behind the bar, where the lights aren't too bright. A bit like you, dear.' Jamie, trained by Serena in the practice of humility, said 'thank you' and walked away.

And so they scraped a living, counting every penny, scrounging food from the club's kitchens when they could, hanging around Tesco for the barcode-cancelled goods when they couldn't. Serena's ambitious plans for a one-woman show had been whittled down to a couple of stripping spots a night; her singing was actually driving audiences away. And so she came on as a shoulder-padded executive bitch with briefcase and chignon, stripped down to lacy bra, stockings and suspender belt, writhed around a little before treating audiences to a quick flash of her primary and secondary sexual characteristics.

But why were our young lovers not living in the lap of luxury, knowing as they did a vital piece of information that could, if dropped in the right ear, send Caroline Wragge to prison and restore Shelley Smithers's freedom? What had happened that fateful night when they fled the Las Vegas Showbar to seek advice from immoral journalist Philip Bray? Surely he had not counselled discretion?

Au contraire: Bray, given the merest hint that there had been a miscarriage of justice, was in favour of full, immediate disclosure – exclusively in *The Daily Beacon*, of course. Serena was on the brink of spilling the beans when she saw something she didn't like in Bray's eyes.

'Come on then, what is it that you know?' he asked.

'Oh... well, I was speaking hypothetically.'

'You came round here in the middle of the night to discuss a hypothetical miscarriage of justice?'

'Call it a woman's whim.'

Jamie was puzzled. 'Serena...'

'Come on, Serena,' said Bray, hoping to browbeat her into a full confession. 'Tell me everything you know.'

'I was merely interested in how you would react.'

'You know something. I've known for a long time that you know something. Why are you holding back? Why are you letting Shelley Smithers rot in a prison cell, another black victim of the white legal system, when a word from you could set her free?'

'And you're the one to make it happen, are you, Philip?'

'I could be. Can you think of anyone in a better position? I have a certain amount of clout, you know.'

'Oh yes. And you'd use it too, I don't doubt. And you wouldn't be too fussy about who got hurt along the way.'

'I'd protect my sources, if that's what you mean.'

'But something just occurred to me.'

'What?'

'If I knew something that would be advantageous to you, Philip, as a journalist, you'd use that information in your newspaper. And if that report suggested that a certain person, we won't say who, was a liar or worse, then you'd be liable for legal action. And in that case, you'd have to substantiate your claims, because there's no libel if you can prove that your information is true. Isn't that correct?'

Curses, thought Philip. Where did she get all this information from?

'And of course justification is an absolute defence in defamation cases. I didn't work in an advertising agency for all those years without learning a little bit about media law. I may have been brought pretty low by circumstances...' Serena noticed to her delight that Philip could not look her in the eye. 'But I was not always as I am now.'

'Serena,' said Philip, in desperation, 'it's your duty as a citizen.'

'I suddenly have a much clearer idea of my duty. I have you to thank for that. Sorry for disturbing you so late at night. Please convey my apologies to Mrs Bray. Goodbye now.'

Walking back towards Elephant and Castle, Jamie bombarded Serena with questions.

'Why aren't we fighting the bitch at her own game? If we threaten to expose the fact that Caroline knew all along who killed Eddie Kander, then she'll do anything to shut us up.'

'But that's blackmail, Jamie.'

'Yeah, so what? It's a dog eat dog world out there.'

'It doesn't have to be that way.'

'But Shelley's going to prison for a crime she didn't commit.'

'And if we allow Philip Bray to run the story in the *Beacon*, we'll end up in prison too.'

'Why? We ain't done nothing.'

'But that's just it, Jamie. We have. We're as guilty as Caroline.'

'Bollocks! She set up the hit.'

'And we witheld evidence.'

'What do you mean?'

'You've known for a long time that Caroline had something to do with Eddie's death, haven't you? And you made sure that she paid for your silence. That's not going to look too good in court, is it? And I assure you that's where we'll end up if we let the *Beacon* expose her.'

'But that's stupid, we're on the right side.'

'It's too late for that now, Jamie. We've made our mistakes.'

Jamie was lost awhile in thought. 'No, Serena, that's not true. It's me that made the mistakes. You never knew about it. I did. I should have gone to the police. I kept the information and I used it to my own ends. That was wrong.' Serena was astonished at this rare display of sequential logic. 'You've only just found out,' Jamie continued. 'You could make a clean breast of it and Shelley would get off and the people that done wrong would get punished.'

'And I know what that would mean for me.'

'Yeah. You'd be a hero and everyone would love you and you could be rich and famous again.'

'No, Jamie. All that it would mean for me is that I'd lose you again. And I don't want to do that.'

'What, you mean you'd sacrifice all that for me?'

Where is he learning these words, wondered Serena.

'Yes. I would.' She squeezed his arm. 'We got into this mess together, and that's how we're going to get out of it.'

'Fuck me.' Jamie's burst of articulacy was over. They retired to Spencer Street, disconnected the doorbell and telephone and spent the rest of the night making love.

Serena Ward, unlike everyone else in this story, had learned from her mistakes. Rather than dive headlong into the obvious course of action, she reflected at the critical moment and saw the primrose path to perdition stretching before her. The alternative route was narrow and rocky indeed, but it was by this unpopulated thoroughfare that she and Jamie would travel towards their happy ending. Had the controller of Channel 6 only known that there lurked this spark of decent feeling in the hitherto benighted breasts of his former stars he might have done something to save *London's Elephant and Castle*. As it was he allowed it to languish, pushing it later and later in the schedules as the viewing figures dropped off. Into its prime-time place he boldly scheduled *Kill Me Slowly* (the expensive drama series, the reader will remember, which had been gathering dust on the shelves for a couple of years) and pronounced himself 'perfectly satisfied' with the 1.4 million audience. Like all his colleagues at Channel 6, he felt happier with failure and mediocrity.

And so our two heroes ride towards an unlikely sunset. But not, surely, at the expense of Shelley Smithers's freedom? Could Serena ever be happy knowing that an innocent woman was banged up for a crime that she did not commit and of which she, Serena, was easily capable of exonerating her?

No.

After that crucial conference chez Bray, Serena wrote to Shelley in prison and announced that she had information that could set her free. Shelley wrote back in despondent mood: 'It's all my fault what happened to Debbie,' she whinged, 'and I deserve to be punished for it.'

This was not enough for Serena, who had watched Debbie's second career as fitness and lifestyle guru blossom and grow over the summer. The publication of her book (*Body and Soul: A Woman's Guide to Growth*) was accompanied by hysterical newspaper coverage, culminating in a five-page feature in one of the Sunday supplements headlined 'Men, Madness, Money, Marriage, Mammaries and Me by tv's Debbie'. Debbie appeared on every chat show available, glossing over her porno past, her parents, her drug problems, talking only about her new-found inner peace. As far as Serena could see, Debbie was having the time of her life, and she told Shelley as much in her next letter.

Eventually, her lacerating guilt allayed, Shelley realised that being in prison was never going to reconcile her with her beloved, and so she informed Serena that anything that could be done to free her would be very welcome.

And so Serena's pet project was green lit. Now all she needed was a broadcaster.

Caroline Wragge, unlike her arch rival Serena, never learned from her mistakes, and decided that *London's Elephant and Castle* was now so nearly extinct that she could afford to concentrate on other things. But this particular old pachyderm still had some teeth left, and just when Caroline wasn't looking rallied itself one last time to give her an almighty bite on the backside.

Nicko McVitie had been left with the thankless task of providing Channel 6 with the requisite 50 minutes of footage to fill the show's late night slot (by the fourth week of the third series it was going out at 0030). Nobody cared much what he filed, as long as it was neither libellous nor obscene, and so Nicko allowed Barry Llannelly, Dave Merryweather, Doreen Dawson and Miachail Miorphiagh to make public fools of themselves with precious little editorial intervention. The cameraman was bored, however; he looked back to the glory days of bugging Debbie's bedroom, of staking out Spencer Street to catch Serena and Jamie in the act, and he writhed in frustration. He spent hours every day on his mobile, trying to rustle up more work, but with his contractual commitments to Kandid he was unable to take up any offers until at least April.

And thus he was a sitting target for wily Serena. She remembered all too well the lascivious glances that he had cast at her décolletage in earlier days, and knew from a life-long study of the type that burly, tattooed Nicko would like nothing better than to be seduced by a sexually aggressive (and possibly ex-male) woman. Nicko was the conduit whereby Serena would bring justice to her little world – and thus it was to Nicko that she addressed herself one slow Thursday afternoon.

Nicko was filming Barry Llannelly's in-store appearance at a newly-opened local pet shop, where he cut the ribbon and cuddled a few rabbits while a handful of elderly shoppers shuffled around the expensive aquaria. So bored was Nicko that he was on the verge of accepting Barry's repeated offer of 'a nosh in the bogs' when to his astonishment he saw Serena walking into the shop.

She was looking good in her 80s power-dressing outfit; Nicko knew, from his frequent freetime visits to the Showbar, that this was her stripping gear. His mouth went instantly dry.

'And so ladies and gentlemen I welcome you all to Fur, Fins and Feathers pet supplies,' shrilled Barry, each sibilant and frictive driving Nicko's indicators into the red. 'Please feel free to look around and enjoy yourselves!' He caught sight of Serena, statuesque in the doorway. 'What's she doing here?' he hissed at Nicko. 'Stop the camera! This is my show now, not hers!'

But Nicko wasn't listening. Mesmerised by Serena's smoky gaze, he followed her out of the shop.

'Nicko, darling,' she said, licking her lips and half closing her eyes, 'it's good to see you.'

'Yeah... right, you too Serena, you're looking great. Love the show, by the way.'

'Oh, that. Well, if it gives you pleasure that makes me happy. So, how's the old series going? You're doing a terrific job...'

Five more minutes and Nicko had agreed to meet Serena and Jamie at Spencer Street the following morning.

'And you needn't tell Caroline anything about this, nor those awful people at Channel 6.'

'No way. Like you said, it's our secret. Thanks, Serena.'

'Are you coming to the club tonight?'

'Well, I'm supposed to be filming with that poof. Sorry, no offence.'

'None taken. Shame. I was going to do a rather special show if I'd known you were going to be there...'

'I'll be there.'

*

When she was interviewed in future years about her extraordinary career in television, perhaps on the occasion of one of the many awards that Bafta or the Royal Television Society would bestow upon her, Caroline Wragge took credit for the extraordinary turn-around of *London's Elephant and Castle* in its third series. 'Yah, I'd been shafted by the suits at Channel 6 who were basically very suspicious of women in the industry in those days, and who were racist and homophobic to boot, hence their willingness to let Shelley Smithers stay in prison for a crime she didn't commit, and their insistence on dropping Serena Ward from the show. But that wasn't good enough for me, and I fought back...'

The truth, of course, was the exact opposite. Caroline washed her hands of the whole business and concentrated on pre-production of *Anthony Trollope's Barsetshire Chronicles*. So, *London's Elephant and Castle* would be pulled before the end of the series; it didn't matter to her. She already had a new job.

But she had reckoned without the independent action of a handful of former employees. Nicko McVitie reported to 1 Spencer Street on the Friday morning, around 15 hours before transmission of the fifth episode. He was shown into the garden by Jamie, where he found Serena looking lovely in a pale blue suit, one of the few vestiges of her respectable wardrobe. It was a mild October morning; the last blooms still glowed on Serena's climbing roses.

'Hello, everyone,' said Serena to camera. 'You might remember us. We were the stars of the last series of *Elephant and Castle*. My name is Serena Ward and this is my partner, Jamie Lord. We've got something to tell you...'

At 0045 the following morning, when this section of the show was broadcast, telephones started ringing all over the country.

Five minutes later, after another dreary interlude in Doreen Dawson's utilities room, Serena and Jamie were back on the screen.

'You will recall that during the last series, Shelley Smithers was found guilty of the murder of Eddie Kander. Well we happen to know that she didn't do it, and we're going to tell you in a moment just who did.'

A few hundred viewers, awoken from sleep by friends who said 'You have GOT to turn on Channel 6 RIGHT NOW!' picked up the phone and did the same to a few thousand more.

Miachail Miorphiagh welcomed Dave Merryweather to his surgery, where they had some amusing banter about Dave's 'Emma Freuds'.

Then Serena was back. The viewing figures, unbeknown to the skeletal night staff at Channel 6, had just crept over a million.

'Eddie Kander was killed by a professional hit man. We don't know the identity of the actual killer, but we know who hired him. Don't go away, because we're going to tell you.'

For the next 20 minutes there was a hastily-assembled sequence of highlights from the first two series, leading up to the death of Eddie Kander. The million and a half... two million viewers were gripped by the biggest whodunnit of television history.

And then Serena was back.

'If there are any journalists watching, please make sure that this story is covered in your papers tomorrow. If there's anyone from the legal profession out there, perhaps you would like to offer your services to Ms Shelley Smithers, currently three months into a life sentence that she should never have started. Because she didn't kill Eddie Kander.'

A series of elaborate tappings on prison pipes alerted inmates to the fact that something strange was going on. Daryn Handy was roused from dreams of tv glory, bundled out of his cell by the guard and ushered without ceremony into the governor's office. He arrived just in time.

'...because she didn't kill Eddie Kander,' he heard Serena say.

'Oh yes, my beauty. You tell them. At last! At last!' Daryn clenched his fists above his head and fell to his knees in triumph.

'The real murderer, the person who hired the hit man, used to be my next door neighbour, until he was taken away for drug-related offences,' said Serena.

'I fucking told you so, you bastards!' whooped Daryn, already looking forward to a lifetime of regular oral pleasure and free cigarettes.

'His son has since been taken into care. His name...'

Serena paused, licked her lips and allowed herself the ghost of a smile.

'His name is Daryn Handy.'

As the viewing figures tipped over 2.5 million and the Channel 6 switchboard was jammed, the duty officer put in a call to Caroline Wragge.

'She can't prove a thing,' Caroline told anyone who asked, secure in the knowledge that Daryn's taped confession was locked away in her safe. But who is this shadowy figure breaking into Caroline's office late one night, guided only by the frail beams of a torch? None other than Nicko McVitie who, acting under orders, has stolen the tape and delivered it into the hands of Serena Ward.

Two

Things moved swiftly after Serena's on-screen denunciation.

Daryn Handy was transferred to a high-security wing pending trial for the murder of Eddie Kander; never, during all his conferences with solicitor or counsel, did he mention the involvement of Caroline Wragge in organising the hit. He wanted all the glory for himself.

Caroline, although she was on the brink of mental collapse throughout the trial, grabbed the publicity and ran with it. Channel 6 pulled the show forward to an 11pm slot, where it continued to do brisk trade with the back-from-the-pub crowd. With a hit on her hands rather than an embarrassing flop that she was eager to disown, Caroline's bargaining power was increased tenfold, and she found that the commissioning process for *Anthony Trollope's Barsetshire Chronicles* was greatly accelerated. At this rate, she thought, I'm actually going to have to read the books. Or at least get someone to read them for me.

Shelley, buoyed up by the fame that greeted her release from prison, took to the talk-show circuit with a vengeance, telling anyone who would listen her theories about the British media and its treatment of minorities. Inevitably, after a couple of months, she encountered Debbie. Their paths crossed in the green room at

Channel House, the irony of which was lost on neither of them, and Shelley was immediately shocked to see how thin her friend was looking.

'Hi Shelley!' said Debbie in an expressionless voice, as if they had spoken only the day before. 'How's it going?'

I went to prison for you, thought Shelley. I sacrificed my freedom, and all you can say is 'how's it going?'.

'Fine, thanks,' she said. 'And you?'

Debbie grinned; her lips looked too big for her face. 'Yeah, it's good, really good. Really, really good.' A waitress hovered with a tray of canapes. Debbie turned her back. Shelley was shocked to see, in the crook of Debbie's arm, an area of bruised, purplish flesh.

'So what have they got you on for?'

'Oh, we're promoting my new relaxation tape. It's great, you should try it if you feel stressed out. I listen to it every night. It helps me to sleep.'

'Thanks, but I sleep pretty soundly since I got out of prison.' Shelley thought it was time Debbie acknowledged her stretch inside.

'Well, it's great to see you.' Debbie was glancing nervously to the side of the room where Bodhi lurked. 'I'd better go and... er... get ready.'

'But you are ready.'

'I've got to do my meditation before I go on.'

'Can I meet you some time, Debbie?'

'Lovely to bump into you.' Debbie's voice was too loud.

'What's the matter?'

'I'll call you,' Debbie whispered, and tottered off towards her ponytailed Svengali.

A couple of days later, when Shelley got home tired after a conference on ethnic minorities and the legal system, she found a message on her anwering service.

'Shelley, it's Debbie,' said the whispered voice. 'I must see you. Tomorrow evening, six o'clock, usual place.'

The months rolled back, and Shelley was an excited schoolgirl once again, looking forward to a tryst at the 'usual place' – the waste ground behind the sports hall at St Agatha's.

It was a pleasant spring evening towards the end of the third series when Shelley strolled up the old familiar streets towards her alma mater. There were the railings, just as she remembered them, with razor wire along the top to keep the perverts out. There was the old school sign, the revised motto 'Condemning Girls to Failure' unaltered still. She squeezed through a gap in the fence that had been conveniently opened up by those very perverts, and skirted the playground with her hands buried deep in her bomber-jacket pockets, her baseball cap pulled low over her eyes. The playground was deserted save for a couple of hard-faced teenagers smoking something by a tree.

But who was that haggard figure hiding in a corner, her tan leather aviator jacket picking up dirt and moss from the crumbling brick wall? Teachers and students from former days might not have recognised her, but Shelley saw through the dark glasses, the stetson covering the bleached tresses.

'Debbie!' She ran towards her.

Debbie jumped, and looked nervously from side to side.

'Shhh! Not so loud!'

'There's nobody here, Debbie. What are you so frightened of?'

'I'm not supposed to be seeing you...' Debbie took her sunglasses off. Around her eyes, devoid of make-up, were the vestiges of two real shiners.

'Did he do that to you?'

'What? Oh, that. No, I walked into a camera.'

'Yeah, right, and I'm Naomi Campbell. I saw other bruises on your body, Debbie. I'm not stupid. He hits you, doesn't he.'

'Don't say that.'

'What else is going on that I don't know about?'

'It's really none of your business.'

'Why not? What's he done to you, Debbie? You look ill. Are you on drugs again?'

'Hah!' For once, Debbie's face relaxed into a genuine smile. 'You're the last person to be lecturing me about that, aren't you?'

'I know, I know, but I worry about you. You should never have gone off and left me, Debs.'

'Left you? It was you, I seem to remember, who were hauled out of the studio by the police.'

'But you didn't exactly stick around to see what happened, did you? The moment I was out of the way you buggered off to California. Fat lot you cared about me.'

'I don't remember much about that time to be honest.'

'So I gather. It's convenient for you to forget about it.'

'I have a career to consider.'

'Peddling that self-help crap?'

'My books, tapes and videos help millions.'

'No they don't. People can't buy the hardcore stuff any more so they settle for what they can get.'

'Prison's made you hard, Shelley.'

'Oh, so you acknowledge the fact that I was in jail, then.'

'Of course I do.'

'I did it for you, Debbie.'

'Did what?'

'Took the blame for Eddie's death. Lied to the court. Protected you.'

'Protected me? What are you talking about? I had nothing to do with Eddie's death. I didn't kill him, and neither did you. This whole situation is ridiculous.'

'I wanted you to know how much I hated what you'd become.'

'Whatever I have become, you're as much to blame as anyone.'

'How can you say that?'

'Shelley, I'm not stupid. I know why you wanted to be around me. I know why you tried to get me away from my parents, why you supplied me with drugs, why you stood up in court and pretended that you'd killed Eddie. You were in love with me. No, don't say anything. I knew it all along, ever since we were at school. I never said anything because I didn't want to hurt you with a rejection, and because I was so fucked up that I was grateful for any scrap of affection no matter where it came from. But the thing is, Shelley, I could never give you anything more than friendship in return.'

'That's all I ever wanted from you, Debbie...'

'No. It's not enough. We're bad for each other. I don't want to be part of your life any more. That's why I came here today. I want you to start again and forget about me, and let me forget about you, and about... this.' She gestured around her.

'What are you afraid of, Debbie?'

'Nothing. I've faced the worst that life can throw at me. I'm not afraid of Bodhi, or of my parents, or of "Uncle" Dudley, and no, Shelley, I'm not afraid of you either. You think I'm a victim, that you can come along and rescue me. Well I'm sorry to disappoint you, but I don't need rescuing.'

Debbie turned and walked away, leaving Shelley shivering in the shadow of the wall.

Within two weeks, Debbie Doubledee was dead.

The 'bruises' that Shelley had noted on Debbie's body were, in fact, the result of blood transfusions and injections. A doctor in California made the diagnosis after Debbie came to him suffering from an inoperable brain tumour. Deterioration was swift. She told nobody, not even Bodhi and Goa, until the symptoms were too obvious to conceal. She made a will leaving her not-inconsiderable estate to the Cancer Research Society, and ensured that neither her parents, nor Bodhi, nor any of her former associates, could get their hands on a single penny.

Shortly after Debbie's death, Bodhi shed his bad karma and fled England, leaving Goa alone in the expensive flat he'd rented for Debbie.

Debbie's death couldn't have been better timed from Caroline Wragge's point of view. Stumped for ideas how to finish off *London's Elephant and Castle*, she was suddenly handed this opportunity on a plate. Of course: the final episode of the final series, before Caroline flitted permanently to WraggeTime Productions and an exciting new raft of drama projects for the BBC, would be a special tribute to Debbie Doubledee, featuring clips of all her footage and a full cast reunion.

And so for the last time in our story, all the principals were gathered together under one roof – a studio at Channel House cleverly decorated to resemble a sanitised version of the now world-famous Elephant and Castle shopping centre. But for the absence of streams of urine, teenage mothers hitting their toddlers and bored beggars huddled in the underpass, it could almost have been the real thing.

They all came to pay tribute to Debbie – some of them out of genuine sorrow and affection, some coerced by money. Serena, Jamie and Shelley huddled together in a corner of the studio, shunning and shunned by the rest of the company. Maureen and Muriel flitted from group to group, handing out fliers for their next Las Vegas Showbar extravaganza, an 'all-male revue' entitled *Guyzone*. Fat Alice cannonaded around in her wheelchair, occasionally lifting her tartan travel rug to expose the bolts that protruded from sore-looking holes in her legs. William and Theresa Wicks sat on a sofa and received condolences from cast and crew, assuaging their grief with the knowledge that a fat cheque from Channel 6 had been banked only that morning.

Daryn Handy, of course, was absent, but had sent greetings on a video tape that would be shown during the course of the episode. This, Caroline assured him, was 'a unique opportunity, an open audition to the entire industry.' Those were the last words she would ever say to him.

Shelley would have boycotted the entire affair had not Serena, with whom she was temporarily lodging, persuaded her otherwise.

'What good would it do?'

'It would register my disapproval of what they're trying to do to Debbie. They're portraying her as some kind of martyr. That's not true. Debbie was murdered.'

'Oh, Shelley, you know that's not true. She had a brain tumour. It's nobody's fault.'

'It is. It must be. Someone's to blame and I'm going to tell the world who it is.'

'And so what good will it do you to stay away from the tribute? Everyone's going to be there. If you have something to say, that's your chance to say it.'

'So you believe me, then?'

'I don't know, Shelley. A lot of things happened in the last couple of years. We've all suffered one way or another. I'm not talking about myself, particularly.' She put a hand round Jamie's waist; he hugged her and beamed. 'All in all, I've come out of this rather well. But look around you. Fat Alice has been in hospital so many times that she knows the consultants on a first-name basis.'

'But she's a pop star now.'

'True, she appeared on *Top of the Pops* singing her cover version of Queen classic 'Fat Bottomed Girls', but then there was that bizarre accident when it appeared that somebody had inadvertantly wired the mike stand up to the mains supply, and she was electrocuted on prime time television. And look at the rest of them. Maureen and Muriel, living off prostitution, just waiting for the day when the Vice Squad comes calling. Daryn in prison, his son in care. Peggy Renders dead, Eddie dead, Jamie and me working in the club, the rest of the cast – Barry Llannelly, Doreen Dawson, Miachail Miorphiagh and Dave Merryweather – rapidly making themselves unemployable. I hate to sound cruel, but I think Debbie's better off out of it.'

'But the truth must be told.'

'Why?'

'There are guilty people who are getting away with it.'

'Who?'

'Caroline Wragge, for instance. She's carved herself a very nice career, hasn't she? But I bet she knows more about Eddie's death than she's letting on. I can feel it in my waters.'

Serena and Jamie exchanged glances.

'Oh, don't look like that. I know you think I'm mad, that this is all some insane conspiracy theory, but I will find the proof one day.'

'Well, Shelley, I wish you luck, I really do. But until you can get your hands on some solid evidence, I think it would be better if you just kept your mouth shut and played the game.'

'It's all right for you, Serena. You've got Jamie. I've got nobody.'

'Oh Shelley,' said Serena, putting a hand on her Shelley's sturdy shoulder, 'if I can find love, I know you can. You're young. You've got so much living to do. Don't let bitterness stand in the way of happiness.'

At that moment, syrupy music swelled in the background. The show was about to go on air.

Thanks to the vigorous persuasion of the Channel 6 press office, the last ever episode of *London's Elephant and Castle* was reviewed in all the main daily papers. What should have been a chorus of approval was marred by one dissenting voice – predictably, that of the *Daily Beacon's* television critic Philip Bray, who now had a page to himself and a picture byline.

'Death of the Docusoap' ran the headline, above 750 words of classic Bray bile. (His robust critical style had earned him the soubriquet 'the bastard on the box'.)

It was not just Debbie Doubledee that we were mourning last night, but the once-great British television documentary tradition. And what killed it off? Greed, lack of imagination, prurience, stupidity and meanness. Shame on Channel 6 for keeping *London's Elephant and Castle* alive for so long – there's nothing particularly edifying about watching a corpse twitching after the brain's stopped working.

The 'stars' of *London's Elephant and Castle* – and we knew they were stars only because the presenter told us so every two minutes – treated the whole thing as their last desperate chance to cling on to a celebrity status that they neither earned nor deserved. And what an unlovely bunch they were. Serena Ward, who doesn't know if she's a boy or a girl; Shelley Smithers, who might as well be a boy because she sure don't look like a girl; Jamie Lord, whose low brow and dragging knuckles suggest that he's only just come down from the trees. Convicted pimps Roy Turner and Vernon Delgado, alias Maureen and Muriel, shamelessly plugged their nightclub, a pathetic front for a prostitution empire now preying on defenceless Kosovar refugees they pick up on the streets. And the rest of them: massively overweight, alcoholic, disabled, insane.

Is this what anybody really wants to watch when they're trying to relax after a hard day at the office, or looking after the kids? I think not. What the viewers of today really want was much better represented on BBC2, where the first episode of new classic drama *Anthony Trollope's Barsetshire Chronicles* brought a breath of fresh air to the fetid, unwholesome tv schedules. With an attractive young cast and an easy-to-follow story upholding old-fashioned family values, this is surely the shape of things to come. The guilty parties at Channel 6 could learn a lot from this uplifting new series that doesn't have to rely on freaks, sex and violence to get its message across...

It didn't suit Philip's thesis to draw attention to the fact that the producers of *London's Elephant and Castle* and *Anthony Trollope's Barsetshire Chronicles* were in fact one and the same person. Caroline

Wragge made sure of that by an irresistible sweetener in the shape of a luxurious holiday for Philip and Mrs Bray in an exclusive farmhouse conversion (with pool) in the heart of Italy's Tuscany.

Three

Six months is a long time in television. *London's Elephant and Castle* was forgotten; *Anthony Trollope's Barsetshire Chronicles*-mania had reached its peak and spawned a profitable sideline in tea-towels, Behind the Scenes books, videos and exclusive jewellery.

Meanwhile, the hand of Fate rained misfortune on our has-been stars. The Vice Squad, as predicted, caught up with Maureen and Muriel, raided the Las Vegas Showbar during the opening night of *Guyzone* and made 45 arrests. Messrs Turner and Delgado once again found themselves up before Lily Law on charges of running a brothel, and faced stiff prison sentences. Shelley Smithers touted her idea for a tell-all book and television series to one uninterested publisher/producer after another. The response was always the same. 'It's very interesting, love, but nobody wants that miserable real-life stuff any more. Can't you think of something a little more... funky?' Eventually, disheartened by her failure to break into the media, and still missing the solid evidence that would have given her wild conspiracy theory some solid credibility, Shelley left London altogether and found happiness with a media studies lecturer from Nottingham, 30 years her senior, who would spend whole evenings listening to her embittered ramblings. (These ramblings later formed the basis of an unpopular course unit on Television, Race and Gender: the Hidden Agenda.)

Jamie and Serena, unemployed since the closure of the Las Vegas Showbar, sat one evening on the roof of Beckford House and watched the sun set over the Elephant and Castle. It had been a long, leaden winter's day, the sort of day that saps hope from even the most optimistic heart. And then, just before darkness fell, the clouds lifted and the sun blazed out for a glorious half hour.

They leaned over the railings and looked down on their kingdom. Serena shivered; Jamie hugged her. Far over the other side of the roundabout, bulldozers were ripping into the Castle Arms, latterly the Las Vegas Showbar, in the first phase of a massive redevelopment that would tear down the shopping centre, the subways, even Beckford House itself, to replace them with already-dated post-modern-eclectic Toytown buildings for the affluent incomers the developers dreamed of attracting to London's never-to-be-fashionable Elephant and Castle.

'There goes a little piece of history, Jamie,' said Serena, her hair blowing around her face.

'Yeah. 'S a shame.'

'Still, we have a lot to be thankful for, don't we?'

'Yeah. We've got each other.' He kissed her on the lips. 'I'm hungry,' he said.

'There's no food in the house.'

'There never is.'

'Have you got any money?'

'No. Have you?'

'No.'

'I could always go and pull a punter.'

'So could I.'

They looked at each other, laughed and shook their heads.

'We could be doing a lot better than this, though, couldn't we?'

Jamie frowned. 'What do you mean?'

Serena pulled a video cassette from her handbag. Daryn's confession.

'We've still got this.'

'Mmmm... And Caroline's got a lot of money these days, ain't she?'

'She'd be very unhappy if it came to light.'

'We could blackmail her, have thousands by the end of the week.'

A few moments' silence, broken only by the grinding and screaming of metal teeth ripping into pre-cast concrete.

'Give it here a moment, Serena.'

She handed him the cassette. Jamie probed into the cavities with his thick fingers, drew out a yard of tape, and another, and another. Then he flung the gutted carcass far out from the walls of Beckford House. It flapped and rustled, the evening sun caught on the shiny surface of the destroyed magnetic tape, and it was gone.

'Oh well,' said Serena, shivering again, 'that's that.'

'Yup.' Jamie looked pleased with himself. It was the first time in his life that he'd consciously done something he recognised as 'right'.

'I suppose we should think about moving on,' said Serena.

'No,' said Jamie, with finality. 'We're going nowhere.'

'Then what shall we do?'

'I can get my old job back in the gym. Rod's all right. He won't mind.'

'Hmmm. No monkey business behind my back.'

Jamie took Serena's hand and placed it on his groin.

'I promise you. This is all yours from now on.'

'Oh, Jamie! How romantic!'

They kissed as the light faded around them.

'And I suppose I can get a job somewhere... stacking shelves in Tesco, or sweeping up in Genesis (The Beginning of Hair Trends) on Walworth Road.'

'Yeah,' said Jamie. 'There's always something.'

'Yes, my darling,' said Serena, slipping her hands inside Jamie's tracksuit bottoms to squeeze his buttocks. 'Now come here, you big ape, and kiss me.'